Praise for Ruth Druart

The Last Hours in Paris

"A wonderful book—an involving, terrifying, heartbreaking story of the power of love and forgiveness."
—Jill Mansell, *Sunday Times* bestselling author of *Should I Tell You?*

"A wonderful, moving, sad, but ultimately uplifting book."
—Lesley Pearse, *Sunday Times* bestselling author of *Deception*

"Engrossing...a tender yet thrilling story of love and family secrets in a time of war, beautifully told."
—Rachel Hore, author of *One Moonlit Night*

"Ruth is an exceptional storyteller. She weaves brave female characters through fascinating story lines. Her level of detail brings the past back to life, shining a light in the darkness. Love, loss, bravery. She's like my favorite history teacher ever! My new go-to author. I recommend her to everyone."
—Ericka Waller, author of *Dog Days*

"These characters command sympathy...A vivid exposé of war and its dislocations."
—*Kirkus*

"The four-year occupation of France by the Germans in World War II must be one of the most intensively fictionalized episodes in history. It takes an inventive author to find a new perspective on this well-surveyed landscape. Ruth Druart is such an author...An engrossing and psychologically complex novel which helps to explain why the Occupation still so fascinates us." —*Historical Novel Society*

While Paris Slept

"As writers, some stories keep us up at night with the need to get them down on paper. Ruth Druart has one such tale. We met in 2006, and I read pages of her story then. She never let go and never gave up. Thanks to this tenacity, her heartbreaking debut will be published in several languages. It will appeal to fans of *The Light Between Oceans* as well as to readers fascinated by novels set in World War II. *While Paris Slept* delves into eternal questions: How far will we go to protect our child? Is love holding tightly or letting go? The characters—and readers—must choose between what is right and what is best in this meditation on love and sacrifice."

—Janet Skeslien Charles, author of
The Paris Library and *Moonlight in Odessa*

"*While Paris Slept* made me think and cry and rage and smile at mankind's capacity for both beautiful, selfless love and terrible, heartbreaking cruelty. It is at once a story of wartime courage and desperation, and of the many ways in which war reverberates through people's lives for years after the fact. Prepare to question yourself and the characters in the novel, to wonder what you might have done in their place; in short, prepare to be thoroughly engrossed in this compelling book in which four adults and one child grapple with the true meaning of love and family."

—Natasha Lester, author of *The Paris Secret*

"What a book…emotional and heartrending…absolutely phenomenal. I was on tenterhooks throughout. A wonderful achievement."

—Jill Mansell, *Sunday Times* bestselling author of *And Now You're Back*

"*While Paris Slept* is a powerful and poignant debut from a brilliant and bold new novelist. Expertly weaving together multiple story lines, author Ruth Druart fills each page with thrilling suspense, uncommon emotional depth, and fascinating characters. Fans of historical fiction should not miss this one." —Imogen Kealey, author of *Liberation*

"Both epic and intimate, this unexpected story of two couples' sacrifices in war-torn France had me completely and utterly enraptured. You'll have your heart in your mouth and tears on your cheeks as it reaches its rich, life-affirming conclusion." —Louise Candlish, author of *Our House*

"I absolutely loved [*While Paris Slept*]. An ingenious plot, wonderful, believable characters, and it moved me to tears. A fabulous read." —Lesley Pearse, Author of *Suspects*

"Good people coping with an impossible situation are at the heart of Druart's [debut] . . . The author succeeds in keeping things moving, particularly in the action-packed first half of the novel . . . Ethical questions raised by the narrative suggest this may do well with book clubs." —*Publishers Weekly*

"The ending is extremely touching, and even the most cynical reader will shed a tear. It certainly brings the story full circle in a very satisfying manner. I can imagine that book clubs will enjoy discussing the intricacies and questions about love and family—and what we would sacrifice in their name—that the book raises."

—BookReporter.com

"Druart examines sacrifice, selflessness, and resilience in this atmospheric debut about the cost of war and the price of love." —*Toronto Star*

"With her accomplished first novel, Druart penetrates to the heart of . . . emotional questions, exploring them in multiple ways through the interlinked stories of two couples . . . The ending is as beautiful as one could wish."

—*Historical Novel Society*

"Ruth Druart has written one of the best novels of the year."
—Red Carpet Crash

The
Last Hours
in Paris

By Ruth Druart

The Last Hours in Paris
While Paris Slept

The Last Hours in Paris

Ruth Druart

GRAND
CENTRAL

NEW YORK   BOSTON

This book is a work of fiction. Names, characters, places, and incidents are the product of the author's imagination or are used fictitiously. Any resemblance to actual events, locales, or persons, living or dead, is coincidental.

Copyright © 2022 by Ruth Druart
Reading Group Guide Copyright © 2022 by Ruth Druart and
Hachette Book Group, Inc.

Cover design by Albert Tang. Jacket images of couple by Collaboration JS / Arcangel.
Cover copyright © 2022 by Hachette Book Group, Inc.

Hachette Book Group supports the right to free expression and the value of copyright. The purpose of copyright is to encourage writers and artists to produce the creative works that enrich our culture.

The scanning, uploading, and distribution of this book without permission is a theft of the author's intellectual property. If you would like permission to use material from the book (other than for review purposes), please contact permissions@hbgusa.com. Thank you for your support of the author's rights.

Grand Central Publishing
Hachette Book Group
1290 Avenue of the Americas, New York, NY 10104
grandcentralpublishing.com
twitter.com/grandcentralpub

Originally published in the United Kingdom by Headline Review,
an imprint of Headline Publishing Group, in July 2022
First North American edition: July 2022
First trade edition: April 2023

Grand Central Publishing is a division of Hachette Book Group, Inc. The Grand Central Publishing name and logo is a trademark of Hachette Book Group, Inc.

The publisher is not responsible for websites (or their content)
that are not owned by the publisher.

The Hachette Speakers Bureau provides a wide range of authors for speaking events. To find out more, go to www.hachettespeakersbureau.com or call (866) 376-6591.

Library of Congress Cataloging-in-Publication Data has been applied for.

ISBNs: 9781538735220 (trade pbk.), 9781538735206 (ebook)

Printed in the United States of America

LSC-C

Printing 1, 2023

To Sandra and Michael, my parents.
Thank you for letting me climb all the trees I wanted.
Ready to catch me if I fell.

"To love or have loved, that is enough. Ask nothing further. There is no other pearl to be found in the dark folds of life."

—From *Les Misérables* by Victor Hugo

The
Last Hours
in Paris

Prologue

"I didn't even look at you, that first time I saw you."

"You just saw a uniform."

"Yes, and it frightened me."

"Well, I didn't look at you much either."

She pinched his cheek softly. "Really?"

"I knew you didn't want to be looked at. Especially not by me. But I noticed you." He played with her fingers. "I found you intriguing."

"Go on," she encouraged him.

It touched him that she wanted to hear him talk about her. "And defiant," he continued. "Brave. I knew you were afraid of those policemen, but you didn't cower in front of them." He let go of her fingers. "I admired that." He ran his hand through her hair. "But I could see you might get yourself into trouble."

"Did you think you would save me?"

"No." He gazed at her. "I knew it would be you who would save me."

Part One

1963

Chapter One

Brittany, May 1963

Élise

I stare out of the bay window at the sea lashing against the slate-gray rocks, white spray bouncing off jagged edges. Impulsively, I unlatch it, letting in the cries of the seagulls and the tireless sound of the tide. A pair of doves balance on a telegraph wire. They cock their heads toward me, looking at me curiously.

"Élise." Monsieur Beaufort walks into the room, his voice cutting through me. "Have you finished? I can give you a lift to the station."

"Thank you." I close the window, dust the windowsill, and turn toward him, putting on a polite smile. Then I remove my working tunic and follow him down the stairs, hanging the tunic on the back of the kitchen door as we walk through to the driveway.

He opens the car door for me.

"*Merci, monsieur.*" He's a gentleman, and I appreciate it.

It makes me feel less like his housekeeper and more like a person.

"Do you have any plans for the weekend?" he asks as we drive along the tree-lined roads to the station at Saint-Brieuc.

"Nothing special, lunch at home with my daughter then probably a walk along the beach."

"How is Joséphine?"

I'm touched that he remembers her name.

"Fine, thank you. She's taking her *baccalauréat* next month. She wants to go to university." I hear the pride in my voice, and just stop myself in time from telling him what a clever girl she is. "She was eighteen last month."

"Already? She was only a baby when you started working for us."

"Yes." I sit back in the seat, wondering if this chapter of my life is over. I've accomplished what I set out to do. Joséphine has safely made it to adulthood, and soon I will tell her the truth. The lies I built around her childhood grew like invisible prison bars, holding me back, trapping me. Only the truth will free me now. At the same time, it terrifies me.

We drive the rest of the way in silence, and I'm relieved when we pull into the station. The train is already there, and I thank Monsieur Beaufort before hurrying onto the platform, where I board an empty carriage and settle down into the old velvet seat. I think about taking a walk with Joséphine this afternoon; on the other hand, I don't want to distract her from her studies. Once her exams are out of the way, we'll have more time to talk. Really talk. I see her getting ready to open up her wings and fly away, but I can't let her go, not until I've told her everything she needs to know.

When the train pulls into Lannion, I get off and walk out

through the station to the road. Soizic's old green Renault 4CV sits in the same parking spot as it does every Saturday when she picks me up at the station. "*Bonjour, Soizic.*" I open the passenger door and get in, kissing her lightly on both cheeks. "How are you?"

"Joséphine won't be back till later today," she says in way of reply.

My heart sinks, but I gather myself before replying, "Did she go to a friend's for lunch?"

"Yes, Hervé's." She turns the key in the ignition, and we pull away.

I glance sideways at her. "She seems to be spending a lot of time with him."

"It's nice for her to have a boyfriend. Don't worry, I've spoken to her about boys and..." She trails off, leaving the insinuation hanging there.

"I'll talk to her too." I try to reassert my position as Joséphine's mother, something I've been doing since she was born.

Focused on the road, Soizic raises an eyebrow. I turn away from her and stare out of the window. The sailboats in Baie de Sainte-Anne have been abandoned by the sea and lie there on their sides, waiting for the next tide. The sea has swept away everything in its path that is not anchored or rooted in the sand. Sometimes I wish I could sweep away the past like that, let the sea take it far out into the ocean where it will never be found again. But the past is part of who we are, and it's time for me to face it. Time for Joséphine to know it.

"I've made lunch." She glances at me. "Onion soup, and there's fresh baguette."

"*Merci.*" I've come to understand this is Soizic's way of

showing she cares. And she does. Despite her caustic retorts and cold manner, I know she cares very much for Joséphine, and even for me. We might not share the same blood, but Soizic has become part of our little family. I'm just not sure whether she's taken the role of mother, grandmother, or father. Sometimes it feels like all three.

We turn the corner and pull in at the side of the old stone cottage that's been my home since I left Paris. The smell of garlic and onions greets me as we go inside, and I'm hungry now. Soizic ladles out the soup; melted cheese strung out among the croutons and fleshy onion rings. Before she picks up her spoon, she makes the sign of the cross. "God, thank you for this food."

"Amen," I murmur.

We eat in a companionable silence, one born of having known each other for so many years. Soizic's never been one for small talk, and I'm used to her ways. Taciturn is the word, but then she has her reasons. We're just finishing our soup when Joséphine bursts into the kitchen, excitement shining out of her bright blue eyes. "Maman, guess what?" She doesn't even say hello.

I'm thrilled to see her so happy and stand to kiss her cheek. "*Bonjour*, Joséphine." Then I hold my hand out to Hervé, who's standing next to her. He turns a shade pinker then takes it, shaking it firmly. He seems like a nice boy.

"Guess what?" Joséphine repeats. She looks at Hervé then back at me. "There's a school trip to England."

Joséphine loves English; she's been dreaming of going there ever since the Beatles released their first album last month. I hear her singing the songs sometimes, "Love Me Do," "Please Please Me." I look at my daughter, her face full of youth and excitement, and, with a familiar pang of longing, I'm reminded of her father. She has the same *joie de vivre*, the same zest for life, wanting to taste it all. But how my heart is heavy, knowing I'll have to disappoint her.

"Joséphine," I say. "I'm sorry. We can't afford it."

Her eyes turn a shade darker and her mouth drops, her dimples disappearing. "But you don't even know how much it is. And I have some birthday money left."

"I know you do." I squeeze her hand. "But we don't have that sort of money."

She lets out a long breath and I feel her whole body deflate. Hervé rolls his lips together, looking away as though embarrassed. Money isn't the sort of thing one discusses outside family.

"You don't even have a passport," Soizic adds.

The word passport sets my pulse racing. She needs to wait a little more, till after her exams, till we've had time to talk about everything calmly and carefully.

"I'm sure I could get one!" Joséphine raises her voice, and I feel her exasperation. Instead of helping her fulfill her dreams, we're hindering her, holding her back.

I turn toward Hervé. "Are you going?"

"I'm going to ask my parents." He looks at Joséphine. "They might be able to lend you some money."

"No! That's out of the question, Hervé!" I'm shocked by his offer; it's not his place to make it. "There'll be plenty of other opportunities." I turn back to Joséphine, bringing the discussion to a close. "You're very young anyway for such a big trip." I attempt a peace-making smile.

"Maman, I'm not a little kid anymore." Joséphine refuses my smile. "I'm sure I could get the money together." She glances at Soizic then back to me again. "But you don't want me to go anyway, do you? You don't even want me to go to Paris. You just want me to stay here in boring Brittany all my life."

"No, that's not true!" Her sudden outburst takes me by surprise. "I know you're not a child."

"Well, why do you still treat me like one?"

"Joséphine!" Soizic's eyes turn stony cold. "That's enough."

Joséphine sighs loudly. "I'm not going to stay here forever, you know."

"I said that's enough." Soizic stands up, crossing her arms in front of her chest, asserting her position.

This is her house, and we live under her rules. We don't shout and we don't fight. I cringe inside, pity for my daughter rising in my chest. This argument isn't really about the money.

Joséphine stands up. "I don't care if I don't go on this trip. I just want to leave this house, and Trégastel. It's so . . . so small. And the people are . . ."

She turns to Hervé, who is looking like he'd rather be anywhere else than where he is right now. She takes his hand and pulls him toward the door.

Chapter Two

Brittany, May 1963

Joséphine

"I won't go either." Hervé puts his arm around Joséphine as they walk along the coastal route to his house.

She stops in her stride, moving away from him then turning to look at him. "I don't care about the trip. I'm just fed up with the way we can't even talk about it. I could find a way of getting the money; I have some saved myself, but Maman doesn't want me to go. She never wants me to do anything. She's afraid of everything. Afraid of life!" She pauses for breath. "I'm not even allowed out on a Saturday night."

"But Saturday's your mother's only evening here."

"Whose side are you on?" *Why can't he see how controlling her mother is?*

"I feel sorry for your mum."

Joséphine narrows her eyes at Hervé. "What?"

"Well, she doesn't have much money, does she? And she's all alone."

"She's got Soizic. Anyway, that's her fault. She never wanted to meet anyone. She had offers, but no one was ever good enough." She starts walking again, a restless energy surging through her when she thinks about how her mother won't even talk about her own father—Frédéric, shot during the liberation of Paris. Whenever Joséphine brings the subject up, her mother adopts a wary expression and looks away, as though taking herself off into her own secret world.

"I could lend you some money," Hervé says. "I need to get a passport too. We could go together."

"What do you need?"

"I don't know." He takes her hand and swings it. "A birth certificate, I guess."

"I've never even seen mine."

"Well, everyone has one. Ask your mum. You can always get a copy of it at the town hall."

Hervé seems to know more about everything than her, and it annoys her slightly. "I'm going back. I want to look for my birth certificate."

"What now?"

"Yes. I'm going to show her I'm not a kid. I'm going to get myself a passport." She kisses him quickly on the cheek and hurries home, thinking that Soizic and her mother will probably be out in the fields, bringing the cows back in for the night. Of course, she could just ask for her birth certificate, but she doesn't want another argument. And she has an idea where it might be—in the little suitcase under her mother's bed, where she keeps old photographs and papers. Joséphine hasn't been expressly forbidden to look in it; it's just one of those implicit rules that you don't meddle in other people's personal belongings.

Her luck is in; the cottage is empty. She goes into the

kitchen then takes the stairs two at a time, up into the only room upstairs—her mother's bedroom. A simple dark oak bed with solid curved ends sits in the middle of the room. Joséphine crouches down, reaching under the bed, pulling out the battered suitcase. In her mind she imagined it to be bigger and grander. In fact, it's just a small case made from thick cardboard and covered in tartan gray paper. She squeezes the old rusty clasp holding it together, but then hesitates, the story of Pandora's box flashing through her mind. For a moment she sits there, her finger on the clasp. She smells lavender, the sweet familiarity of it bringing back memories, snuggling down with Maman on Sunday mornings while Soizic clattered about below in the kitchen.

Her mind has wandered. Impulsively, she pulls at the clasp and opens the case. A few scattered papers, letters, and black-and-white photos lie inside. Joséphine leafs through them, intent on her birth certificate, but her curiosity gets the better of her and she can't help pulling out the photos. Her mother as a young girl, standing between her parents, a shy smile playing on her lips. Her mother in a beautiful long dress, holding a man's hand. Why hasn't Maman shown her these pictures before? She's asked for photos of Frédéric, her father, but her mother was always evasive, saying they didn't take photos back then. So who is this man? Maybe he was a lover, not her father. She turns it over. Three words make her heart jump. Frédéric, February 1939. He must be her father. But why wouldn't Maman have shown her this picture?

She picks up a book of poetry by Victor Hugo, wondering why her mother would hide a book. She opens it at the first page, and there's an inscription written in clear cursive handwriting.

My Love, Lise,
My life began with you.
Yours forever,
S

"S"? "S" isn't "F" for Frédéric. Who could "S" be? And why hadn't he written his whole name? She finds old letters but resists the temptation to read them. It's her birth certificate she's after, and she shouldn't let herself get distracted.

An official-looking letter catches her eye. It's so short, she's read it before she's even thought about it.

> We regret to inform you that Frédéric Dumarché was killed while carrying out his loyal duty in defending his country.

Something at the top of the letter catches her attention. The date: May 1940. Five years before she was born! How could that be? She reads it again. It must be another Frédéric.

The click of the kitchen door opening makes her drop everything back into the case. Quickly, she closes it and shoves it back under the bed. She smooths down her dress and tries to breathe calmly before going back downstairs.

"What were you doing in your mother's room?" Soizic stands at the bottom of the stairs, her arms folded across her chest.

"Where is she?" Joséphine answers with a question.

"I asked what you were doing." Soizic's tone is cold.

"I need my birth certificate." She has a right to have it, so why does she feel as though she's asking for something she shouldn't have?

The blood drains from Soizic's face. "What do you want with that?"

"I want to get a passport."

Soizic lets out a long deep breath. "You don't need a passport yet. Wait till your exams are over."

"My exams? What have they got to do with it?"

"It's what you should be focusing on right now." She turns away, tutting. "I don't know! Trips abroad and boyfriends. You're letting yourself get distracted."

"It doesn't matter." Joséphine tries to sound casual. "Hervé says I can ask for a copy at the town hall."

"No. No." Soizic looks her in the eye. "No need to do that. I'm sure we can find it. Just give us some time." She lets out a long sigh. "You young people are so impatient."

This last remark strikes Joséphine as particularly unjust. She's been so patient, never pushing her mother or Soizic to talk about the past, the war, not when she saw how much it upset them.

"Do you know who Frédéric Dumarché was?" Joséphine asks.

Soizic closes her eyes for a second, then shakes her head. "You shouldn't be going through your mother's things like that! Dragging up the past. It won't do anyone any good." She hesitates. "You should know better."

Joséphine looks down at her feet, ashamed now, feeling horribly guilty for making Soizic remember. Because Joséphine knows what happened to Soizic's daughter. Everybody knows, but nobody talks about it.

The door opening breaks the tension, and Joséphine's mother comes in. "It's cold tonight." She takes her coat off. "The weather might be changing." She doesn't seem to have noticed the atmosphere she's just walked into and takes a step further into the kitchen, bringing her open palm against Joséphine's cheek. Joséphine shudders at the icy-cold touch.

Chapter Three

Brittany, May 1963

Élise

If I didn't know my daughter better, I'd think she was sulking. But she's not a sulker. She's a thinker. And right now she's thinking about that trip to England. I can almost hear her mind whirring away, making a plan.

"I'm sorry about the school trip, Joséphine." I try to find a way in as we sit down to eat. "To make up for it, you could go to Paris after your exams. You could stay with your Aunt Isabelle; she'd love to take you out and show you around."

Joséphine shrugs. "Maybe."

"Wouldn't you like to go to Paris?"

"I guess so."

Soizic dishes out the boiled potatoes in silence.

"You'll go to England one day." I try to lighten the atmosphere. "You have your whole life in front of you."

Soizic lifts the lid of the casserole and I breathe in the rich, meaty smell of her beef bourguignon. She serves it then makes the sign of the cross. "God bless this food we are about to eat."

Joséphine and I murmur, "Amen."

Even though it's mostly carrots and celery, and the cheapest cuts of meat, it's full of flavor and the beef is so tender it falls from my fork. But Joséphine only picks at it, prodding a potato with her fork, breaking it in two.

"Do you like poetry?" she asks out of the blue, looking at me quizzically.

I'm taken aback by her question. "Not really. Why?"

Soizic pauses, her fork halfway to her mouth as she looks at me.

"I think I might if I read some." Joséphine drags a piece of bread through the sauce. "Have you got any?"

"Me?" I look at Soizic. We only have twelve books between us, and Joséphine has read them all. And then I remember. The book in the suitcase upstairs. Surely, she hasn't been going through my things. She wouldn't do that, would she? "No," I answer carefully. "I don't believe I do."

Joséphine drops the bread into the sauce. "That's a shame." She plunges her fork into a morsel of meat, bringing it to her mouth and chewing it slowly as she watches me.

And I know. I know she's gone through my suitcase upstairs. My suitcase of memories. She's seen the book of poetry Sébastian gave me, and his messages, but he never signed his name. She wouldn't know who he was. There's nothing dangerous in there. Not really.

"Someone once gave me a book of poems." I attempt a smile. "And I read a few of them."

"Who was that?" Her question is short and direct.

"Just someone I once knew."

She sighs, picking up the soggy bread, putting it in her

mouth. I'm aware that my answers are inadequate, and I want to tell her more. I want to tell her everything. But not now. Not like this. It isn't the right time.

"I think you'd have a lovely time in Paris." Soizic's voice breaks in, sounding off-key and falsely bright.

"It will give you a chance to get to know your Aunt Isabelle." I smile, but it feels like my face is cracking.

"And my grandparents. I hardly know them. I've never seen my grandfather. Is he even still alive?"

"Yes, he is." I try to speak steadily. "But he was never the same after the war." *The war.* The forbidden subject in this house. I glance at Soizic, concerned for her now we're treading on fragile ground.

"But don't you want to see him?" Joséphine pushes it. "He probably won't be around much longer."

"He doesn't want to see me. I told you that."

"Just because you weren't married when you had me?" Joséphine rubs her nose. "It wasn't your fault my father was killed."

I feel my cheeks burn up. I should never have told her that. It will take a lot of undoing. I try to swallow whole the piece of carrot in my mouth, but it gets caught. I cough, bringing my hand to my throat. I cough again, my eyes watering. Soizic stands and hits me on the back between my shoulder blades. I try to stop coughing and grab my glass of water, taking a large sip.

Joséphine stares at me as though she's seeing me for the first time. I feel exposed. She knows. She knows it's all been a pack of lies.

Chapter Four

Brittany, May 1963

Joséphine

Sunday night, after her mother has gone back to Saint-Brieuc, Joséphine is drifting off to sleep when it comes to her. A childhood memory of her mother stuffing a folder behind a set of dinner plates they never used, as though it were part of the back of the cupboard. There had been something secretive about the way her mother had put the folder away, as though it wasn't to be removed again. And even as a child she'd sensed its importance. She's sure she'll find her birth certificate in there.

With this thought she falls asleep. But these are not thoughts to fall asleep on, and the next morning she's woken early by a nervous energy surging through her. Creeping out of bed, she finds the cupboard in the kitchen where the old plates are stored. She looks carefully behind the crockery. A pale green folder lies against the back of the cupboard.

Quickly she pulls it out and opens it up. She peeps inside, pulling out the first sheet of paper. Her name is at the top.

Name: Joséphine Chevalier
Name of mother: Élise Chevalier
Name of father: Sébastian Kleinhaus

The paper drops from Joséphine's hands. A shudder runs down her backbone, turning her cold. Time moves into a different frame, backward, forwards, but not here, not where she is now. She's lost all sense of where she is. Clenching her eyes shut, she tries to get a grounding. What does it mean? *Name of father: Sébastian Kleinhaus.* It's not possible. Her father was a Frenchman named Frédéric. Did he have another name?

A memory comes flooding back. It made no sense at the time, but the words ring in her ears now as though they've been sitting there all these years waiting for this moment, waiting for her to understand what they meant.

It was one Sunday morning as they were leaving church, when she was about eight years old. "What's the difference between a Boche and a swallow?" The question was directed at her by an older boy. She shrugged, not sure what a Boche was back then, only that it was a bad word. "When a swallow has babies in France, he takes them with him, but a Boche leaves them behind." He said it spitefully, and she always remembered his words, not sure what they had to do with her.

Sébastian Kleinhaus. A German! A Boche! All at once she understands the silences surrounding the topic of her father. Her mother had to run away to Trégastel to have her Boche baby, where no one knew anything about her. It explains why she's never taken Joséphine to Paris, why Joséphine has only met her grandmother and Aunt Isabelle four times in her entire life, why she's never even met her grandfather; the man who was sent to a work camp in Germany during the occupation, and came back with only hatred in his heart for all things German.

A Boche bastard.

Her mother has been lying to her all her life. Who else knows? Does Soizic know?

Surely not, she'd never have taken her mother in if she knew. Her mother must have lied to Soizic too. *La honte*— the shame of having slept with the enemy. "*Putain!*" she swears under her breath. "My lying mother!"

Footsteps make her freeze. Her lungs cave in, the air circling them too thin to fill them. Struggling to breathe, she brings her hand up against her sternum. Then clenching the birth certificate in the other hand, she turns around to face Soizic.

Soizic is deathly pale, and her eyes are wide and frightened. She knows. She always knew.

"Why didn't you tell me?" Joséphine's voice trembles. Tears well up. But she's not going to cry. She blinks them away. "I had a right to know!"

Soizic has gone very still, her lips mouthing something, but no words come.

"You knew my father was a Boche?"

"Don't use that word!" Soizic grips the sideboard with a shaking hand, her face drained of all its color. For the first time, she looks the full seventy-seven years she is. "You shouldn't go through other people's affairs."

"Other people's affairs!" A gross sense of injustice inflames Joséphine. "It's *my* birth certificate!"

"It's up to your mother to give it to you. You don't just go and take it!"

"You knew? And you never said anything?" The hurt of Soizic's deceit shoots through her. The two people who brought her up, who loved and cared for her; together they kept this shameful secret from her, as though she couldn't be trusted with it. With knowing who her own father was.

"Yes." Soizic's voice is firm. "Yes, I knew."

"Why?" Confusion crowds Joséphine's thoughts. "Why did you even take her in?" Without waiting for an answer, she asks another question. "Did he rape her?" Somehow, she knows he didn't, but she has to ask. "Did he?" she insists.

Soizic shakes her head vigorously. "No! No!" Her hand drops from her throat, leaving a small red mark where she was gripping it. She reaches out to Joséphine. "I'm so sorry. She wanted to tell you, but I wouldn't let her."

Joséphine moves back, against the wall, as far away as she can get. But she wants to know. She wants to know how bad her father really was.

Her father. Unshed tears sting her eyes. She tries to blink them away, but they're coming from a well deep inside and she can't hold them back.

"Joséphine, *mon coeur.*" Soizic steps forward. She tries to put her arms around Joséphine, and Joséphine almost lets her, but she doesn't want to be comforted. She pulls back, roughly wiping away her tears with the back of her hand. "Just tell me who he was. What did he do?" She has to know. She has to know if her father was a monster.

"I don't know. I don't know, Joséphine. I wouldn't let your mother talk about him."

Chapter Five

Brittany, May 1963

Joséphine

Instead of going to school, Joséphine walks to the payphone in the village. She wants to get away from Trégastel before her mother comes back next weekend. She'll find out the truth for herself.

She has to call the operator to get her Aunt Isabelle's number. Isabelle answers in a voice still heavy with sleep. "I'm sorry," Joséphine starts. "Did I wake you?"

"Joséphine, is that you? Is everything okay?"

"Yes. Everyone's fine." Now she doesn't know how to ask. "It's just that, well, I wondered—could I come and stay with you for a few days?" She cringes at the boldness of her request.

"What now? You want to come now?" Isabelle's surprise echoes down the line. "What about school?"

"It's only studying at the moment."

"This is a surprise."

Joséphine's heart sinks. She's going to say no. But then Isabelle's tone brightens. "That would be lovely. When do you want to come?"

"Tomorrow?" she suggests tentatively. Really, she'd like to go right now.

"Tomorrow!" The line goes silent. Then her aunt speaks again. "Yes! Why not?" She lowers her tone. "How is your mother? Is she all right?"

"Yes." Joséphine lets out a white lie. "I'll call back when I've got my ticket, tell you what time I'll arrive."

"Wait. I have a timetable here."

Joséphine puts another franc into the money slot.

"There's one at eight thirty tomorrow morning. Could you get that one?"

"Yes!" A thrill of excitement rushes through her as this impulsive idea becomes reality.

She'd like to go and see Hervé, tell him everything, but she doesn't want to go to school, so she walks along the beach for the rest of the morning, trying to work out how this new knowledge has turned her inside out, why she feels so raw, so exposed. She returns to the cottage for lunch and tells Soizic she's going to Paris.

"But what about your mother? She'll be so upset. You can't go running off like that!"

"I need to find out what happened. I'm eighteen now, and I have enough money saved for my ticket." She takes a deep breath. "You can't stop me from going."

"What about school, your exams?"

"I can take my books with me." Joséphine sighs. "I can study there."

Joséphine is firm, leaving no room for Soizic to dissuade her, and on Tuesday morning, Soizic agrees to drive her to the station. The rain lashes down, the wipers squeaking as they swish from side to side.

Soizic stares out into the rain as she speaks. "Don't be so harsh on your mother. She's always done what she thought was best for you."

Joséphine throws her a withering glance. "For me?"

"Yes, for you. She wanted to give you a safe, happy home." She shifts gear, turning the car round the corner. "That's always what came first for her."

Joséphine doesn't answer, but stares at the tall trees along the roadside, their branches succumbing to the strong wind, their delicate blossoming buds battered.

They pull up outside the station, and Joséphine puts her hand on the door handle, but then hesitates. There's a calm stillness inside the car as the wind and rain pummel the roof and windows, making Joséphine feel cocooned. Once she opens that door, she'll be exposing herself to the elements, and she'll be all on her own. Soizic's always been her rock; always there for her when she's needed her, ready with practical advice and help, but tough too. If she didn't agree with Joséphine, she'd say so. She wouldn't bother beating around the bush with niceties. *Honest*, Joséphine thinks ironically. This would have been the word she would have credited Soizic with, but not anymore. It makes her wonder how well you can ever really know anyone. From now on, she'll always be wondering what part of themselves people are hiding. She glances at Soizic's profile, and half of her wants to throw her arms around this tough, kind woman, but the other half is still reeling from a sense of betrayal and hurt.

Soizic rests her hands on the steering wheel as she stares out into the rain. "I've already lost a daughter." Her voice sounds faraway. "I couldn't bear to lose you too."

But I'm not your daughter, Joséphine wants to scream. *I'm not your dead daughter.* But she can't. She can't hurt her like that. "I'm sorry," Joséphine murmurs, and she is. She's sorry for them all, for the things that were never said, for the stories never told. But right now, all she wants to do is get away.

Taking a deep breath, she puts her hand on the door handle and opens the door. *"Au revoir."*

Joséphine sits alone in the carriage on the train to Paris. Despite the emotional turmoil flooding through her, she can't help but enjoy the sensation of being on the fast train. She stands up, pulls the window down, and leans out. The wind takes her breath away, reaching into her hair, pulling it back with its force. She opens her mouth, gulping for air, her heart beating fast with the exhilaration of speed. A train flying toward her on the other tracks makes her want to pull her head back in. But she doesn't. Instead she absorbs the terror. Then she takes a step away from the window, and it all goes quiet again. She sits back on the lumpy velvet seat, feeling every spring through her skirt. She likes this sense of being between places, neither where she was, nor yet where she's going. It feels like a safe place, where she can be anyone she wants to be.

Maman wants her to be somebody she's not. She wants her to study engineering at university; she doesn't understand how Joséphine is drawn to letters and languages, that she loves putting words together, creating images with them, finding rhythm in the phrases, using them to stir emotions. Joséphine has felt the acute absence of words at home, as though they were hiding behind cupboards, under beds, inside drawers, gathering dust. What Joséphine has learned about life has been through books. Once she could read, she devoured them; in her bed, secretly under the covers with a torch after she was told to turn out the light, on the beach in the summer, lying on her tummy, chin cupped in her hands, sand lightly blowing across the paper. In between these pages she learned about life, about love, about courage and cowardice. Words are power. They can bring you down, they can lift you up, make your heart soar, make you fall in love. Or make you hate. She thinks about those two simple words—Sébastian Kleinhaus—and how they have had the power to change who she is.

Five hours later, the train draws to a stop at Montparnasse station. As soon as Joséphine steps out of the carriage, she's hit by the level of noise; people hurrying by, talking loudly, announcements bellowing out, the shunting of trains and the blowing of whistles. Thankfully, she spots Isabelle at the end of the platform.

"*Bonjour! Bonjour,* Joséphine. Here you are at last!" Isabelle kisses her, then glances at Joséphine's small suitcase. "Good thing you've traveled light, we can walk."

"*Bonjour, Tante* Isabelle."

"Don't call me aunt, let's pretend I'm your big sister. Auntie sounds so stuffy, and I'm only ten years older than you. I'm more like a sister. Do you like jazz?"

Joséphine's head spins with Isabelle's chatter. "Yes, no, I don't know."

"Well, you can find out Saturday night. We're going to a jazz club! You're going to love Paris!" She stares at Joséphine's skirt. "I'll take you shopping too. I'm going to spoil you rotten. But lunch first. I'm starving."

Joséphine looks down at her skirt, her heart sinking when she sees it through Isabelle's eyes. Dowdy. Back in Trégastel, her skirt looked chic on the mannequin in the window, but here in Paris, it labels her as a *plouc*. Parisian women glide by in tight straight skirts, tailored jackets, smart heels, little leather handbags hanging from their elbows. She's seen the magazines with the latest fashions, but she didn't think everyone would actually be wearing them. And here she is, in a frumpy skirt, lugging her suitcase, sweat beginning to collect under her hairline and her armpits.

Isabelle seems to notice her unease. "Here, let me take your case."

Gratefully, Joséphine passes the case to her aunt. Traffic whizzes by as they walk down a wide street; sports cars, cars without roofs, cars beeping, buses with open backs— passengers leaning out, smoking. Isabelle turns around, looking at the tall buildings, the wrought-iron balconies, and the faces of stone staring down at her.

"Let's go in here." Isabelle abruptly turns into a brasserie, and soon they're sitting at a little round table on the terrace, Joséphine's senses overwhelmed with all the new sounds and sights.

The waiter soon arrives with the menu, and Joséphine stares at the large choice in front of her. "The *menu du jour* looks good," Isabelle comments. "The *plat du jour* is *magret de canard*. Do you like duck? *Oeuf mayonnaise* for starter and *mousse au chocolat* for dessert."

"Yes," Joséphine replies, though she would have liked to have tried the snails and the lamb.

"And a *demi-carafe* of red. A meal without wine is just a snack." Isabelle laughs and orders quickly before the waiter has time to move away.

Some of the women walking by have chic little bobs, while others have their hair wound up high on their heads, held tightly in place. Once again, Joséphine feels like the country bumpkin with her thick wavy hair.

"Eric has given me some money to take you shopping." Isabelle seems to read her mind. "He's a darling." She winks. "He's really excited that you're here. You've only met him twice, haven't you? But he remembers coming to Brittany, seeing you. He's always asking after you." Putting her hand on Joséphine's knee, she continues. "We were both so disappointed you couldn't come to our wedding."

Joséphine attempts a smile, but her lips refuse to move. She doesn't want to be reminded of that day when she and her mother were stuck in Trégastel, while Isabelle walked down the aisle with Eric. Her mother pleaded poverty, saying they couldn't afford a trip to Paris.

"I told Maman you were coming," Isabelle continues, "and she's dying to see you again. How many times have you seen your grandmother?"

"Four."

"Only four! Never mind. You're here now!" Isabelle stops and rummages in her bag. "And I have something for you. A birthday present!" She passes Joséphine a package, beautifully wrapped with silver paper and a classy black bow. "I wish I could have seen more of you when you were growing up, Joséphine. But I plan to make up for it now."

"*Merci*." Joséphine leans forward, kissing Isabelle on the cheek. She thinks about telling Isabelle that she knows now why they've hardly seen each other, why she's been hidden away in Trégastel. *La honte*. The shame of the family. But she doesn't want to spoil this moment, so she opens her present instead. A small box with "Chanel N° 5" written on it peeps out. Joséphine has never had perfume; it's such a luxury, decadent even. "Oh, Isabelle, thank you so much." She stares at the Chanel symbol, her eyes watering. *For goodness' sake*, she tells herself, *it's only perfume!* But it feels like so much more than that; like an entry into womanhood, like a whole new world opening up.

Isabelle smiles. "Try it."

Joséphine opens the box, taking out the delicate bottle; a work of art in itself. Tentatively she sprays her wrist and waves it in the air before sniffing it. It smells of light and freshness, of new beginnings, of sensuality and adventure. She breathes it in.

"You like it then?"

"I love it!"

They're interrupted by the waiter bringing their first course.

"How's your mother?" Isabelle asks when he leaves, as she picks up a forkful of egg, bringing it to her red lipsticked lips, chewing softly as she studies Joséphine.

Joséphine takes a piece of bread from the basket and picks at it, feeling uncomfortable under Isabelle's scrutiny. She'll tell Isabelle what she knows, but not yet. It will change everything and probably ruin her visit. It can't be the first thing they talk about. "Fine," she lies. "Where's the Eiffel Tower?" She moves away from the subject of her mother. "Is it far?"

"Don't worry. I have all the sights planned for tomorrow. Today I thought we'd take it easy—meander back through the Jardins du Luxembourg."

After lunch, when they stroll through the park with its perfectly aligned avenues of chestnut trees, Joséphine gazes at the dark green leaves fluttering in the gentle breeze and wonders how her life will be different now. She feels oddly

disconnected. Who is she in this big city? Can she be anyone she wants to be?

They pass by a lake where children holding long sticks
are prodding at small wooden sailing boats. She turns to
Isabelle. "Did you come here when you were a child?"

"Yes, Élise—your mother—used to bring me here." She
pauses. "Then we stopped coming. During the occupation
the gardens were swarming with Germans and their lady
friends. Élise didn't want to come any more."

"But..." Joséphine's dying to ask how that could have
been so when her mother had a German boyfriend herself.

Isabelle looks at her, a frown lining her forehead. "But
let's not talk about those times." She takes Joséphine's hand.
"I know I keep saying it, but I'm so glad you're here!"

Chapter Six

Paris, May 1963

Joséphine

When they get to the apartment, they have to climb six floors up a narrow, winding wooden staircase before Isabelle takes out the key. "Here we are. Home sweet home." She opens the door and Joséphine realizes it's well worth the climb. The view over the rooftops makes her feel as though she's on top of the world.

"It's amazing!" She puts her case down and opens the window to lean out.

"We only have one bedroom, so you'll have to sleep on the couch in here."

"It looks lovely. Thank you." Joséphine throws herself onto the cushions lining the couch. She doesn't care where she sleeps. She's just happy to be in Paris.

"I have to make dinner now. Eric will be home at seven."

Joséphine's impatient to see the sights and thinks about

suggesting she take a walk on her own, but that seems rude. Instead she offers to help prepare the meal.

On the dot, at seven, Eric walks in, looking handsome in his brown suit, his dark hair slicked back. He kisses his wife then Joséphine. He smells of expensive cologne.

"Welcome to Paris." He takes a step back, looking at Joséphine. "Quite the lady now."

She smiles, appreciating the compliment.

"I'll get changed then we can have an aperitif."

When he comes back in, he looks slightly less handsome in a plain T-shirt and loose pants. Walking over to the open kitchen, he takes out three flute glasses and pours a dash of *crème de cassis* in each. "*Kir royale?*" Without waiting for an answer, he takes a bottle of champagne from the fridge and, pointing it at the ceiling, unwinds the wire holding the cork in. The cork bursts out, pale froth flowing down the sides of the bottle. Laughing, he quickly fills their glasses. "To Joséphine," he toasts. "And her first time in Paris." It's delicious; light and air bubbling their way to Joséphine's head.

"I'll put some music on." Eric swings around and leafs through a selection of records. "What do you like? Johnny? Jacques Brel? Gainsbourg?"

"'La Javanaise'? I love that." Joséphine has only heard it twice, but it comes straight to mind.

"Me too!" Eric pulls the record out of its sleeve, blowing on it before setting it down on the turntable, then he lifts the needle gently and drops it down into the groove.

"*J'avoue, j'en ai bavé, pas vous, mon amour,*" Gainsbourg's sexy husky voice rings out. Eric sways gently from side to side as he sings along. Isabelle joins in, and Joséphine takes a large sip of her drink before accepting Eric's open palm as an invitation to dance. Oh, to be in Paris! It feels like decadence itself. Eric and Isabelle seem so far removed from Maman and Soizic and their little life in Trégastel, and so much more exotic.

Later they sit down around the dining table, and the conversation turns polite. "How's your mother?" Eric asks.

Joséphine shrugs. "Fine." She really doesn't want to talk about it now. Not tonight.

"Still working in that big house, is she?"

"Mondays to Saturdays." Joséphine feels giddy from the wine and the dancing. "Sometimes I imagine she has another family there."

"Whatever makes you say that?" Isabelle's tone is sharp.

Joséphine has surprised herself—that she actually said it out loud. She finishes her glass. "Well, she does spend most of her time there. She could have a whole double life. A husband, other children."

Eric laughs and refills Joséphine's glass. "What a vivid imagination you have! A man, yes, I can imagine a man leading a double life. But not a woman. What a thought!"

Isabelle frowns at Eric. "Can you indeed?"

Joséphine isn't sure if Isabelle's playing with him, or if she means it.

"It's been hard for your mother." Isabelle turns back to Joséphine. "It's not easy being a single mother. She's always had to work. You shouldn't hold that against her. It was difficult finding work after the war. She took what she could."

"Good thing I had Soizic. She's been more like a mother to me."

Isabelle's eyes turn cold. "Soizic was good to take your mother in, but everything your mother has done has been for you."

This is too much! Joséphine's ready to tell them the truth; the alcohol is giving her the courage. She gulps back her second glass. Eric serves her again.

"Eric, go easy. Joséphine's probably not used to drinking." Isabelle stands, clearing their plates, leaving Joséphine alone with Eric. She'll have to wait for her to come back now.

Joséphine takes a small sip from her glass, working out how to begin. "I know why I never met my grandfather." She looks at Isabelle as she walks back in with the cheese platter. "Why Maman never wanted to bring me to Paris."

Isabelle glances at Eric as she puts the plate down then turns back to Joséphine. "What do you mean? Your grandfather has been ill since his time in the German camps."

Joséphine raises an eyebrow. "Yes, that must have been hard for him." She pauses. "Even harder to get home and realize your own daughter..." She can't say the words.

The blood drains from Isabelle's face. Eric coughs as though embarrassed. And the silence hangs heavy like the calm before the storm.

"I know about my father," Joséphine soldiers on.

Isabelle sits down heavily. "What do you know?"

"That he was a Boche."

"Don't use that word." Isabelle brings her hand to her mouth.

"But he was, wasn't he? He was a Boche." She can feel the champagne bubbling in her head, making her more daring than she should be. "Why did you all hide it from me? Don't you think I had a right to know who my father was?" Joséphine's aware that her tone is aggressive. But resentment mixes with her newfound daring. "It explains so much, so much I never understood." She can tell by the look on Eric's face that she should just shut up; she's said enough. She tries to compose herself.

Isabelle leans over and lays her hand over Joséphine's. "What did your mother tell you?"

"I found my birth certificate."

"Found it?"

"Yes, I looked for it actually. It named my father. Not a man called Frédéric as Maman had told me. It was a German name! Sébastian Kleinhaus."

Isabelle's voice turns to a whisper. "She named him? I always assumed she put 'father unknown.'"

Joséphine is confused. "But he wasn't unknown. You all knew!"

"Don't you see? She knew you'd find out one day. She wanted to tell you, she just wanted to wait till you were ready."

"Ready! She should never have hidden it from me."

"I know how upsetting it must have been for you to find out like that." Isabelle presses gently on the back of Joséphine's hand. "But you have to understand how hard it was for your mother. She had nowhere to go when she found she was pregnant with you. Soizic was the only person who was ready to take her in. But she didn't want to hear one word about your true father."

"It doesn't make much difference." Eric helps himself to a large slice of Brie. "It's all in the past. It doesn't change who you are."

Joséphine removes her hand from under Isabelle's and rests her chin in her open palms. It's as though they think she's behaving like a spoilt kid having a tantrum. She imagines that's how Eric sees it, anyway. They don't understand how her whole world has been turned upside down; she can feel it, she just can't explain how. "It does," she starts. "I'm not the person I thought I was. I'm not the daughter of a French hero. I'm a…" She can't say the word. "It changes everything."

"You're exactly who you were before." Eric puts a slice of Brie onto a piece of baguette. "It's your father who's different. Not you." He speaks with authority, and Joséphine begins to wonder if she really is making a fuss over nothing.

"And look, you've turned out great," Isabelle adds. "You have a mother who loves you, and you have Soizic. And you have us." She pauses. "And you're in Paris!"

"But…" Joséphine's heart beats harder. "I can't think of myself in the same way." She needs to voice these thoughts charging through her head. "I feel…I feel cut off from who I was before. It wasn't me."

Eric frowns as he chews on his bread.

"Like I thought I was one person," Joséphine continues. "And now I find out I'm not that person. I'm someone different."

"Oh, come on. You're the same person you've always been." Eric stops chewing.

"I'm not!" Joséphine blinks back tears. "I'm not," she repeats in a whisper.

"Joséphine," Isabelle speaks softly. "Your mother and father loved each other. That's all you need to know."

"No! How can you say that? He was a Boche!"

"Please! Don't use that word. I hope you didn't say it in front of your mother." Isabelle hesitates. "What exactly did your mother tell you?"

Joséphine feels the heat rise to her cheeks. "Not much," she mumbles, intending to explain how she ran off before giving her mother a chance to explain anything.

But then Eric interrupts. "Listen," he says assertively. "Let's not argue. It was probably a shock for Joséphine to find out her father was a Bo— a German, but it doesn't change who you are, Joséphine." He smiles at her, using all his charm. "Don't let this spoil your time here." He picks up the platter of cheeses, passing it to Joséphine. "The Brie is delicious."

Joséphine shakes her head, swallowing the hard lump in her throat, as she turns toward Isabelle. "Do you know what he was doing here? What was his role?"

"Didn't your mother tell you? He was a translator."

"A translator?" It doesn't sound evil, in fact it sounds quite mundane, and Joséphine feels a wave of relief.

Isabelle squeezes her shoulder. "Don't be sad, please Joséphine. He wasn't a bad man." She gets up and stands next to Joséphine. Bending down, she puts her arms around her. "My poor little Joséphine. Would it help if I told you what I know about your father? Would it help to talk about him? About that time? About all of us?"

"Yes." Tears flood down Joséphine's cheeks. Tears of relief and gratefulness. "Yes." This is what she wants. She needs to know who her father really was. And who her mother really was.

Part Two

1944

Chapter Seven

Paris, April 1944

Élise

Paris was quiet. The Boches didn't beep like the Parisians used to. They drove quickly and silently in black cars and, like hearses, they signaled death. When they walked, they didn't stroll, they strutted, their hobnailed boots echoing through the empty streets. Paris was no longer Paris. It was an occupied city, and even the buildings seemed to be holding their breath, waiting. There were no flowers on the balconies, no light laughter spilling out, no music on the streets. The German soldiers based here probably didn't even realize they'd taken the heart out of Paris. All they saw were the impressive Haussmann buildings, the forward-thinking architecture drawing a star around the Arc de Triomphe, the restaurants, the cabarets, the shops, the champagne, the wine. And it was enough for them. They loved it. But it wasn't Paris. Paris was sleeping, waiting to be rescued.

My stomach rumbled as I crossed the square at

Saint-Sulpice. I paused at the fountain, looking over at the tall church, saying a silent prayer to myself. *Please make it be over soon.*

"*Bonsoir, mademoiselle.*" A young soldier walked up to me. "Do you have a light?" He held out a cigarette.

I wanted to smack it out of his hands. I knew he had a light; he just wanted to see if I was one of those girls who would accept a cigarette, then a drink, maybe dinner, and then who knows what else. I shook my head and walked away, my hands trembling as I put them in my pockets, my heart thumping hard. He could come after me, arrest me for nothing.

I hurried across the square and down our little street, quickly pushing on the big heavy door into the entrée and through to our apartment on the ground floor. As soon as I opened our front door, the smell of cooking cabbage hit me. Closing it behind me, I leaned back on it, breathing a sigh of relief and inhaling the familiar rotten odor of cabbage.

"*Bonsoir*," I called, going straight through to the kitchen.

Maman wiped her soapy hands on her apron before kissing me on the cheek, then she looked down at my empty hands. "Wasn't there any bread?"

"No."

She smiled a half smile that didn't quite reach her eyes. "Just soup tonight then. Shall we eat?"

I followed her into the dining room, where my little sister, Isabelle, was setting the table for dinner. Maman thought she couldn't have any more children, and then Isabelle arrived like a little miracle thirteen years after me. Her hair hung in one long plait that swished from side to side as she placed soup bowls on large white plates, as though there would be another course to follow the soup. I pecked her on each cheek.

"Did you have a good day at work?" she asked in her put-on, grown-up voice.

"Yes, thank you. And how was school?"

"Boring. Marc has gone." Maman and I exchanged glances. Another deportation? Isabelle caught our look. "He's probably not coming back. Madame Serriers said he's got Jewish grandparents."

"God, when will it ever stop?" My chest burned with rage and a sense of powerlessness. Innocent people were being arrested every day and sent to God knows where, while most of us stood by helplessly, just grateful it wasn't us.

Maman sighed and turned away. "We just have to wait. It will stop eventually."

"What? When they've all been deported?" I spoke to her back.

She stopped and everything went still, a heavy silence creeping into the room. Isabelle glanced at me anxiously. I'd upset Maman.

Maman was doing her best to keep up appearances, pretending life was normal, never complaining, never asking questions, just keeping her head down. It was bad enough that I insisted on volunteering at the UGIF—the *Union Générale des Israélites de France*, where orphaned Jewish children sometimes ended up. I took them old clothes and sometimes food, if we could ever spare any, which we couldn't, but every little helped—the odd potato or carrot, some cabbage leaves.

If she knew what else I was doing at the UGIF, she'd be furious.

Isabelle carefully placed knives and forks at the sides of the plates.

"Isabelle, we don't need knives and forks," I couldn't help saying. Why couldn't I just keep my mouth shut?

"You know I like to set the table properly." Maman interrupted before Isabelle had a chance to answer. Isabelle must have felt like she had two mothers to boss her around; maybe it made up for not having a father at home. Papa was in Germany—forced labor for the Boches. When we'd seen the poster calling up men his age, we'd been horrified. Papa, working for the Boches. It was unimaginable. But then one morning after much shouting and cursing and slamming of doors, he'd left. We'd been devastated to see him go like that, but in truth our lives were more peaceful after he'd gone. No more of his dark moods, no more shouting, no more living on tenterhooks hoping he wasn't going to explode at any moment. I wondered how Maman felt. One never really knew with her.

"*Asseyez-vous, les filles.*" Maman put on a bright cheery voice and went into the kitchen.

When she returned, she put the large soup dish in the middle of the table, then sat down, putting her hands together. "God bless this food we eat. Keep us safe. Amen."

Isabelle and I murmured, "Amen," and passed our bowls to Maman. She ladled out the watery yellow liquid with the occasional piece of potato, then when we were all served, we placed our napkins on our laps—as if we might spill a drop.

"*Bon appétit, mes filles.*"

"*Bon appétit.*"

"I only used a little salt, so you might like to add some."

"Pass the pepper please."

"Would you like water?" Maman held out the carafe as if it were wine, and Isabelle and I held out our glasses to be filled.

And so we went through the routine of dinner, sipping on our soup slowly, making the most of every mouthful. I took the salt mill, turning the worn wooden handle, watching the almost transparent crystals fall into my soup—dissolving. Like us, I thought to myself, trying to make ourselves invisible.

Isabelle lifted her spoon, tilting it, so the watery soup fell back into the bowl. "I wish we could have something nice to eat."

"We'll have to get rid of the Boches first." I picked out a piece of potato from my soup.

"When will that be?" Isabelle sighed. "Have they always been here?"

She was only six when they came marching down the Champs-Élysées, and now she was ten; she could hardly remember a time before they came. My thoughts turned to Frédéric, my fiancé, sent four years ago with the other French soldiers to defend the Maginot Line. But it was undefendable against the German tanks. He never came back. The thing that had upset me the most was the way he'd left for war; so willingly, so enthusiastically. So stupidly naive. What a waste of a life.

I often dreamed of food; soft madeleines that melted in my mouth, croissants that I'd pull apart, watching the dough stretching out. This morning I was dreaming of *pains aux raisins* when something woke me up. I closed my eyes again, hoping to fall back into the dream, but my empty stomach wouldn't let me. I got up instead and wandered into the kitchen in search of our special brand of coffee, acorn and chicory, hoping it might ease my hunger pains.

"*Bonjour,* Élise," Maman greeted me with a peck on the

cheek. "Madame Dumaison brought some clothes over yesterday; she was fed up with them taking up cupboard space. If you want, you could take them over to the UGIF."

"*Merci*, Maman."

She acknowledged my thanks with a small nod of the head, but her lips were pursed. "If you must insist on volunteering there." She stared at me hard. "I know you think you're helping those poor Jewish orphans, but they've only set up those places so they can keep tabs on the Jews, and they'll be keeping tabs on you too if you keep going there."

"I know that, but it's all they've got, they'd starve without it."

"Just be careful, Élise. We don't want any trouble."

I paused a minute, wondering if she had an inkling of what I was up to, but dismissed the idea. If she did, she wouldn't let me go. I quickly drank my ersatz and set off with two boxes of clothes. As I turned down Rue Saint-Jacques, I saw a group of women sitting outside a hairdresser's, having their hair wound up into turbans. It saved washing it, and it looked quite chic in a way, not that I cared about looking chic myself. I preferred to have short hair and wear pants whenever I could; anything to avoid the attention of the German soldiers.

"*Vos papiers!*" Two of them stood in front of me, blocking my path.

I stopped, my heart thumping hard. Lost in thought, I hadn't seen them. "*Oui, messieurs.*" I dropped the boxes on the pavement and dug into my pocket for my identity card. The taller one snatched it from me. Holding my breath, I watched him scrutinize it and waited for him to give it back, but he held onto it. "What's in the boxes?"

"Clothes for the UGIF." I tried to keep my voice steady.

"Open them."

My fingers trembled as I pulled back the card folded over the top, holding out the open box for him to search. He handed my identity card over to his partner and plunged both his hands into the box. A trickle of sweat ran down my ribs as he fumbled through the soft material, probably hoping to find something harder, like a radio or maybe papers containing secret messages. He seemed disappointed when his grasping hands came across nothing but children's clothes.

His partner passed my identity card back. "Come on." He nudged the other one. "We have more important matters to attend to."

They didn't even bother with the other box and left me standing there as they strolled away, probably looking for bigger trouble. I waited for my racing pulse to slow before picking up the boxes, but the sweat continued to trickle down my ribs as I walked toward the orphanage. Why had they stopped me like that? Was I under suspicion? Did they know what I was up to? Maman's words this morning rang in my ears: "Just be careful, Élise. We don't want any trouble." I knew it wasn't only myself I was putting at risk, but her and Isabelle too, without their knowledge or consent.

I turned down Rue Claude Bernard with a heavy heart. The front door was locked, and I had to knock to be let in. Leah opened the door, and I put the boxes into her open arms. Without a word, she nodded in the direction of Anaïs, who was hovering over two small boys. Holding hands, they stood in front of a plain gray wall, where the paint was beginning to peel. The younger one bit on his lower lip as if concentrating hard, while his other hand picked at the paint where it had curled at the edges. The older child's tears had dried into streaks of salt running down his cheeks, and I knew he would hold on to the rest of his tears for his sibling's sake. He stared at me with an assertiveness well beyond his years, already assuming his role as head of the family.

"What's your name?" I asked him.

"Isaac."

"And how old are you, Isaac?"

"Eight."

"And your brother?"

"Four."

"I'm Élise." I held my hand out for him to shake, treating him like the man he had to be.

"And what's your name?" I turned to his younger brother, who'd removed his hand from the wallpaper and put his thumb in his mouth as he watched me suspiciously.

"His name's Daniel." Isaac spoke for him.

I gave them a hard candy each. Isaac stuffed his into his pocket, barely glancing at me. I was giving him a tiny patch for a gaping wound and we both knew it—a sweet for a stolen childhood. Daniel struggled to unwrap his, and his brother took it from him, taking the sticky paper off carefully before handing it back. The way Daniel stuffed it into his mouth and crunched it made me think he was hungry. I remembered the apple I'd saved in my pocket since yesterday. Just the thought of it took away the edge of hunger that never left me. I took it out, watching their eyes grow wide. It made me wonder when they'd last eaten. I held the apple out to Isaac.

"*Merci.*" Without even looking at it, he gave it to his younger brother. I watched as Daniel took a big bite and then another. He was about to dive into a third when he stopped and looked at Isaac with large doleful eyes, then passed it back to him. It made me want to hug him, but instead I opened the boxes I'd brought, passing the clothes out to the women.

"These two are leaving next," Anaïs whispered as she took a small shirt from me. "This Sunday."

My stomach lurched. *This Sunday?* I was still jittery after my encounter with the police this morning, and I would have liked to wait a little longer. I couldn't help feeling something was amiss. Just nerves, I told myself. Nothing more. I looked at Anaïs and nodded. I would be there. I would be there on Sunday to escort the two boys to the Bois de Boulogne, where they would meet their *passeur*, who would take them out of Paris and down south, eventually to the Swiss border. My part was tiny, my risk nothing compared to others'.

Chapter Eight

Paris, April 1944

Sébastian

Paris in spring. Sébastian had always dreamed of visiting the "City of Light" at this time of year. But not like this. Not when it shrank back from him, defeated and lifeless. Paris had become a city of dark uniforms, of sinister black cars silently sweeping past, hobnailed boots echoing through the empty streets. It was no longer the city he'd visited eight years ago, when he'd been an impressionable young lad of sixteen. He felt lost and alien in this place that had once opened its doors to him. He'd rather be home in Dresden than here right now.

He wandered along the *quai*, glancing at the *bouquinistes'* collections of old books and photos in the dark green wooden cabins that lined the banks of the Seine. He'd have liked to strike up a conversation with one of the old men who kept the stalls, but he knew they'd just grunt at him and look the other way. He didn't blame them, and he tried not to take it personally. It was his uniform; that was all. He wished he didn't have to wear it in his free time, but that was exactly why they made them wear it at all times; a reminder that they were the property of the Third Reich. All of his life, he'd belonged to someone else, but never himself. He wondered what it would be like to be free. To have choices.

Sébastian leaned over the bridge, staring at the Seine; dark blue in the spring sunshine. It was warm, but a soft breeze from the river kept it from being too hot. He decided to head over to his favorite bookshop before it closed.

The bell rang as he pushed open the door, causing the owner to look up from his book. He nodded at Sébastian.

"*Bonsoir, monsieur.*" Sébastian removed his cap, stuffing it under his elbow. Immediately two women left the shop, making a point of not acknowledging him as they walked by, their heads held high. A familiar wave of loneliness washed over him, their reaction having exactly the effect they had certainly intended, leaving him feeling ostracized, making him wish he wasn't there.

Sébastian glanced round, taking in an old couple by the atlases. A heavy silence filled the shop, and he couldn't help wondering if there had been chatter before he'd entered. He stood still for a moment, gathering his thoughts, wondering what he should read. He'd already read *Madame Bovary* and most of Victor Hugo's novels. But this evening he felt restless; he didn't know what he wanted. Something that would take him away from himself. Maybe he should try poetry.

Wandering past the first set of shelves, Sébastian caught sight of someone bent over a book. Short, dark hair flopped forward, hiding the face, and baggy pants held up by a thick brown belt hung loosely. He stopped for a minute, taking in the thin, slight figure. Then the person looked up, and Sébastian saw it was a young woman. She stared at him coldly then went back to her book. He continued on to the next set of shelves.

The door opened, and two policemen walked in. Sébastian stepped back behind the shelf, out of view, curious as to what they might be doing in this particular bookshop.

"*Papiers!*"

Sébastian peered out from behind the shelf as the old couple produced their identity cards, but the policemen hardly glanced at them. Instead they strutted past the shelves as if they might catch someone hiding between them.

"*Vos papiers!*" Sébastian couldn't see, but he guessed they were talking to the woman he'd seen.

"*Messieurs*, I'm sorry. I left them at home."

He heard a man's laugh, loud and mocking. "Left them at home? That's a good one."

"It's true. They're in my jacket pocket. I came out tonight without it."

"Without your jacket? Where's your yellow star?"

"But...but I'm not Jewish."

"Well, if you don't have your papers, we have to assume you are."

"I'm not! Monsieur Le Bolzec here—he knows me. He can tell you."

"Monsieur Le Bolzec? Now, don't try getting someone else in trouble. You'd better come with us."

Sébastian sighed loudly, stepping into view. "Why don't we just ask Monsieur Le Bolzec?"

The policemen stared at him wide-eyed, obviously surprised to hear a German speaking perfect French, then their eyes flickered over Sébastian's collar and left sleeve, where his rank was displayed. Sébastian was just an ordinary soldier, but still he was German, and they were French. The pecking order was clear.

"They're liars. They always lie." The policeman laid his hand on the woman's shoulder as if staking his claim.

"I suggest you take your hand from her shoulder." Sébastian surprised himself with the authoritarian tone of his voice.

The policeman's hand immediately fell to his side. The woman rolled her shoulder as if freed from a huge weight. Sébastian looked at her. Her hair was cut short, barely reaching her chin. Her features were fine, and her eyes shone out like a cat's; green, speckled with dots of yellow. Everything came together to give her a kind of elfin appearance, and there was an energy about her.

"She doesn't have her papers." The policeman started again. "It's the law! She's broken the law!"

"Don't tell me the law!" Sébastian raised his voice, taking a step nearer. He deliberately avoided looking at the woman. It wasn't about her. It was about these petty policemen abusing their position. How he despised them. He turned to the man at the counter. "Monsieur Le Bolzec?"

"*Oui, monsieur.*"

"Do you know this woman?"

"Yes, I've known her and her family since she was old enough to read. Her name is Élise Chevalier."

"Can you vouch for her then?"

"Yes, I can. She comes from a good Catholic family."

"Well, that's settled." Sébastian turned back to the policemen. "There is no need to bother the authorities with this. Don't you think they have enough work?"

"But...but it's...it's the law." The tall one couldn't help it. The shorter one looked down at his feet; he obviously had more sense.

"Who made these laws?" Both policemen gaped at him. "Well?"

"The Nazis," the short one answered.

"Exactly. Now get out before I have you arrested."

Without another word they shuffled out of the shop.

Sébastian turned back toward the woman. "You shouldn't forget your papers." He tried to show a stern face, but the light in her eyes seemed to see straight through him, and he had to look away. Lost for words, he coughed.

"It was so warm today; I left my jacket at home."

"Yes. It has been very warm this week." Sébastian tugged at his collar, feeling suddenly suffocated. She nodded then turned away. Sébastian sensed that she just wanted him to leave. Without stopping to think he grabbed a small book of poems from the shelf just in front of him.

At the cash till, Monsieur Le Bolzec took the book from him and raised an eyebrow as though questioning Sébastian's choice of book. "Do you like poetry?"

It was the first time a Frenchman had addressed him with a question, and it made him feel normal. Almost. "I don't know much about poetry," he admitted. "I thought… I thought I might try some."

"Victor Hugo. A good place to start." Monsieur Le Bolzec handed the book back, then rang it up on the till. "Three francs fifty please."

Sébastian paid and turned to leave, but the thought of leaving the little shop and wandering through the streets of Paris alone filled him with dread. He wanted to stay and talk with Monsieur Le Bolzec about books, about anything. He craved conversation, a friendly face. He didn't want to see the sun setting on Notre-Dame all on his own. These spring evenings were poignant with longing, as the light gently faded from the day. For a moment the emptiness inside him seemed to expand till it was all that was left of him, and the vastness of it terrified him. Impulsively, he turned back to Monsieur Le Bolzec. He was watching him, as though he'd just read his mind.

Chapter Nine

Paris, April 1944

Élise

In the early hours of the morning, I sat at the kitchen table, going over the plan again in my head, checking I'd remembered the false details for the two brothers. Eight o'clock dragged around, and I set off without breakfast, leaving Maman and Isabelle to sleep late on Sunday mornings—their treat of the week. Walking through the silent streets only accentuated my unease, and when I got to the orphanage, I glanced round at the apartments overlooking it. Something moving in my periphery made me look back, but there was nothing. It was just my nerves. Taking a deep breath, trying to calm myself, I knocked on the door.

Leah opened it immediately. "We've got Alfred today."

I sighed with relief. He was our most trusted and reliable *passeur*, already having made seven successful journeys to the Swiss border.

Isaac and Daniel stood against the wall again, staring at

me with large, solemn eyes. They understood only too well the danger they were facing. Anaïs and Leah looked pale and anxious. The sooner we got on with it, the better for all of us. But before we could set out, protocol obliged me to ask the boys a series of questions. I was glad to see they'd been cleaned up and made to look like good little school-boys with their leather satchels and shiny shoes.

"What's your name?" I asked Isaac.

"Pierre."

"Good boy. And where are you going?"

"To stay with my auntie in the Alps." He paused. "Because I have ax...asthma." He looked relieved to get the word out. Then he coughed, holding his little fist against his chest. All part of the act.

"And who's this?" I pointed to his little brother.

"This is Marcel. He's only three." I understood why they had made him a year younger than he really was— a three year old could get away without talking. The less the younger ones talked, the better. They could be so unpredictable.

"Three?" I repeated. "When's his birthday?"

"July thirty-first."

"And yours?"

"December fifth."

"Show me your papers."

Isaac took the satchel from his back and opened it up, handing over their identity cards with a sweet smile. I felt a surge of pride in him. He was doing well.

"Will Maman and Papa be there?" Daniel asked in a tiny voice.

Isaac turned to face him. "I told you already. They have to stay here to work."

"But why didn't they say goodbye?" Tears began to fall down Daniel's cheeks.

"They said goodbye, but you were asleep."

Daniel wiped his face with his sleeve. "Why didn't they wake me up? I wanted to say goodbye."

Isaac put his arm around his brother. Daniel looked so small, so lost, and he was going to have to be so strong. "Marcel," I spoke softly. Daniel didn't respond. "Marcel," I repeated, louder this time. I looked at the two women, holding my breath. This wasn't going well. I wouldn't be able to take them if there was a risk, and then they'd be open to deportation at any minute. When the police couldn't provide enough for the quotas, they always came here to make their numbers up.

Isaac nudged his little brother. "Answer her. Say your secret name."

"I don't want a secret name." Daniel's lower lip stuck out stubbornly.

"But it's the game," his older brother insisted. "You have to play the game so we can see Maman and Papa again."

"It's best if he doesn't speak." I turned to Isaac. "Tell him to stay quiet. Tell him to pretend he can't talk."

"Okay." Isaac blushed as though embarrassed for his younger sibling. Or was it fear?

It was risky. It was always risky. I wasn't sure they were ready, and I knew Alfred would question them further before embarking on the dangerous journey.

"You should go. It's time." Leah spoke with authority. "Take six other children with you."

"Yes, of course." I always took a larger group out, so that I could still return with a group of children rather than not returning at all, just in case someone was keeping watch.

You never knew. There were always people on the lookout for someone to denounce, hoping to gain favor with the Germans, to help them climb that ladder to get a bigger apartment or extra food rations.

Leah went to fetch six other children and together we left the building, Isaac holding his brother's hand as we walked toward the Métro, where we separated. Leah got on the last carriage of the Métro with the six other children, as was the rule for Jews, while I got on a carriage in the middle with the brothers. I prayed our papers wouldn't be checked, but if they were I knew what to say and so did the boys. It was still early and not even the Boches were up yet on a Sunday. I held the younger brother's hand as we sat down, taking in two other passengers. "Marcel," I said, reenforcing his false name. "We're going on an adventure today." He looked at me with wide innocent eyes, and I squeezed his hand. "It will be fun." I wished he'd smile, to appear like any other child going to the woods for the day. "We'll play some games." He just stared at me as though I was completely mad.

"Yes," his brother helped me out. "And we'll have a picnic."

The other two passengers stared out of the window as though they were miles away, but you never knew.

When we left the Métro at Michel-Ange—Auteuil, we regrouped and walked toward the woods. The trees were in early blossom, but the air was still cold. I breathed in deeply, trying to ease the cramps in my stomach. Some of the children began to jostle each other, as though they were feeling a little safer now we were out in the open. The lake ahead shimmered in the morning sun, and the rowing boats were out. I wished I could have taken the children out in a boat, but of course, Jewish children were forbidden such pleasures. One of them stopped to pick up a stick, throwing it into the lake.

A man sitting on the bench stood up. "Beautiful day, isn't it?"

I turned to look at the man. It was Alfred, our *passeur*.

"*Oui*," I replied. "And we have two boys here who are very excited to be going to stay with their auntie."

"*Bien, bien*. Are these them?" He turned toward the two brothers.

I nodded. "Pierre and Marcel."

He held out his big paw of a hand, shaking the brothers' hands. "Pleased to meet you, Pierre and Marcel." The boys kissed him on each cheek as they had been instructed to do, as though he were family. Then Alfred turned back to me. "Leave them with me," he whispered. "Go around the lake. If I don't think they're well enough prepared, I'll come back around in the opposite direction."

The other children kissed the brothers goodbye, and then we walked away. They knew what was up, but they were never allowed to talk about the children who left like this. Once they were gone, we all had to pretend they'd never existed. The children were surprisingly good at this, and they never asked why. I guess in their hearts, they knew. They were far too wise for their years.

We wandered around the lake for a while, the children kicking despondently at loose pebbles. I was too preoccupied and anxious to engage with them. I half expected to see Alfred returning with the two boys. Mission abandoned. But I didn't see them again.

Chapter Ten

Paris, April 1944

Sébastian

Sébastian got up from his desk at the old Louis-Dreyfus bank, which was no longer a bank, but instead housed the Commissariat Général aux Questions Juives—the CGQJ. Without saying goodbye to his colleagues, he walked out onto Place des Petits Pères. It was just six o'clock and it was still light. He pulled at his tight collar, loosening it slightly as he took a deep breath, breathing out slowly as though he could exhale all the bitterness and venom of the denunciation letters he'd had to translate today. His stomach gurgled and there was an acidic burning in his throat. He'd never suffered from heartburn before and had the feeling that it was due to all the words he'd had to swallow today. It didn't make him feel like eating, so instead of sitting outside one of the cafés and ordering dinner, he decided to take a stroll. As had become a habit of his, he walked toward the river, crossing Pont Louis Philippe to Île de la Cité, wandering around the back of Notre-Dame. He preferred this view of the cathedral: it was far less grandiose; the gardens like those of a large house, the arches reaching forward to support the smaller end of the cathedral. Religion, he thought to himself, the so-called cause of many wars.

In a way Nazism was itself a religion, the difference being that there was no forgiveness, no redemption, and certainly no resurrection. But one God? Hitler? And if you didn't obey his orders, you would be punished, probably killed, but not before you'd been made to suffer for your sins. There was no room for misunderstanding, or even understanding. It wasn't about the individual; it was all for the good of the group. Hitler understood the psychology of the masses and had even written that all propaganda must be directed at the intellectual level of the least intelligent, truth being far less important than success. The propaganda he'd spread so successfully about the Jews was the perfect example, and they were to be discriminated against according to their "race," not their religion. He'd managed to unite people against a common enemy. Like others, he imagined, Sébastian had nothing personal against the Jews, but he'd been powerless to go against the current. *Putain!* He should have seen what was coming. He swallowed more bile, wishing there was a way out. He crossed the river again, stopping to lean over the bridge, staring down at the flowing water, at the stray pieces of broken wood carried forward by the current. He imagined falling into the river, letting himself be carried away. Turning back, he leaned against the bridge, refusing to entertain such dark thoughts. He reached into his breast pocket and pulled out a pack of Gitanes, and with his back to the wind, cupped his hands around his lighter as he tried to light up. But the breeze coming off the river was swift and blew out the tiny flame before it could catch. Damn! He couldn't even light a cigarette properly. In frustration and anger, he scrunched it up and threw it into the water.

He shouldn't smoke so much anyway. He never used to. As he continued through the narrow, winding streets, he glanced at the cafés, tables and chairs spilling out onto the sidewalk. A few elderly men sat around, enjoying a glass of red, and he would have liked to join them, but their eyes burned into his back as he passed by. Sighing inwardly, he carried on toward the Panthéon.

The bookshop was on his way, and on impulse he pushed open the door. The smell of dust and old paper greeted him. He was aware of a hush descending upon the place and couldn't help wondering if the bell served as a warning so they could wrap up quickly any illegal activities. What if the bookshop was a Résistance meeting place? He hoped it wasn't.

"*Bonjour, monsieur.*" The bookseller stepped out from behind the center shelves, breaking the silence.

The greeting warmed Sébastian, lifting his spirit. "You're open late."

"Until curfew."

The hush fell again as the last few customers silently sidled out of the shop. Sébastian watched them leave, knowing it was because of him, and certainly aggravated by the way the bookseller had greeted him instead of ignoring him. Sébastian understood the way people used silence as a weapon. He pitied them, conscious that it was all they had left.

"What are you looking for?" The bookseller stared at him.

"Something to read."

"Really? Well, this would be the place then." The older

man didn't smile, but his words felt like light teasing, as though, even if they were not quite familiar with each other, they were at least amicable.

It encouraged Sébastian to continue the conversation. "I'd like to learn more about French writers, maybe read some poetry."

"Oh yes. Poetry. Words from the heart. But didn't you buy a poetry book last time you were here?"

Sébastian felt the heat rising in his cheeks. "Yes," he admitted. "I just thought you might have something else you could recommend."

"Poetry's at the back."

Sébastian followed him to the dingy corner at the back of the shop, the smell of dust reaching the back of his nostrils, making him want to sneeze.

"I'm afraid poetry's not really my thing; getting into another person's head like that." The bookseller ran his finger down the dusty spines of the books in front of him, as though distracted by the thought. "How about short stories instead? Maupassant?"

"Yes, I haven't read anything by him." Sébastian followed him to the next stack of shelves.

Abruptly the bookseller stopped and turned around, facing Sébastian. "I don't believe we've introduced ourselves properly."

"Kleinhaus, Sébastian."

"Yannick Le Bolzec." He held out his hand toward Sébastian. "I must say, Sébastian Kleinhaus, I liked the way you handled those policemen the other evening."

Sébastian felt a rush of pride. It was the first time someone had said something nice to him for years. "Well, some of them are a little big for their boots."

"Indeed they are." Monsieur Le Bolzec paused. "You know I wasn't lying. I've known that woman since she was a child."

Sébastian wondered why he felt he had to tell him this. "How do you know her?"

"Her mother used to bring her into the shop. She learned to read here."

Sébastian found himself hungry for more information. "Is she a student?"

"No." He paused, as though deciding whether to continue the conversation or not. "She works in a bank," he finally continued, pulling a book off the shelf. "Here. A selection of short stories." He passed the book to Sébastian. "Is this your first time in Paris?"

"No, I came when I was sixteen." Sébastian opened the book at the title page, but his mind was in a different place. Had he really been sixteen? He remembered it as though he were remembering someone he'd once known in a different life. "My French grandmother brought me for my birthday," he murmured. "It was 1936."

There had been a small birthday celebration in the kitchen of their home in Dresden, where he'd been handed a tall glass containing something sparkly and alcoholic, though not champagne, as Mamyne had pointed out, but a German Sekt. She'd clinked his glass with hers, leaning over to whisper in his ear. "Sixteen! You're almost a man now. It's high time I took you to Paris."

Mamyne had moved to Germany to help her daughter who, against her firm advice, had married a German; a man she'd met on a train, not long after the Great War. "How do people meet on a train?" Mamyne had asked a million times.

Much to his parents' disapproval, Mamyne had used

her savings in France to buy train tickets for Paris. Money which, in their opinion, would have better served to feed her German family. Nevertheless, they'd arrived in Paris in the early evening and had headed straight to her favorite restaurant, L'Escargot, in the 1st arrondissement.

As soon as they'd walked through the dark red velvet curtains that draped the main door, Sébastian knew he was entering another world. The dining room oozed luxury and pleasure, the smell of warm pastry and garlic welcoming them in. More red velvet hung from gold curtain rails, while lightly embroidered white tablecloths covered the tables. The ceilings were of dark oak embossed with gold, and the room was lit only by candlelight that flickered softly from every table. It felt intimate, and even now he could remember every little detail.

Mamyne had ordered for him, snails to start with, then tender meat covered in pastry that melted in his mouth, accompanied by full-bodied red wine. His head had spun to a pleasant rhythm while she educated him on life and love. "Sébastian," she said, "don't forget your heritage. France is my real home, and one day I hope you'll think of it as yours. The French know how to live. Look at that couple over there." His eyes followed Mamyne's gaze. "Nobody minds that he doesn't have his hands on the table, but on her instead. We enjoy seeing couples in love; it's nothing to be ashamed of. The only time you should take your hands off your lover is when you need to cut your meat, or pay the bill." She laughed. "Well, you have plenty of time for that. Now, tell me which writers you're reading at school."

He'd been relieved to move away from the subject of girls, feeling that this was not quite the kind of thing boys discussed with their grandmothers. "We're only allowed to read German writers now," he replied. "But I still read Victor Hugo, I've hidden *Les Misérables* under my bed."

Mamyne tutted loudly. "*Bien!* How do they imagine they can dictate what we read? What ignorance! Tomorrow we shall visit Victor Hugo's apartment. And we shall buy another of his books."

The next day, in the Place des Vosges, they'd sat outside the café next to Victor Hugo's apartment, sipping espressos. In the green square in front, a couple of old men sitting on a bench spread out a game of chess between them. It all looked so civilized, and Sébastian could well imagine Victor Hugo strolling through the park, stopping to chat with his neighbors.

Inside the apartment, they'd visited Victor Hugo's dining room, where he saw a poem on the wall. Mamyne read it out loud to him.

Demain, dès l'aube, à l'heure où blanchit la campagne,
Je partirai. Vois-tu, je sais que tu m'attends.
J'irai par la forêt, j'irai par la montagne.
Je ne puis demeurer loin de toi plus longtemps.

Tomorrow at dawn, when white covers the countryside,
I will leave. You see, I know you are expecting me.
I will go by the forest, I will go by the mountain.
I cannot stay away from you any longer.

Mamyne explained how Victor Hugo's daughter had drowned in a boating accident at the age of nineteen. Sébastian felt the father's grief and yearning for his lost daughter almost as if it had been his own, and he'd had to swallow the lump in his throat, turning away to compose himself before he could look at his grandmother again. They'd continued through the rooms, to the bedroom, where his grandmother pointed out the presence of a second door, covered in wallpaper to make it look like part of the wall; the secret door through which the great man's lovers discreetly came and went.

Later, as the sun was sinking, Sébastian and his grandmother wandered around the Louvre where the beauty and genius of the Impressionists' paintings spoke to him. He'd understood their quest to capture the light. He was looking for it too and, filled with the optimism of youth, he'd been sure opportunities would come along. He just had to be ready to seize them.

When they returned home the following day, his father told him it had become mandatory to join the Hitler Youth.

"And what did you think of our city back then?" Monsieur Le Bolzec brought Sébastian back to the present with his seemingly friendly question, but Sébastian couldn't help noting the possessive use of the term "our."

"I thought it was beautiful. The light was different, different to Germany."

"Paris—the City of Light." Monsieur Le Bolzec sighed. "Such a cliché."

"No, it's not. It was true."

"It *was* true?" Monsieur Le Bolzec raised an eyebrow, a half smile playing on his lips.

"It's the white stone they use here," Sébastian continued. "It makes everything look lighter. The buildings in Germany are darker."

"I've never been to Germany," the bookseller stated. "Well, not past the front line anyway." He smiled ironically.

Of course, he must have served in the last war, and here

he was, caught up in another. He could be forgiven if he sounded a little cynical.

"May I ask you where you learned to speak such fluent French?"

"My mother's French."

Monsieur Le Bolzec raised an eyebrow. "And a German father?"

"Yes. I'm here as a translator," Sébastian volunteered.

"A man of words then."

"I suppose you could say that, though they are hardly poetic words." He paused, wondering whether to go on. "Just paperwork, documents, nothing of great importance." He didn't want to give away more. Monsieur Le Bolzec seemed harmless enough, but even though he had detected some warmth toward him, it would be naive to assume that it was sincere.

Abruptly, Monsieur Le Bolzec turned around, pulling another book off the shelf. "Here, you might like this."

Sébastian took it from him, looking at the cover. *The Picture of Dorian Gray.* "Oscar Wilde. He's not a French writer."

"No, he's an Irishman, but it's been translated into French. A very interesting book. I think you might enjoy it."

Chapter Eleven

Paris, April 1944

Sébastian

"Shch!" A droplet of blood oozed out onto Sébastian's cheek. Taking the razor away from his chin, he leaned forward, the basin jutting uncomfortably into his stomach as he tried to get a better view in the grimy mirror. The whites of his eyes had turned a watery yellow and the irises were a murky blue, like a stormy sea. He was sure they used to be brighter. As he ran his fingers across the sharp stubble, he thought about how much he'd changed over the last four years. He'd lost his brightness—his spark, his *joie de vivre*— whatever you might call it. He stared into his dull, expressionless eyes, remembering how they used to shine with the excitement of life. But now he knew too much about life, too much about himself.

His thoughts slipped back to the woman in the bookshop. She had it—that inner light. She wasn't exactly beautiful, her features were too sharp, but there was something about her. A certain defiance, a strength of will. And it intrigued him.

He continued to drag the razor over his chin, wincing as the blade scraped across his hard, dry skin. It was difficult to get a good lather with the useless soap they gave him. Shaving unsatisfactorily finished, he threw his shirt onto his damp body, dressed, and left his hotel room on Rue du Temple. At least he wasn't housed in barracks somewhere like the rest of the Wehrmacht were. As he was part of the administrative staff, he was entitled to his own room, and there were plenty of rooms in the requisitioned hotels.

Once in his office, he found it difficult to get down to work. He sat at his desk, staring at the large pile of denunciation letters waiting to be translated into German. It might not be him who ransacked homes in the middle of the night, dragging children from their beds or hiding places, pushing them into waiting trucks. He might not be the one to pull the trigger. But he was certainly their accomplice.

With a heavy heart, he picked up the next letter.

To whom it may concern,

As concerned citizens, we thought we should bring it to your attention that the UGIF orphanage on Rue Claude Bernard appears to be "losing" children. I live across the street and have been observing movements in and out of the building over the last few weeks. The children are sometimes taken out for a walk on a Sunday morning, but the number of children returning is often less than the number that set out.

Sébastian stopped reading and rubbed his tired, dry eyes, a knot of despondency tightening in his stomach as he imagined the scene that would follow at the orphanage: the women being taken away in handcuffs for interrogation, the sniffling, uncomprehending children being driven to Drancy. He didn't understand how French citizens could denounce people who were saving the children; children who could have been their neighbors.

The door to his office was open, and when he glimpsed through he saw everyone engrossed in their work; typewriters banging away like pistols being fired, round after round. He put his palms against his temples, trying to think calmly. His pulse quickened as an idea wormed its way into his head. It was a dangerous idea, and if anyone ever discovered what he'd done, it would be the end of his posting. Probably the end of him. He wasn't sure he had the courage to go through with it and so, delaying any decision, he folded the letter into four, squirming in his seat as he pushed it down into the seat pocket of his pants.

The rest of the day he worked mechanically, trying not to think, and by five thirty he was exhausted with the effort of it. He hadn't finished his usual quota of letters for the day, but he stood up anyway and grabbed his cap. It was time to make a decision, and he couldn't think straight in that place. He passed his colleagues on the way out, and he sensed a few of them looking up at him as he strode by, but he kept his eyes fixed on the door.

Once outside, reality hit him like a fist to his gut. What the hell was he thinking? Cold sweat broke out on the back of his neck as he imagined what they might do to him if they ever found out he'd removed a denunciation letter. A black Gestapo car sped around the corner. Sébastian instinctively shrank into the wall till it had passed by, then he took the nearest street, walking without direction, trying to decide what to do with the letter.

Soon he realized he was on Rue Montmartre, and he guessed it must lead to the small village of Montmartre, where the white church of Sacré-Coeur stood at the top of the hill, overlooking Paris. He hadn't seen it yet and, though he wasn't one for churches, it might be a good place to think. He carried on for another ten minutes before spotting the famous windmill, lit in red—Le Moulin Rouge. A line of German soldiers extended along the sidewalk, and he passed by quickly then continued along the street to one side, soon reaching a steep staircase leading to the church. He gripped the metal banister running down the middle of the double-sided staircase as he climbed, his breath coming quickly as the steps went on and on. Further up, he heard music. He soon came across the source: an old man bent over a guitar while two women stood next to him, humming quietly. When they saw him, the music stopped abruptly. He turned away and carried on, vaguely aware of their humming starting again.

When he reached the top, he followed the narrow winding street round the side of a park to the church. The domes gleamed white, like a fairy-tale castle.

As he entered the church, the silence hit him. It wasn't only an absence of noise, but a peaceful and purposeful silence. Despite the high vaulted ceilings, it felt welcoming. Tentatively, he walked around the edge, taking in the confession boxes and the odd candle lit under the alcoves. Looking over at the pews, he saw about twenty people kneeling, heads bent over in prayer. He sidled over to one of the benches near the front and sat down. As a child, he'd gone to church at Christmas and Easter with his family and, though he found it boring, he liked to imagine God watching over him. It had made him feel safe. What nonsense it was! No one was looking out for him, neither mortal nor immortal. He thought of the Greek gods, and the way they played with the people as though they were pawns on a chessboard. This seemed more realistic to him.

As he absorbed the peace and quiet, an unfamiliar sense of calm spread through him. He looked at the ceiling; Jesus with outstretched arms stared down upon him, but his eyes were blank, indifferent even. If there was a God, he wasn't there for people like Sébastian. No, he was there for the victims and the innocent, those looking for comfort, not reason. Sighing, Sébastian stood to leave, and as he did so, he felt the letter in his back pocket crinkle, as though it were whispering to him, telling him there were always choices even when you thought there were none. Suddenly, he knew what he was going to do with the letter.

Sébastian's fingers trembled as he held the letter over the offertory candle, watching the paper glow orange then turn to black as it disintegrated into ash. He blew on it, dispersing the tiny fragments across the church floor, using the sole of his boot to rub them into the grooves between the flagstones.

He walked out of the church into the night. *Putain!* What had he just done? Closing his eyes, he took a deep breath, forcing the air down into his lungs, exhaling it slowly. An unusual sensation of pride swept through him. He'd only done a small thing, but still, he stood taller and straighter, as though he were a man in control of his destiny. But had he done enough? More letters could follow. They were like weeds; when you pulled one out, more would grow back. He'd have to keep a watch out for them, now he'd crossed the line. He should warn the people at the orphanage, but how? No one would trust him; anyone he told would think it was a trap. The only French person who might listen to him was Monsieur Le Bolzec, but he barely knew the man. For all he knew, he could be a collabo, and hadn't Sébastian already stuck his neck out far enough? He'd have to think about it carefully.

The sun was slowly sinking behind Sacré-Coeur when Sébastian walked back down the steep staircase. Two soldiers came up the steps, laughing loudly. *"Heil Hitler!"* They stopped, raising their arms in salute. Sébastian smiled instead of raising his arm. The younger man frowned but the other one asked if he wanted to join them for a drink.

"Not tonight, thank you." Sébastian tried to look amicable. He didn't want any trouble with them.

"Suit yourself," the younger one replied. "But watch out for the girls, *mein freund*, they've all got the clap."

The other soldier slapped his friend on the back. "Well, you would know, wouldn't you?"

Sébastian left them to their laughter and continued down the steps.

A girl called out from the shadows. "Hey, soldier." Like a cat, she slunk up to him, a light hand reaching out to his shoulder. "Are you looking for company tonight?"

It was getting too dark to see her properly and a large hat partly shrouded her face. The smell of vinegary wine hit him. He ignored her and walked on, but then, only a second later, he felt a twinge of regret. Company would have been nice, and what was so bad about a woman selling herself to make a little money? There were worse things. Far worse things. Men and women prostituted themselves every day, just to survive. As a boy, he'd sold himself without even realizing it, winning all those athletic trophies for the Hitler Youth, soaking up the praise, marching in uniform, feeling like one of the chosen few. What an idiot he'd been. Worse than a cheap whore.

Impulsively he decided to stop for a drink at one of the cafés at the bottom of the steps. As he sat on a stool and ordered a cognac, he noticed two women at the other end of the bar. Their legs were bare, and their dresses were hitched up to display their pale thighs, smudged lines drawn down the backs of their legs pretending to be stockings.

Suddenly they were next to him. "How would you like to buy us ladies a little drink?"

He rather admired their audacity and asked the barman for a carafe of white. It was unceremoniously pushed across the bar, and Sébastian had to pour it himself.

They clinked their glasses together, making eye contact. "*Santé.*" One had a fine black line drawn inside her lower eyelashes and dark red lipstick merged into purple along the contours of her lips. The other one had no makeup, but her lips were full and sensuous. She pouted as she placed a cigarette in her mouth, taking a deep drag. He watched her as he downed his glass of wine, feeling her hand slowly but firmly massaging its way up his thigh. Then she leaned toward him, and he felt her soft bosom against his chest. She breathed in his ear, "Two are better than one. We can make you very happy." Her mouth traveled down his neck, biting him softly. He closed his eyes for a moment, enjoying the awakening feeling of arousal. Then he felt the other one draw a line across his cheek with a sharp nail. "What do you say, *soldat?*" she whispered.

It was the word *soldat* that did it—that and an unexpected whiff of familiar cologne. It smelled like the one the commandant used. His rising desire was quickly dampened. "Listen, ladies, I have to go, but enjoy the wine." He threw some coins on the counter and turned around to leave.

"You don't know what you're missing, *soldat*," one of them shouted after him.

It was past curfew, and there was a different kind of atmosphere. Anyone out now had a right to be there, meaning they were German or had been assimilated. Prostitutes were tolerated, though the Nazis preferred that they work in one of the established brothels.

As he wandered toward the Métro, a girl leaning against a wall caught his attention. There was something different about her, as though her mind were miles away, and there was an attractive flush of color in her cheeks.

He paused.

She looked up and smiled. It was an open easy smile, and he found himself smiling back. He was about to walk on when she stepped toward him, and without a word slipped her hand into his. It felt light and fragile, like he could crush it with one tight squeeze. He tightened his fingers around it.

"Eh!" she gasped.

Loosening his grip, he turned to her and smiled. "*Pardonnezmoi.*" The fear in her eyes instantly turned to relief. How vulnerable she was. He could do anything to her, and there'd be no one to protect her. It was wrong, all so wrong.

"Do you want to have a drink with me?" she asked.

He put his hand in his pocket and pulled out his wallet. "I can't tonight," he said. "But here, take this." He put a five-franc note into her hand.

"*Merci, monsieur, merci,*" she called after him as he walked away.

Chapter Twelve

Paris, April 1944

Sébastian

Sébastian glanced at the clock on the wall—only 5:00. Leaning back on his chair, he stretched his arms out behind his head, rolling his stiff neck from side to side as he looked at his busy colleagues, their heads bent over typewriters or stacks of papers. He was restless, and the thought of eating alone again depressed him.

Sighing, he gazed down at the pile of letters waiting for him to translate. He'd do two more and then he'd leave. His eyes felt dry and tired, and so he picked out one of the typed letters; always easier to read. He scanned the page, signed by *Un Homme Honnête*, claiming someone they knew to be a communist. If it wasn't a Jew, it was always a communist. He inserted a clean piece of paper into the typewriter and began the translation, word for word.

It was barely 5:30 when he left, and a few of his colleagues looked up when he walked out. As he crossed

Pont Neuf, he stopped to watch a long cargo boat gliding by, low in the water due to its heavy load. Continuing along the *quai* on the other side, he walked by German soldiers who were sitting out on café terraces with Frenchwomen. He couldn't help wondering what these women really felt for the men. Did they just see them as meal tickets? Or did they have feelings for them? Did it even matter?

He found himself walking toward the bookshop again. The bell went as he entered the shop, and the bookseller looked up from the shelf he was stacking. Sébastian saw a flicker of recognition cross Monsieur Le Bolzec's eyes, but then they turned cold. He probably wasn't as welcome as he liked to think he was.

The bell went again. An old lady came in, nodding her greeting.

"*Bonsoir, madame.*" Monsieur Le Bolzec smiled at her.

"*Monsieur,*" she replied curtly, turning to Sébastian, a deep frown growing across her forehead.

"*Bonsoir, madame,*" Sébastian made a point of saying.

The old lady looked at him, long and hard, then without another word she turned on her heel and walked straight out of the shop. Sébastian heard Monsieur Le Bolzec sigh loudly, and for a moment he stood there awkwardly.

"I'm sorry. I seem to be frightening your customers away." Sébastian wondered if he should leave.

"Don't worry. She never buys anything anyway. I don't usually sell more than two books a day at the moment."

The atmosphere lay thick, Sébastian's feelings of alienation and loneliness becoming more painful by the minute. He wasn't ready to leave. He removed his cap and tucked it under his arm, then wandered over to a shelf, where he picked up a book at random, flicked through the pages without taking them in.

"I hope you don't mind me asking." Monsieur Le Bolzec followed him, breaking the silence. "Do you have to wear your uniform when you're off duty?"

Sébastian closed the book and looked at him. "We're never off duty."

Monsieur Le Bolzec raised an eyebrow. "Never?"

"That's right. Never."

"They don't make you sleep in it, do they?"

"No. But I could be court-martialed if they caught me in civilian clothes."

Monsieur Le Bolzec studied Sébastian for a moment. "You're no freer than we are, are you?"

"Not really." Sébastian shook his head. "We just get better food."

"And soap."

"Yes. We get soap." The two men looked at each other for a minute, and if he wasn't mistaken, Sébastian felt something pass between them: a kind of mutual understanding.

"Did you read that book by Oscar Wilde?" Monsieur Le Bolzec finally asked.

"Yes, I finished it yesterday," Sébastian replied, remembering how Dorian's debauched lifestyle had caught up with him in the end. "I enjoyed the descriptions of London."

Monsieur Le Bolzec just perceptibly raised an eyebrow, as though suggesting he found Sébastian's reply a little superficial. "What did you think of the ending?"

"Clever. Sooner or later the surface is bound to crack." Sébastian wondered if the bookseller was trying to draw a parallel between Nazism and Dorian Gray's life. It was true— the high officials were always impeccably dressed, the model of politeness itself, using euphemisms such as "resettling" and "questioning," often without even raising their voices, as if these were perfectly civilized concepts.

"Indeed." Monsieur Le Bolzec pulled a book off the shelf. "Last time you came in you were telling me you were just a young lad of sixteen when you first came to Paris."

"Yes, my French grandmother wanted to show me the city she grew up in."

"When was that? If you don't mind me asking."

"1936."

"The year Germany won the most Olympic medals."

"Yes."

"Wasn't that also the year Hitler made it compulsory for children to join his army?"

"The Hitler Youth? Yes."

"Anyone under the age of eighteen."

Sébastian nodded.

Monsieur Le Bolzec studied Sébastian. "I must admit, I thought that was very clever of him." Sébastian was unsure how to respond, but he found he didn't need to. Monsieur Le Bolzec continued, "It gave him a loyal army, didn't it? I bet they gave you smart uniforms. And filled your bellies." Sébastian looked down, worried that he was being disloyal in having this conversation with a Frenchman who was practically a stranger. "You must have had some good times, all you boys together. Bet you had some games."

Good times? Games? Sébastian's mind flew back to one of their "games."

It had involved "platoons"—groups of boys who were supposed to be on the same side, except one was chosen to be the victim. The victim was given ten minutes to run away and hide, before the rest of them were sent out to track him down. When they brought the miserable child back to the commandant, they had to deal out his punishment. One time, the commandant had noticed Sébastian wasn't joining in with the beating. "Kleinhaus, a little soft-hearted, are we? Kick him in the face! That's an order!"

Sébastian stared down at his big, hard boots and then at the boy's terrified face. He pulled his leg back, ready to kick, but then something else inside him took over, and he sprinted off, running as fast as his legs would carry him. He was the best athlete in the group, and for the next few hours he ran for his life. Finally, night drew in, and he stayed out in the forest till dawn broke.

When he returned to the group the next morning, the commandant's face was hard and unwelcoming. He signaled to one of the older boys, who swaggered over to Sébastian with a mean look in his eye. Sébastian's blood raced through his veins, and once again he had the urge to run, but he'd got no energy left.

The punch to Sébastian's face came swiftly and efficiently, knocking him sideways, pain shooting through his jaw. He tried to stand upright, but his head was spinning, and he stumbled, vaguely aware of laughter breaking out.

"Punishment block for Kleinhaus!" The commandant's voice rang out loud and clear.

The older boy tugged at Sébastian's shoulder, pushing him out in front of him and booting him in the rear.

"Well, Kleinhaus, if you can't fight, you can always run." The commandant's laugh vibrated through Sébastian as he was led away.

Sébastian gazed at Monsieur Le Bolzec, still half-lost in his memory. "Yes," he replied. "We played games."

Chapter Thirteen

Paris, April 1944

Élise

I thought I'd stop in at the bookshop on my way back from work tonight as I wanted to get Isabelle a book for her birthday. Monsieur Le Bolzec didn't usually close till just before curfew, so I had time. It was empty when I walked in.

"Élise, my dear. This is a pleasure." Monsieur Le Bolzec came out from behind a shelf. He was followed by a man in uniform. The German from the other evening.

"*Bonsoir, mademoiselle.*" He had the audacity to hold out his hand as though we were acquaintances.

My hands didn't leave my sides as I stared at him. He even had the cheek to look right back, but I was damned if I was going to be the first to turn away, and I held his gaze with stony eyes. It must have only been a second or two, but it felt like time stretched out on a tight piece of elastic. I noticed his irises were a clear blue, like the aqua stone I had in a ring. Eventually he lowered his eyes. "I should go," he said.

It made me feel triumphant. I wasn't going to let the way his shoulders slumped, nor the sad tone of his voice, taint my feeling of victory.

"You don't have to leave." Monsieur Le Bolzec spoke quickly, glancing at me.

But the German shook Monsieur Le Bolzec's hand, nodded at me, put his cap on, and walked out.

As soon as the door shut behind him, Monsieur Le Bolzec turned to me. "You don't have to be quite so hostile."

"We're at war with them!" My heart thumped hard with outrage. "He's a Boche!"

"But he's not responsible for the war."

"They're all responsible! Every last one of them."

Monsieur Le Bolzec shook his head and sighed. "He's not much more than a boy really."

I rolled my eyes, wondering if he was going to make more excuses for the Boche.

"His name is Sébastian, Sébastian Kleinhaus. He's half-French. His mother's French and his father's German."

"*Je m'en fous!* What difference does it make? He's wearing a Nazi uniform!" I met his gaze and held it, challenging him. It made me feel uncomfortable, facing up to him like that.

The bell went, making us both turn toward the door. A young man walked in with an elderly lady on his arm. "*Bonsoir, mademoiselle, monsieur.*" They greeted us, then walked to the next shelf, browsing the books.

Monsieur Le Bolzec turned to me. "It's a funny thing, nationality. What does it really mean to be French? Or to be German?"

I wasn't sure where Monsieur Le Bolzec was going with this, and I wasn't keen on continuing the discussion with other people around. I thought about leaving, but didn't want to part on a bad note either. And I still wanted to buy a book.

"Have you heard of the Hitler Youth?" he continued.

"Yes." I was aware of the other customers, but they seemed engrossed in a book they were looking at together.

"The indoctrination of a whole generation. Hitler's brain-wave." He lowered his voice slightly. "It was all based on nationalism. And he gave them no choice. Everyone from the age of twelve had to join."

"I don't understand why you're insisting on making excuses for him," I whispered.

He put his hand on my elbow. "Not excuses, Élise. Reasons. When you get to my age, you see the world differently, you realize there's the story and then there's the story behind it." He leaned in nearer to me. "Don't be so quick to judge."

The elderly lady coughed loudly, and when I looked over, I saw the young man rubbing her back. It didn't seem to help. She coughed again, and again, her hacking making me wince.

Monsieur Le Bolzec went into his back room, returning quickly with a glass of water. He held it out to the lady, placing his hand on her shoulder. She took a sip, looking at him through watering eyes. "Merci, monsieur. Merci."

"Come and sit down." Monsieur Le Bolzec took her arm, guiding her to one of the stools he kept behind the cash till. I watched as he sat her down, his hand not leaving her as he talked to her now in low, soothing tones. Then I caught the young man's eye and saw his relief. Monsieur Le Bolzec's kindness left me feeling clumsy and awkward.

When they left, Monsieur Le Bolzec addressed me again. "Élise, you can't afford to be so . . . so transparent."

"What do you mean?"

He scratched his sideburns while studying me. "I've known you since you were a little girl. I know how you feel about the occupation, about the Germans." I sighed loudly. This was no secret. "And I can see you're living on your nerves; I can feel it. You don't have to tell me what you're up to. All I'm saying is that you never know when someone might be useful to you, when it might be good to have the enemy on your side."

"Are you saying we can use him?"

"You never know. Forgive me for my arrogance, but I believe I'm a good judge of character. That boy is plagued with guilt and loneliness—a fatal combination."

"Boy? He's a man!"

"Yes, you're right. But he's still so young; he hardly knows himself. He's never been free to make his own choices. He was an obedient son who became an obedient soldier. But there's more to him than that. He's a troubled soul."

"And so he should be!" I still couldn't believe Monsieur Le Bolzec wanted me to sympathize with a Boche.

He smiled a half smile. "It won't hurt you to talk to him a little." He paused. "Only when the shop is empty, of course. We both know how people gossip. He's far from home, and he's lost and lonely. I was the same age as he is now when I was sent to the front during the last war. Do you think I wanted to go? Do you think I wanted to go and kill young men whom I'd never met, who'd been sent there just like me? No. But I still went, didn't I? It's no different than what he's doing now: following orders because the alternative is too frightening."

I let out a long breath. Though I could see his point, it wasn't my problem. My problem was standing up against the enemy, and that's exactly what this Sébastian Kleinhaus was. The enemy.

Chapter Fourteen

Paris, April 1944

Sébastian

Est-ce à nous qu'il prête l'oreille?
Est-ce aux anges? Est-ce aux démons?
A quoi songe-t-il, lui qui veille
A l'heure trouble où nous dormons?

Is it to us that he lends his ears?
Or to the angels? Or to the demons?
What is he thinking, he who watches over us
In this troubled time when we sleep?

Sébastian closed the book of Victor Hugo's poetry. He was tired, but sleep refused to bring him release. He switched off the lamp, then turned onto his side, but he was hot. Too hot. It was stifling in his little room. A door slammed. His colleague must have just returned from a night out. A woman's light laughter rang out. *Damn!* Now he'd have to listen to the bedsprings creaking all night long.

He put the lamp on, glimpsing at his watch: 2:30. The sound of hobnailed boots interrupted giggles coming from the room next door. He got up and opened the windows, undoing the latch holding the shutters together, then he leaned out, breathing in the cool night air. Three soldiers strode by, their rifles pointing up. They stopped in front of a block of apartments further down the street. With the butt of his rifle, one of them forced the door open, and they entered.

After a few minutes they came back out, pointing their rifles into the side of a man's head. The man was still in his pajamas, and his hands were on his head. A woman in a nightdress walked next to him, holding a small child by her hand. As Sébastian leaned further out of the window, he heard the cries of the child fading into the distance.

He wanted to run out onto the street, stop them taking away a family like that. But he was powerless, a nobody. He turned away and sat down heavily on the bed. Balling his fists, he thumped the mattress repeatedly, a feeling of helpless despair sweeping over him. The walls of the room were closing in on him, suffocating him, and the bed in the room next door was creaking away. He glanced at his uniform hanging from the wardrobe door. In the semidarkness it seemed to mock him, as though it were saying, "Yes. I belong to you, and you belong to me."

Grabbing the pack of Gitanes from the bedside table, he lit up, staring at his uniform. "I'll show you," Sébastian muttered. Taking the cigarette from his mouth, he stood and held it against the dark gray material of his jacket. Mesmerized, he watched it burn a hole. He removed the cigarette, stepping back to observe the perfectly round empty circle it had left. The creaking of the bed next door abruptly stopped and everything went quiet. Sébastian held his breath, waiting for the door to open and close—for the woman to leave. He didn't have to wait long. She slammed it on her way out. At least now, he could go back to bed.

He dropped his cigarette stub into the ashtray on his bedside table and switched the light off, then lay down in the dark. He felt his mind slow down, waves of sleep beginning to rise and fall. He welcomed them, hoping to be carried away on them. But one of the waves crashed over him. He woke with a start, his heart pounding. Henrik. He was dreaming about Henrik again. Russia. Sitting up, he wiped the sweat from his clammy forehead. He would never be free from it. Never.

He got up, threw his pajamas off, flinging them onto the floor, then roughly he pulled his uniform on, not bothering with a shirt. He just had to get out of the room.

He wandered the eerily quiet streets then, in the early hours, watched the sun rise above the Haussmann buildings before slipping into a café for coffee and a croissant. It was Saturday and he had nothing to do, and so he found himself wandering toward the bookshop once again, desperate for a half-friendly face.

The shop was empty, and Monsieur Le Bolzec was busy doing something at the till. Sébastian walked over to the dusty corner where the poetry books were kept. The bell went, sending a jolt through him. It was her. Élise. He noticed her hesitate, and he knew she wanted to turn around and walk right out again. *Let her*, he decided. That was her prerogative.

But Monsieur Le Bolzec was too quick for her. "Élise." He kissed her quickly on each cheek. "It's a pleasure to see you." Sébastian pulled a book off the shelf and pretended to read it. "How are you?" he heard Monsieur Le Bolzec ask her. "I've got something for you to take over to Rue Claude Bernard."

Rue Claude Bernard? He knew that name. *Merde!* That was the name of the street of that orphanage. The UGIF center. He was sure of it.

Monsieur Le Bolzec went out to the back room and came back with a brown paper bag. "Some books and a few cookies for the children." Sébastian held his breath, waiting for her to reply, but she didn't say anything. He had to force himself not to turn around and look at them, then he heard her say, *"Au revoir,"* and the bell ringing. She was gone. Monsieur Le Bolzec was busying himself at the till again. *Merde!* What should he do?

He approached the till, waiting for the older man to look up, his throat thick with emotion as he thought about what he could say. Images of the Gestapo raiding the orphanage flooded his mind. "I couldn't help overhearing," he started.

"What?" Monsieur Le Bolzec observed him cautiously.

"Rue Claude Bernard."

Monsieur Le Bolzec's eyes turned a shade darker. "What about it?"

"It's the UGIF center, isn't it? The orphanage."

"I believe so." He paused. "It is legal. Where do you want them to put all the children whose parents have been deported?"

"That's not the problem." Sébastian's skin crawled as he tried to think of a way to explain himself. "They might be in trouble."

"What do you mean?" Monsieur Le Bolzec leaned forward on the till, his face ashen gray.

"I can't say." Sébastian was in too deep. He couldn't afford to give any more away. "Tell her to be careful. Tell them all to be careful."

Monsieur Le Bolzec gripped his arm. "What's going on?"

"They might be watching it." Sébastian pulled himself away. "You should warn them."

"What do you mean? Why are they watching it?"

"I don't know."

"But Élise has done nothing wrong." For a moment the two men stood staring at each other, each aware that this had nothing to do with anything.

"Okay, I'll tell her. I'll tell her to tell them all," Monsieur Le Bolzec conceded.

Sébastian left abruptly, before he was tempted to say anything else.

Chapter Fifteen

Paris, April 1944

Élise

The regular whack of a tennis ball resounded in my ears as I walked through the Jardins du Luxembourg on my way to work. It felt incongruous, as did the early blossoms budding. On the surface, it all appeared normal, but if you looked closer you would see that most of the happy strollers were German soldiers, and then you might also notice the signs stuck into the grass: *Interdit aux Juifs*—Jews not allowed. The Jewish people had been ostracized from our community, then gradually but surely removed.

I froze, my pulse racing. A German soldier stood in front of me. "Would you take a photo for us please?" He smiled.

I nodded without speaking, wishing I had the courage to ignore him and walk away. Taking my silence as my agreement, he passed me a large box camera, explaining in bad French which buttons I needed to turn and press. I didn't say another word, though he didn't seem to notice, and when I glanced at the woman hanging off his arm, she looked away. As I stood back, pointing the camera at them both, she smiled widely, her eyes twinkling, her red lipstick shining, like a slash across her face. If she was only pretending to be happy, then she was making a great job of it. It made me want to throw the camera down, but instead I turned it at an angle, so I only got their legs. It gave me a small sense of satisfaction, and as I handed the camera back, I smiled. "*Guten Tag.*" I paused, taking in the soldier's round happy face and spoke softly, half under my breath. "*J'espère vous aurez ce que vous méritez.*"

He beamed at me. "*Danke schön! Merci, mademoiselle.*"

I strode away quickly, almost tripping over the sign, *Interdit aux Juifs.* I pulled myself back up and stared down at it, remembering my friend Ellen, who'd been arrested along with her family in the big roundup in '42. They'd taken them to the Vélodrome d'Hiver, and from there I'd heard they'd been taken to Drancy, a transit camp. I'd written to Ellen three times, but never got a reply. I had no idea where she was now. Rage and frustration welled up inside me. I had an urge to rip the stupid sign out from the earth it stood in. I almost did it, but I knew it wouldn't help anyone, and it would only satisfy me for a brief moment. And so I continued on my way to work.

"*Bonjour, les filles.*" I took my beret off as I entered the bank, hanging it up with my light summer jacket on the hat stand, then went to greet my colleagues, pecking them on the cheek.

"*Salut*, Élise." Françoise raised an eyebrow. "Apparently, the Boches are paying us a visit today."

"Germans, Françoise!" Monsieur Desgardes walked into the room. "You can't call them Boches. Not in here. And yes, they want to check some of the accounts. Who's in charge of the Dreyfus account?"

"I am," I answered.

"Well, make sure you have it to hand."

The atmosphere was tense for the rest of the morning, and it was almost a relief when one single German officer walked into the bank just before lunch break. He surveyed the room, then clicked his heels together. At least he hadn't done the *Heil Hitler!* salute they usually did. None of us responded verbally, but we all looked up in acknowledgment of his presence. He was tall and slim and had a healthy color in his cheeks. I bet he'd been out strolling around the Jardins du Luxembourg at the weekend.

"The Dreyfus account," he announced.

"I have it here." I felt the slight tremor in my voice and hoped he hadn't noticed. I didn't want him to think I was afraid of him—it immediately gave them the upper hand—but I saw it already in the way his eyes flickered greedily over the room, in the way he put his hands behind his lower back as he strutted toward me. They always had the upper hand.

"*Bien, bien.*" He had a heavy accent, and I realized his French was probably quite limited, which took the edge off my fear, though it shouldn't have. I stood up, holding the file out to him. "*Assis, assis.*" His French really was awful, and I wondered if he always repeated his words like that, or was it a nervous tic? Without even opening the file, he held it against his chest as he leaned down over me. "Empty it."

I shifted away from him. "Where should I transfer the money?" I looked at him, feigning innocence, while seething underneath. So this was what they were up to, why they were paying us a visit today.

"*Ici, ici.*" He handed me a scrap of paper with an account number on it.

"This is a different bank. I'll need to type a letter."

"*Oui, oui.*" He sounded impatient.

I pulled my typewriter toward me and inserted a clean sheet of paper. Though there was hardly any room, he squeezed his bottom onto the edge of my desk, peering over the typewriter as I typed, as if he didn't trust me to get the numbers right. A hush fell on the office, the sound of my keys typing out numbers and letters that would rob a family of all their wealth, the only sound, apart from his breathing—heavy, labored breaths, like an animal leaning over its prey. The sound of it sent a wave of anger through me. Here he was, stealing one of our clients' money right under our noses, and we could do nothing about it.

For the rest of the day, I immersed myself in tables of figures and numbers, calculating percentages, growth rates, and taxes. It took me away from the present, into a world of numbers. Numbers could be relied on. Numbers didn't lie, not if you knew how to read them. And I knew how to read them. I understood only too well how the Germans had fixed the exchange rate, giving them an inflated number of francs for one of their Deutschmarks. It meant that the soldiers based here, who were paid in Deutschmarks, were a lot richer than they should have been, which enabled them to eat in our restaurants, while we couldn't. They could buy expensive perfumes, Hermès scarves, and silk stockings for their wives back home, while we had to make do with altering the clothes we already had. They flashed our money around as if they'd earned it, as if they had a right to it, when really, they'd stolen it from right under our eyes. They were robbers. Murderers and robbers. God, how I despised them.

That evening, when I left the bank, I walked briskly, my blood still boiling with anger at the Nazis and at myself for being complicit. *Merde!* I'd promised Maman I'd get some bread. Turning back, I remembered she'd told me where I might be able to find some today. She was right. When I got to the boulangerie, there was already a long line. I joined it, standing behind two elderly women. They were talking so loudly I couldn't help but overhear their conversation.

"There'd be enough food to go around if the Boches weren't such greedy pigs."

"Shh!"

"Oh, don't worry. There are none in this line." Her friend looked around, laughing cynically. I caught her eye and smiled. "And you can bet your last centime that there won't be any collabos in this line either. It's just us mugs."

"Shut up, Micheline!"

"Don't worry. They don't care about us old ladies. We're invisible to them." She turned back toward me. "Is that why you cut your hair?"

"Pardon?" I knew what she meant, but her directness put me off.

"You don't want them to notice you, do you?"

My hand flew defensively to my head. "I like it short."

"Yes, it's not bad. It makes your eyes stand out." She paused. "But men prefer long hair."

"I don't care."

She laughed again, throwing her head back. "*Bien dit!* Well said! If it wasn't for men, well, we wouldn't be standing here in this damned line, would we?"

"No," her companion spoke. "We'd be dancing, singing... eating."

"Curse the lot of them!"

"They're all the same."

I joined in their laughter, happy to see the line was moving forward. It turned out to be one of those rare occasions when one could buy bread in the early evening. Clutching my half baguette, I walked home through the Jardins du Luxembourg. The lake shimmered in the late afternoon sun and, as usual, several German soldiers strolled about with their girlfriends as if they owned the place. I sighed loudly as I walked past one of them kissing his girlfriend. My blood rushed through my veins as I held back the urge to slap her around the face, to scream at her. What the hell was she doing, kissing the enemy?

It was hopeless. Too many of us had accepted them, appeasing them instead of resisting them. It was impossible to know who you could trust and who might betray you. It shouldn't have been like this; we should have stood together. But some people had realized they could profit from the situation, and then there were the anti-Semites who were only too happy to get rid of the Jews. There was that sign again—*Interdit aux Juifs*. It was the same one I'd almost tripped over this morning. Impulsively, I pulled my leg back and kicked it. It couldn't have been so firmly stuck in the ground because it fell straight down with a thud. *Merde!* I quickly walked away.

"What are you doing?" The German I'd just passed marched toward me.

My heart stopped. Then instinctively, I took flight. Surely, he wouldn't bother coming after me, not while he was with his lady friend.

I was wrong. Pounding footsteps behind me grew louder. I sprinted around the next corner.

I ran straight into a policeman. "What's the hurry, mademoiselle?"

I tried to pull away, but he had his hand on my shoulder. He tightened his grip. "*Vos papiers!*" I dropped the bread. "*Vos papiers!*" he yelled again. With trembling fingers, I fumbled with the catch on my handbag. It was a mess. Papers, books, pens all jumbled together. I rummaged through them, desperately looking for my ID.

The German appeared, his chest rising and falling heavily with the effort of running. "You're under arrest," he hissed between breaths. My ribs contracted around my lungs. I gasped for air, dropping my bag, its contents spilling out. The German took out a pair of handcuffs and clamped my hands behind my back. I gaped at my things scattered on the ground, my head spinning. This couldn't be happening!

"Put her things back in the bag," he shouted at the policeman.

It was happening! I had to stop it. I swallowed, forcing words out of my tight throat. "I tripped over the sign. I didn't mean to knock it over. I'm sorry!" I looked at the German. He paused for a second, staring at me coldly. "I'm sorry," I repeated.

He raised his hand, but I didn't see it coming. The slap across my face. I stumbled backward. Out of the corner of my eye I was aware of his lady friend, staring at me. "I'm taking her to Rue de la Pompe!" he shouted.

Oh God, no! Not the Gestapo headquarters! In desperation, I looked at the policeman, but he turned away, distancing himself.

"Rue de la Pompe?" The lady spoke softly. "But I thought we were going to spend the evening together…"

The German glanced at her, sighing loudly. "Can't you see I have matters to attend to now?"

"But couldn't the policeman take her in?"

I held my breath, dreading his next words. But still hoping.

"No! How can I trust him? I'll have to do it myself. She's destroyed German property."

I looked at the woman and saw her hesitation. "But Stefan, I was so looking forward to our time together." She put her hand on his arm. "It is your evening off."

"I'm never off duty!"

She caught my eye, and I saw a sad look of apology. She had tried.

He dragged me by the elbow through the gardens, out to where a black car was parked. He roughly pushed me into the back seat, hurting my shoulder. I broke out in a cold sweat. Were they going to interrogate me? *Interrogation.* Just the word terrified me. I closed my eyes, trying to block out images of them beating me, pulling my nails out, electrocuting me. Stop! It wasn't going to happen. I would admit to kicking down the sign. Then they would leave me alone, maybe send me to prison for a few days. Another spasm of fear shot through my stomach.

When the car stopped at Rue de la Pompe, he pulled me out by my elbow and directed me into the building. SS men strutted about, shouting orders. My knees buckled under me as he led me down the corridor. I stumbled. I nearly fell. He pulled me back up, then pushed me onto a metal chair outside an office. I closed my eyes, praying to a God I no longer believed in.

Chapter Sixteen

Paris, April 1944

Sébastian

It was already six o'clock, but Sébastian was still at his desk. Today had been particularly busy, and his head was throbbing with the treacherous words oozing from the letters he'd translated. How could people denounce their neighbors like that? They might as well take a gun and go and shoot them. This underhand way, where someone else would all too flippantly dispose of their Jewish neighbors under the guise of being a "concerned citizen," made him physically sick. And it gave him a migraine.

The phone next to him rang, making him jump. He picked it up. *"Heil Hitler!"*

"Heil Hitler! Officer Wenner here. We need you for an interrogation, Rue de la Pompe. Our interpreter is ill."

"Yes, Officer Wenner."

"Report direct to me, ground floor."

Sébastian stood up, grabbing his briefcase. His pulse raced

as he imagined what lay in store for him. They'd only asked him to do one interrogation before, and it had ended so badly he'd thought they would never ask him again. He'd thrown up when they'd tied the prisoner's arms to the table and taken the plyers out.

He took the Métro, getting into the first carriage, always reserved for Germans. He noticed a few Jews shuffling into the last carriage, and he couldn't help wondering how they'd survived this long with the quotas for deportation that needed to be filled every month.

As he entered the Gestapo headquarters, the hairs on his arm rose and a shiver ran down his spine. Uniformed men and women thumped down keys on typewriters, so engrossed in their work they didn't even look up as he walked by. Then a commotion behind him made him turn around. A man was swearing and shouting in French as a group of German soldiers dragged him in, forcing him down to the ground. Sébastian turned away as the soldiers' heavy boots pummeled into the man's kidneys. A German officer ran out of his office. "Stop!" he shouted. "I need to get information out of him. Bring him to my office." Gradually the agonizing sounds of boots hitting a body subsided, and the soldiers gathered the man up from the floor and dragged him toward the office, his feet trailing behind at unnatural angles.

As Sébastian's eyes followed the movement, he noticed four French citizens sitting outside another office. Then he looked back again. That woman was there. Élise. She glimpsed at him, a flicker of recognition crossing her eyes. Sébastian looked at her coldly, hoping she'd understand what he was trying to tell her; that she should give no indication she knew him.

Everyone was absorbed in watching the other prisoner

being dragged away. He saw his small window of opportunity. And he seized it. He walked over to her and addressed her in an authoritarian voice. "Follow me."

Without a word and with her eyes on the ground, she stood up. She followed him as he walked back out the way he'd just come in. His heart thudded in his ears, beating in time with the clinical clicking of the typewriter keys. He told himself that if anyone stopped them, he would pretend he had nothing to do with her.

She followed him out of the heavy wooden doors, down the road, and around the corner. Once away from the building, he stopped and turned around. She almost walked straight into him. He gripped her arms and felt her body trembling, her black pupils expanding into large pools of fear. Quickly he pulled her across the street into the entrée of a block of apartments, then through into a courtyard.

"What were you doing in there?" He held her arms tightly. Then realizing his fingers were digging into her arms, he loosened his grip.

"I knocked down one of those signs," she stuttered. "*Interdit aux Juifs.*"

"What? What are you talking about?"

"It was in the Jardins du Luxembourg. A German officer saw me."

"But..." He didn't understand.

"I kicked it. I didn't know it would fall down."

"You were sent here for that?" Why would they send her to the Gestapo headquarters just for that?

"The officer was mad. I couldn't find my ID."

He had an absurd urge to laugh out loud. "Again?"

"It was in my bag, but everything fell out. I panicked."

"Where is it now?" His hands still gripped her arms.

"I don't know. Somewhere in my bag."

"Didn't they ask for it when you were brought in?"

"No. There was all that shouting. They just made me sit on that chair."

Relief swam through Sébastian, making his head spin. He took his hands off her and put them over his eyes. She'd just had the narrowest of escapes.

"Thank you." She paused. "Sébastian."

She'd used his name! He didn't even know she knew it. He stared into her green eyes, and everything became sharper, accentuated; the smell of the jasmine creeping up the wall next to him, the sound of the trucks on the streets outside. Time slowed down, almost as if he could escape it.

Then time caught up. "Go straight home." He put his hands on her shoulders. "Don't say a word to anyone. Just go home and stay there."

She nodded, and he saw her swallow before she turned around and walked away.

He let out a long breath, his heart still beating hard and fast. He'd probably saved her life. Maybe he was losing his mind. Maybe he should lose his mind. Instead of going back into the Gestapo headquarters, instead of assisting at the interrogation, he could go after her, grab her hand, and they could make a run for it.

Stop fantasizing! No, he had to go back in there, as though he'd just arrived. He took a deep breath, filling out his chest as he took on the role he would have to play.

Chapter Seventeen

Paris, April 1944

Élise

My legs trembled all the way home, and it was as much as I could do to put one foot in front of the other without stumbling. A shudder took hold of my whole body. What if someone had seen Sébastian leading me out? What was he doing there anyway? I never even asked him.

I felt too tired and shaky to walk all the way back home, so I took the Métro at Passy. As I put my ticket in and went through the turnstile, I kept my eyes on the ground, terrified. When I got on the train, I sat next to the window, staring out into the dark tunnels as the Métro rumbled along under the streets of Paris. In my hand I gripped my ID card, ready to hand it over if any soldiers got on. It was silent even though the carriage was half-full. Before the occupation, we used to speak to each other, sometimes catching another person's eye. But now it was as though everyone was pretending to be somewhere else. We had become wary of each other.

Only children didn't understand this unwritten rule, and in the seat opposite me, I felt a child's eyes boring into me, making me uneasy.

I cried with relief when I finally walked through the front door into our apartment.

"Did you get the bread?" Maman came out of the kitchen.

I swallowed my tears and lied. "There was no bread, Maman. I'm sorry."

She sighed. "Strange. I heard there was."

"I'm going to lie down," I said. "I have a terrible headache. I need to rest in the dark. Don't wake me for dinner. I'll try to sleep it off."

I didn't wait for her to answer but went straight to my room, where I opened the window and leaned out to close the shutters. Immediately it felt cooler and safer. I sat on my bed, removed my shoes, and lay back on the pillow, staring at the ceiling in the dim light. My left upper arm throbbed where Sébastian had gripped it so tightly. I turned on the little lamp next to my bed and removed my blouse, checking for bruises, surprised to find none. I ran my fingers along the skin, feeling its warmth as if his touch had stayed with me. I turned the lamp off, then as I lay back down I heard his voice ringing in my ears; his urgent questioning. "Where's your ID? Didn't they ask for it when you were brought in?" His words played in my head as I ran through the scene again. The visible relief when I told him I'd only been arrested for knocking that stupid sign down. He'd put his hands over his eyes like a child might. It was in that moment that I think he fully understood the enormity of the risk he'd taken for me. Like a child, I don't think he'd weighed up the consequences when he'd seen me sitting on that chair outside that office. But he'd known what was waiting for me on the other side.

My dreams that night were vivid and confusing; Sébastian and the soldier who'd arrested me, all mixed up. I woke several times, hunger eating into me, but I didn't get up. Why had this man I barely knew taken such a risk for me? Maybe Monsieur Le Bolzec was right; he was troubled with guilt, and saving me was the one thing he could do. I felt myself softening toward him, and I had to remind myself he was still the enemy.

Chapter Eighteen

Paris, April 1944

Sébastian

Sébastian knew it wasn't good to have regular habits in wartime. It meant people knew where you were and who you were mixing with, but he couldn't help it. He couldn't keep away from the bookshop, where he knew Monsieur Le Bolzec would give him a friendly welcome. And where he might see Élise. He was worried about her. This evening, as he pushed the door open, he wondered if she might be there. But the shop was empty; he couldn't even see Monsieur Le Bolzec.

"*Bonsoir*," he called.

And then he saw her, coming out from the back room. Her hair was messy, as though she'd been running her hands through it, and when she spoke there was a slight tremor in her voice. "Monsieur Le Bolzec had to go out. He asked me to keep an eye on the shop." He looked at her, and silence fell on them, the only sound the ticking of the clock echoing around them. Then she moved, and he heard the light brush of her dress swishing against her legs. He tried to think of something to say. Anything. But she took the words away from him. "I should thank you for the other day, for getting me out of that place."

Sébastian nodded, noting the way she'd used the word "should." Of course she couldn't really thank him; that would be too ironic.

"Monsieur Le Bolzec told me they're watching the orphanage on Rue Claude Bernard," she continued.

"It's possible."

"How do you know?" Her green eyes pierced him.

The directness of her question shocked him. "I can't tell you that."

She studied him. "I shouldn't be talking to you." Her eyes left him, and he waited for her to walk away, but she didn't move. "I shouldn't have needed rescuing in the first place." In one breath she'd said she wasn't going to talk to him, and in the next, she was. She was full of contradictions.

"I know. I'm sorry."

"Sorry?"

"Yes, I'm sorry to be standing here in this uniform." He hesitated, then took the plunge. "It's not who I am."

"Who are you, then?"

Sébastian felt his cheeks glow warm. This wasn't the kind of conversation he should be having. Still, they were alone, and this might be his last chance to talk to her, so he soldiered on. "I'm just an ordinary man."

A tiny line crossed her forehead, and she raised her hand, scratching it with her little finger.

He found this gesture endearing and carried on where he knew he shouldn't be going. "Ordinary, and not brave. I was very young when the war began, young and naive. I had no idea it would come to this. I even thought that France and Germany together could build a better, stronger Europe."

"Together?" She laughed cynically. "That would be funny if it wasn't so tragic."

"I never imagined..." He hesitated, trying to find the right words. "I'm not trying to make excuses. This position I'm in...I hate being here like this."

"Don't say anything then."

She was right. He should just shut up. The gap between them was too large. He took a step back.

"Where did all the hatred come from?" she asked abruptly.

The air grew charged. She was asking him another question, giving him a way in. "The hatred?" Every word he chose would be harshly judged, and so he thought carefully. "It was poverty. People were starving. Families couldn't afford to feed their children. I'm not excusing anything."

"Good," she stated simply, looking directly into his eyes.

"I'm just trying to answer your question." He took a small step forward. "Germany was crippled after the First World War. Parents watched their children starve. Hitler provided a scapegoat, a common enemy." She scratched her forehead with her little finger again as she studied him. He had to make her understand, before someone walked into the shop. "It was hard." She didn't move, and so he forged on. "Our money was worth nothing."

"Yes, I know about the hyperinflation."

Their conversation felt like a game of chess; small moves by the pawns to begin with, while he worked out which strategy to use. But he was wary of offending her. "We weren't able to recover after the last war."

She raised an eyebrow. "So you had to start another?"

"I didn't start this war."

"No, but you're here now in uniform—representing your country."

"I wish I wasn't." He had an urge to take it off, right there and then. He removed the jacket and put it on the cash till, exposing himself in his beige shirt, his hands by his side, his palms facing her.

Her eyes widened and the color rose in her cheeks. For a moment they stood there, looking at each other, and he felt the attraction like an electric current running through him. His breath quickened, as he imagined what it would be like to be the man he wanted to be, with her.

The bell shattered their intimacy. The same two policemen from the first time walked in. They stopped in their tracks, leaving the door swinging open, their mouths gaping. Sébastian saw Élise look down, her cheeks growing red. They glanced from her to him, and back again, then, having reached their conclusion, looked at each other with that knowing look. "Monsieur Le Bolzec not here this evening then?" the taller one ventured.

"He's coming back any minute." Élise's voice trembled as she answered.

"I'm waiting to speak with him myself." Sébastian spoke with authority. "What business do you have with him?"

"We're just doing our rounds."

"It's good to know you're keeping us safe." Sébastian's tone was ironic.

An awkward silence followed. Sébastian stared hard at them, willing them to leave.

When they walked out a few minutes later, Élise slammed the cash till. "You know what they think now, don't you?"

"I'm sorry. I shouldn't have come here."

"No. People gossip."

He turned away but couldn't bring himself to leave.

"Are they going to raid the orphanage?" She spoke under her breath without looking at him.

"They might." He put his jacket back on. As he did the buttons up, he watched her anxiously. "I'm sorry, Élise."

"Just go," she hissed under her breath.

Chapter Nineteen

Paris, April 1944

Élise

I no longer walked to work through the Jardins du Luxembourg. In fact, I deliberately avoided the gardens; there were always too many well-fed German soldiers strolling about with their French girlfriends, and I was terrified of bumping into the one who'd taken me in. I was worried about the orphanage too. I'd warned the women there, and they'd agreed not to send any children out for the moment, but that only meant they were more likely to be rounded up when the police couldn't fill their quotas for deportation. One night when I couldn't sleep, a crazy idea crept into my head. It was too dangerous and risky to share with anyone else, but the more I thought about it, the more feasible it seemed to become, but I needed to talk to Monsieur Le Bolzec before I did anything.

After work I made my way over to his bookshop. Monsieur Le Bolzec looked up from the cash till when I walked through the door. "Élise, how are you?"

"Fine thank you." I walked past a young woman browsing the books on the front shelf.

I waited for her to leave, then when the shop was empty, I spoke. "Can you lock the door?"

Without a word, he turned the closed sign around and locked up. Then he turned back to face me.

"I did something stupid the other day," I started. "I kicked over one of those *Interdit aux Juifs* signs." The words leapt from my mouth as though they were burning me from within.

"Élise!" His eyes became perfect round circles, wide with shock. "Did anyone see?"

"A soldier."

"What?"

"He arrested me. He took me to Rue de la Pompe."

"Oh my God!"

"He left me outside a room. They were going to interrogate me."

The blood drained from Monsieur Le Bolzec's face, and he went completely still. "Interrogate you?"

"That German, Seb...Sébastian, who was in here the other night, he came to my rescue. He took me out. Right under their noses."

"Sébastian Kleinhaus?"

I nodded.

"Your ID. Did they get it?"

"No. I couldn't find it."

He laughed; a deep throaty laugh full of relief. Then as abruptly as he'd started laughing, he stopped. "What did Kleinhaus do?"

"He told me to follow him, and he led me out. He told me to go straight home."

"My God! He saved your life!"

"I don't know what would have happened if he hadn't been there." We were both silent for a minute, imagining what we knew to be certain. I would have been thrown into a cell, probably never to be seen again. "I think...I'm starting to think that maybe we can trust him."

"Maybe." He ran his index finger down the bridge of his nose. "Probably."

"He warned me about the orphanage."

"I told you they were watching it." Monsieur Le Bolzec spoke under his breath, glancing quickly around the empty shop.

"But if they raid it, they'll take the children away." He looked at me with sad eyes but said nothing. "I've been thinking about what you said," I continued, trying to gauge his reaction, aware that once I told him what I'd been doing and what I was thinking, there'd be no going back. "About him feeling guilty and lonely. About using him."

"Using him? Did I say that?"

"In so many words."

"I feel sorry for him. He seems so lost, and yes, lonely, far from home, far from his family. He's shown himself to be brave too, braver than I thought he was." He studied me. "He must like you very much, to have taken a risk like that."

I felt myself blush. "Maybe." In fact, I knew he liked me; I could tell by the way his eyes locked onto mine, as though searching for something from me. In other circumstances I would have been attracted to him too. I liked his boyish manner, the intensity in his eyes, his expressive mouth. But this wasn't what I was here to talk about. Or even think about, for that matter. "I'm wondering whether I can ask him to help."

"Help? What do you mean?"

"What he said about the orphanage, that they think children are being smuggled out—it's true. I've already taken eleven children out. I handed them over to a *passeur*." Monsieur Le Bolzec's eyes grew rounder, and the atmosphere grew stifling. I let out a long breath. "I've been doing it for the last six months. No one knows. Only the women in the orphanage."

"But Élise." His voice trembled. "If they arrest them, they'll talk. They'll give your name."

I nodded, fear rising from my belly. "I had to take that risk." Closing my eyes, I swallowed my terror. "I think we could use Sébastian. He could bring the remaining children out himself. There are just six left. Nobody would be suspicious of a German soldier coming out with children. They'd think he was taking them to a camp."

"You can't ask him to do that!"

"I think I can." I paused. "I think he would."

"No! It could turn him." He put his head in his hands, shaking it.

"Turn him?"

"Yes, if he thinks we're using him, he could turn against us."

"I don't think he'd do that. He wishes he wasn't here in that uniform."

"It's one thing wishing. It's quite another to actually do something. He'd be risking his life."

"As we are! Every time I take children out, I'm risking my life, but then I think of them, and how I'd feel if I did nothing. We have to do what we can."

"You're right, but..."

"We have to ask him. We can't risk waiting."

"I don't know, Élise. We have to be sure."

"I think it would be worth the risk. For the children."

"Maybe, but even the best men talk when they're afraid."

"You yourself said he's braver than he looks."

"Don't use my words against me. I know he took a huge risk for you the other day. But it doesn't mean he'd do it again."

"I want to ask him." I spoke decisively with more confidence than I felt. "If he can get a car, he could put the children in it, they could change their clothes in the car, then he could drop them round the corner from here. Once they're here we could hide them till we can get a *passeur*. Think about it. No one would think twice about children going into the shop. And we can have people we trust picking them up if we can't get a *passeur* early enough."

"No, Élise. No. It's too risky. Imagine what people will think if they find out children are staying here."

"What shall we do then? Just wait for the next roundup?" My eyes stung with unshed tears.

He scratched his sideburns, shaking his head. "It's too dangerous. Far too dangerous."

I swallowed hard. And waited. I knew he'd come round.

"Let me think about it. I need to think. How will we get the *passeurs*? We might have to find safe houses first. We have to do this carefully. Very carefully. And we need to make sure he's really on our side."

"I'm sure he is. The women at the UGIF can arrange the *passeurs*. We don't have much time. What if they raid it tomorrow?"

"Patience, Élise. Patience. We have to be absolutely sure he's with us."

Chapter Twenty

Paris, April 1944

Élise

Every evening after work I went to the bookshop, hoping to see Sébastian Kleinhaus. On the third evening he showed up. This time I smiled at him when he walked in. If it hadn't been him, if he'd been a Frenchman, it would have been touching to see the way his eyes lit up when he saw me.

"*Bonsoir.*" I couldn't quite bring myself to say his name. I felt uneasy enough greeting him as it was. Two young women at the back of the shop whispered to each other then looked over at me. I felt the color rise in my cheeks. *This isn't what you think*, I wanted to tell them, *I'm a loyal Frenchwoman.*

"*Bonsoir*, Élise." The sound of my name on his tongue made me feel like a traitor, but I wasn't sure who I was betraying; myself or him. I was doing it for the children, I reminded myself. Only for the children.

The two women walked out of the shop, past Monsieur Le Bolzec, who was on his ladder, sorting out a shelf, past Sébastian and me. They left without a word and without looking at any of us. *It's not what it seems*, I wanted to scream after them. Instead, I turned back toward Sébastian, aware that we were alone with Monsieur Le Bolzec. "I can't stop thinking about those children in the orphanage." The words shot out of my mouth. "I'm worried sick. What do you know?"

He looked down at his feet then he spoke quietly. "Only what I told you the other day." He took a deep breath, looking back at me. And something passed between us. An unspoken knowing. He knew what I was doing, and I knew I could trust him.

"Sébastian," I said quietly. "Do you really wish you weren't standing there in that uniform?" I was careful to keep eye contact.

"Yes," he answered plainly.

"Do you want to prove it?" It was a dangerous question, and a shiver ran down the back of my neck.

"Yes," he repeated with conviction.

"We need to take the children out of the orphanage."

He took a sharp intake of breath. "You want me to get them out?"

Without taking my eyes off him, I nodded. "You'd bring them here." I paused, waiting for his reaction, but there was none. "That's all we'd need from you. We can take care of the rest."

"You trust me to do this?" I heard the wonder in his voice. And the joy. His eyes let in more light, and I could feel his happiness as though he'd thrown his arms around me.

"You saved me from the Gestapo," I reminded him. "It couldn't have been a setup."

"It's probably the bravest thing I've ever done."

I nodded. "You'll need to get hold of a car."

Chapter Twenty-One

Paris, April 1944

Sébastian

Getting the car turned out to be the easy bit. All he had to do was swallow his pride and ask the officer in charge of translation. He pretended he wanted to impress his girlfriend.

"Thought you'd been distracted lately." The officer raised an eyebrow. "As long as you don't get too involved. Remember marriage is forbidden." He winked at Sébastian. "But anything else is permitted of course, as long as you take precautions. Go, sow your wild oats, and then I want you back at work! No more slacking off." So, he had noticed Sébastian leaving work a little early. His thoughts turned to the letter he'd destroyed. If they ever found out, he was a dead man.

He dropped into the bookshop two evenings later, as they'd planned. As soon as the shop was empty, Monsieur Le Bolzec turned the sign around to *Closed*, and they huddled together at the far end of the shop, near the poetry books, as they discussed how to proceed.

Sébastian's nerves were raw, and he was jumpy, but he felt alive in a way he hadn't felt since he was a boy. "I can get a car tomorrow night."

Monsieur Le Bolzec patted him on the shoulder, and Élise raised an eyebrow. He couldn't help the feeling of pride that surged through him, having overcome the first obstacle. "We'll have to keep up pretenses." Sébastian looked at Élise. "I told him I wanted to impress my girlfriend. We'll have to use the car in the evening."

Élise swallowed hard, biting her lower lip. "Use the car?" she repeated.

"Yes." He thought about it for a moment. "I could take you to a restaurant."

"No!" She shook her head, her hair swishing from side to side. "I couldn't do that."

"If we don't, and they find out, they'll be suspicious." He had to keep risks to a minimum, though he couldn't imagine they'd bother with him. If they did, he was already in serious trouble. "I can pick you up somewhere discreet, we can have dinner at a restaurant, then I'll drop you off somewhere out of the way."

"I'd get back before curfew?" Élise narrowed her eyes.

Sébastian was both relieved and surprised that she seemed to be accepting the idea. "Yes, then I'll drive back to my hotel and go out again at four in the morning to pick the children up. How many are there?"

"Six," Élise murmured.

"And you'll bring them here in the early hours of the morning?" Monsieur Le Bolzec asked.

"Where else can I take them at that time?" Sébastian was surprised at the question. "If someone sees a German car outside your shop, they'll assume you're in trouble, and they won't report that. It will only be a problem if the Nazis see me and wonder what's going on; that's why five in the morning is the best time. Any Nazis out at that time will be busy with their roundups."

"Yes, I'm sure you're right. You must know their movements better than us." Monsieur Le Bolzec looked reassured.

"Who would be in this restaurant?" Élise quizzed Sébastian.

"Only Germans, and their lady friends. No one else."

"No one must see me with you. I mean no one on the streets."

"Of course not. There's a driver at the restaurant who parks the cars. You can get straight out and inside the restaurant before anyone sees you."

"Have you been before?" Élise looked right through him.

"No. Never. I've just heard about it. It's a well-known German restaurant."

"German?"

"Only for Germans."

"*Les salauds!*" Élise whispered under her breath. "The swines!"

Sébastian returned her hard stare. "You'll have to pretend... you'll have to pretend to be a collaborator. Can you do that?"

She pushed her hair off her forehead. "If I have to."

"And you'll have to wear a nice dress." Monsieur Le Bolzec smiled a small smile. "And do something with your hair."

Élise ran a hand over her unwashed hair. "Do you have any soap?" She looked at Sébastian.

"I'll get you some. What else do you need?"

"Stockings, if I want to look the part."

Sébastian nodded. "I know a shop."

"Right." Monsieur Le Bolzec spoke affirmatively. "We're

set then. The children will hide upstairs in my rooms till we can get them to a safe house, or until a *passeur* is available."

"What? You don't have anyone yet?" Sébastian frowned. "What if they make a noise?"

"They won't," Élise replied immediately. "They know how to be quiet."

"What if one of them cries?"

"They're not like other children." The green light left Élise's eyes. "They're terrified for their lives."

Sébastian's heart shrank when he thought of what they must have gone through already. "We can't take any risks."

"We're well aware of that." Monsieur Le Bolzec spoke coldly.

"Of course." Sébastian's stomach fluttered with fear. It was all becoming real. "Where shall I pick you up, Élise?"

She blushed, and he instantly regretted his choice of words. He'd made it sound like a date.

"Somewhere far from where I live or work." She paused. "Le Marais. Saint-Paul on Rue de Rivoli."

"Fine. I'll get soap and stockings then." Sébastian turned toward Élise. "I'll drop them off here in the morning, and I'll see you at six thirty tomorrow evening. Saint-Paul." Without another word he left, his heart thumping hard against his ribs. If he'd stopped to weigh up the situation, he wouldn't be doing it. And that's exactly why he hadn't stopped. He was following his heart, not his head.

Chapter Twenty-Two

Paris, April 1944

Élise

At 6:30 sharp, I stood outside the church of Saint-Paul, hair freshly washed and a pair of real stockings in my handbag. I'd decided not to put them on till I got in the car, just in case I ran into someone I knew. Any woman who could get hold of stockings would be immediately suspected of collaboration.

I didn't have to wait long for a black car to pull up. Keeping my head down, I got inside and without a word we drove off.

Sébastian hardly looked at me but drove as if deep in concentration. "Is everything okay?" I wondered if he was regretting his decision to get involved.

"Yes, of course. But I'm nervous about going to this restaurant. It's only for Germans. You'll hate it." He paused. "And so will I."

"It doesn't matter, it's all part of the plan. You're right, we need to keep up pretenses and minimize our risks."

It didn't take long to drive through the empty streets, and we were soon parked alongside a large red door. A man in a porter's hat opened the driver's door and Sébastian got out, handing him the keys. With my scarf over my head, I stepped out of my side. Immediately Sébastian was next to me, putting an arm around me, guiding me to the door. A frisson ran down the back of my neck, and for that brief moment I felt protected, happy even, as though we were any couple going out for dinner together.

He opened the door, and I was hit with warmth, light, and music; joyful noises I'd almost forgotten: people laughing and chatting, someone playing a piano. A waiter led us to a table without a hint of disapproval, and after we were seated another appeared, flourishing large menus. *"Un apéritif, monsieur?"*

"Oui, deux verres de champagne, s'il vous plaît." Sébastian ordered for us both.

After the waiter disappeared, I glanced at my menu. "It's in German!"

"Shh, I'll translate for you. Don't worry, the food is still French!" He laughed softly then read the menu out. "Snails or foie gras for starters, then there's beef bourguignon, *confit de canard*, or pork."

Three different meats! How was that possible? Where on earth did they get it all from? I looked round at the other diners; all Germans in uniform, most of them accompanied by well-dressed Frenchwomen. The thought crossed my mind that I was one of these women now. They laughed loudly and overenthusiastically, and I couldn't help but feel a wave of shame. An attractive woman with a mass of shiny dark hair cascading around her pale face caught my eye and smiled. I found myself smiling back, and in that tiny second, a mutual understanding of unspoken complicity passed between us. We were both playing a part, for reasons best known only to ourselves.

The waiter soon reappeared with our champagne, ready to take our order. Having been so long deprived, I chose the richest food on the menu; foie gras followed by duck. When the waiter left, Sébastian lifted his glass. "To peace."

"To peace." I raised my glass, touching it against his, looking into his eyes. It would have been rude not to. I couldn't help but notice their aqua shade of blue. Looking down at my glass, I took a sip. Light airy bubbles burst onto my tongue. I closed my eyes, remembering the special occasions when we used to drink champagne; a joyful drink, full of hope and expectations, and even there in a room full of Nazis, I felt its magic. And in that moment, I knew that one day soon France would be ours again. I looked back up at Sébastian and smiled, my heart lifting.

He returned a wide boyish smile. "When this war is over, we'll open a bottle of champagne together." He didn't say who was going to win it, but we both knew Germany's days were numbered. Hitler's greed and unquenchable thirst for power were going to be his downfall.

We'd only just sipped on our champagne when the wine waiter reappeared, cradling a bottle, its label concealed under a thick white napkin, which he proceeded to flourish in the air as if performing some magic trick. "Sauternes, 1939," he announced.

Sébastian tasted it solemnly then nodded his approval, playing his part too. No one would guess what we were planning. The foie gras arrived next with a basket of thin toast. Sébastian cut a piece of the soft liver, placing it on a piece of toast then sprinkling it with a few grains of sea salt.

I followed his example, but when I added the salt, I was reminded of Maman and Isabelle at home, having nothing but cabbage soup again. I thought about putting some food in a napkin and slipping it into my handbag. But Maman had no idea where I was. And she'd be horrified if she knew I was in a German restaurant.

Feeling uneasy, I took a bite of toast laden with foie gras. It melted on my tongue, leaving a rich warm feeling in my mouth. I took a large sip of Sauternes. I hadn't eaten like this in years, and I had to force myself to slow down, or I'd make myself sick. I realized Sébastian had hardly said a word. "Tell me more about Germany." I preferred to let him talk so I could enjoy my food. "What was it like growing up there?"

His eyebrows came together as he looked at me intently. "I should tell you about my grandmother then. She was French. And quite a character. She loved to read. She always had hard candy in her shiny leather handbag." He grinned. "We used to suck away on them for hours, while poring over her precious collection of books. She made me read to her: *Les Trois Mousquetaires*, *Les Misérables*, *Le Comte de Monte-Cristo*..."

"*Le Comte de Monte-Cristo*? I love that book. Everything that happens, but he keeps coming back."

"Yes, good conquering evil. What all great stories are made of."

"Just stories?"

He paused then continued. "We used to spend a lot of time together; my parents were always so busy. We used to call ourselves '*Les Deux Complices*.' '*Où est mon petit complice?*' she'd say in a singsong voice when she was looking for me. That would really annoy my parents." He hesitated, looking at me for a moment. "She was a brave lady."

"What do you mean?"

"Well." He leaned nearer, lowering his tone. "One day we were walking in town, back home in Dresden, when an SA parade, Hitler's storm troopers, marched by. When this happened, you had to raise your arm in salute, or you'd be in big trouble, probably arrested, but she pulled me into a building's entrance and whispered, '*Pas ça!*' I was so scared. I didn't want to disobey them."

"You were just a kid." To my surprise I found myself making excuses for him. "Is your grandmother deceased?" I changed tack. "You used the past tense."

"No." A tiny crease appeared between his eyes as though he hadn't realized until I'd pointed it out. "It must be because that all feels like another life, back in Germany, as though it only exists in the past. I find it hard to believe I might see her again."

I wanted to tell him that he would, that this war wouldn't last forever, that one day we'd be free again to be with our families and live life the way we wanted, but how, in my place, could I offer such words of comfort? So I said nothing.

"Of course, it was very hard for my parents. We had so little money." He smiled a crooked smile. "I used to go apple scrumping with my brother. My mother would pretend to be cross, but she was happy to get the apples." He took a sip of wine. "Money, money, it was a constant worry. It literally vanished before your eyes. People joked that you needed to take a wheelbarrow to the bank; a loaf of bread that cost one mark in the morning could cost you eight thousand by the afternoon. Our notes became worthless overnight. Some people got paid three times a day, and their family would collect the money then rush out to spend it in the next five minutes. You had to carry huge amounts of useless notes to be able to buy anything at all."

"I heard it was bad."

He nodded. "Luckily for us, my father was a civil servant, so at least he knew he'd get paid every month. The morning after he received his salary my mother would wake us at five and we'd go to market, even my grandmother. I was only about three or four, and my father pulled me along on a trailer he'd made. On the way back I had to walk because the trailer was used for the food—food for the whole month. We had to spend the money before it lost its value, and we bought what we could—tinned meat, dry beans, things that would keep." He looked into the distance. "I loved those mornings. We were all together, and my mother seemed happy for a change."

I was totally absorbed in his words and hadn't noticed a singer approaching our table. The piano stopped abruptly, starting up again with a different rhythm. Placing a hand on Sébastian's shoulder, she looked over into my eyes as she sang.

Elle fréquentait la Rue Pigalle...

She frequented the Rue Pigalle...

It was about a prostitute! The other diners looked up, some tapping their fingers in time. The Germans probably didn't understand a word.

To my relief, the woman twirled away, leaving me wondering what it had all been about. Did she think I was a high-class prostitute? Did I care? I was doing what I had to do.

The waiter removed our plates, reappearing minutes later with our main course, carefully placing a plate in front of me, turning it round so that the leg of duck cradled the beans and potatoes.

"*Bon appétit.*" Sébastian slipped the fatty skin off his duck with his knife, exposing the meat underneath.

I watched the butter melting over the hot green beans, leaving a trail of yellow fat, and I picked up my fork, tasting one; it was firm and fresh. I tried a potato; it was crisp outside and soft inside, just how I liked them. Taking my knife and fork, I pulled the skin away from the duck, then cut into the dark meat.

Chapter Twenty-Three

Paris, April 1944

Sébastian

Sébastian drove back to his hotel and parked outside. Once in his room, he lay fully clothed on the bed and lit a cigarette, watching the smoke spiraling toward the ceiling. Even though he had a dangerous task ahead of him, he felt light of heart. The evening had been magical; Élise and he had talked as though they were any normal couple getting to know each other, and he'd enjoyed speaking about his past, though he was aware she'd given very little away about herself. He'd understood her reticence and hadn't pushed her.

He rolled over and set his alarm for four that morning just in case he dropped off. But when the alarm rang, he hadn't slept a wink, his mind racing between thoughts of Élise and nerves about picking the children up. He reminded himself that no one would stop a German soldier in a German car. He was hardly taking a risk at all. Not really.

It was deadly quiet when he went down to the car, not

a soul in sight. He got in quickly and drove through the deserted streets, coming to a stop at a red traffic light. A tapping on the window made him jump. A young soldier stood there. But Sébastian didn't have time for this. He ignored the man and sped off.

He pulled to a stop in Rue Claude Bernard, wondering if the "concerned citizen" would be awake now, watching the orphanage. It wouldn't matter if they were. They might be glad to think their letter had been taken seriously, and here was a German soldier on a night raid. The front door was open as Élise had said it would be, and he walked straight in.

A group of small children, huddled together in front of a thin-faced lady, shrank further into her legs when they saw him. A girl of about seven years with long dark hair was sobbing. "Shh," the lady whispered. "I told you, he's come to help you. He's going to take you somewhere safe."

The girl shook her head vigorously, her large brown eyes wide with fear.

Sébastian crouched down, thinking he might look less terrifying if he was their height. But they just backed further away, clinging to the lady's skirt. Then a taller skinny girl, with skin so pale it looked translucent, stepped forward. "Where are you taking us?" She stared directly at Sébastian, as though challenging him.

Sébastian smiled in what he hoped was a warm way. "I'm taking you to a bookshop."

"A bookshop?" The girl frowned. "Why?"

"Because if you're very quiet, no one will guess you're there. And you can read as many books as you like."

"I want to stay here." A small boy tugged on the lady's skirt, looking up at her. "Please."

"Come on now, we've talked about this." The lady's voice

was warm and coaxing. "If you want to see your parents again you have to be very quiet and do exactly as you're told."

A whimper escaped from one of them. Sébastian just wanted to get on with it, afraid that their fear would escalate into something uncontrollable if they waited much longer. "Follow me to the car outside," he said.

The lady pushed the children forward, and without another murmur they followed Sébastian. He opened the back-seat door. "Get in and lie down." He held the door with one hand while he put his other on their backs, pushing them in, hurrying them along. Soon they were all squashed in. "Stay low. So no one can see you." They did as they were told, thin limbs entangled across the back seat.

He glanced up at the windows overlooking the orphanage before driving off. He thought he saw a face at one, but it must have been his imagination. No one would be looking now, not at four in the morning. Sébastian held his breath as he drove up Rue d'Ulm, past the university, taken over by the Germans now. The only sounds were the children's breathing and the gentle purr of the motor.

He rounded the next corner when a man stepped out of nowhere. Sébastian slammed on the brakes. The children made a soft thudding sound as they were thrown against the back of the seats. Two of them cried out.

"Shh," Sébastian hissed. "Be quiet."

It went silent as though the whole car had stopped breathing. Sébastian's heart beat loudly in his eardrums. Then the man laughed, thumped the hood, and walked round to the driver's window.

Sébastian's foot hovered over the accelerator. Should he hit it? He could see from the man's coat and hat that he was an officer. A drunken officer. Would a drunken man remember a license plate? He couldn't risk it. He removed his foot and wound down the window.

"*Guten Abend.*" Sébastian drew his words out as though he were totally relaxed.

"*Guten Abend,*" the officer slurred. He bent down, looking into the car, breathing whiskey fumes into Sébastian's face. A whimper came from the back. Immediately Sébastian coughed to hide it, sweat breaking out under his hairline. Thank God it was a dark night and the lights were out.

"Lost my car." The man laughed loudly. "Drive me home, would you?" He was already walking round to the passenger door, letting himself in. He collapsed into the seat letting out a long sigh. "The Majestic," he said as though Sébastian were a cab driver.

Shit! Sébastian's pulse raced. Now he'd have to cross the river and go all the way along Rue de Rivoli. "Of course, sir." He put the car into gear and drove off, silently begging the children to stay quiet. With a deeper pang of fear he realized they wouldn't understand this exchange in German. They might think he was handing them in. God! If the officer saw them, he would be; they'd be sent straight to Drancy.

"Been having fun tonight?" The officer laughed again. "I have!"

"Yes, thank you, sir." Sébastian wanted to keep talking, to hide any noise from the back. "It was a great evening. Had dinner over in Montmartre. How about you, sir?"

The man was already snoring.

Sébastian let out a long breath. "Don't worry," he whispered as much to himself as the children. "It will be all right."

The officer mumbled, shifting in his seat.

Sébastian held every muscle taut as though he could stop

time. The snoring started again. Not a sound came from the back.

When he pulled up in front of the grand hotel, a porter ran up to the car to help the officer out. He leaned down, taking him by the arm, twisting his head as he did so, toward the back of the car.

The hairs on the back of Sébastian's neck stood up. A chill ran down the back of his head.

Then the porter straightened up, the officer on his arm. "What's that smell?" the porter asked. "Smells like piss back there." He didn't wait for an answer but turned away quickly, leading the officer toward the hotel.

The acidic stench of urine reached the back of Sébastian's nostrils, and he breathed out with one long exhale, then pressed on the pedal and pulled away. Now he'd have to clean the car before he gave it back.

"Well done," he whispered. "You were very good. We're going to the bookshop now." He felt a rush of pride in these children he didn't know.

When he pulled up in front of the bookshop, he got out and opened the back-seat door. "You can get out now." Sébastian spoke softly. "Go on into the shop." Round eyes shining in the dark stared back at him. "It's okay, it's safe here." He pulled at one of the hands. The little hand grasped his and soon a girl was standing next to him. "Daniel peed himself." She looked at him, hesitating. "It's not his fault. It's because he was scared."

Monsieur Le Bolzec opened the shop door and stood there in his pajamas, beckoning the children toward him. The girl's hand slipped out of Sébastian's, and she walked into the shop. Sébastian pulled four more children out, pushing them forward toward the shop. What if another German car drove up? He couldn't stay parked like this. Someone could come along at any minute and want to see what was going on. They had to hurry.

The last child lay curled up in a tight ball, whimpering. He reminded Sébastian of the tethered dog that used to live in the house down the road. Everyone knew his owner beat him, but no one ever said anything to him, just looked the other way when they passed in front. Sébastian had once poked a leftover chicken bone through the fence, and the poor animal strained at his leash trying to get to it, but it was just out of his reach. Sébastian had felt terrible, realizing he'd only caused more suffering.

The smell of urine grew stronger. "We have to go." Sébastian pulled at the child, but he resisted, his bird-like shoulder blades quickly drawing back. Sébastian put his hands around the child's waist and hoisted him out. Surprised at how light he was, he carried him into the bookshop and put him down. "He's had an accident." Sébastian looked at Monsieur Le Bolzec.

"Come on, son, let's get you some clean clothes." Monsieur Le Bolzec led the child away by the hand.

Sébastian looked at the quivering huddle of children. He wanted to offer them words of comfort, of encouragement, of admiration even for their courage. But anything he thought of saying died on his lips. Instead, he knelt down and held out his hand toward them. The taller girl stared at it a minute then placed her delicate bony hand in his and shook it. The others followed suit and in silence they each shook his hand.

Sébastian nodded at them, then stood up and walked out, blinking back the tears in his eyes.

Chapter Twenty-Four

Paris, May 1944

Élise

Five days gone by, and no news. I tried to carry on as normal, going to work, lining up for food, but the children were constantly at the back of my mind. Were they safe? Had they been moved on yet? I began to regret agreeing to keep away from the bookshop and the orphanage; I needed to know. But Anaïs was organizing the *passeur*, and they didn't want me involved. I was the lead that could connect the orphanage to the bookshop.

On Friday afternoon when I was sitting at my desk going through some accounts, Françoise approached me. "Are you okay?" she asked. "You look so worried."

"I am!" I blurted out. "There's a war on, for goodness' sake!"

She took a step back. "And life goes on!" She smiled. "We're going to a *bal clandestin* tonight. Why don't you come?"

I couldn't help shaking my head. "I'm really not in the mood for dancing."

"It will do you good." She paused and looked at me quizzically. "Don't you see? They win if we let them impose their rules on us, making us stay at home, never going anywhere, never having any fun." She sighed loudly. "How can they ban us from going to dances? They make us dance for them. But we should be dancing for ourselves!"

Her energy enthused me, and I couldn't help grinning. "You're right. But I just feel...I'm so tired with it all."

"Oh, come on, Élise. Don't give in to them!"

Her last words got to me, and what did I have to lose? "Okay, okay," I conceded. "I'll come."

At seven o'clock that evening, I walked to the Métro at Saint-Sulpice, my wooden wedges tapping along the sidewalk giving me more height than the flat shoes I usually wore. It was a beautiful early autumnal evening, the sinking sun casting long shadows. A few Germans were out, patrolling the streets in their sinister dark uniforms, probably looking forward to a night of entertainment in Paris.

As I walked to the Métro, I was careful to avoid them, then when I reached the station, I scuttled down the steps, eager to get to Bastille, where it would be less busy. The platform quickly became crowded, and I noticed two women wearing yellow stars waiting at the far end of the platform, ready to get into the last carriage, while the Germans gathered at the other end, ready to jump into the front carriages. The Germans laughed loudly together, without so much as a glance in the women's direction. But it made me anxious to see Jewish women so near the very men who could have them arrested and sent away for no other reason than being Jewish.

When the train finally drew in, we all took a step back, but as soon as it came to a halt we crowded on. The seats were quickly taken, and I stood, holding onto one of the vertical metal bars. As the train lurched forward, the sudden force caught me unawares, and I swung around on the bar, accidentally bumping into one of the men in uniform. "Sorry," I mumbled.

"Don't worry!" He turned around, smiling at me. "It's quite all right." He was young and his smile looked genuine and open.

I almost caught myself smiling back. Then I silently cursed myself. I must never, never accept their presence here. I must never allow myself to see them as individuals. It was bad enough I'd got to know Sébastian, and that was only since he proved to be useful.

"Would you like my seat, mademoiselle?" Another soldier stood up, opening his arm to indicate the free seat he'd just left.

"No, thank you," I replied, avoiding his eyes.

"Are you sure?" he insisted.

I nodded, turning away from him so I wouldn't have to watch his humiliation as he sat back down. A Frenchman standing on the other side caught my eye and just perceptibly winked. It wasn't a leery wink, but one of complicity, and I found myself smiling back.

When I hopped off at Bastille the Frenchman jumped off too. "Well done!" He walked next to me as I left the platform. "That's the way to treat them."

"Just trying to do my part." I turned to look at him; his eyes were dark brown and sparkling with mischief.

"Where are you going?" he asked.

"I'm meeting some friends."

"Would you and your friends like to join me and my friends?" He paused, lowering his tone as he leaned nearer. "We're going to a *bal clandestin*."

"It doesn't sound very clandestine to me." I strode ahead. "*Au revoir,*" I shouted back. The brief flirtation lifted my spirits.

Françoise was waiting for me at the café on the corner of Rue de la Roquette. I kissed her on the cheeks, and she linked arms with me as we walked and talked. "The others will meet us there. It's not far, just around the corner on Rue de Lappe."

I rarely ventured out into this part of Paris and was surprised by its shabbiness and dingy-looking cafés. Françoise must have noticed my reaction. "I know it's not the most beautiful part of Paris, but I like it, and it has the added advantage that the Boches don't bother coming here." She looked at me expectantly.

"No, it's fine. Anywhere the Boches don't go is good for me."

"Quite." She slowed down. "This is the address." We stood in front of a small café, its window frames worn down, exposing pale wood. She pushed the door open, and as our eyes adjusted to the dim light, I saw that it was more of a bar than a café; one long zinc counter extending the length of the room. A few older men, nursing their *ballons de rouge*, stared at us as we walked in.

"*Mesdemoiselles?*" The barman greeted us coolly.

"*Bonsoir, monsieur,*" Françoise replied just as coolly, as she walked to the end of the bar. I followed her, wondering if we'd got the right place, and if we had, whether I really wanted to be there.

The barman met us at the end of the bar. "Here for the dance, are you?" he whispered.

Françoise looked at me and nodded. Without another word he came out from behind the counter and walked to the back of the room, where he pushed open a door, motioning for us to go through. We walked right into a thick velvety curtain, but when we pushed it aside, we found ourselves in a much larger room. In one corner a group of musicians stood chatting, while a few women waited around the edges. As we walked further in, we sized each other up, like women do, checking out the clothes we'd managed to put together. Most of us were simply dressed in straight skirts and plain blouses; it would have been unseemly to have more material. There were no windows, and the walls were covered in the same thick velvet as the curtain we had come through. The only light came from small lamps placed on tables set out around the edge of the room. There were only a few men, and I wondered how they'd managed to avoid the forced labor in Germany. Maybe they had essential jobs here, whatever they might be.

"I think we're a bit early," Françoise whispered. "Let's see if we can get a drink."

We wandered around the room and soon came to a table laid out with tumblers containing a clear liquid. "What's that?" I asked the man standing behind the table.

"My very own invention," he said proudly. "Alcohol made from potatoes."

"Isn't that vodka?" Françoise raised an eyebrow.

"Not exactly. Try it."

We took a glass each, knocking them together before looking each other in the eye as we both took a sip.

"*Mon Dieu!*" My throat burned and my eyes watered. "It tastes like pure alcohol!"

"Why don't you mix it with something?" Françoise asked the man.

"I would if I had something."

"You could try water." I gave my glass back to him. "I can't drink it like that."

He added some water from a carafe that was already on the table, and I realized he was just having a laugh at our expense.

We gave him a franc and wandered off. Just then the musicians started up, filling the room with a lively but soft beat.

Then I felt a tap on my shoulder. It was the Frenchman from the Métro, holding out his hand to me. His over-confident smile and the expectant twinkle in his eye made me decline. "No thank you." I turned away from him, just in time to see the look of surprise on Françoise's face.

"Why didn't you dance with him?" She nudged me with her elbow. "He's cute, and there are so few men around. I would have."

"I guess I'm just not in the mood."

Out of nowhere, Sébastian entered my thoughts.

Chapter Twenty-Five

Paris, May 1944

Sébastian

Sébastian sat alone on the café terrace after work, thinking about the children, wondering if they'd been moved on yet. He sighed loudly, attracting the attention of the waitress.

"*Oui, monsieur?*" She looked nervous, and he realized she must have interpreted his sigh as displeasure. The carafe of wine was still half-full, and he'd only half finished his *confit de canard*.

"Can I have the bill, please?"

While he waited for it, Sébastian glanced around the café. Two Frenchwomen sat with a group of four German officers, and three other women sat together at another table, sharing a carafe of wine. He guessed they wouldn't be on their own for long. He hated the way the Germans treated Paris, as though it were their playground, most of them hoping to pick up a French girlfriend while they were here. The Frenchwomen seemed exotic and mysterious in a way that German women weren't. Despite the war, they dressed well, and they had a certain dignity, as though refusing to admit that they were living under an occupation. Well, most of them dressed well, Élise being the exception in men's pants and plain shirts, her hair cut short, her face not made up. In a strange way it only emphasized her femininity. It was in the contrasts; her waist accentuated by the brown belt, her hair thick and shiny, her cheekbones highlighted by the natural light, her eyes softer than a man's.

His thoughts returned to the children, and he decided that five days was long enough to wait. It wouldn't be too risky for him to go back to the bookshop, browse a little, possibly pick up a message. The waitress returned with his bill. He left a generous tip then got up and started walking toward the 5th.

Monsieur Le Bolzec looked surprised to see Sébastian, and not too pleased. His face was drawn and pale, and his eyes, which were usually lively and curious, darted toward the other customers anxiously as he greeted Sébastian with a slight incline of the head instead of his usual cheery *bonjour.*

Sébastian wandered over to the shelves in the middle, where he'd first seen Élise, hoping that Monsieur Le Bolzec would make his way over when he saw the opportunity. The shop appeared to be busier than usual, and he had to wait a while. He wished they'd devised a secret plan of leaving messages tucked inside certain books. He needed to know if the children had got away safely. Eventually Monsiuer Le Bolzec came to stack some books on the shelf in front of Sébastian. "Excuse me," he said as he leaned past Sébastian. "I just need to add these." He slipped a thin book in between two larger books, tapping it on the spine with his first finger.

Sébastian got his meaning and removed the book. He opened it carefully, and there inside the front cover was a piece of paper, on which were written the simple words. *Ils sont tous partis.*

Monsieur Le Bolzec had known what Sébastian had come for, and there was his answer. The children had already been moved on. Sébastian's heart soared with relief. It was working. It had all been worth it. He closed the book with the paper still inside and went to pay for it.

With a lighter heart now, he left the shop and walked toward the Panthéon, then the Sorbonne—silent witnesses to so much history. He carried on and soon found himself standing in front of the fountain at Saint-Sulpice, looking at the large, imposing church. A woman hurried across the square, her wooden wedges echoing through the night, her short hair bouncing from side to side. He was reminded of Élise and, his curiosity aroused, walked toward her receding back. When he was level with her, he glanced at her profile. Her nose was just visible behind the shaft of hair which flopped forward, half hiding her face.

She turned to look at him. Fear flashed in her eyes, quickly turning to relief as she recognized him.

"Élise," he whispered.

She turned away from him, continuing even more quickly on her way. He looked at his watch. "Curfew starts in ten minutes."

"I know. That's why I'm going home." She strode away from him.

He caught up with her, his stomach contracting as he found the nerve to speak again. "I can walk back with you, just in case you're stopped."

"No!" Her eyes darted around, and he realized she was

worried about who might see them together, but it was so close to curfew, the streets were already deserted.

"You look nice." He fell into step with her. "Have you been out?"

"Yes, to Bastille," she replied amicably enough, giving him the confidence to go on.

"To a dance?" They both knew that dances for the French citizens had been forbidden.

But still she replied, "Yes."

A pang of regret shot through him, as he imagined her dancing, laughing, happy, without him. "I wish I could have gone with you." The words shot out. He stared at her profile, longing to run his finger over the bridge of her nose, to her forehead where, in the moonlight, he could see a small crease forming.

"The children are already out," he whispered, grateful he could give her some good news.

Her hand flew to her chest. "Thank God." She paused in her stride, turning toward him. "You did a good thing." Her eyes met his for a brief second. He wanted to hold her there, but he felt her tense up when a couple of women hurried by; she looked away, quickly carrying on across the square. He kept pace with her, then she slowed down in a small street off to the side, in front of a burgundy-colored door.

She turned to face him. "Thank you for seeing me home, Sébastian."

She'd thanked him! And used his name again! A thrill of excitement vibrated through him. "You're welcome." He glanced at his watch. "Would you walk a little more? You'll be safe with me." He knew he was pushing his luck, but under the moonlight he saw little dimples appear on her cheeks. Then in a flash they were gone. She shook her head.

"Just five minutes," he persisted. He watched her glance around and knew she was anxious about who might be watching. It was deadly quiet, though curtains could always be twitching. He waited, aware that too much insistence would put her off. Then he had an idea. He took his jacket off and put it round her shoulders, pulling the collar up, his fingers brushing against her neck, sending a spark of electricity through him. "You can hide in this." He smiled.

Her eyes widened.

Merde! He'd made a huge mistake, putting a German jacket on her. What an ass he was!

She threw it off, stepping further away.

He caught the jacket in his hand. "Sorry! God, I'm an idiot! I'm so sorry!"

She turned to look at him, a deep line across her forehead. "It's okay," she whispered.

He waited for her to open the door and leave him, but instead she took a step down the street. A rush of joy lifted Sébastian's heart, and he had to hide his smile as he matched his step to hers and walked next to her.

Chapter Twenty-Six

Paris, May 1944

Élise

It was only five minutes. What harm could it do? He'd risked his life getting those children out. I could risk five minutes for him. Maybe I'd had too much of that alcoholic potato drink. My head felt light, and the world didn't seem quite so dark. I felt him walking next to me, like a force pulling me in, and I could hear his breathing in the silent street. It felt intimate. Dangerously intimate. Thrillingly intimate. I was unprepared for the wave of exhilaration that rippled through me. Or was it fear? Whatever it was, it made me feel alive. My pulse fluttered and my heart beat hard, leaving me slightly breathless. Something in the air was mystical, as though the worries and terrors of life had evaporated, leaving me caught somewhere between reality and dream-state.

"I think I like Paris best when it's sleeping." Sébastian spoke in a low voice. "When it's quiet like this." He hesitated.

"When there are no soldiers." He said nothing for a moment, and I could hear him thinking. "It's a city full of secrets, isn't it?"

"It is now." I kept my eyes focused ahead, though I thought I could feel him smiling his small smile. "I never asked you how you got your posting here," I blurted out. "Did someone owe you a favor?"

He didn't answer straight away, and I was wondering if he was going to answer at all when he spoke, almost in a whisper. "I was in a bad way after Russia."

"Russia?"

"Yes, I was sent to the front. I was a foot soldier. A nobody." I'd heard about the massive German defeat in Russia, how the Germans had lost hundreds of thousands of men. We'd rejoiced when we'd heard of their huge loses, but now I thought about how each individual life lost was grieved for—how the large numbers had dehumanized the deaths. "My father managed to pull a few strings," he continued. "He got me this posting here." I waited for him to continue, but loud shouting and laughter shattered the calm. A group of drunken German soldiers stumbled toward us. A large man crashed right into me, his enormous belly knocking me off the sidewalk. He put his arms out to catch me. Then holding me, he laughed. "*Habe ich dir Angst gemacht?*"

I pulled his paw-like hands off me and stood back.

"*Du bist direkt in ihr hineingelaufen!*" Sébastian shouted.

"*Excusez-moi, mademoiselle.*" The fat soldier smiled at me, his teeth glinting in the semidarkness. Then he turned back to Sébastian. "*Wieviel nimmt sie dafür?*" The other soldiers laughed out loud. I didn't know what the man had just said, but out of the corner of my eye I saw Sébastian stand straight, pulling his shoulders back. I held my breath, shrinking back against the wall, trying to make myself invisible. Everything went abruptly silent and still.

Sébastian balled his hand into a tight fist.

"Don't!" I grabbed his arm.

He turned around. His eyes were burning wild with fury. The soldiers laughed again. Then as suddenly as they'd appeared, they disappeared, putting their arms around each other, loud, leery voices fading away as they staggered off.

I stared into Sébastian's wild eyes, my fingers still digging into his arm. Then as if it had burned me, I dropped it. "It's okay," I whispered. "It doesn't matter."

The fury in his eyes slowly faded. "Doesn't matter?" He ran his hand through his hair. "I'm ashamed of them." He sighed. "And I'm ashamed to be here, like this."

"I know you are." I looked at him directly for the first time, and he looked back at me, holding my gaze.

"What did the fat man say?" I asked, breaking the moment.

He turned away and carried on walking. "Nothing worth repeating."

"Tell me."

"You don't want to know."

"Yes, I do."

He sighed. "He said you've got beautiful eyes."

"And you were going to hit him for that? That's not what he said."

"Élise, his words are not worth repeating. I wouldn't do him the honor. Forget it. Please."

Of course, he'd insulted me, but I dropped it. "It's a good job you didn't hit him."

"Yes, good job for him!" He laughed, and it felt so child-like, so spontaneous, I laughed back, and the tension lifted. Our laughter must have disturbed a sleeping rat; it scuttled across the street, diving down a drain. I took a leap backward, stepping on Sébastian's toes. His hands gripped my waist, and a frisson rippled through me. "It's okay. It's just a rat." He laughed, letting go. "Paris is full of rats these days." He didn't take his hands away, and for a moment neither of us moved. His touch vibrated through me, pulling me toward him. I had an urge to lean into him, to soak up the warmth of his body.

Instead I moved away. "What happened in Russia?" I remembered what we'd been talking about. But my question was met with silence, left dangling awkwardly, the only sounds now my wedges and his hobnailed boots, echoing out into the night like two out-of-time clocks ticking.

We continued to walk in silence, my breath thudding in my ears.

"I had a friend," he murmured. "His name was Henrik."

I slowed down, noticing his hunched shoulders, hearing the tremor in his voice. "Don't tell me if you don't want to."

"No, I want to," he continued. "Henrik and I grew up together." I held my breath, closing my eyes. "We did everything together." His voice floated into the darkness. "Then the war came. We were both sent to Russia, in the same unit. Because it was the two of us again, we thought nothing bad could happen, as though together we were invincible; stupid boys that we were!" He stopped, leaving his words hanging there. I swallowed painfully, dreading what was coming next. "We were ambushed. Henrik and me. Everyone." His voice grew hoarse. "It was snowing, falling thick. We couldn't see. They came out of nowhere. Russian soldiers with guns. They shot at us." He took a breath. I covered my face with my hand, as if I could protect myself from his next words. "Then it went quiet." His voice dropped to a whisper. "And the screams started. Henrik was screaming my name."

He paused, pulling out a pack of Gitanes from his breast pocket, holding it out to me. I shook my head, watching him light up. After taking a deep drag, he carried on, his eyes fixed on some invisible point ahead as he started walking again. "I crawled along. The other screams—I ignored them all. Then I found him. He'd been shot in the stomach." He stopped walking, tapping the ash from the end of his cigarette onto the ground. I waited. "So much blood. I could smell it. The hole was too big to cover with my hands. He was falling out of his body. I tried to lift him up, to carry him." Sébastian stared at me, but his eyes were distant, as though he were only half seeing me. "The Russians were advancing again. There were more shots. More shouting. Henrik was so heavy." He paused, beads of sweat shining on his upper lip, as though the words were burning him from within. "I stumbled. I fell with him in my arms, on top of him. He was shaking all over. I didn't have the strength to pick him back up and run. I could hear the Russians getting nearer. He told me to finish him off." He dropped his cigarette, rubbing it into the ground with his boot. "How could I shoot him? I tried to pick him up again. But he cried. He begged me." He wiped his face roughly with the back of his hand. "I held his head in my hands, and I...I..."

"You shot him?" I shuddered, a sickening feeling of revulsion rising from my belly. Staring at the stone wall in front of me, I tried to block out the image of Henrik lying in a pool of blood in the white snow.

Sébastian turned toward the wall. He put his arms out in front of him, pressing his hands against the stone, bending over now, his back horizontal. His arms began to tremble.

Was he crying? Was this how men cried? I waited for him to take control of himself, but his trembling turned to shaking. I was terrified he was going to collapse as spasms racked through his whole body. Taking a step nearer, I put my arms around his back, trying to steady him. "Sébastian." His name burned my lips. "It's over. It's over." I leaned my head against his back, holding onto him, till the tremors began to lose their viscous energy and his body slumped, but I didn't take my arms away. I felt him take a deep breath, then he turned around, gripping me, like a drowning man. I let him cling to me, his cheek against mine, his tears damp and warm. "I'm sorry, Élise." The hot ragged breath of his words vibrated through me. I felt myself dissolving, losing myself in him. Losing everything.

It took all my resolve, all my will, but I managed to take a step backward. A bitter wind seemed to swirl up, blowing between us, separating us. I took another step and the wind swept through me, leaving me cold and empty.

The crossroads opened up in front of me. The moment that would change everything. I took his hand, pulling him back toward me, closing the space. And I kissed him. I kissed him with every breath in my body.

Chapter Twenty-Seven

Paris, May 1944

Élise

Sébastian knew where I lived, a fact that both terrified and excited me. Every day when I came home after work, I was on tenterhooks, swaying between hoping he would come by, then praying that he wouldn't. I didn't think he'd come to my home, but then again, I'd seen his impulsive side. I thought back to how careful he'd been when he took me to the restaurant, ensuring no one saw us together. But then again, I'd witnessed his impulsivity when he'd rescued me from Rue de la Pompe, his courage when he'd agreed to help get the children out, and his vulnerability the other night. I thought of our wild embrace, as though we were the only people left in the world.

The doorbell ringing cut into my thoughts. My heart leapt into my throat, even though I didn't believe it was him, but just the possibility was enough to set my pulse racing. "I'll go," I shouted. Grabbing my jacket, I ran out to the main door.

My stomach sank. A woman with a package stood there. "Madame Chevalier?"

"I'm her daughter," I answered, taking the package from her. Irrational disappointment seeped through me as I returned to the kitchen to give it to Maman without staying to see what was inside.

A week went by.

No, I decided, adding it all up, Sébastian wouldn't come. I would have to find him.

I'd agreed not to go back to the bookshop. But Isabelle could go. Couldn't she? I wouldn't be putting her in any danger, not really. She wouldn't have to do anything. Monsieur Le Bolzec would realize why I'd sent her, and if there was a message for me, he'd be able to pass it on, maybe in a book.

I asked her to go in the very next day, saying I wanted a book of short stories. She seemed happy to go off on her own, Saturday afternoon, and came back looking quite excited.

"Guess what?" She walked into the kitchen, holding a wrapped brown package under her arm.

"What?" I asked tentatively, looking up from the rutabaga I was grating.

"There was a Boche in the shop."

My throat grew tight.

"Don't use that word, I've told you before." Maman wiped her hands on her apron, turning to face Isabelle.

"What was he doing?" I couldn't help asking. It could have been anyone, but I knew it was him, Sébastian.

"Talking to Monsieur Le Bolzec," Isabelle answered.

"What's he doing talking to them?" Maman sighed. "He shouldn't encourage them to go into his shop. Once this war is over, people will remember things like that."

"Germans are allowed into bookshops too, Maman." I bit my bottom lip, anxious that I might say too much. "No one would ever think Monsieur Le Bolzec was a collabo."

Maman frowned. "You don't know what people might do."

I heard what she said, but my mind was on the package Isabelle was still holding. "Is that for me?" I asked her.

She held the package out. "Monsieur Le Bolzec said you'd asked for this book." She paused as I took it. "What is it?"

I shrugged, faking indifference, as I turned it over in my hands. It was tied with string, obviously only meant for me to open. But how could I sneak off and open it in private? Already I could feel Maman's eyes digging into me. I sat down at the kitchen table, trying to breathe more calmly as I put the package in front of me and untied the string. The brown paper fell away. "Yes," I said. "I remember, I asked him to put it aside for me." My heart beat faster when I remembered Sébastian buying this book the first time I'd seen him in the shop.

"What is it?" Maman leaned over my shoulder.

"Poetry." The word felt false on my tongue.

"Poetry?" Her surprise was obvious in the inflection she put on the end of the word.

"I thought it might be nice to read some for a change."

Maman hung over me, waiting for me to open it.

"Is that all?" Isabelle sounded disappointed.

"What else did you think it would be?" I made my voice light, breezy-sounding.

"I don't know. Something better than poetry." She twirled around on her foot as though bored with the matter now.

"Why don't you read us a poem?" I detected a hint of irony in Maman's words.

I opened the book in the middle—a safe place, I assumed.

I had the distinct feeling that Sébastian had read this very page not long ago. I started reading aloud.

"Est-ce à nous qu'il prête l'oreille?" Is it to us that he lends his ears?

"Est-ce aux anges? Est-ce aux démons? A quoi songe-t-il, lui qui veille." Or to the angels? Or to the demons? What is he thinking, he who watches over us.

I stopped reading. Sébastian must have given this book to Monsieur Le Bolzec to pass on to me, and somewhere inside there was a message from him, but I couldn't look for it with Maman hanging over me like a vulture. I closed the book, desperate to get to the privacy of my bedroom.

"Why have you stopped reading?" Maman raised an eyebrow. "I was quite enjoying it."

"I'll choose one to read tonight then, after dinner." I put the book down and went back to grating the rutabaga.

I waited a whole hour before excusing myself to go to my room. Then I closed the door and sat on my bed. At last I was alone. This time I opened the book on the first page. There was an inscription.

My Love, Lise,

My life began with you.

Yours forever,

S

I lifted the open book up against my face, breathing in the smell of paper, print, the thrill of a world opening up, trying to catch the smell of him. Then a piece of paper fell out. I picked it up—a sketched map of the Bois de Vincennes, arrows drawn by the Saint-Mandé side of the woods, next to the little lake, and a note at the bottom. *Follow the white paint on the trees. Seven o'clock. Saturday and every day after till you come.*

My heart lifted. The world felt bright and full of hope. Glancing at the clock, I saw it was already seven o'clock. He could be there now, waiting for me. A thrill raced through me. Tomorrow. I would go tomorrow.

The next evening, which happened to be Sunday, I told Maman I was going to meet a friend and that she shouldn't wait for me to eat.

"I'll be back before curfew," I reassured her.

"I know you will," she snapped back. "But where are you going in such a rush?"

"Meeting a friend." I turned around and hurried out before she could say anything else.

I splashed out on a pedi-cab to take me to Châtelet, urging the wiry cyclist to peddle faster, then I picked up the Métro toward Vincennes. Once I got to the woods I breathed more calmly, listening to the birds calling out their evening song as I walked past the lake, toward the trees. When I reached them, I peered at their trunks, looking for a sign of white paint, but I saw nothing. With a sinking feeling I looked around at the hundreds of trees, wondering how I would ever find the ones he'd painted. Moving among them now, separating the branches as I went along, I desperately looked for signs of white. Then I saw a daubed splotch of white paint on the trunk of a thick tree. I ran my hand over the mark, my heart pulsing in my throat. He was here! I looked around, searching for the next mark. It was just two trees away, then there was another five trees further on. But then nothing. There didn't seem to be many people around, and I had to stop myself from shouting out for him as I moved from tree to tree, pushing my way through the low-hanging branches and the small bushes. When I looked up, a single white rose caught my eye. "Sébastian," I whispered, reaching out for it, feeling its delicate silky petals.

A rustling came from somewhere. I froze. A hand grabbed mine and pulled me through a narrow gap in the bushes, scratching my legs and arms. Swallowing my scream, I let Sébastian lead me through to a small clearing, where a coarse brown blanket lay spread over the rough ground and nettles, a bottle of red and a whole Camembert set out in the middle. He pulled me close, his hands tight around my waist. My breath came quickly, our faces almost touching.

"You came," he murmured. "I thought you never would."

For a moment neither of us moved. It didn't seem real, as though I'd stepped into a secret garden. How could we be standing so close I could hear him breathing, could smell his skin? I wanted to touch him. I raised my hand toward his face. He grasped my fingers and lifted them to his lips. His other hand found the small of my back, pulling me further into him, his stubble grazing my cheek.

I had no words. Instead I caressed his lips, parting them gently, knowing that once we kissed, there would be no going back. No before. And so I lingered, prolonging this exquisite moment, before everything exploded into a million fragments we'd never be able to put back together. I felt the fervent urgency in his breath, but he waited. He waited for me.

The kiss, when it came, was tentative at first—exploring, testing, but rapidly growing desperate, wild. There wasn't enough of him, and I wanted it all. Whatever shred of rationality I might have had left, vanished.

Chapter Twenty-Eight

Paris, June 1944

Élise

The only way to keep a secret is not to tell a soul. But how to hide the love that ran through my veins, that brought light to my eyes, color to my cheeks? I practiced in the mirror, trying to make myself look miserable, trying to extinguish the light. But anyone who knew me well would see through it. Maman knew, I could see it in her sidelong glances and pursed lips. She saw something had changed in me, and rather than making her happy, it worried her. Of course, it did. These were times when secret smiles and a lightness of spirit aroused suspicion.

But she didn't say anything that first evening when I came back. Nor the next time, or the time after. But she knew I was hiding something from the way I averted my eyes when I came back after she and Isabelle had eaten, not hungry myself. I brought them back bread and cheese, even strawberries once. That was a mistake. Maman wouldn't take them from me, and I had to give them to Isabelle, who gobbled them up without any questions, Maman watching with folded arms and pursed lips while I stood by cursing myself for being such an idiot, for making it so obvious.

"What's his name?" she finally asked while Isabelle sucked on the strawberry heads, her eyes closed in sheer ecstasy.

I stared at Maman, knowing that I couldn't avoid this conversation now. "Sébastian," I finally said.

"Sébastian what?"

I couldn't say his surname. How could I bring a German name into our home? "He's half-French," I said instead, remembering Monsieur Le Bolzec's words when he tried to make me see Sébastian in a different light. And my reply: *What difference does it make? He's wearing a Nazi uniform!*

"Half-French?" Her words were slow and deliberate, the unspoken question lying between them.

"His mother is French. His father is ... German."

Isabelle looked up, and the air in the kitchen swelled with a thick silence, making it hard to breathe. I sat down heavily at the table, but I held my chin up. I wanted to defend him, but how could I? I couldn't tell her about the children he'd saved. I couldn't tell her he was different than the others.

"Isabelle." Maman straightened her back. "Go to bed."

Isabelle, clearly sensing the tension, was wise enough not to argue and silently slipped out, leaving me alone with Maman.

"What do you think you're playing at?" she hissed. "If only your father were here. For the love of God, what are you doing?" Her words poured out like a torrent of rain. "A German? I thought you hated them. Have you lost your mind?"

"It's not his fault he's German."

She stared at me incredulously. "And it's not our fault we're prisoners, in our own country. I don't give a damn whose fault it is. What happened to your loyalty? He's the enemy."

"He's just a man. He didn't want this war any more than we did."

"You've lost your mind!" She pressed her hands into the sides of her head as if it were all too much to take in. "This war will be over soon." She paused for breath. "And then what? Have you thought about that? You'll be sorry. We all will be. Have you thought about Isabelle? Have you stopped to consider us? Who knows what might happen to people, to people who...?"

"No, Maman. Please, it's not like that. You don't know him." I longed to tell her what Sébastian had done in helping the children, but I couldn't talk about such things. It was just too dangerous.

"How can you be so naive? So stupid?"

"Maman, please. No one knows where I'm going when I meet him. And it's only for an hour, never more."

She picked up a bowl from the draining board. For a moment I thought she was going to throw it onto the floor, but then she dropped it into the sink. "I'm exhausted." She wiped her eyes with the back of her hand. "I'm tired of living in fear. Tired of being hungry. Tired of trying to find enough for us to eat. And all you're thinking about is your German. How can you be so selfish?"

"He's not all I'm thinking about. No one knows about him."

"Why do you have to take such risks now, for God's sake? The Allies have already landed on the beaches in Normandy. Armies are on their way. We just have to hang on a little longer."

"I know, Maman. I know." I took a step toward her and reached out for her hand. I held it in mine. "I feel it too, Maman. Liberation will come. But please, let me have this time with Sébastian." I squeezed her hand. "I love him."

She pulled her hand away and glared at me. "Don't ever tell your father that," she said in a threatening voice as she stormed past me, out of the kitchen.

Chapter Twenty-Nine

Paris, August 15, 1944

Sébastian

Sébastian could tell Élise was still asleep by the soft regularity of her breathing. Their hands were clasped under the sheets; he gently untangled his fingers from hers. Turning onto his side, he looked at her as shafts of light from the early morning sun shone through the slats in the shutters, highlighting her face, her cheekbones. This was the first time she'd stayed the whole night since they'd fallen in love, just four months ago. They were taking a risk, and it meant she'd had to lie to her mother. But it had been worth it. Every minute had been precious.

He traced a line from under her ear, along her collarbone, his fingers coming to rest in the dip of her clavicle. She stirred softly. "Shh, Lise," he whispered. "Sleep." This part of her felt intimate, private. Others might see it, but no one else would touch her here. Was there a name for it? If there wasn't, there should be. This special place. Like her secret self. She had let him in, trusting him completely, and he had revealed himself to her, along with all his terrors. Leaning forward, Sébastian touched this warm hollow with his lips, knowing he would never betray that trust.

He stroked her hair, hoping to soothe her back into her dreams. He wanted to soak up these moments, etch them on his mind, every last detail; the way her eyelids twitched when she dreamed, the way her cheeks glowed rose when she was excited, the way she reached for him in her sleep. He needed to store it all away so that when they were separated, he would be able to play these memories back. These moments with her were fleeting, slipping out of his grasp before he could get a firm hold of them. He yearned for something he could hold on to forever. He wanted to write poetry about her. Semi-formed words grew in his mind, struggling to escape, unsure of themselves. He was afraid of their impact once released. The power of words. Words lied. Words betrayed. Words killed. What if they frightened her? What if they made her feel trapped? Responsible for him in some way? What if the words killed the magic?

Élise stirred again; this time turning her hips slightly, coming to lie on her side, facing him, then without opening her eyes, she reached her hand around the back of his neck, pulling him toward her, her mouth searching out his.

Later, when they lay side by side, their bodies sleek and damp, she stroked his cheek. He waited, knowing she wanted to dig deeper, to know him completely.

"Do you believe in love at first sight?" she asked softly.

He closed his eyes for a second, thinking. "No." Of course, he didn't. It was plainly just a mating instinct. What fool would trust an animal instinct like that?

168 • **Ruth Druart**

"Nor do I. I didn't even look at you, that first time I saw you in the bookshop."

"You just saw a uniform."

"Yes, and it frightened me."

"Well, I didn't look at you much either."

She pinched his cheek softly. "Really?"

"I knew you didn't want to be looked at. Especially not by me. But I noticed you." He played with her fingers. "I found you intriguing."

"Go on," she encouraged him.

It touched him that she wanted to hear him talk about her. "And defiant," he continued. "Brave. I knew you were afraid of those policemen, but you didn't cower in front of them." He let go of her fingers. "I admired that." He ran his hand through her hair. "But I could see you might get yourself into trouble."

"Did you think you would save me?"

"No." He gazed at her. "I knew it would be you who would save me."

"Save you for myself." Dimples appeared as she smiled at him.

"I'll never belong to anyone or anything else." And in that moment, he believed himself to be a completely free man. Free from his country. Free from his family. "We belong to each other," he murmured. "And whatever happens we'll have our memories." He was thinking of the lengthening spring evenings when they'd meet in the Bois de Vincennes, in the place behind the brambles where the stinging nettles grew wild, how he'd carefully placed the blanket on the ground and taken off his boots, his cap, his jacket, and his shirt. Free from almost everything that labeled him, he'd felt he could be himself. He'd known then that these moments were few and so he'd treasured every one of them, savoring them, like one might taste a vintage wine. Only a million times better.

"Remember the lovely evenings we had." She seemed to have read his mind. "You thought of everything. I was terrified the first time. Terrified but excited. Then you were so well hidden, it was as though we were in another world." She looked at him intently. "I'd go anywhere with you. I feel safe with you."

"Anywhere?"

"As long as we're together." She sighed. "Let's escape. Go far away."

He knew where this conversation was going; they'd had it before. "But where would we go? I don't have a car, and even if I did, there's no gasoline."

"We could get horses."

He laughed. This wasn't something she'd suggested so far. "And what would they eat?"

"Grass. Leaves."

"But the grass has all dried up. It's been a hot summer." He kissed her ear.

"We could stop at farms. They must have hay."

"And where would we go, on these horses?" His voice was light and teasing.

"South." She ran her finger lightly down his thigh. "Somewhere far from here. Somewhere in the middle of nowhere."

"There's no middle of nowhere. They're everywhere." The Allies were coming, and the Résistance were gathering their forces. It wouldn't be long before the fighting began and the Germans would be forced out, one way or another.

"We'll hide," she insisted.

"What about the Maquis and the Résistance?" In truth he feared them more than the British or the Americans.

"You just don't want to run away with me, do you?" She pinched his chin.

He caught her hand, bringing it to his lips. Unformed words swimming into his throat then sinking down again. His emotions too raw, too unruly, too immense. He just wanted her to absorb all the feelings he had for her. Circling her waist with his hands, he brought her closer to him, holding her tight while he kissed her on the mouth, breathing into her, as though he could breathe his thoughts into her.

The next words he spoke would not be words of love. They would be hard words that he'd have to drag out from the back of his mind, where all his worries lay. "Lise, you've taken a risk coming here."

"But no one saw me. It was dark."

"The walls have ears. You know how it is; we can't trust anyone. You mustn't be found here. It won't be long before the Germans lose Paris." He pulled away, sitting against the headboard. "It could be a matter of days, and once the French get the upper hand, many of them will be on the rampage, desperate for revenge. It will be violent. Anyone who collaborated or sympathized with the Germans will be made to pay the price."

"But I didn't!"

"Do you really think they'll stop and listen to you? People have seen you talking with me in the bookshop. Those policemen—they'll remember you. They won't stop to ask questions." A sickening feeling started in his stomach when he thought what could happen to her. "You mustn't be found here. You have to go home." He paused. "Did you tell your mother you were coming here?"

"No."

"What did you say?"

"I told her I was staying with my friend Françoise, from the bank. I told her we had work to do at home since the banks have closed up." She turned to look at him. "I'm not sure she believed me though."

"She knows you've been seeing me."

"Yes."

"You didn't tell her about the orphanage?"

"No, of course not. She only thinks I've been taking clothes there."

He held her head against his chest. "She'll know not to talk."

Élise pulled back, looking at him. "We've still got today, haven't we? Tell me we still have today."

"I don't know how long we have. We're waiting for new orders, but some men have started moving out already. They're more afraid of the French getting hold of weapons, and the Allies getting here, than they are of getting court-martialed."

"Maybe you should get out too."

"No. I'll wait for orders."

"Then we have today!"

"Yes, we do. I wish I could take you somewhere special."

"Where would you take me?"

"To the sea," he replied. "We'd swim, and then we'd have a picnic on the beach."

"Go on," she encouraged him.

"We'd go on bicycles," he continued. "No," he corrected himself. "Just one bicycle. You would sit on the crossbar, so I could wrap my arms around you."

"And what would we have in our picnic?"

"A bottle of wine. Red. Bread and cheese, and fruit,

yes—apples and grapes." He paused, kissing the top of her head.

"What about chocolate?"

"Of course. How could I forget? Chocolate too." He took her hand. "Lise, I have an idea."

"What?"

"Let's take this day, just for us." He lifted her hand to his mouth, looking over the top of it as he spoke softly. "But then you go home." He looked at her, checking she'd agree. "I could go out, get some food, and we could have a picnic right here in this room. We can sit by the open window and pretend—"

"Like children," she interrupted. "Pretending to be adults."

"Like adults." He smiled. "Pretending to be children."

She laughed lightly. "Is it safe to go out? Where will you get food? There's nothing left in the shops."

"Lise, my darling, I have connections." He tapped the bridge of his nose with his index finger, exaggerating that odd gesture people make when they have a secret, smiling to himself.

"Go on then." She kissed his hand. "Go out and bring us back a feast."

He kissed her cheek and let her go. He pulled on his pants and put on a shirt, but no jacket and cap, and he left the room. As he walked down the sidewalk, he hugged the buildings closely, heading to the little passage where he sometimes bought food on the black market. A truck thundering by made him jump. Turning to look at it, he saw it was packed high with mattresses. It was closely followed by a tank camouflaged with leaves and branches. The Germans were leaving Paris, and they were taking supplies with them. He hurried to get their picnic. Time was running out.

He was relieved to find the little shop was open, and they were still willing to serve him. He bought as much as he could, wanting to spoil Élise.

"Welcome back." Élise kissed him on the cheek when he returned to the room, like a wife welcoming her husband home. "What have you got?"

He glanced over at the blanket spread out below the open window and laughed. "What a lovely spot for a picnic." He took out the bottle of wine. "A *petit* Bordeaux, Château Margaux. I think you'll like it." He put it down on the blanket and took out a whole Camembert.

"Where on earth did you get that?"

"Oh, I know a couple of racketeers." He smiled, pulling out another item wrapped in brown paper, which he proceeded to open slowly, teasing her.

"Chocolate!" She pulled the tablet out of his hands, hugging it to her chest. "I haven't seen chocolate since... What else have you got in there?" She tried to peak into the bag.

"Ha, just you wait and see." He settled down on the blanket, spreading his legs out in front of him. "Would you like to try the wine?"

"But it's eleven in the morning," she protested.

"Indeed it is. But we have something to celebrate." He took out a corkscrew and pulled the cork out with a satisfying pop, then poured the wine into the two cups from the bathroom.

It might have felt strange, being stuck in a hotel room on a glorious summer's day, drinking red wine from bathroom cups, but in that moment Sébastian couldn't think of anywhere he'd rather be.

"To peace." Élise raised her cup.

"Peace." He knocked his cup against hers. "Whatever

happens now, Lise," Sébastian's tone grew serious, "I'll always remember this day. Thank you."

"You don't need to thank me."

"Yes, I do." The words caught in his throat.

She leaned over him, kissing the rest of his words away. Then she pulled back. "I'm starving!"

The sound of artillery fire in the distance made them jump. "It's okay." Sébastian sat up straight. "It's far away."

Élise laid her head against his chest. "Why don't we just leave? When winter comes this will all be over." He stroked her hair but didn't speak. "We'd be safe," she continued. "I know we would. And we'd be together."

"Lise," he took her hand, "we're meant to be together. We'll find a way."

Chapter Thirty

Paris, August 16, 1944

Élise

I slipped out of bed, gathering my underwear, which lay strewn across the floor. I should have gone home yesterday. Poor Maman, she wasn't stupid; she'd have guessed where I was, and she'd be worried sick.

Sébastian sat up, picking up a packet of Gitanes from the bedside table. Without a word, he tapped one out and lit up. He didn't usually smoke in bed. I wondered if the same thoughts were going through his head as mine. Were we throwing away what little time we had left together? Were we doing the right thing? My heart was screaming at me to stay, but who would trust their heart at a time like this, when our lives were at risk?

When I walked out of that door, we might never see each other again. How could we let each other go like that? I wanted to spend every last minute with him; it was all that mattered. The rest could go to hell. Turning away from him, I closed my eyes, my heart sinking into the pit of my belly. I took a step away from him, just to see what would happen. Nothing happened; he didn't speak or move. I bent down to pick up my bra and, with my back to him, I did it up. Then I found my shirt and put it on. Still Sébastian didn't say a word, he just carried on smoking. I buttoned my shirt then took my pants from the back of the chair and pulled them on.

I felt the distance opening between us like a chasm I was about to fall into, while he stood on the edge, watching. I longed to pull my clothes off and throw myself back into his arms, naked, laughing, and brave. These were the moments worth living for—the moments with him.

It was my sandals next. I slipped my feet into them, then I took another step toward the door. *Stop me! Stop me!* I begged him in my head. *Don't let me go. Not ever.* But the room was silent, the only sound the thudding of my heart. Some self-destructive impulse stopped me from turning around as I lifted my hand toward the door handle.

"Lise. Don't go like that." I stopped, my hand in mid-air. I heard him getting off the bed, moving toward me, then I felt his hand on my shoulder. He turned me around to face him, softly pushing his nose against mine.

"Just promise me you won't die," I whispered.

He kissed my tears away, then he put his mouth against my ear. "Trust me, Lise. We're going to be together."

I wanted to believe him. I needed to believe him. I couldn't bear the thought of us separating like this, saying goodbye in his hotel room, with nothing left to hang onto. I reached behind my neck and unclasped the necklace my parents had given me for my eighteenth birthday: a single red ruby rose on a silver chain. I slipped it into his hand.

"Make sure you return this to me." I kissed his closed lips softly.

"Lise," he whispered. "I promise. Admin staff like me will be evacuated before the Allies get here. I'll be back in Germany before the war ends. Once the fighting has stopped, I'll come back to you. It won't be long."

He made it all sound so simple, I almost believed him.

"It's safer than trying to escape," he added. "I don't want to put you in more danger than I already have." He closed his eyes and kissed me on the forehead. "Now go."

I turned back toward the door, this time my hand touching the handle. And I pulled it open.

I walked along the corridor then down the stairs, my heart cracking with every step. Concentrating only on putting one foot in front of the other, I forced myself into a state of numbness, knowing that if I allowed a single emotion through, I would run right back.

It was almost a relief to step out onto the street; the noise of cars, trucks, and people shouting hitting me like a reminder that I was still here in this world. The bright sun shone into my eyes, and I shielded them with my hand as I looked around. A lorry rumbled past, jam-packed with German soldiers, their rifles and machine guns pointing at the windows of the apartment blocks. I squeezed myself flat against the wall as more cars and trucks streamed by; honking, stopping, loading up. I hesitated, wary about going out there. Taking a deep breath, I stepped back out into the street and continued toward the Métro. I wasn't surprised to find it was closed, and I carried on walking. An open lorry blocked the road, and when I crossed behind it, I saw German soldiers loading it with bedside tables. I stopped, my heart beating hard with fury. They were still stealing from us—taking furniture home! One of them paused, setting his table down on the ground as he stared at me. I held his gaze. And he winked, as though making me complicit in his thievery. Then he leaned back against the table, casually taking a cigarette from his trouser pocket, lighting up as he continued to watch me.

Holding my head high, meeting his eye, I walked past him without a word. I heard him whistle behind me, but I didn't turn around. It had taken a monumental amount of courage to walk away from Sébastian. Anything else would be easy now.

Chapter Thirty-One

Paris, August 16, 1944

Élise

I took the long way home and crossed the bridge at Île Saint-Louis. A girl of about ten stood in the middle, a tray full of brightly colored objects hanging around her neck. She caught my eye and I walked over. "What are you selling?" "Brooches," she answered. "Blue, white, and red."

I looked around, worried for her, but there were no German soldiers patrolling. "Be careful," I whispered anyway, digging in my pocket for some change. "I'll take three." My heart raced as I took them from her. It was dangerous, but it felt like a step toward victory. It was only a matter of time.

At Odéon, a poster on the corner caught my attention. The *Front National* were calling all Parisians to join the FFI (Forces Françaises de l'intérieur—De Gaulle's troops) or patriotic militias and fight the Germans. My heart leapt at the thought of joining the fight, but how could I now?

The thought of Sébastian all alone in his hotel room made me ache with longing and despair. What did I have left for the fight?

I stood for a minute in Place Saint-Sulpice, gazing at the church, gathering my strength before facing Maman. Then I rounded the corner and went home.

Maman opened the front door before I'd had a chance to push on it. Then she quickly closed the door behind me before starting on her tirade. "You've been with him! Not with Françoise! She came here asking after you. I had to say I didn't know where you were. The shame of it!" She stood there, her arms crossed in front of her, blocking my path, like a barricade.

"I'm sorry." I felt depleted and emotionally exhausted. I just wanted to be left in peace. But this was not an option. I followed Maman into the kitchen.

"Sit down." She pulled out a kitchen chair. I fell into it, readying myself for a lecture. She sat next to me, and for a moment said nothing. Then quietly, she said, "I know how you feel about him." I waited for her to continue with a series of reprimands, but instead she said, "I may have a solution." She let out a long breath, her chest deflating. "I've been thinking about it. About you and...and Sébastian." She used his name for the first time. "He's half-French, isn't he?"

I nodded.

"And he speaks French like a Frenchman?"

"Yes."

"I know how much he means to you, Élise." She studied me, but I didn't move. "Who knows what will happen once the Allies get here? It will get nasty for sure. He'd be safer here."

"What do you mean?"

"You could bring him here. We can pretend he's a cousin."

"What? What about the neighbors?" She hadn't wanted to hear me speak of him, and here she was offering to harbor him. I was confused rather than happy.

Maman sighed. "I'll manage them. I'd rather have you here under our roof than out there with him."

She didn't know I'd come home for good, that I'd left Sébastian. I almost said so, but the thought of him being here with me was too tempting. Was it really possible? I let myself imagine it for a moment, my heart lifting, then it sank again when I thought about the neighbors. "You only have to breathe in the wrong direction for madame la concierge to get the wrong idea. She's a snitch."

"Don't worry about her."

"But she'll see him come in. She'll ask who he is." Had she really thought it through?

"I'll meet him outside and come in with him, while you distract her with something. You could give her some of those potatoes we got from Georges. That will be enough to take her mind off anything else."

"Are you sure, Maman?" I didn't want to put us all in danger. "What about Papa? What will happen when he comes home?"

"We'll worry about that when it happens. In fact, you can take him some of your father's clothes. A flat cap, some of his old pants, and a jacket. He'll look like any other Frenchman."

Poor Maman, she'd just been concerned for my safety, and now she was willing to take a risk like this for me. My misjudgment of her left me feeling small and ashamed. Swallowing the hard lump in my throat, I put my arms around her, but she felt rigid. Of course, this was a tough and dangerous decision for her, and it must have been hard for her to put her own worries aside and realize what Sébastian meant to me. A pang of guilt shot through me as I thought about her and Isabelle and what I'd be putting them through. "Thank you, Maman. Thank you! We'll be very careful, I promise." I paused, thinking of the extra mouth we'd have to feed. "I can ask him to bring some food."

"We'll manage." She folded her arms and frowned. "There's no time to lose. There'll be fighting on the streets soon."

Both excited and uneasy about the arrangement, I left the kitchen and went to my bedroom to get a clean shirt before leaving again.

"Élise." A little whisper behind me made me turn around. Isabelle stood there in a pale blue summer dress, her long thin arms dangling down at her sides. "Where were you?"

"I was with a special friend."

"Your boyfriend." She smiled a secret smile. "He's that man, isn't he? From the bookshop. That Boche."

How could she have worked this out? Damn Maman! She must have said something. I frowned, reminding myself that she was only a child. It was hard enough for us adults to make sense of it all.

"He's half-German, half-French."

"But he's still a Boche, isn't he?" she insisted.

I let out a breath, frustration rising through me.

"The Boches are really bad, aren't they?" She shifted her weight, coming to stand on one leg, as though testing the ground.

"You shouldn't use that word, Isabelle."

"Boche? But you used to say it." She studied me for a

moment. "When de Gaulle gets here, he's going to kill them all."

"The Nazis. He's going to fight the Nazis."

She frowned. "What's the difference?"

"Not all Germans are Nazis, Isabelle. They're people, just like us. Some good. Some bad." I held my arms open to her, expecting her to come to me.

But she didn't move. "Why do you like him anyway? Why can't you like someone who's just French, like us?"

I closed my eyes as I searched for the right words. "You don't choose who you love. It just happens, and sometimes you fall in love with someone you're not supposed to fall in love with."

Isabelle wrinkled her nose as though this was a most distasteful idea. "I'm never going to fall in love. I'm going to stay here with Maman."

"That's because this is where you belong right now. Come and give me a hug." I opened my arms for her again. Tentatively, she moved toward me, and I held her against my chest, burying my nose in her hair, breathing in her child's smell—lemon and sunlight. "You'll change your mind one day," I whispered.

"No, I won't." She took a deep breath in. "If you have children, will they be German?"

I pulled back from her and looked her in the eye. "They would just be children, like all children." Her question worried me. "Isabelle," I said softly. "Have you talked to anyone about him?"

She shook her head, but her cheeks burned red, and I knew she had. "I can't remember." She shifted onto the other leg.

"Isabelle," I said in a firm tone. "I need to know if you told anyone about Sébastian."

"I can't remember."

"Isabelle." I put my hands on her shoulders, forcing her down onto her two legs. "Who did you tell?"

"Just Marie. She's my best friend." She squirmed under my grip.

I let go, repressing the urge to yell at her. She was just a child. It wasn't her fault. Maman should never have told her. Children don't know which secrets are the important ones to keep. Beads of sweat broke out under my hairline as I imagined the neighbors talking about me, their suspicions growing as they gossiped about what I might have done.

Maman poked her head around the door, holding out a bag of clothes. "Go, Élise. Go and get him."

Chapter Thirty-Two

Paris, August 16, 1944

Élise

The relentless sun scorched the pavement and burned the back of my neck, while warm dust spun around my ankles as cars and lorries hurtled by. My stomach growled, reminding me I hadn't eaten. I glanced at an open café as I walked by; it looked dark and cool inside. Impulsively I walked off the hot, noisy street and stepped through the open door.

A handful of people stood around the polished zinc bar, and a couple of heads turned to look at me.

"*Bonjour, madame.* Are you serving food?" I spoke as I approached the bar.

The woman turned to look at me. "*Jambon beurre.*"

"Could I have one, please? And a coffee, and a glass of water please."

She placed a glass of water on the counter along with a small coffee, then turned back round to make the sandwich. I could tell by the sound of her breadknife sawing away that she only had old hard bread, probably made with sawdust. I didn't care. It was food.

A man sitting at the counter folded his paper and looked up. He took a breath, and I knew he was going to say something about what he'd just read. "The Americans have bombed the coast," he started, "east of Toulon. Brittany has been liberated, Blois too, and Orléans and Chartres. We'll be next."

An older man standing up at the bar coughed as if to get our attention. "Once the Boches lose Paris, it will be over for them." He sighed loudly. "But they're not just going to walk out. *Mais non.* We'll have to fight them."

I gulped back the water then took a sip from the cup. The aroma hit me immediately; it was real coffee! Not the foul ersatz we were normally served. To me, this felt more significant than any headline. We no longer needed to keep it for the Germans.

The first man waved his newspaper. "Yes! It's time to pick up arms and fight. *Aux armes, citoyens.*" He hummed the tune to "La Marseillaise." "*Formez vos bataillons.*" He prodded the paper with his first finger. "They're calling for insurrection."

"*L'Humanité!*" The older man snatched the paper out of his hands. "Where did you get that commie paper? I'm not listening to the communists. I'm waiting for de Gaulle."

"God only knows when he'll get here." The man stood, glancing around the bar. "Probably just in time for the victory parade." He snatched his paper back.

The older man raised his shoulders, opening his hands, pale fleshy palms facing upward. "He was always fighting for us. And I, for one, won't be celebrating anything till he comes back."

"Whatever happens, you'd better be ready to pick up your weapons and fight the bastards."

I had to get to Sébastian before the fighting began in earnest. I grabbed my sandwich, glancing at the men. *"Au revoir, messieurs."* I hurried out of the café, through the hot crowded streets, heading for Sébastian's hotel.

As I carried on my way, I constantly checked behind me, thinking where the safest place would be to cross the river. Around the next corner I saw two Frenchmen with hammers and screwdrivers pulling down a road sign written in German Gothic script. I glanced around, afraid the men would be shot at, but just one German car drove past, without even slowing down. I hurried on.

Chapter Thirty-Three

Paris, August 16, 1944

Sébastian

Three hard taps on the door set Sébastian's heart racing. Grabbing his pistol from the bedside table, he jumped off the bed and opened the door.

"*Wir werden evakuiert! Hôtel Majestic!*" His colleague from the room next door stood there in uniform.

"Evacuated today?" Sébastian ran his hand through his hair. "Okay, I'll get ready."

He was busy packing his knapsack when Élise burst into his room. She closed the door then flung her arms around him, searching out his mouth with hers, but he pushed her away. What the hell was she doing back here? It had been hard enough to say goodbye the first time.

"Élise, we're being evacuated. Today! You can't be here! I have to leave."

Ignoring his words, she grabbed his hand. He pulled it back, fear and confusion racing through his head. "Sébastian!

Come home with me!" Her eyes shone with excitement. "Maman said you should come back with me. You can dress like a Frenchman. We can sneak you in past the concierge. You can pretend to be a cousin." Her words came out in a mad rush.

"Your mother wants me to come to your apartment?"

Élise bit her bottom lip and nodded solemnly.

"But Lise, your mother wanted you to have nothing to do with me!"

"She was just worried for me. But now…now she wants to help. She wants you to come today. The fighting is going to start. It's in the papers! The Americans are on their way. De Gaulle will be here soon!"

De Gaulle or the Americans? Who would get here first? Who would claim Paris? It might not be that simple. Politics was a tricky business. Sébastian moved over to the window, peering out through the gap between the shutters as though they might be just around the corner. He turned to face Élise. "It's too dangerous. It's not a good idea. Not for any of us."

The look of disappointment in her eyes sent a pang of longing through him. He wished he could make her happy, make all her dreams come true.

"I've brought you some clothes and a cap to hide your hair." Élise stubbornly ignored his last comment. "And while you're with us we can dye your hair."

"What made your mother change her mind about me?"

Élise put the bag of clothes on the bed. "She knows how I feel about you. And she'd rather have you under our roof than me in Paris with you somewhere else."

"But you'd gone back to her."

"She didn't know that."

"Your family shouldn't take such a risk for me." Sébastian

crossed his hands around the back of his head as he studied her. "I can't put you and your family in danger like that." He didn't tell her he didn't want to be labeled a deserter, a crime he could be shot for.

She looked at him defiantly. "It's worth the risk; I'm going to stay here with you if you won't come with me." She sat down heavily on the bed.

He let out a long breath and sat close to her, but without touching her. "Lise," he whispered. "I can't. You have to go back now. Without me."

"*Jamais!*" He heard the determination in her voice. "Come home with me," she whispered. "You'll be safe with us. No one would ever imagine that you were German. Not once you're in our apartment." She rested her head against his. "Please. I need you."

Chapter Thirty-Four

Paris, August 16, 1944

Élise

I watched from the bed as Sébastian put on Papa's old pants and gray shirt. They fit perfectly, and the cap hid most of his fair hair. If we waited till dusk, no one would notice, and anyway everyone was busy preparing either to fight or take flight. Most of the Germans were only concerned with getting out, and the French were busy gathering arms, praying the Allies would get here quickly. No one would look twice at a French couple hurrying through the streets.

We waited for dusk and left the room at nine that evening. "Bicycles," Sébastian announced as we walked down the staircase. "There are a couple in the courtyard."

"*Mais oui*, let's take them." It made sense. We'd be less vulnerable on bicycles. It would be easier to fly past people before they had time to wonder who we were.

We found one unlocked black bicycle leaning against the

wall as though it had been abandoned. Sébastian lifted it away, spinning the wheel. "It looks good to me. And one is enough." He wheeled it out into the street and held it out to me. "Can you balance on the crossbar?"

I sat across it, gripping it tightly, then I lifted my feet off the ground just as he jumped on the saddle, pedaling away, and we were off. I stifled a scream when we wobbled, my feet landing back on the ground, and then we were off again, finding our rhythm as we sailed through the empty streets. I couldn't help feeling disappointed when we arrived at the corner of my street so quickly. We got off the bicycle without talking. It was eerily quiet, and I had the awful feeling we were being watched. I told myself I was just nervous, that was all.

"Wait here," I said. "I'll get Maman, and you can go in with her like we planned."

I hurried past madame la concierge's room, glancing through the window. She was nowhere to be seen. Hopefully, she was in bed. When I got into our apartment, Maman was waiting in the kitchen for me. Her face was pale, and she rushed her words without looking at me. "Is he on the corner, like we said?"

"Yes." I noticed she didn't use his name.

"Madame la concierge is already in bed, so we don't need to provide a distraction for her," she continued. "You wait here."

Before I had time to answer, she dashed out of the kitchen. I held my breath as I looked around the empty room. It was unnaturally quiet. Usually there were noises of some kind, though I couldn't recall exactly what they were as I stood there, my pulse beating in my throat, my breath resonating in my ears.

Maman burst back into the kitchen with Sébastian by her side. Thank God! He was inside. I threw my arms around him as though we'd been parted for weeks, not just three minutes.

"I'm off to bed then," Maman said abruptly, turning to leave.

I reached out for her arm. "Thank you, Maman."

She mumbled something but didn't meet my eye, and then she was gone. Not even a kiss goodnight.

Sébastian looked at me, raising an eyebrow. "Are you sure she wanted me to come?"

I nodded. "It was her idea."

With a loud sigh, Sébastian slumped into a chair. "Well, she doesn't seem very happy about it now."

"She's just nervous." I sat on a chair next to him, taking his hands in mine. "It will be okay, I promise." He didn't answer but looked around nervously then got up and went to the window, opened it, and closed the shutters. "We don't usually shut the kitchen shutters, Sébastian."

"I'd feel safer." He paced the kitchen. "Where will I be sleeping?"

"In my room. Maman made you a bed on the floor."

"That's very kind of her." He stopped pacing and smiled at me. "Though I don't think I'll be using it!"

I was relieved that he seemed less stressed, but then he started pacing again. "Have you got the hair dye?" He pulled out a packet of crumpled Gitanes from his breast pocket and, with shaking fingers, lit up. I held my hand out, wanting one too, though I never usually smoked. He lit it for me, and I inhaled the coarse dry smoke, waving it away as it curled upward. Maman wouldn't want the kitchen smelling like an ashtray tomorrow, so I opened the shutters he'd just closed, and then the window. Sébastian shrank further into the room, his back against the cupboard. "I think we should dye my hair tonight, just in case."

"I'm not sure we have dye yet. Maman didn't mention it again." I took another drag, my fingers shaking. "You'll have to stay in meanwhile. Don't worry, no one will come."

He stubbed his cigarette out in an empty coffee cup on the sideboard. "Close the shutters then. It will be safer." His tone was flat, and I knew he was expecting us to have planned this better, but Maman had only just thought about it, and items like hair dye weren't easy to get.

"Let's go to bed." He took my hand and we left the kitchen, both of us uneasy.

Silently we undressed and slipped into my single bed. He held me in his arms, our breath ragged at first then calming to a synchronized rhythm as we closed our eyes. We didn't talk and we didn't make love, but we drifted in and out of sleep, sometimes stirring, waking, then slipping off again. All night long I stayed in his arms. It gave me a feeling of protection, though I knew it was only an illusion. Danger hung in the air, and we breathed it in all night long.

Very early in the morning I opened my eyes to see the rays of sunlight shining though the slits in the shutters. Sébastian's breath was regular and shallow, and I knew he was sleeping so I closed my eyes too.

A loud knocking woke me with a start. Immediately Sébastian opened his eyes. "Where's that coming from?" he whispered.

It sounded like the front door. I gripped him tightly. "Don't move." I covered his head with the sheets, wrapping my arms around him, praying that there was some other reason for the urgent knocking.

They knocked again.

"*J'arrive, j'arrive,*" I heard Maman shout.

I held my breath as I held Sébastian, tears welling in my eyes. *Please, Maman, get rid of them.*

In the deadly silence I heard the front door open. Heavy footsteps resounded in my ears, then a loud voice shouted, "*Il est où?* Where is he?"

I gripped Sébastian's head tighter. There was nowhere to run. No time to escape. I wrapped my body around his. *God, please don't come into my bedroom.*

Footsteps came down the corridor. The bedroom door flew open. A large man stood there.

"He's in here!" he shouted.

Another man ran in. He kicked the bed. "Out now! Get out!"

I held Sébastian tighter, panic seeping through every pore. I clung to him with all my strength. A man's hand loomed in front of my face. It grabbed Sébastian and pulled him out. I pulled the sheets around me. "Please!" I screamed. "He's on our side!"

Another man put his face right up against mine. "Shut up, whore." His breath stank of vinegary wine. I recoiled, clutching the sheet against my face.

"Put your clothes on," one of the men shouted at Sébastian.

"*Sale Boche!*" another shouted.

"This is one dead Boche." The third man's voice was terrifyingly cold and assertive. Fear shot through every nerve in my body. Shaking hard, I gripped the sheet, powerless to help Sébastian.

"Maman!" I screamed. "Maman! Do something!" I couldn't see her. She wasn't there. "Maman!" I screamed again. "Please!"

Chapter Thirty-Five

Paris, August 19, 1944

Élise

Two days later, I still hadn't eaten a thing and had only slept in bursts when exhaustion took over. I couldn't talk and I couldn't think straight. My mind spun round in crazy circles. How the hell had they known Sébastian was here? Someone must have tipped them off. They were too close on our heels. It was my fault. I should never have persuaded him to come back with me. It must have been Isabelle, telling Marie.

The man's voice rang again and again in my head. Every time I closed my eyes it came back louder. *This is one dead Boche.* It was the way he'd said it, with such conviction, that set me trembling, terrible visions crowding my mind. I saw Sébastian being led away, taken to some small back street, on his knees, his hands behind his head. One shot to the back of his neck. His body left there till they cleared the streets. I bunched up the sheet and stuffed it into my mouth, stopping the scream soaring from the depths of my soul. It came out as a muffled wail, long and low. It was my fault. I had brought him back here, against all his misgivings. What arrogance! What ignorance! God, how I hated myself.

Maman tiptoed into my darkened room, putting a tray of food down next to my bed. I pretended to be asleep but when she tiptoed out again I opened my eyes and turned over, looking at what she'd left. Another pang of guilt shot through me when I saw two slices of thinly cut bread and a spoon of plum jam on the side of the plate. We'd been saving that jam for emergencies. But there was no way I could eat it. Though hollow, my stomach twisted in agony as fear wound its way through every nerve. Curling back into the fetal position, I closed my eyes, a wave of exhaustion washing over me.

The bedroom door creaked open. "Élise," Isabelle whispered. "Are you asleep?"

"Yes," I murmured.

She came in anyway, shutting the door behind her. "Do you hate me?" I turned over, looking at her as she stood there awkwardly, still such a child but trying to grapple with adult problems. In that moment, I almost did hate her. "I'm sorry I told Marie about your boyfriend." I sighed. This wasn't a conversation I was ready to have. But I moved over on the bed, leaving room for her. She lay next to me. "I didn't mean to tell Marie. I'm really sorry, Élise."

"Did you tell anyone else?"

"No! I promise I didn't!" Her voice cracked and I knew she was telling the truth. "Will you be better soon?" She reached for my hand under the covers.

I didn't think I would ever be better. The pain of thinking about Sébastian was physical. I turned away from Isabelle, burying my head in the pillow. Isabelle put her thin arms around me and laid her head on my rounded back. I felt her trembling and I knew she was crying. I would have to pull myself together, pretend that I was okay when I was dying inside. Breathing deep into my abdomen, I ignored my pain as I rolled back over to face her. I couldn't speak, but I held her tight, letting her cry. When her trembling subsided, I stroked her damp face.

"It's my fault. It's all my fault. Élise, I'm sorry."

It was true. It probably was her fault. It could have been Marie telling someone who told someone else, and Sébastian had probably been vilified as SS or Gestapo. "Let's get up, Isabelle." I tried to speak decisively, as though I were in control. It was a role I would play now. But it was painful, lifting myself from the bed.

I went into the bathroom and washed with a cool flannel, trying to soothe the burning pain inside me. Then I went into the kitchen. Maman was standing over the sink.

Immediately, she turned round, catching my eye. "How are you feeling?" Her tone was soft and gentle, but she looked away quickly, as though she were merely asking if a cold was better.

I couldn't answer. Instead I took the rutabaga she was washing out of her hands. "Shall I cut it up?" I needed something practical to do. Removing the cutting board from the cupboard, I placed it on the kitchen table and put the rutabaga on top. Then I took a sharp knife from the wooden knife block and pushed down hard into the fat round lump. It sliced into two parts quite easily and I carried on slicing, the bits getting smaller and smaller.

"That's enough." Maman touched my elbow. "Stop, Élise. Stop!"

Chapter Thirty-Six

Paris, August 22, 1944

Élise

I lay awake in my bed, trying not to think about what they might have done to Sébastian. But how could I not think about it? How could I stop the images flooding my mind? His lifeless body lying in a pool of blood. Instead, I tried to remember the way his eyes lit up when he saw me, the way I pretended to sleep when I felt his eyes caressing me, the impulsive way he laughed, like a child, the way he cried. I held on to my memories, knowing that with time they would fade, that they were all I had. Memories.

Maman tried to tell me they might use him in a prisoner exchange; a member of the Résistance in exchange for Sébastian, but what would she know? I would have given anything to find out, but we had no connections, no one to ask.

We were waiting in no-man's-land, without supplies coming into Paris, and no idea when the Allies would get here. Some said the Nazis would destroy Paris before they left, that they were capable of that kind of barbarism. But all I could think was that cities could be rebuilt. People couldn't.

Sighing, I turned over. At the same moment, an explosion shook the whole building.

"Maman! Maman!" Isabelle's screams rang out.

I held my breath while the windows and doors rattled.

Maman came into my room, holding Isabelle's hand. She pulled me up with her other hand, and the three of us went into her bedroom, where we lay huddled together on her bed, clinging to each other. Eventually, in the early hours of the morning, the explosions faded away. We dozed until the sun shone too brightly through the slats in the shutters. Then we dressed and stepped outside.

The world had changed.

A woman went by, wearing men's pants, a rifle slung over her shoulder, an FFI band on her upper arm. As we walked down the street, we saw posters pinned to the white stone walls calling us citizens to arms. Résistance newspapers were openly on sale. The atmosphere was electric.

Our neighbor Yvette pushed past us. "We're going to the Champs-Élysées," she shouted. "Are you coming?"

Maman looked at Yvette. "Isn't it dangerous?"

Yvette shrugged. "Less so now. The Boches just want to get out."

"But the explosions last night. Was that them?"

"Must have been. There are still some left in the Jardins du Luxembourg." She stared at me for a minute, but I couldn't read her expression. "Everyone's coming out on the streets now," she continued. "The Allies will be here any minute."

"Please, Maman. I want to go." Isabelle's eyes shone with excitement.

Maman took my arm. "We'll put Isabelle between us. They're not going to shoot at two women and a child."

Yvette took Maman's other arm, and we walked down toward the Seine. Maman, Yvette, and Isabelle started singing, *"Allons enfants de la Patrie, le jour de gloire est arrivé..."* I tried to join in, but my throat was too tight. Liberation was finally coming after four long years, but my heart felt like a lump of lead. It made me feel disloyal to my own country. I felt untethered. Lost to myself.

"Contre nous de la tyrannie," Isabelle sang out loud and clear.

We walked down toward Café de Flore, past the closed cafés and boarded-up shops, past the barricades. The street heaved with people singing, shouting, and we were swept along with the crowd, surging onto Pont Alexandre III, toward Place de la Concorde.

An explosion shot through the air. People screamed. Then they tried to run, but only ran into each other, bodies blocking bodies. I gripped Isabelle's hand. The crowd stopped. Thick gray smoke rose in columns from the roof of the Grand Palais.

"Allez!" The crowd rippled forward again, toward the fire, like moths drawn to a light. I glanced over at the Hôtel de Crillon. Large German tanks stood in front of the hotel. Were they going to fire on us?

"Come on!" Yvette shouted, pushing my shoulder. "Let's go."

"No! Look at the tanks!"

But the crowd streamed forward, making it impossible to hold our ground. Pulled along with it, we craned our necks, staring in horror at the flames roaring through the roof, at the thick columns of gray smoke strangely tinged with pink. The sound of horses neighing in terror made me shudder.

The circus horses must have been trapped inside. A group of firefighters rushed into the Palais. A horse stampeded out. German soldiers raised their rifles and shot at the firefighters but hit the horse. It thudded to the ground, collapsing like a grotesque puppet. I turned away. Isabelle screamed.

"*Grand Palais!*" a woman shouted. "How could they? I hate them! They are not men. They are monsters, and I will hate them till the end of time."

"We have to leave!" Maman tugged at Isabelle's other hand.

I turned around, shocked to see people sitting out on deckchairs on the grass-covered traffic circle at the bottom of the Champs-Élysées. They were watching the scene as if they were at the theater. Was I dreaming? Were they ghosts? I closed my eyes, screams and shouts echoing around me. *Sébastian! Sébastian!* Why didn't you run with me? Where are you now?

"I want to go home," Isabelle cried.

I opened my eyes and pulled her into my arms, clinging to her thin frail body, hot tears streaming down my face. Through my watery eyes a blurred image appeared, of people surrounding the fallen horse. *No! Surely not!* I turned away, shielding Isabelle's eyes from the scene. People with penknives and other implements hacked at the horse's flesh, tearing off pieces of meat that they stuffed into their bags. This was what hunger did to people.

Chapter Thirty-Seven

Paris, August 23, 1944

Élise

Shame, fear, and revulsion pumped through my veins as we made our way back home. People had been hungry enough to tear the flesh off a dead horse. We'd been hungry, but never that hungry. It made me wonder how some had survived the last four years, those without connections, without any income. At least we'd had my salary from the bank.

Near Place Saint-Michel we passed by a group of men gathered in the street, pickaxes in their hands. They were hacking into the paving slabs and had a chain going; two people would remove the slab of concrete, then pass it along to the next in line, who in turn would pass it along, and so on, till it reached the men who would add it to the barricade they were building.

"Want to help us?" one of the men shouted over.

I shook my head. The man looked disappointed, and I

noticed a few of the women looking over at me, adding to the shame and disloyalty I already felt.

"You stay and help," Maman said. "I'll take Isabelle home." I was exhausted and still in pain, my stomach constantly cramping up. I just wanted to go home too. But she insisted. "Go on, Élise. You should be with them, building the barricades." Her tone was assertive, and she was right. It was time for me to show where my loyalties lay.

Without another word, I walked toward the group. "I'd be glad to help." I addressed the man who'd called me over. And as soon as the words left my mouth, they became true. I did want to help. Despite my empty heart, I wanted to be part of this. The group opened up a space, letting me in, and I felt immediately welcomed, already part of their team.

"*Salut*. I'm Thérèse." The woman on my left side spoke. She was wearing what looked like men's shorts, held up with a thick leather belt, and heavy brown boots. I couldn't help staring at her bare legs.

"Élise," I answered as the next slab landed in her hands. She passed it to me. The weight of it shocked me, and I felt my knees buckle, but I lifted myself back up, helping to pass it along. The sun was beating hard, and I wiped away a trickle of sweat sliding down the side of my face. Then I looked at her. "Did you see the smoke from the Grand Palais?"

"*Oui! Merde!* The Boches are still here! And they have some strongholds—those posh hotels around Concorde, where they've been holed up." She glanced at me. "But don't worry. We just heard that American generals have arrived at the Hôtel de Ville. It won't be long now before their armies and tanks get here. Then we start the offensive."

The offensive? I was impressed by her assertiveness. Would

women like her meekly return to looking after their husbands and families after the war now they'd had a taste of action? This war had broken down social barriers, between men and women, and between classes. We were all in this together. "You have to be careful though," she continued. "The Boches have snipers up on the roofs. Two women were shot dead yesterday, and the other night there was a shooting on Boulevard Saint-Michel, just next to the cinema."

The next slab arrived in my hands, and I had to take my eyes off her while I got a grip on it.

The man who'd first called me over walked up to us, handing me a cup. "You must be thirsty. We're going to take a little break now."

"Thank you." I took it from him, gratefully gulping down the water, conscious of his eyes on me as I drank it.

Then he turned to Thérèse. "Did you know the bastards sent out another train from Drancy only a few days ago? We should have stormed the camp. If only we had more weapons." He paused. "At least we've got our police back."

"They took their time." Thérèse put her hands on her hips, arching her back.

"Better late than never." The man raised an eyebrow.

"Do you think the Germans will put up much of a fight?" I spoke up, looking around at the people who had stopped for a minute to rest, thinking they looked more like friends building a house together than soldiers getting ready to kill. Or die.

"Von Choltitz will defend the city to the last man. Just depends how many men he'll have."

"And they could well plant bombs before they retreat," Thérèse added.

"Yes. We can't rule that out."

"I just wish the Allies would hurry up and get here." Thérèse wiped her brow.

"As long as they don't take over when they do." An older woman on the other side of me interrupted. "I don't trust the Americans any more than I trust the *rosbifs*."

"Yes. We'll have to get our own government together quickly," the man answered. "Or they'll fill that vacuum. We can't afford a battle of power between de Gaulle's forces and the communists."

"Surely we'll all be behind de Gaulle." I'd always assumed he would take the lead once he got here.

The old woman shrugged a shoulder. "The communists have been doing a lot of the fighting. De Gaulle hasn't been here on the ground. Not like us."

The way she said "not like us" made me think she might be a communist herself, and I found myself defending de Gaulle. "He was one of the only politicians willing to fight for France. He had no choice but to do it from London."

"As long as he recognizes the fighting we've done here. And the people we've lost." The man looked into my eyes, making me think he must have lost someone close. We'd all lost someone.

He was right; we should recognize the men and women who'd been fighting underground all these years, risking their lives, losing loved ones.

After the break, I worked until my arms and back ached with the constant lifting. I didn't have a watch on, but I felt the minutes ticking away into hours as the sun began to sink. Finally, the pace slowed, and people started to move away.

"Where do you live?" the same man who'd first called me over asked as I was preparing to leave.

"Saint-Sulpice."

"I'm heading that way," he replied. "Do you want to walk together?"

The blood rushed to my cheeks. "I'm meeting a friend," I lied.

"Maybe see you tomorrow then." He looked a little dejected.

I walked home alone. Though I was exhausted, I stopped at the church on the square and went in to light a candle for Sébastian.

Chapter Thirty-Eight

Paris, August 24, 1944

Élise

"*Bonjour, les filles,*" Maman shouted out, walking through the front door and into the kitchen. "I went out to get some food." She pulled off her headscarf, shaking it out. "It's pouring, and all I could get was this." She stood there, holding out two potatoes.

"For breakfast?" Isabelle turned her nose up.

"It's better than nothing. Let's cook them." My stomach was so hollow from lack of food, and I felt dizzy and weak.

"But there's no gas," Maman reminded me. "We can't eat them raw."

I almost cried in frustration. Surely, there must be something to eat. It almost made me wish we'd put our squeamishness aside and had helped ourselves to some of the horsemeat yesterday. I remembered the picnic Sébastian and I had shared in his hotel room—the cheese, the bread, the chocolate—and I would have done anything to turn back the clocks and be there now. And not bring him back here.

"We'll just have to eat our emergency supplies." Maman opened the cupboard door, where once we had jars full of different preserves. "There's still one jar of white beans."

By the afternoon, the rain had finally stopped, leaving a humid stifling heat, and I peered out of the kitchen window, wondering what the Allies were waiting for. The long afternoon dragged by, then just as dusk was falling, a loud knocking on the front door roused us from our lethargy. Maman went to open it.

Nathalie's voice rang out with excitement. "Our soldiers are here! I've seen them! In their tanks. French soldiers!"

We ran out of the apartment, sandals unbuckled in our haste to get out. As soon as we turned down Rue de Seine, the noise of the crowds hit us. People surged toward the river, children bouncing up and down on adults' shoulders. At Place Saint-Michel young men and women hung off the wings of the statue of the saint, shouting out, "*Notre jour de gloire est arrivé! Paris est libre!*"

We lost Nathalie in the crowd, but it didn't matter; we were all headed in the same direction—toward the Hôtel de Ville. A row of tanks covered with French flags slowly drove by. Young FFI fighters and women perched on the top waved as they passed us. Other women ran alongside, their arms outstretched, wanting to be pulled up to join the others as the tanks slowly inched forward.

I bent down. "Get on my shoulders, Isabelle." She clambered onto my back, wrapping her skinny legs around my neck, and we strode along next to the tanks. Some of the soldiers were busy scribbling notes, then rolling them and throwing them into the crowd. One young soldier bent over, handing a note to Isabelle. She passed it to me, and I read it under the light of a street lamp. It was just one line:

Ma chère Maman. Je suis rentré! Je t'embrasse très fort. Ton fils. Jean

A Parisian address was written on the back. I stuffed it in my pocket, planning to deliver it myself tomorrow, to bring Jean's mother the happy news that her son was home.

We followed the tanks to the Hôtel de Ville, where they joined others that were backed up to the building, their guns facing into the square. A voice boomed through a loudspeaker. A hush came over the crowd.

"Open the road to Paris for the Allied armies, hunt down and destroy the remnants of the German divisions." The speech rang out into the night. It was Colonel Rol-Tanguy, a Résistance leader and a communist. "Link up with the Leclerc Division in a common victory."

The bells of Notre-Dame, silenced during the occupation, tolled in celebration. Church bells heard the call; they rang out all over Paris—like God's own song reaching into my soul, telling me not to lose faith. I gripped Maman's hand tightly. Was this really the end of the occupation? Tears ran down my face as I stood there with my compatriots, united against the tyranny of the last four years. It didn't matter who was a communist, who had joined the Free French, and who had done nothing but wait. We were all French, and in that moment, we were one. How I wished Sébastian could have been by my side.

Lights flooded the square. Our voices joined the thousands of voices crying out like a hurricane. Crying out for liberty.

Chapter Thirty-Nine

Paris, August 25, 1944

Élise

The next morning, Isabelle jumped on my bed, waking me from a dreamless sleep. "Maman says come!" she shouted with excitement. "She's got something special for us to wear."

When I walked into the living room, Maman was standing there with a large reel of red ribbon in her hands. "We should get dressed up. De Gaulle is due any minute."

Isabelle's dark eyes shone with excitement as Maman wound some ribbon around the little white summer dress she was wearing, then placed a bright blue beret on her head. She looked beautiful, like the future shining in front of us. Maman wore a red dress, a white handkerchief tied around her neck, and on her feet, shiny blue shoes.

"Now you." Maman smiled at me. "Go and find something."

I stood frozen to the spot. I felt I could hear Sébastian's voice echoing around me, his eyes gently watching me as though aware of every thought that troubled me, as though his spirit lived on inside me. And I knew he would want me to celebrate this moment.

"What about your navy-blue dress?" Maman encouraged. "We'll brighten it up with this." She held out a wide strip of red ribbon.

The three of us looked at ourselves in the full-length mirror, Maman standing in the middle, an arm around each of us. We were all so skinny, and so pale. But Isabelle's smile stretched across her whole face, lighting it up. This would be a moment she would remember forever; one she would tell her children about. We were living history, right there and then.

Maman bent down to kiss Isabelle on the head, and then turned to me, kissing me on the cheek. "Your father will come home soon, and we'll all be together. It's all that matters." I looked into her eyes, understanding her hidden message. But it wasn't all that mattered. Not to me. Did she really think I would just forget Sébastian?

Too nervous and wound-up to eat, we didn't care that there was nothing to have for breakfast. Instead, we went straight into the streets. Everyone was out, and the noise had doubled since yesterday. We could hardly walk down Rue Saint-Jacques. Tanks covered in flags and bouquets had come to a standstill as women clambered onto the caterpillar wheels, arms outstretched, waiting to be pulled up to join the American soldiers. One soldier jumped down from his tank, throwing himself into the crowd as the girls swarmed round him, smothering him in kisses.

We stopped on Pont Alexandre III, staring over at the German tanks outside Hôtel de Crillon. One of them fired. A cannon shot straight up the Champs-Élysées. The crowds shrank back, screaming in terror. Maman, Isabelle, and I huddled together, holding our breath, dreading another cannon shot. "It's still dangerous," Maman whispered. "We should go home."

"No!" Isabelle drew away from us. "I want to stay." We waited a few minutes longer. No more shots were fired, and the crowd grew bolder, moving up the tree-lined avenue. The swastika flags had been removed, and French flags blew in the breeze. They gave us a feeling of protection as we continued to make our way along the Champs-Élysées. It was crazy and dangerous, but I understood how we all had to be a part of it. I imagined this was how soldiers might feel when they charged onto the battlefield—invincible and brave beyond reason.

For the rest of the day, random shots were fired, but people carried on singing, dancing, kissing. Me too, I sang, I smiled and laughed. I did it for Isabelle. I did it for France. I did it for all the people who had given up their lives for us, for freedom.

When the news reached us that de Gaulle would be at Hôtel de Ville, we made our way along Rue de Rivoli, getting there just in time to see him mount the staircase and go inside. Speakers out on the square relayed his words to us.

"*Paris!*" he shouted.

The crowd went wild, cheering and shouting. *Paris.* Our beloved city. My crushed heart soared on hearing that one word, spoken by our true leader.

The crowd went quiet as his next words came through.

"*Paris outragé! Paris brisé! Paris martyrisé!*"—Paris outraged! Paris broken! Paris martyred!

"*Mais Paris libéré!*" But Paris liberated!

Our hearts beat as one with pride for our country. De Gaulle came out onto the balcony, where he stood tall and proud. The man who had never lost faith, never doubted France, never deserted his people, nor given in to tyranny, was here, uniting us in victory. He was our hero. De Gaulle *was* France.

Maman put her arm around me, whispering in my ear. "We've won the war, Élise!"

Won the war? Were there really any winners? It seemed to me that we'd all lost something. Everything from now on would only be a show. No one could ever know what was truly in my heart.

Chapter Forty

Paris, August 26, 1944

Élise

The next day was bright and sunny, and when I walked out with Isabelle in the early morning to get some bread, it felt like a new dawn for France. Even the light was sharper, the white stone of the Haussmann apartments gleaming in the late summer sun, the leaves of the tall chestnut trees twisting and turning in the light breeze, showing off shades of green.

That evening, just before dark, I went out into the courtyard to empty the trash. Nathalie was already out there, squeezing some paper into the garbage cans that were full to overflowing. She didn't smile and neither did she greet me, she just looked at me coldly.

"*Bonsoir*, Nathalie," I said, remembering politeness was the best form of defense. I lifted the lid off one of the garbage cans.

"Élise," she replied in a low voice. "I should tell you something."

"Yes?" My pulse quickened, dread seeping through me.

"I've heard. I've heard your name is on the list."

"What list?" My stomach shrank in on itself, knowing exactly what list she was talking about.

"The list of women who..." She couldn't finish her sentence. "They're coming in the morning. You've still got time to hide."

Hide? I shook my head, anger replacing my fear. The thought of them coming to our home, frightening my little sister and Maman, filled me with outrage. "How do you know?"

"Someone told me."

"Who? Nathalie, who! Who told you?"

She looked at me tight-lipped. "I'm only telling you, to help you."

I bashed the lid back onto the garbage can. "To help me! Tell me who you've been talking to."

But like a fox, she slipped away, leaving me standing there, trembling with fear and fury. I had harmed no one. I had given away no secrets.

I crept back into the apartment. Isabelle was already in bed, and Maman was reading the paper in the living room. She looked up as I walked in. "Are you all right?" she asked. "You look so pale." She closed her paper. "I'm worried about you. You've been so sick."

I thought about telling her what Nathalie said, but I couldn't. I would have to deal with this alone. That night, I lay fully clothed in bed. I almost got up and left, ran away. But the thought of them dragging Isabelle from her bed, demanding to know where I was, terrified me more than anything.

Before dawn broke, I knew what I was going to do. On trembling legs, I slipped out of bed, listening, but the only sound was my raspy breathing echoing back my terror. I walked through to the bathroom and looked in the mirror.

"*Courage*," I whispered at my reflection, stroking my smooth dark hair. I opened the cupboard under the sink and took out the little basket. The scissors poked out from under a hairbrush; I pulled them out by their rounded handles, opening them up then closing them with a clean slicing movement. I looked into the mirror again, lifting the lock of hair that fell over my forehead. Holding my breath, I brought the open scissors toward the roots and quickly cut the hair away, watching the dark strands slip into the sink. *It's only hair*, I breathed when silent tears ran down my cheek. *It's only hair.* Without taking my eyes off the mirror, I continued to cut around my whole head till I had no hair left. My reflection stared back at me like a stranger, all bones and hollowed gray cheeks, eyes dark and large.

A window smashed. I dropped the scissors into the sink and clutched my naked head. *Oh my God, they were here!* Blood thumped through my veins. The air in my lungs froze.

Maman appeared in the doorway. "No! Élise!" She reached out to me. "What have you done?"

I stepped back, against the sink. I didn't want her to touch me. I tried to breathe. "They've come for me, Maman!" I gasped. "They're here!"

"No!" She stepped back, pushing her palms into her cheeks. "No!"

"*Salope! Salope! Salope de Boche!*" The cries from outside grew frantic and louder. I pushed past Maman, terror spinning out of control.

Don't stop. Don't think. Just go. I walked toward the living room, toward the shouts and cries.

Isabelle stood in the semidarkness at the end of the

corridor. She looked so small, so frail. "I'm sorry, Élise, I'm so sorry," she gulped between tears.

I couldn't let them break in. I shot back to the living room, throwing the door open. Broken glass lay glinting on the floor, and there they stood outside, below the iron balustrade—about ten men. "*Putain de Boche! German whore!*"

They wanted blood. Mine. I was so cold, freezing cold. Wrapping my arms tightly around myself, I tried to stop the violent shivering that had taken hold of me.

A man's head rose up above the others, his face contorted with hatred. They were lifting him up so he could climb over the balustrade.

"Élise!" Maman ran into the room, grabbing my arm, trying to pull me away from the window.

"No!" I pulled my arm back. Out of the corner of my eye I glimpsed Isabelle, her dark eyes wide with fear, her ribs showing through her pale pink nightgown. "Maman," I whispered. "Get her out of here."

Maman moved toward her, shielding her.

I stepped nearer to the window. *Courage. Don't think. And don't look.* I took two large steps. I was in front of the raised man.

"The whore's cut her hair herself!" He spat at me through the smashed windowpane.

I put my hand around the knob of the unbroken window, turning it slowly. A wasp trapped between the lace curtain and the window buzzed angrily. It flew out as I pulled the window open. *Don't look at them!* I watched the wasp fly up into the sky. And I hoisted myself onto the window ledge, one leg over the balustrade.

Hands reached out, grabbing me, pulling me down. With a sickening thud, I hit the hard concrete below. Pain shot through my elbow. Arms hoisted me up, fingers digging into me. Someone clenched my face, crushing my cheeks. Spit landed on my nose. "*Salope! Sale pute!*" Vicious hands pulled at my blouse, ripping it open.

I screamed. My knees buckled. I slid down. Hands heaved me back up, leaving me dangling, not quite touching the ground. Like a ragdoll. A slap across the face sent me reeling backward. My head spun wildly. I was losing control.

They dragged me to an open lorry and threw me in. Other women were already there, sitting squashed together. Some cried. Some screamed. Some were silent. My bones shook as the lorry hurtled through the streets, bringing me back to myself. Where were they taking us? Abruptly it came to a stop. I was thrown forward violently, but not one of us made a sound.

Outside, a crowd was gathering around a square, jeering and shouting, "*Putain de Boche!*" The square was a blur, and I didn't know where I was.

They pulled us out of the lorry and pushed us toward a plank of wood suspended between two piles of bricks, where they made us sit in a line. A large man pulled the first woman away. But I didn't look. I didn't look at the stage they'd mounted, nor the people who had gathered to watch. I closed my eyes and I prayed, *Please God, make it be over quickly.*

My turn came. Rough hands gripped me, dragging me up the steps, onto the wooden platform. A long shiny blade glinted at me. The man holding it laughed. "Thought you'd do it yourself, did you?" He shoved my head down, gripping the back of my neck. Then he gripped me under my chin, forcing me to look forward into the crowd. I stared blankly when he drew the cold metal across my scalp. I tried not to flinch when it caught my skin, drawing blood. Instead, I pictured Sébastian, sitting in his room, looking at me. I held the image in my head. I held on to it when they took out the brush and painted the swastika across my forehead. Branded a whore and a traitor to my country.

They didn't stop there. They pushed us into a wooden cart pulled by horses, parading us through the streets of Paris in our underwear, our heads naked.

Chapter Forty-One

Paris, August 27, 1944

Élise

I was vaguely aware of the cart stopping, then Maman wrapping a scarf around my head, helping me up. Leaning into her, I walked home, the jeering from people lining the streets ricocheting off me. I was numb. Unreachable. Even to myself.

When we reached home, Isabelle stood in the doorway crying. "I'm sorry," she sobbed. "I'm sorry, Élise."

I couldn't look at her. I didn't want to look at anyone. Maman ran a bath while I stood mutely by, staring blankly ahead. Gently, she removed my underwear and helped me step into the water, silent tears running down her face. It was cold, but I didn't care. I just wanted to wash everything away. Maman washed my body softly with a sponge, then she scrubbed the swastika off with a scrubbing brush and soap. She didn't talk and neither did I. Isabelle sat outside crying.

When she'd finished, Maman wrapped me in a large

bath towel, holding me tight, as though I were a child. "I'm sorry, Élise. I'm so sorry."

I couldn't speak. I shook my head instead, not wanting to invite her words, just wanting to be left alone in silence. I stepped away from her and walked down the corridor into my bedroom, where I lay on the bed in my damp towel, curled into a tight ball. In that moment I wanted to leave it all behind. I wanted to die.

I didn't leave my bed for the next few days. But I couldn't sleep either. Every time I closed my eyes the image of the man wielding the long sharp razor was waiting for me. I took to sleeping in fits and starts during the day, but I couldn't stop touching my bare scalp, couldn't stop remembering. How could they have done it to me? People who didn't know me. People who didn't know what Sébastian and I had really done.

Isabelle and Maman went out to get some food, but I wasn't eating. Maman tried to talk to me, but her voice echoed through my head, her words meaningless. Every motion, every noise, every smell only sought to remind me that I was still alive. There was not a single part of me that wasn't raw with pain.

On the third day, Maman came into my room, holding a letter. "It's from your father," she said. "He asks if we can send socks and a wooly hat. I suppose the letters are vetted and he can't say what's really going on, but I'm sure he's thinking of his journey home."

The thought of Papa's return filled me with fear instead of joy.

"Élise, come and have something to eat. Please."

I followed Maman into the kitchen. Isabelle sat at the table, playing with her dolls. I didn't think I was still playing with dolls at her age, but it was hard to remember. So thin and waif-like, she didn't look like the eleven years she was. It felt as though we were all disappearing into ourselves. I hadn't even bothered to call work. They knew. Everyone knew. I sat next to her, but she was engrossed in her dolls, in her own little world of make-believe, and she hardly looked at me.

Maman put a plate and a cup in front of me. I took a sip of coffee, but it burned my throat. I pushed it aside and bit into the plain baguette. It tasted like dust.

Maman picked up a newspaper. "De Gaulle's making collaboration an official crime. He's calling it '*indignité natio-nale.*' He claims it's to stop indiscriminate attacks. Now there will be trials. They've arrested the opera singer Germaine Lubin for performing Wagner for the Wehrmacht. They've sent her to Drancy!"

I stared at the bread on my plate, wishing she'd shut up.

But she continued. "And Arletty. You know, the film star. She had an affair with Hans-Jürgen Soehring. They're sending her to Drancy too! Do you know what she said? You have to admire her audacity."

I waited.

"*Mon coeur est français mais mon cul, lui est international.*"

"My heart is French, but my ass, that is international," Isabelle repeated. "*Mon cul! International!*" She laughed, a sound I hadn't heard for a while.

I closed my eyes, a headache mushrooming from the nape of my neck. I stood up, scraping my chair back with a horrid screeching sound. I had to get out of the apartment. "I'm going out."

Maman's eyes widened in alarm. "No, Élise! You can't go out."

"I'll wear a scarf."

"No! People will see you. Things could get nasty."

"Things are already nasty."

"Give it more time, Élise, please. Wait for your hair to grow back."

I looked at her in disbelief. "I can't stay here, just waiting." I walked out to the corridor.

Maman jumped to her feet, blocking my path. I shoved past. But she grabbed my arms. I tried to pull her hands off me. "Élise! You can't go out!"

"Stop it!" Isabelle stood there, tears running down her face. And something inside me broke. A sharp pain shot through my chest. I couldn't breathe. My knees went from under me, and I fell.

Maman caught me. She held me, gripping my arms, her fingers digging in. "Élise. Élise, please." But I was too heavy for her. She tried to hold me up, but I felt myself sliding down. I was vaguely aware of Isabelle still crying, but I felt myself letting go, losing consciousness. Then a burst of air seared through me, breath exploding into my lungs. I pushed Maman's arms away, collapsing into a heap on the floor, a wail escaping from me.

I felt Maman's body on mine, wrapped around me, holding me tight as wild uncontrollable sobs racked through me. When they began to subside, Maman guided me back to the living room where she laid me down on the couch. "Get a blanket," she whispered to Isabelle.

Chapter Forty-Two

Paris, November 1944

Élise

I ran to the bathroom again, reaching the toilet just in time to throw up, sweat running down my face. I stood back up on wobbly legs, holding on to the walls for support. It had been the smell of eggs that did it. Maman had wanted to treat us to a proper breakfast for a change, but I couldn't stand anything that smelled strongly, and the thought of eating turned my stomach. I'd lost more weight and hadn't had a period for four months now, not since July. That wasn't unusual for me; they'd been stopping and starting since the beginning of the occupation. But the vomiting was.

I walked into the kitchen, watching Maman at the sink scrubbing dirty clothes with a brush. She couldn't have heard me come in because she didn't turn around, and I took a minute to observe her, noticing her thin hunched shoulders. What had become of us? Paris was free, but our little family was falling apart. Our friends were few and far between, the neighbors looked the other way when they saw us—harder to bear than the strict rationing and constant hunger. I felt Maman's loneliness and worry seep into me, adding to my own. Knowing that I had brought this on my family filled me with guilt, but still I couldn't bring myself to regret Sébastian, I only wished I'd kept him secret from everyone, including my mother. I should have been more careful. I should have been more careful about many things.

Abruptly Maman turned around, wiping her hands on her apron before placing them on her hips. "You've been sick again," she stated. "Élise, I've had enough pregnancies to know the signs."

I looked away, sadness filling me as I remembered all the miscarriages she'd had. Instinctively I put my hand over my abdomen. "I'm sorry." I didn't know what else to say.

She shook her head. "Who are you sorry for? You? Us? Or the baby?" She took her hands from her hips and leaned against the sink as though the weight of her aging body was too much for her. "How could you have let it happen?"

The look of disappointment and regret in her eyes made me lower mine. "I didn't think I could get pregnant." I raised my eyes to meet hers. "My periods were so irregular."

She shook her head. "How could you be so stupid? And what about him, your boyfriend? He should have had more sense."

My boyfriend? She couldn't even say his name. I'd told Sébastian not to worry, that I couldn't get pregnant, that my cycles had stopped. He'd looked surprised but didn't argue with me—after all, what would he know?

She stepped forward and put a hand on my shoulder. "We might be able to find a doctor who can help."

"No! I can't do that!" I stepped back. How could she

imagine for a minute that I'd want to get rid of his baby? Only a year ago, under Pétain, a woman had been guillotined for performing abortions. And she was suggesting this!

She let out a long heavy breath. "Élise, you can't keep it." She took a step toward me, and I felt her trembling hand on my head, touching my stubbly short hair. "Why do you think they did this to you?" Her voice cracked. "We've already been ostracized by our neighbors. It will take years to regain their trust, and now this." She paused. "The nuns will take it."

She was right. A child born of the enemy would only serve as a reminder of how we'd surrendered, how we'd lain down and taken it. *La honte*. The shame was deep and destructive.

But this was my child. And all that I had left of Sébastian. "No!" I put my hand over my belly again, a feeling of love and protectiveness toward my unborn baby already growing.

"You can't keep it! Think of your father, a prisoner in Germany for three years. How do you think he'll feel to come home to find one of their babies in his own home? And you could still be arrested. The trials haven't finished; some women are getting a whole year's sentence."

"I can plead my case."

Maman rolled her eyes. "Don't be so naive. Do you really think they'll listen to you, out of all the girls in the same predicament? After what they did to you, how can you even imagine that—"

"You don't know everything about Sébastian! He was a good man. A brave man."

Maman put her hand up as though to stop my words. "Don't, Élise! He was part of the occupying forces. Our enemy."

"Why then? Why then did you want him to come here?" My pulse beat and my voice trembled. "You didn't really want to help him, did you?"

She pursed her lips, shaking her head.

And then I told her what I'd promised never to tell her. "Sébastian helped. He helped me get the children out."

"What do you mean?" She glared at me.

"I couldn't tell you before. It was too dangerous." I took a deep breath. "I was helping smuggle children out of the orphanage."

"Élise, what are you talking about?" She pressed a hand into her cheek.

"The UGIF center, the children there. Sometimes I'd take one or two to a *passeur*, who'd take them down to the south, over the frontier."

She stared at me, wide-eyed and speechless. Then she wiped her hands on her apron. "Élise! Are you mad? You put us all in danger! And what about Isabelle? Did you stop to consider her?"

"Yes, of course I did!"

"You could have got us all killed!"

"But I didn't, did I? And we saved lives. I couldn't tell you. It had to be that way. But then Sébastian found out that they were watching the orphanage. It was too dangerous for me to take the children to the *passeur*, so he did it. He took six children out. They would have been sent to Drancy, then..."

Maman turned away from me, burying her head in her hands, her shoulders shaking. I put my arm around her, but she pulled away from me, as though my touch had scorched her. "Why didn't you tell me?" she yelled, turning back to face me. "You should have told me!"

"You didn't need to know. I couldn't tell you."

"Yes, I did! I needed to know! I'm your mother, for God's sake."

She was my mother, but she felt like a stranger. She wouldn't have wanted to know what I was doing. And if she had known, she'd have stopped me. I couldn't have told her.

Chapter Forty-Three

Paris, November 1944

Élise

Maman was right about one thing; Papa would never be able to accept the thought of his own daughter having slept with a German, let alone having his baby. We didn't know when the war would officially end, nor when he'd be back, but I realized I had to leave before then. It was the only way. And there was only one person who might be able to help me. Monsieur Le Bolzec. He'd been there from the start, when I'd first met Sébastian.

I slipped out of the apartment unnoticed, a scarf covering my spikey short hair. The bell rang as I entered the shop, bringing back memories of the times I'd find Sébastian there. His absence now cut into me like a knife.

"Élise!" Monsieur Le Bolzec looked at my covered head before taking me in his arms and holding me tight. "I was just going to close up," he whispered. "I have fewer customers now than before liberation."

Glancing around the shop, I saw it was empty. Still, I waited for him to turn the sign to *Closed* before removing my head scarf. I waited to see his reaction at my stubbly ugly hair, but he didn't flinch. Instead he pulled out a stool for me. "Sit down. I've been so worried about you. I came by after... your mother told me everything."

"I didn't want to see anyone."

"No. Of course not." He paused. "Revenge attacks." He took my hand. "I wish I could have done something."

"There was nothing you could have done."

"No, you're probably right. I'd only have got myself into more trouble."

"What do you mean, more trouble?"

"Oh nothing really. Just a couple of remarks, you know the kind of thing: *Where's that German friend of yours today?*"

"What? People say that?"

"Well, Sébastian was in here quite often. People are bound to talk. Most of them will know I was no collabo. But others... you know how people can be." The color rose in his cheeks. "I'm sorry, I didn't mean to belittle what happened to you, not after all that you've gone through."

"What about those policemen? Have they been back?"

"No. They've probably got more sense than that, I expect they're lying low for the moment. You won't have been the only person they tried to intimidate."

"Do you know anything about Sébastian? About that night they came for him?" I asked impulsively.

"No." He shook his head.

"Somebody must have given him away."

He raised an eyebrow. "Do you have any ideas?"

"Isabelle told her best friend I had a German boyfriend."

"Poor Isabelle, she must feel so guilty."

"Yes, she does, but I'm not sure it was that." I shifted on my stool. "I have to get out."

He squeezed my hand and looked at me intently. "Those men who attacked you had no right. They felt powerless—castrated, having lived under the enemy for four years. They were raging against themselves more than anything. I'm not excusing anything. It's inexcusable. Unforgivable. And unworthy of us." He paused. "You don't have to leave, it will calm down." He scratched his sideburns.

"I still have to get away, far away. Before Papa comes back." I looked down at my belly. "I'm pregnant." I raised my eyes to meet his.

His pupils dilated as he took it in. "*Mon Dieu!*" He took a gulp of air, running his hand over the back of his head and neck. "Are you sure?"

I stood, opening my coat and gazing at my belly. "It doesn't show yet. But yes, I'm sure."

"How many months?"

"About four, I think." I paused. "Have you got any wine?" I asked impulsively.

Without a word he reached into the cupboard under his cash till, bringing out a bottle of red. He uncorked it and poured it into two smudged glasses. I gulped mine down. "Thank you." Some of the tension left my body, and I let out a long breath. "I want to keep it," I said abruptly.

His Adam's apple bobbed up and down. "Does your mother know?"

"Yes. But I can't stay here in Paris. What will happen when my father gets back?"

He gripped my hand. "I understand."

"Can you help me?" I looked into his eyes. "Please."

"If you really want to keep it, we'll find a way."

"How?"

A deep frown crossed his forehead as he studied me a minute, as though working something out. "My sister, Soizic," he finally said, "lives in Trégastel, Brittany. It was liberated just before Paris. She might take you in. She has a small farm; just a few cows and some land. I know she could do with the help since . . . since her husband was killed at the beginning of the war." He gazed down into his glass of wine. "Her daughter too."

"Her daughter?"

He nodded without looking at me. "It will be hard work."

"And you think she might take me in?" I finished the rest of my glass.

"She might. I think it would help her."

"What do you mean?"

He smiled sadly. "A baby could help." He hesitated. "She won't talk about her daughter. It's best if you don't mention her." He took my hand. "And you won't be able to mention Sébastian."

"But he's the father. How can I not talk about him?"

Monsieur Le Bolzec shook his head. "No, Élise. We'll have to make up another story."

"But he helped us! He helped the children escape. I can't just pretend he never existed." I stared at him. "You can't ask me to do that."

"Élise, please listen to me. People are prejudiced; they won't want to hear your story. Everyone will have stories, but they'll only hear the word 'Boche.'" He squeezed my hand. "When Soizic sees your stubbly hair and your belly, she'll work it out, but we need to give her a lie she can live with. If we came right out with the truth, she'd have to turn you away."

I stared at my empty glass, a deep sadness washing through me as I thought of all the secrets we had to keep from each other. "Are you sure she'll take me in?"

"She will if I ask her." He refilled my glass. "And Brittany is a good option. Lots of people there have blue eyes, some even have fair hair."

I nodded solemnly, seeing no other option. "I'll be glad to leave Paris."

He squeezed me hands. "I know. A fresh start will do you good."

Chapter Forty-Four

Paris, December 1944

Élise

We had our city back, and soon we'd have our country too. We were almost free. So why did I still feel like a prisoner? I turned away from the broken window, held together with sticky brown tape.

I hadn't heard Maman come in. I only knew she was there when I heard her cough.

I turned to face her. She looked like a ghost in the dim light of dusk. "I suppose we should get something for dinner." Her voice was listless. "There are a few potatoes left. It's getting dark already."

Sometimes it's easier to talk in the half-light. "Maman," I started. "I'm going away."

I saw a flash of relief in her eyes. "Where? Where will you go?"

"Monsieur Le Bolzec has a sister in Brittany, Soizic Le Calvez. She's going to take me in."

"Brittany," she repeated, staring out of the broken window. "Yes." She turned back to face me, her eyes narrowing. "Does this woman know the truth about the father?"

"No." The word felt cruel and hard on my tongue, but it was part of the deal.

"What story did he tell her?"

"That Frédéric was the father, that he was killed during the liberation." The words came out in one breath, as though in saying them, I would be relieved of the lie.

"Yes, that could work. You can always take a picture of Frédéric with you—make it more believable. Though you shouldn't let anyone see you till your hair's grown back and that baby is born." Maman's shoulders slumped. "What will I tell your father?" Without waiting for an answer, she went on. "He'll know. One of the neighbors will tell him. Or the concierge. And then there's Isabelle, she's no good at keeping secrets." She put her head in her hands. "Oh my God, he'll kill me."

In an awful moment of realization, it dawned on me that she was hoping he wouldn't return. He was the reason I had to leave. But she was his wife, of course she wanted him back.

Chapter Forty-Five

Brittany, January 1945

Élise

One month later, I stood on the platform at Rennes, hugging myself tight and tapping my feet in a futile attempt to get warm. There was no waiting room, and my connecting train was late. A family of five was also waiting, but I didn't approach them, and they didn't approach me. They only glimpsed at me now and again out of the corner of their eyes. I had a beret on, but there was no hair poking out or hanging down my back. I knew they were wondering if I was one of the *tondues*—the shaven ones.

The stationmaster strolled down the platform, and I shrank back into the shadows. But he'd seen me. He paused in his stride, glancing at me, mumbling under his breath, "Shame on you."

I shrank further back. But where was my dignity? I was ashamed of my own shame. Taking a large step forward, I looked him directly in the eye. "*Bonjour, monsieur.* When is the next train to Lannion?"

He hesitated before answering. "A quarter past three, mademoiselle," he eventually replied.

"*Merci, monsieur.*" I watched his receding back, my dignity returning. I would not be forced to live in the shadows. And neither would my child.

As soon as the train arrived, I jumped on, relieved to be out of the cold wind, but the empty carriage was unheated. I pulled the woolen scarf tightly around my neck, huddling down in my seat. I was grateful for the flask of coffee that Monsieur Le Bolzec had kindly prepared, and I poured myself a cup, breathing in its warmth before I drank it, wondering what kind of a welcome I'd receive when I eventually got to Trégastel.

When the train finally pulled into Lannion station, night had fallen, and one solitary street lamp lit the platform. I stood there, watching people being met, being hugged, being kissed, but it didn't look like anyone had come to meet me. A knot of anxiety tightened in my stomach. I was all alone in a new place. A pang of loneliness shot through me, and I missed Sébastian with a physical pain that left me feeling hollow. He should have been with me; we should have been expecting our first child together.

I picked up my suitcase in one hand, my other wrapped around my waist, trying to keep warm, and I walked out onto the street. A horse and trap trotted by. Was that her? I'd assumed she'd come in a car; stupid of me really. Tentatively, I walked over toward where the horse and trap had pulled to a stop. The driver's head turned toward me. It was a woman. "Madame Le Calvez?" I ventured.

"*Oui. Montez.* Get in." She glanced at me before turning back to her reins.

I hurried around to the other side and climbed the two

steps into the seat next to her, pulling my case after me. But before I had time to greet her properly, she'd already turned the horse around and we were trotting away. I studied her profile in the dim light; she had a pointed nose and small round chin. She was frowning. "Thank you, Madame Le Calvez, for coming to meet me, and for—"

"No use thanking me," she interrupted before I had time to finish. "I'm only doing it for Yannick."

"Yannick? Monsieur Le Bolzec?"

She glanced at me, giving me time to catch the coldness in her eyes. "Yes. He told me you had nowhere else to go."

I looked at the faint shadows of large looming trees and shivered, the hollowness inside me expanding. "It's very kind of you to take me in."

"Hmm." She coughed, ignoring my remark. "You'll have to work hard. I need someone to take care of the cows."

"The cows?"

"Yes, the cows," she repeated as though I was some kind of imbecile. "I'll show you how to milk them."

"Yes, of course." In fact, I quite liked the idea.

"When's the baby due?"

"April."

"Three months to go. You showing yet?"

"Not really."

"Bet there's still not much food getting through to Paris."

"No, not much."

"Who's the father?" She fired the question at me in the same cold tone as the other questions.

"Frédéric," I lied. "He was shot, by a German sniper, during the liberation." The lie Monsieur Le Bolzec and I had agreed on came out uneasily, making me cringe as the words left my mouth. It felt disloyal to Sébastian, and

I loathed myself for it. She didn't reply, and we drove on in silence, the cold wind biting through my thin coat. I glimpsed her profile again; in the dim moonlight her thin pointed nose stood out from the rest of her face. She looked like a proud woman, and I couldn't imagine much warmth between us. I buried my face in my scarf, trying not to let my loneliness engulf me.

"What was he like?" she asked abruptly.

Her question took me by surprise, and I hesitated, unsure whether to describe Sébastian or Fréderick. I had to stick to the lie. "He had brown hair, brown eyes. He was kind." An awkward silence hung heavy. I shivered, burying my face deeper into my scarf. The cold felt like it was setting into my bones, and a feeling of dread seeped through me. "Have you told anyone I'm coming?" I worried that she wasn't even on my side.

"I don't see many people, only the old man next door and the ladies who own the *maison de la presse*. I told them about you."

"What did you tell them?"

"Exactly what Yannick told me. What did you expect me to tell them?" She clicked her tongue loudly as we turned the next corner. The horse trotted forward as the road straightened out, and I braced myself against the icy wind.

We came to a driveway, drawing to a stop outside a small stone cottage. Madame Le Calvez took out a torch, shining it around as we descended from the trap, highlighting the empty fields surrounding the cottage. "You go on in. I'll get the horse sorted."

"Can I help?" I offered, though I was freezing cold and just wanted to get inside.

"No," she replied curtly. "Just go in and get warmed up."

Gratefully, I took my case and opened the door to the cottage. The kitchen's warmth immediately hit me. It was coming from a large stove on which two saucepans stood. Drawn toward it, I took my gloves off and held my hands above the stove's heat. Gradually the blood returned to my fingers.

She came back in, banging her hands together. "*Ma Doué!*" The words were foreign to me; they must have been Breton. "It's cold tonight," she continued in French, as she peeled off layers of coats, hanging them on the back of the door, then she looked at me still standing there in my thin coat. "I made soup." She moved over to the stove, picking up the large saucepan. "Take your coat off and sit down."

"Can I do anything?"

"No. Just wash your hands and sit."

I did as I was told, taking off my coat, hanging it on the back of the door as she did, then washing my hands at the kitchen sink and drying them on a rough towel hanging by the stove. I looked around, but the walls were bare, providing no clues about this woman.

I took my place at the long narrow table, made of thick dark wood and covered in burn marks of dishes gone by—large circles and smaller ovals. She placed the saucepan in the middle, and I winced when I thought of the additional mark it would leave, wondering why she didn't use mats. She ladled the soup out, and my stomach rumbled when the smell of herbs, black pepper, and chicken wafted up my nose. When our bowls were full, I attempted to be friendly. "*Bon appétit.*"

"God bless this food we are about to eat." She ignored my meaningless *Bon appétit*, instead making the sign of the cross as she looked down at the table. I followed her example.

In silence we took our first spoonful. "It's delicious, Madame Le Calvez. Thank you." She nodded and passed me a piece of baguette. It was rock hard, but dipped in the soup, it softened, soaking up the flavor of the chicken. We ate in silence. "How far are we from the sea?" I attempted to make conversation.

"Five minutes." She slurped her soup.

"I haven't seen the sea for five years now."

"You can go for a walk tomorrow. But you'll have to dress well. The wind whips round the coast here. And you'll have to tie that beret on with a scarf." She laid her palms firmly on the table. "But maybe you shouldn't go out at all. Not until you've had the baby."

I let the spoon drop into my bowl. "That's another three months!"

"I know that." Stony cold eyes bore into me. "Now, girl, are you going to tell me the truth about the father?"

I felt my cheeks redden, and I couldn't meet her eye. An awkward silence hung heavy. Then she sighed loudly. "Does Yannick take me for an idiot?" Her voice cut through me. "As soon as I got the letter, I knew. Why else would you need to come here?" She studied me. "Was he blond?" she asked abruptly. "Were his eyes blue?"

I swallowed before answering, trying to keep my voice steady and calm. "Yes, his hair was very fair. And his eyes were blue, aqua blue."

"Aqua indeed!" She snorted. "Yannick knew I wouldn't take you in if I knew the father was a Boche. And he was right. I wouldn't have." She sighed. "And he begged me, if you want to know. He always knows what buttons to press. He knew I wouldn't throw you out, not once you'd got through the door." She turned away, her lips twitching.

"We'll do our best to make this lie work. But I don't want to hear anything about your Boche. Ever. Understood? As far as I'm concerned, he never existed."

I nodded, but in my heart, I held on to Sébastian, making a silent promise: *I'll never let you go.*

She removed the soup bowls, taking them over to the sink. I stood up. "Let me wash those."

"No. You can do it in the morning. I'll show you to your room."

I took my case and followed her up a narrow wooden staircase. Just above the kitchen there was one little bedroom, its floorboards worn and uneven, gaps between some of the boards showing through to the kitchen below. A dark wooden bed with high curved ends sat under a small window cut into the sloping roof, and there was a lamp on the table next to the bed. I took solace in the fact that she'd made the bed for me.

"The bathroom's downstairs, next to the kitchen," she stated.

"Thank you; it's very nice."

"*Alors, bonsoir.*" She turned and left.

I sat down on the bed, feeling more alone than I'd ever felt before in my life.

Then I placed my palm over my swollen belly, feeling my baby—our baby—and a feeling of love and gratitude swept through me, replacing my loneliness with hope.

Chapter Forty-Six

Brittany, February 14, 1945

Élise

I was waking earlier and earlier, always in the dark. But then, we were tucked up in bed before nine every night. There was little else to do, and anyway, at seven months pregnant I was always exhausted, relieved to get into my little bed under the rafters at the end of the day. The baby growing inside me had become real; I knew when he or she was sleeping or awake. I had the feeling it was a girl, and I talked to her in my mind, telling her all about her father. I felt his absence sorely, like a gaping hole in my soul, but I comforted myself with the thought that soon I'd have a part of him, and someone to love completely.

Madame Le Calvez had organized our routine so we'd have minimal contact, asking me to milk the cows before daybreak, and to get them out to the fields as soon as the sun rose, so we couldn't even have breakfast together. Switching on the bedside lamp, I looked at my watch:

five o'clock. I slipped my feet out of bed and went down to the kitchen.

She was already there, making coffee. I could see I'd upset her morning routine by the way she stared at me with pursed lips and cold eyes. "I won't be here today," she said before I even had time to say *bonjour*. She filled a silver flask with coffee. "Can you collect the eggs and make the bread this morning?"

"Yes, of course." I wanted to ask where she was going but didn't dare.

"I'll be back before dark. You'll have to bring the cows back in too."

I finally found the courage. "May I ask where you're going?"

She stared blankly at me, then she shook her head. Without another word, she put the flask and some bread into a basket, and she left. Who went out before daybreak? Where was she going?

In a way, it was a relief to be alone in the cottage. I threw the big woolen coat over my shoulders and pulled my rubber boots on. If I got on with the milking quickly, I'd have more time to enjoy the place alone before she got back. Though I'd learned the hard way that it was no good rushing the milking; the cows liked to be coaxed gently into giving up their milk, and it could easily take me two hours to do all six, sometimes longer. This morning I started with my favorite, Jessie. She nudged me gently as I entered the stall, mist blowing out through her nostrils. I stroked her wet nose, murmuring to her as I ran my hand down her velvety neck, burying my nose in the flaps of her skin, breathing in her smell. There was comfort in the cows' solid, silent presence and though it was crazy, I felt like Jessie could read my emotions. Sometimes joyful, sometimes melancholic, sometimes anxious. Always lonely. I patted my belly, glad that in a couple of months there would be two of us.

I pulled out the little stool and sat down, blowing on my hands to warm them before taking her teats, humming softly as the milk started to flow. When I'd done all six of them, I carried the heavy pails of milk into the kitchen, ready to bottle later. Then I went back and led them out to pasture.

When I finally returned to the warm kitchen, I put the water to heat for my first coffee of the day. A tap on the door made me jump. Tentatively, I opened the door. An old woman stood there, looking me up and down. "*Bonjour.*" I hesitated, not sure whether to ask her in or not.

"You're Élise." She said it as though it were an accusation. Then she walked straight in. "Madame Le Calvez not here, then?"

"No. I'm not sure when she'll be back. Not till this evening, I think."

She closed the door behind her and took a step further into the kitchen. "February fourteenth. Knew she wouldn't be here today."

"Valentine's day?" Maybe she had a secret *amant* somewhere.

"Naught to do with Valentine's." She stared at me coldly. "Aren't you going to offer me a coffee?" She sat down, and seeing I had little choice in the matter, I took two bowls from the cupboard behind me.

"What's your name?" I ventured.

"Give a cup, not a breakfast bowl." She shook her head as if exasperated with me.

I put some coffee beans in the grinder and turned the handle while I waited for her to tell me who she was. But she just sat there, her eyes following me, burning into my back when I turned away from her. Finally, she spoke again.

"Did she tell you where she was going?"

"No." I turned to look at her. "She didn't."

"Hmm, she's not told you much then."

"No. We've been working hard."

She ignored my comment, continuing to stare at me through narrowed eyes. "I know about you though."

I felt the color rush to my cheeks and turned back around, taking the saucepan off the ring, pouring her a coffee, resolved not to say anything.

"She had to take you in," she continued. "Because of her brother." I put the cup down in front of her. "He tried to save her daughter. Did you know that?" She didn't wait for an answer. "Yes. He came all the way here. Didn't do no good in the end though."

"What happened to her daughter?"

"The Gestapo got her." She took a sip of coffee, her lips puckering around the rim of the cup.

I froze, a cramp shooting through my stomach. Pulling out a chair, I collapsed onto it, breathless. "What happened?"

"I saw her that very morning, St. Valentine's day, cycling past the church. That same afternoon I heard she'd been arrested, something to do with making false papers, or carrying them." She looked at me dispassionately. "She was in the Résistance, you know."

I closed my eyes, trying to dislodge the image of the Gestapo taking her away.

"Yannick Le Bolzec came three days later. He went straight to the police station." She hesitated. "But it was too late."

I screwed my eyes tight shut, holding on to my stomach as waves of nausea rose through me.

"She's buried over at the cemetery in Perros-Guirec. That's where Madame Le Calvez will be now." She took another sip of coffee, looking over the rim of her cup at me. "Yes, it's hard for her, to have you here. Very hard. She's a saint, for sure."

I concentrated on not throwing up, trying to breathe down into my abdomen, breathing into my unborn child.

"She told me that cock-and-bull story about that so-called fiancé of yours. I didn't say a word, just pretended to believe her. She knows I don't really. But that's not what matters. What matters is what everyone else believes. So, my girl." She paused as though for effect. "You are going to have to behave yourself. Rumors have already started. Probably ain't far from the truth neither, but we'll nip 'em in the bud."

I nodded. I'd go along with anything now, to keep us safe. All of us.

"Soizic has been through hell," she continued. "Lost her husband to the Boches, then her daughter. She has good friends here. Loyal friends. We'll stand by her. And no one will guess that after what she's gone through, she would take in...take in you and your..." She sighed loudly. "When that poor child is born, Soizic will be the one to take it out and show it around. It's the only way people will accept it." She stood up. "People just need to see you're a good worker, that Madame Le Calvez is happy with you, that you know how to keep your head down and out of trouble." She squinted at me. "Do you get what I'm saying?"

I nodded again.

"We're not complicated folk, and we won't ask for more than that." She puffed out her chest. "Well, that's all I came to say. You be on your best behavior. We'll spin your story about that fiancé of yours, and people will believe it, or they won't. But we'll make sure they treat your child right. For Soizic's sake." She stood and took a step toward the door. Then without saying goodbye, she opened the door and left.

Chapter Forty-Seven

Brittany, April 14, 1945

Élise

The mornings were getting lighter as spring pushed winter out, and I was no longer getting up in the dark. I enjoyed the calm and peace of milking the cows before the sun had fully risen. But this morning Jessie was restless and wouldn't stand still for me. A twinge shot through my abdomen as I raised myself from the stool, the pail only a quarter full of milk. I carried it into the cottage, just in time to see the postman cycling off; probably a letter from Maman or Isabelle, maybe news of Papa.

But when I walked into the kitchen, I knew it wasn't. Madame Le Calvez was at the table, hunched over a telegram. She was very still, and the air around her felt heavy. For a moment I stood there, hoping she might look up at me, but she didn't move.

Instinctively, I sat next to her, glancing at the two lines written on the piece of brown paper. A shiver ran down the back of my neck. I froze, unable to digest what I'd just read.

Yannick Le Bolzec died last Monday. A single shot to the back of his neck.

"Who?" I mumbled. "Who killed him?"

"They thought he was a collabo." She spoke in a flat monotone.

My blood ran cold. I didn't understand. And yet I did. I did. "Who? Who thought he was a collabo?"

"I don't know who, do I? One of the factions looking to settle accounts. How do I know? It must have been because of that Boche who kept going into his shop. Your Boche!" She spat the last word out.

A sharp pain shot through my side. Gasping for air, I put my hand on my pounding chest. Kind, wise Monsieur Le Bolzec. Murdered. His words rang in my ears. *Unworthy of us.* It was unimaginable. Unthinkable. Barbaric. I thought of that dear old man lying there, a pool of dark blood under his head. And clear as day, I knew that's what they'd done to Sébastian. Cold silent tears ran down my face, and I let them fall.

"Please," Madame Le Calvez said. "I want to be alone."

I wished we could have found comfort in each other, but she'd erected a wall between us. I got up and went back into the cowshed, where I buried my head in Jessie's warm flank and cried for Yannick Le Bolzec, for Sébastian, for me, and for my unborn child. When there was nothing left inside me, I lay down on the straw, exhausted and empty. I dreaded going back into the cottage, and if I'd had anywhere else to go, I would have left. We didn't speak for the rest of the day, and that night I went to bed even earlier than usual, collapsing onto my bed.

In the middle of the night, I woke, feeling cold and wet. Sitting up, I pulled back the sheets, reaching for the lamp. The bottom sheet was wet through. My heart raced. This was it. My baby was coming. I removed the sheet and rinsed it in the bathroom, then hung it over the back of my bedroom chair to dry. I made a bed on the floor with a blanket under me, and I lay down, staring at the ceiling as I placed my hand over my abdomen, feeling my baby. "Please come safely," I whispered.

I must have drifted off because the next thing I knew, Madame Le Calvez was opening the curtains. "What are you doing on the floor?" she asked. "It's already six."

Immediately my hand flew to my belly. "My waters broke in the night."

She turned around. "Have the contractions started?"

"No, I don't think so. I'm not in pain." I sat up, pushing my hands into the floor, lifting myself onto my feet with difficulty.

Madame Le Calvez watched me in a detached manner as though trying to work something out. "Those contractions need to get going. You should move around. Your waters have broken, infections can get in."

"What shall I do?" I tried to keep the panic out of my voice.

"Get up and get on with your chores. It will come when it's ready." She turned to leave. "Come down. We'll carry on as usual."

I followed her down the stairs, trying to steady my rasping breath.

"Don't sit down," she said as soon as I entered the kitchen. "It will slow things down."

My belly felt heavy, the ligaments stretched, and I put my hands under it, supporting its weight as I walked out to the cowshed, trembling with a mixture of cold and fear. Pulling out the milking stool, I sat down in front of Jessie, warming my hands before feeling her full udders, then moving my fingers down to her teats. She let out a low deep moo and kicked out a back leg. I pulled my hands away.

I stood up, breathing into my abdomen and my baby. The cow nuzzled me with her wide flat head, pushing me backward, making it clear she didn't want me there today. I left the cowshed and walked back into the kitchen.

Madame Le Calvez was making coffee on the stove. I breathed in the warm comforting aroma, looking at her rounded shoulders as she took the bowls out of the cupboard. "I can't milk the cows today," I said to her back.

She turned around, fixing me with a cold stare. "What do you mean?"

"They're playing up."

She put the bowls on the table. "Playing up indeed? I suppose I'll have to do it then." She sighed. "As if there isn't enough to do."

"Should we call the midwife?" I needed someone to tell me everything was going to be all right.

"No." She poured the coffee. "We don't need to bother her yet. She'll just tell you to keep moving. Your body needs to wake up."

For the rest of the day, she kept me busy, cleaning out the henhouse, collecting the eggs, taking the cows out to graze. Even after lunch, she wouldn't let me rest, but had me making bread and churning butter. That evening when we finally sat down to supper, I was exhausted.

"Can you still feel it moving?" she asked as she broke off a piece of baguette.

"I don't know. No, I don't think so." I put my hand over my hard abdomen, feeling out the roundness of the baby's bottom, praying it would turn soon, that it would find its way out.

"We'll give it twenty-four hours. If nothing's happened by morning, we'll call the midwife."

"Can't we call her now?"

"Not yet. Sometimes it can take a while for the contractions to start."

After supper, even though it wasn't cold, she lit a fire in the small living room, and we sat on the worn couch. I pretended to read a book and she pretended to read the paper. I didn't understand why she couldn't call the midwife, just to check on me. Terrible thoughts wormed their way into my head. What if she didn't want this baby to be born? What if she wanted both of us to die? Since learning of Monsieur Le Bolzec's death yesterday, she'd become even more distant, turning her nose up at me as though I were some filthy animal she wanted to get rid of.

"Yannick was my friend," I said impulsively.

She looked startled. "And he was my brother."

"He always saw the best in everyone." I looked into her stony eyes. "But I wish he hadn't sent me here. It was too much to ask of you." There, I'd said it now. Her heart wasn't as forgiving and kind as her dear brother had thought it might be.

She folded her paper, looking at me for a moment. I hoped she might say something, but her lips remained tight. Then she said. "Maybe we should try castor oil. I think I have some."

"Why don't we just call the midwife?"

She looked at me out of the corner of her eye. "I have done this before, you know."

I wasn't sure if she was referring to when she gave birth, or whether she meant she'd delivered babies before. "What do you mean?" I asked.

She stared at me as though her mind were miles away, then she spoke very softly. "I had a child." Her words were whole, but at the same time, I felt their emptiness. "A girl," she whispered. "She took a long time coming."

At last, she was talking to me about the daughter she'd lost. I nodded, not wishing to interrupt as I waited for her to go on. Staring into the flames, she continued in a slow monotone as though the words didn't really belong to her. "Her fingers were wrinkled when she finally came out, like she'd been in the bath too long." She took a stick and poked the fire. I waited, wanting to hear more, but she was silent, lost in her memories. "She was just seventeen," she finally continued, "when her father died. His death hit her really hard. She started going out a lot, at odd times, disappearing for days at a time. I thought she had a lover somewhere. She wouldn't talk to me. We argued a lot." She paused, staring into the fire. "It wasn't a lover though. I wish it had been. No, she was involved with the Résistance; carrying messages. I didn't know until it was too late."

I watched her playing with the fire, remembering what the old woman had told me, dreading her next words. But Madame Le Calvez stood abruptly, and her tone changed back to the harsh practical one she usually used with me. "To bring on the birth, I took castor oil. It helped." She left the room, returning with a small brown glass bottle and a soup spoon. "Two spoons should do it." She held out the bottle and poured a spoonful of the transparent liquid. When she passed it to me, I took it without a word, trying to stop my fingers from trembling as I put it in my mouth and swallowed the sickly rich oil.

That evening before I fell asleep, I prayed for my baby to come soon. And safely. I didn't sleep well, dreams of Sébastian mixed up with thoughts of him, reality merging with fantasy. At one point I saw him there, holding our baby. Was I dreaming? Or was I just imagining it? I ached for him till it pulled at my soul, ripping me apart.

Chapter Forty-Eight

Brittany, April 1945

Élise

Shooting pains in my abdomen woke me. This time it was no dream. It was real. Thank God, my contractions had started. I got up immediately and went down to the kitchen, thinking to make myself some coffee. But on the stairs a stronger, more violent pain gripped me. It took my breath away and I stopped abruptly, leaning into the wall, holding my breath as I waited for it to pass. I made it into the kitchen, where I took a saucepan and filled it with water. Another wave of pain shot through me. I gasped, holding on to the sink for support. When it had passed, I sat down, wiping the sweat from my forehead and the tears from my eyes. I was at the mercy of my body now, and I shouldn't be fighting it like this. I would have to breathe with it. I readied myself for the next contraction.

Madame Le Calvez appeared in the doorway. "It's started then?"

"Yes." I looked at her through wet eyes.

She made the sign of the cross. "A baby is a gift from God. We must never forget that." She paused, contemplating me. "Come through to my bedroom. You'll be more comfortable there."

With my arms wrapped around my abdomen, I followed her through to her bedroom. A large bed dominated the room, an armchair in the corner.

"Do you want to sit or lie down?"

Before I could answer, another contraction seized me. I held on to the back of the armchair and tried to breathe with it. But the pain stole my breath, and I moaned in agony instead.

Madame Le Calvez took her watch from the bedside table. "It's only four o'clock. I don't like to call the midwife this early in the morning. We'll see if we can wait."

We? I wanted to scream. *I'm the one having the baby!* I turned around and stared at her, feeling the pain ebbing away. "Wouldn't it be safer to call her? She must be used to getting woken up."

"She's only twenty minutes away. Let's time the contractions first. You could still be hours away from giving birth."

"What!"

"I'll cover the bed. Don't want you messing that up." She lifted off her bedspread and blankets and threw a thick cotton sheet over the bed. "Wait, I'll get some towels too."

I felt the next wave rolling in. Gripping the back of the armchair, I vowed not to give in to the pain, but it took all my energy, and when it passed, I collapsed against the chair, breathless and exhausted. Unwelcome thoughts flooded my head; stories of women in labor for days, women who'd died from their suffering. Babies born blue.

Madame Le Calvez came back with a pile of burgundy-colored towels that she placed on the bed. "Better get on the bed."

Awkwardly, I maneuvered my cumbersome body onto the bed then I sat up, resting back against the headboard. I glanced around her room and saw a picture of a young girl with long dark hair, smiling into the camera with confidence and happiness. Her daughter, I supposed.

Madame Le Calvez handed me a cup of tea. "Camomile."

I shook my head. I couldn't take it. The next wave was on its way.

She put the cup down by the bed and took my hand. I squeezed it with all my strength. I saw her wince but couldn't let go. I needed her. When the pain had passed, she looked at her watch. "I'm going to time them." She passed me the tea, and I took a sip, trying not to tense up as I waited for the next contraction. When it seared through me, she stood up, looking at her watch. "Two minutes between."

"Is that good?" I gasped, wishing I could reach for her hand again, but she was standing too far away.

"They're not that close, could be a while. I should get on. I don't s'pose you'll be helping me today. I'll have to do the butter myself."

I wanted to laugh at her even considering I might work today. And I wanted to cry, *Don't leave me!* But I knew it would do me no good, so I said nothing.

Only a couple of hours could have passed by the time the sun came up, but I was worn out. I felt another presence in the room and, glancing at the doorway, I saw Madame Le Calvez standing there, looking at me with an expression I couldn't decipher. "The contractions are still two minutes apart," she said. "Your baby ain't in a rush to get out."

"She must know she isn't welcome here," I said quickly, knowing the next contraction was on its way. This one lifted my back off the bed with its force, and I screamed out.

She came next to the bed. "Don't fight it."

"Please! Call the midwife!"

She put her cool hand on my hot forehead. "You'll be okay. Childbirth can be painful."

Fresh tears burst from my eyes. She was going to let me and my baby die here.

"Let me have a look." She moved down to the end of the bed and placed one hand on my abdomen, while she put the other between my legs. She stood back up, looking at me. "Your cervix isn't opening yet."

I threw my head back on the pillow, tears choking me. I didn't know how long I'd be able to take this. My head was spinning, and I felt sick with pain. Again, she left the room.

My world swirled in a blur of wretchedness and agony. I couldn't say how much time passed, but it felt like hours. Panic seized me and I screamed out. "Please! Call the midwife!"

I felt a cool damp towel on my forehead. "Shh now. Let me have another look."

I tried to calm myself as she bent down to look between my legs again. She stood up. "I'll call now."

"Can you see the head?" I asked desperately.

But she was already gone. I lay back, grateful that at last she was calling. Everything would be all right once the midwife got here. She'd know what to do.

Madame Le Calvez came back minutes later with a wet flannel for me to put between my teeth. I sucked out the moisture from it as the next contraction seared through me. This time she didn't leave me but stayed to mop my sweaty brow. I closed my eyes, summoning all my courage.

A knock on the door was like music to my ears. Madame Le Calvez left the room and returned with a man. The sight of him sent a wave of terror through me. Why hadn't she called the midwife? Why did I need a doctor?

He took one look at me. "*On va vous aider, madame.*" I was aware of him opening a box of tools. I closed my eyes and prayed.

"Push!" he shouted. "Push!"

With my last reserves of strength, I pushed with all my might, till my eyes throbbed with the effort. A burning spasm coursed through me, making me scream again.

"Again!" he shouted. "Push again!"

I was pain. It had consumed me. But I pushed again.

Then like a wave breaking over me, it was gone. I collapsed back onto the bed.

Then I heard a cry. My baby was alive! Tears of pain turned to tears of joy.

"It's a girl," I heard Madame Le Calvez say.

"Can I hold her?" I croaked.

"I'll just clean her up." It was the doctor again.

"No!" I shouted. "Give her to me." I had to see her. I had to know she was real.

He placed the naked child in my arms, and I buried my face in my daughter's warm body, my tears melting into her. "I will keep you safe," I promised.

Part Three

1963

Chapter Forty-Nine

Paris, May 1963

Joséphine

When Joséphine wakes, she looks around at Isabelle and Eric's apartment and wonders if she could be happy here, in Paris. A fresh start might help. She could reinvent herself as a chic *Parisienne* instead of the country bumpkin she feels she is.

"Croissants!" Eric walks in with a paper bag. "Nothing like fresh croissants for breakfast, is there?"

Isabelle wanders in wearing her dressing gown. "How lovely." She kisses Eric on the cheek and removes the bag from his hand. "I'll make coffee."

Joséphine stretches. "I'll go and get washed first."

When Joséphine gets back from the bathroom, Isabelle has laid out the table with a pot of coffee, croissants, and strawberry jam. Joséphine sits down, and Isabelle pours her some coffee. "I made a decision last night," Joséphine announces, looking from Isabelle to Eric. "I'm not going to study engineering, like Maman wanted. I'm going to do literature."

Isabelle smiles. "How exciting! You'll love it, and you'll be the first one in the family to go to university."

"Will I?" The word *family* seems to have taken on different connotations since she found out who her real father was. "We can't be sure of that. Maybe my father went, or someone from his family." She bites her bottom lip, thinking about her family she's never met, like her grandfather right here in Paris. He probably hates her just for having a German father. She's not really missed having grandparents, after all she's always had Soizic. It's not like she's been lonely, but she can't help wondering what he might be like—the only man in the family, apart from Eric, and he's not even a blood relative. Dare she ask to see him? What harm could it do? He can only say no.

"Do you think I could meet my grandfather?" Her words come out clear and concise, hiding the anxiety behind them.

Eric splutters. "That old goat! I wouldn't advise it."

"Eric!" Isabelle glares at him.

"He's lost his marbles. Though, in fact, I think it's improved him." Eric spreads jam over his croissant. "He doesn't rant like he used to, or he forgets what he started ranting about."

"He just gets muddled sometimes." Isabelle defends him.

"Does he ever mention me?" Joséphine asks.

Eric and Isabelle look at her. "No," Isabelle finally replies. "He doesn't. I'm not sure he remembers he has a grand-daughter. And he never talks about your mother."

"He might not know who I am then."

"That's true." Isabelle seems to be considering the idea. "I could ask your grandmother—see what she says."

"What else have you girls got planned for today?" Eric

swiftly changes the subject as he wipes the crumbs from the corners of his mouth.

"*La Tour Eiffel, Le Louvre,* lunch. Shopping in the afternoon." Isabelle smiles at Eric.

"Make sure you get something nice." Eric stands and bends down to kiss the top of Isabelle's head. "Remember I'm taking you girls out tonight." He rinses his hands in the kitchen sink and puts a jacket on. "I'll see you about seven."

"*Au revoir, chéri,*" Isabelle calls after him as he leaves the apartment.

As soon as he's gone, Isabelle turns back to Joséphine. "If you do meet your grandfather, I should warn you, he can be quite grumpy. And he shouts a lot; he's quite deaf."

"I'd still like to meet him."

"Of course." Isabelle pours more coffee then looks at Joséphine. "I'm sorry we haven't been much of a family to you. I hope we can make up for it. I'll call Maman now."

Isabelle shuts the kitchen door behind her as she goes out to the corridor where they keep the phone.

Joséphine pulls a buttery croissant in half, watching the dough stretch, wondering if he'll agree to see her, imagining Isabelle on the phone, trying to convince her grandmother, and she's already filled with a sense of rejection. She almost gets up and tells Isabelle not to bother. She can't bear to hear that he doesn't want to see her, because of who her father was. The injustice of it sends a burst of rage through her. She's not sure she even wants to meet him any more.

"It's okay." Isabelle comes back into the room. "We can go there this morning. Your grandmother says he probably won't realize who you are anyway, but at least you'll get to meet him. We'll introduce you simply as Joséphine, see what he says. He's not really interested in people."

Joséphine puts a spoon of jam on her croissant and eats it while she thinks.

"He's quite diminished," Isabelle continues. "He's dependent on your grandmother for everything."

Joséphine swallows the piece of croissant. "What's the point if he doesn't know who I am?"

"It's up to you, Joséphine. I thought you wanted to see him."

"Okay." She pushes aside her misgivings, thinking that at least her grandmother will be happy to see her, so Isabelle said.

An hour later, they're walking through the Jardins du Luxembourg on their way to her grandparents' apartment. Isabelle takes Joséphine's hand. "It's a gorgeous day. I can't wait to show you Paris."

"Out!" someone shouts, making Joséphine jump. Then the sound of a tennis ball being whacked picks up again. They carry on walking along the chestnut-tree-lined paths, pausing to look at a group of men in berets playing *pétanque*. When they pass by the lake in front of the large mansion, couples on metal chairs sit opposite each other, games of chess between them.

"Are you okay?" Isabelle squeezes her hand.

Not really, would be the correct answer, but Joséphine says, "Yes, I'm fine, thank you."

They soon leave the park, turning onto Place Saint-Sulpice, where water cascades from a fountain. Isabelle points to a little street on the opposite side, and they move away from the fountain toward the far corner. She feels breathless as she follows Isabelle across the square and down the side street. They soon stop outside a large burgundy-colored wooden door, and Isabelle pushes the small bell, releasing the catch so they can walk through to the entrée, then she buzzes the bell next to the name *Chevalier.* Joséphine's name.

Her grandmother comes through the door, her arms open to greet them. Her dark brown eyes are warm, and small dimples appear in her sagging cheeks. "*Bonjour, Joséphine. Bienvenue.*" She kisses her. "I'm so glad you've finally come to Paris."

Joséphine is relieved that she seems so happy to see her, and her apprehension fades. She kisses her grandmother's soft doughy cheek, enjoying this feeling of being welcomed.

They follow her through to the kitchen. "I'll make coffee," she proposes. "Sit down. How was your journey, Joséphine?" she asks. "It's a long way from Trégastel."

"Fine, thank you. I love trains." Really, she'd like to talk about her father.

"Isabelle told me you know about your father now." Mamyne seems to have read her mind, and Joséphine feels exposed, as though all her turmoil and heartache were printed on her forehead. "It must have been a shock for you."

"It was." Joséphine hasn't managed to explain to anyone that her mother doesn't even know she knows, or even that she's here. The unintentional lie just got harder to break.

Her grandmother squeezes her hand. "I'm glad you know. I never agreed with keeping the truth from you."

Isabelle sighs loudly, as though annoyed with her mother, and stands up. "Shall we go through to the living room now, so Joséphine can meet her grandfather?"

"Of course." Her grandmother takes Joséphine's hand. "But be prepared. He can get quite confused." She leads them through to the living room, where an old man sits in an armchair, a newspaper lying on his lap. He looks up with large brown eyes.

"Isabelle's come to visit." Joséphine's grandmother approaches him, bending down to shout in his ear.

He nods, and Isabelle leans down to kiss him on his mottled cheek. Then she stands back. "I've brought someone to see you." His eyes immediately move to Joséphine, focusing on her, fixing her with a hard steely stare. "This is Joséphine." Isabelle smiles a strained smile. "Your granddaughter."

Joséphine wasn't expecting her to tell him this much. She looks down at the floor, feeling self-conscious under his scrutiny, wondering if he might imagine she's Isabelle's child. He tries to stand, but his legs are so thin, they hardly seem able to support him. Her grandmother steps forward, taking one arm while Isabelle holds the other, and together they help him up.

"Come here!" he shouts. "Let me see you."

Tentatively, Joséphine takes a step nearer, afraid of his large eyes, which seem out of proportion with his small frail body. It makes her feel awkward and clumsy. His breath wheezes in his chest as he studies her. "This is my granddaughter, eh?" He looks over at his wife. "Do I just have the one grandchild?"

"Yes."

"What did you say her name was?"

"Joséphine," his wife says quietly.

"Élise," he murmurs. "Yes. I see her in you." He stretches out a shaky hand as though he wants to touch her, but it doesn't quite reach her. "You have the same…" He trails off, coughing into a cotton handkerchief. Then abruptly he stops and looks up, his eyes alert. "I hope you have a better head than she did. She was always so…so headstrong. Got her into trouble in the end. I knew it would." He squints as he looks into her eyes. "You have your father's eyes. I've never forgotten his eyes."

"But you never met him, Papa." Isabelle steps forward, touching his shoulder.

Confusion swims in his eyes and he frowns. Then the frown disappears, and he laughs. Falling back into his chair, his laughter turns to wheezing.

Isabelle disappears, returning with a glass of water. She passes it to him, and the loose skin on the back of his hands trembles as he takes the glass, an awkward silence filling the room while he takes a sip. He swallows loudly, his Adam's apple moving up and down. "It was a long time ago." He speaks up. "But I've never forgotten."

"What, Papa?" Isabelle grips his shoulder.

"Do you remember?" He raises his voice, looking at his wife. "When I came back?"

"Yes," she answers. "I remember. You were so thin and so tired, I hardly recognized you."

"Yes! The damn Boches tried to kill me."

He turns back to Joséphine, his eyes fixing on her again. "He had those same blue eyes. Just like yours."

Joséphine's grandmother steps forward. "Who?" Her voice is sharp. "Who had the same blue eyes?"

The sharpness of her voice makes him jump. "Who?" He sounds unsure of himself as though he's losing track of his thoughts. Then his eyes light up. "Her father." He stares at Joséphine. "Her father."

Chapter Fifty

Joséphine

Joséphine puts her hand over her chest. It feels like her grandfather reached right inside her and wrapped his cold withered fingers around her heart.

"*Mais c'est pas possible!*" Her grandmother says in a half whisper. "You can't have seen him!"

"I met him!" he shouts, turning back to his wife. "He came here!"

"He couldn't have come here!" she shouts. "He was dead!"

Joséphine's world is slipping away. She doesn't understand how he could have met her father. No one does. "When?" Joséphine asks. "When did he come here?"

"Let me think." He frowns again, a deep crease appearing between his eyebrows. "It was wintertime, after Christmas. You were away." He looks at his wife. "In Brittany. He came here, looking for Élise."

"What are you talking about?" Mamyne's voice cracks.

The old man makes a sweeping movement with his hand as though brushing away her words. "You never listen to me." He slumps heavily back into his chair as though all his energy has left him.

Joséphine crouches down and puts her hand on the old man's knee. "Can you remember the year?"

"After the war. Two years." He pauses. "Or maybe three. It was a long time ago. I can't remember exactly."

Joséphine's grandmother stumbles backward, holding out her arms as though groping for support. Isabelle puts her arms around her mother.

The old man looks at them both. "For God's sake, what's wrong with you women?" He sighs, turning back to Joséphine. "He had bright blue eyes. *Putain de Boche.* I sent him packing. Lucky for him I didn't kill him."

Joséphine swallows as she stares at her grandfather. "That was my father." *He hadn't died!* He'd been alive then. He might still be alive. This thought sends a ripple of shock down her spine, spreading through her whole body as though someone has just picked her up, shaken her around, and replaced her back on the ground—a different person.

"Yes! Your father! The Boche! I told him Élise had been shot! Served the bastard right. He left after that. Never saw him again."

Isabelle turns to face him. "How could you?" she shouts. "Do you know what you've done?"

Joséphine's grandmother extracts herself from Isabelle's arms and takes a step nearer to her husband. She's trembling and her face is red. "You told him Élise was dead?"

"Yes!" he shouts. "Then all those damned letters stopped coming."

"What letters? What letters?" his wife shouts.

His shoulders slump, and he leans back in the chair as if this conversation has completely drained him.

"What letters?" Joséphine repeats.

The old man shakes his head. "No letters. I'm mixing everything up."

Joséphine's grandmother sinks onto the couch. "What have you done? What have you done?"

He shakes his head, the loose flesh on his cheeks wobbling. "Women!" he shouts. "What's wrong with you? Always making a drama out of nothing. You should have been there! You should have seen what they did to us." He closes his eyes as if it's all too much for him.

Isabelle grabs Joséphine's arm and pulls her up. "Two years after the war. He could still be alive!"

The blood throbs loudly in Joséphine's ears. Her father could be out there. Anywhere. "What letters is he talking about?"

"I don't know." Isabelle squeezes Joséphine's arm. "Leave him for a minute. He's exhausted."

Joséphine watches the old man's chest rise and fall as if the effort of breathing is too much. His eyes are closed, and he looks like he's fallen asleep. But she's impatient. "My father must have written letters. He must have written to Maman."

Isabelle nods but doesn't say a word.

Joséphine swallows painfully. If they can find the letters, they'll know his story.

Chapter Fifty-One

Paris, May 1963

Joséphine

"We have his name. The Red Cross will be able to find him." Joséphine thinks she can track him down without the letters, and a thrill of excitement ripples down the back of her neck. She hesitates: but why didn't her mother try to find him? "Why didn't Maman look for him after the war?" Joséphine's voice feels small and distant to her ears— timid-sounding, as though she shouldn't be asking such questions, as though she has no right to ask.

Her grandmother shakes her head. "We thought he'd been killed. We were sure of it. When they took him away...the violence. It was frightening. And she never heard from him again."

Sharp, hard coughing coming from the living room resonates through to the kitchen. "You stay here," Joséphine's grandmother says. "I'll go."

The violence. At the same time as Joséphine wants to learn the truth, she is afraid. What might her father have done? What might he have suffered? But her desire to know him is stronger than anything else, and now she's this close, her impatience grows. She gets up and walks to the living room, peeping from behind the door. Her grandmother is passing her grandfather a glass of water, wrapping his fingers around the glass. She's surprised at the tenderness in the gesture. "You drifted off," she hears her say. "You were just telling us about those letters."

"Letters?" He grips her hand. "Did I tell you about them?"

"Yes, you did." She strokes his bald head. "The letters from Joséphine's father. Where did you say you put them?"

"Put them?" he repeats, shaking his head. Joséphine stops breathing, terrified he won't remember where they are, or won't tell. Or worse, that he destroyed them. "Yes," he says so quietly she can only just hear. "I put them away."

"That's what you said," her grandmother lies. "Where did you put them?"

He frowns at her, as he digs under his shirt with his leathery hands, lifting out a key on a piece of string. He stares at the key. "I had to hide them." He wraps his fingers around the key. "I had to, or you would have given them to her."

"Yes," she coaxes him. "You were protecting your family."

He nods. "Yes. Yes, I was." But even Joséphine can hear the doubt and confusion in his voice.

Gently Mamyne takes the key out of his hands and lifts the string over his head. "Is this the key to your drawer, next to the bed?"

He nods, slumping back in his chair, letting out a long breath, as though relieved of a great weight.

Joséphine's grandmother walks toward the door. Joséphine steps back, letting her out. "Were you listening?"

"Yes." Joséphine's heart beats erratically, like a trapped bird's wings. She follows her grandmother into the bedroom. With trembling fingers, her grandmother inserts the key, twisting it to open the wooden drawer. Joséphine holds her breath. Light blue envelopes lie scattered. They all bear the King of England's head on the stamp. Joséphine leans forward, running her hands over them, knowing that here lies the story of her father. She strokes them, as though she's discovered something precious.

Her grandfather's rasping breath breaks through the silence. He's standing in the doorway. His whole body is shaking, and he's looking at her with uncomprehending eyes, as if he can't remember who she is or what she's doing there.

"Élise." He stares at Joséphine. "I hid them for your own good." He frowns, his forehead collapsing into deep lines, and then he shakes his head. "Couldn't have a Boche in the family."

Chapter Fifty-Two

Paris, May 1963

Joséphine

The hatred of all things German that Joséphine's grandfather has harbored in his heart must have been all-consuming, and anything that fell in its path was just collateral damage. Joséphine *is* collateral damage. Her mother too.

She lies awake that night, thinking about all those letters, hidden for years; letters that could have found her father, that could have reunited her mother with him. What *is* in those letters? They're in a large brown envelope at the bottom of her suitcase, ready to take home to her mother. But what if she opened one? The last one. There might be an address inside; a clue as to whether her father is still alive, even where he might be. Doesn't she deserve to know? Isn't this her right?

Pushing the sheets aside, she lifts herself off the couch, and in the dark, feels her way along the wall, fumbling for the light switch. Once the room is flooded with light, she walks toward the case. She opens it, and her hands dig in greedily, pulling out the large envelope. She tips it up, scattering the thin blue envelopes across her bed, then she checks the postmarks and puts them in chronological order. The first one is dated May 14, 1945, just a month after she was born, six days after the Germans surrendered. And the last one is dated January 15, 1948. Nearly three years of letters. One hundred and one in total. Each letter is a single sheet of very thin paper, folded on itself to make the envelope, as light as possible for airmail. There's no way she can open one and close it again without ripping it. She collects them together and stuffs them back in the envelope.

When Joséphine wakes the next morning, Isabelle is sitting in the armchair, sipping a bowl of coffee. She stands and kisses Joséphine. "Coffee?"

Joséphine stretches her arms high above her head and yawns. "Yes, please." She follows Isabelle into the kitchen.

"Today I thought I'd take you to the Tuileries. We can walk through the gardens to the Louvre." Isabelle pours her a coffee. "Do you want to see the *Mona Lisa*?"

"The *Mona Lisa*?" Joséphine couldn't care less about the *Mona Lisa* anymore. "I'm not really in the mood for sightseeing. I'd like to get back and give the letters to Maman." Joséphine needs to know what's in them.

"But you've hardly seen Paris!" Isabelle looks disappointed. "You can't go back already. Those letters have waited this long. They can wait another day or two. Your mother won't be back till Saturday anyway."

"I need to get to the bottom of this." Joséphine feels bad disappointing her aunt, but she can't stop thinking about what might be in those letters; on the other hand she can't open them till the weekend. "My grandfather's completely crazy, isn't he? And cruel. He kept them apart."

"He suffered. And he was angry. You have to remember what he went through. He was a prisoner for three years. It certainly didn't improve him." She turns to the stove, pouring the heated milk into Joséphine's coffee. Joséphine takes it from her, and they go back to the living room, where they sit in the armchairs, their feet curled under them. The picture of her grandfather is vivid in Joséphine's mind; his large unfocusing eyes, his deep frowns, the confusion, the shouting. To lie like that, to pretend his own daughter was dead. How could he have done that?

"Please don't go back yet, Joséphine. You should be here enjoying Paris, not worrying about what happened so long ago. It's all in the past." Isabelle looks at Joséphine with pity. "I know you want to find out about your father, but you'll have plenty of time for that later."

"I need to know if he's alive or not."

"I'm sorry to be so harsh, but it's too late, isn't it? He wasn't there when you were growing up."

"No! It's not too late." Unexpected tears fill her eyes. No one seems to understand how she feels.

"I'm so sorry." Isabelle puts her coffee on the side table and takes Joséphine's from her, putting it down too, then she wraps an arm around Joséphine's shoulders, squeezing her tight. "I'm being insensitive. Of course, this has turned everything upside down. If you want to go home, we'll find you a train. Paris can wait."

"Thank you," Joséphine murmurs, gathering herself together and wiping away her tears. She disengages herself from Isabelle. "I could go back Friday."

Isabelle smiles and kisses her on the cheek. "Yes, that's much better. Don't go rushing off when you've only just got here."

"No one talks about what happened, do they? During the war." Joséphine still wants to talk about it; she can barely envisage what it must have been like, how it must have affected people.

Isabelle sighs as though this isn't the conversation she wants to be having. "There was too much we wanted to forget. And this is a new era. We have so much freedom. You can't begin to imagine what it was like back then." She lowers her voice. "We were reduced to second-class citizens. Worse than second-class citizens. We had no rights. We were always hungry, but the worst thing was the fear. We could be arrested for nothing, or just on a suspicion. We were just grateful we weren't Jewish." She pauses. "Have you ever asked your mother what she did during the war?"

"Apart from sleeping with the enemy?"

"You haven't spoken to her about it, have you?"

"She never wanted to talk about it."

"You should ask her. Ask her when you get back."

Chapter Fifty-Three

Brittany, June 1963

Élise

I wake with a start. It's that recurring dream again. The one where I can't find Joséphine anywhere. I'm running around and around the rocks, desperately searching for her, but each time I think I've found her, there's only a dark empty place in the shadow of the rocks. I cry out her name, but it's lost in the wind. It's the cry that brings me back to the real world, and I wake with her name dying on my lips.

Of course, I'm terrified I'm losing her. It's a deep-seated dread that comes from when she was only a baby, and I had to leave her every week. She had to learn from a young age how to live without me. Maybe she just became too good at it. I wish she needed me more. She means everything to me; she's my whole world.

The seagulls are squawking loudly, and I know I won't sleep again, so I slip out of bed and go down to the kitchen. Monsieur Beaufort is already up, making himself some toast.

"Saturday," he states as though I didn't know. "I can give you a lift to the station at twelve today."

When I get to Lannion, Soizic is waiting in her usual spot outside the station. I open the door and climb into the passenger seat.

"Élise," she says before starting up the motor. A cold dread spreads through me on hearing the heavy emphasis she puts on my name. "Something happened this week."

"What?" The sense of dread grows.

"Joséphine found her birth certificate."

"What?" The sense of dread solidifies into a hard lump in the pit of my stomach. "How?" Oh my God, how could I have been so stupid, not to see this coming.

"She went looking for it. You should have hidden it better."

"She saw her father's name." Waves of guilt and fear wash through me as I imagine her shock. "Is she all right? What did she say?"

"She's upset."

"She must hate me!" What an idiot I'd been, hiding the truth for so long.

"I told her you were going to tell her—that it was me who stopped you." She pauses, her hand on the ignition, but she doesn't start the engine. "There's more, Élise. She went to Paris. She went to see Isabelle. She's already back."

Paris? Already back? How could all this have happened in five days? "You let her go to Paris?" It sounds like an accusation, and it is.

"I couldn't stop her. You know what she's like."

"I should have told her ages ago." I bite my bottom lip hard. "I should never have listened to you."

"It was impossible." Soizic shakes her head as though

trying to convince herself. "We did the right thing. You'd have been ostracized, and Joséphine—look at how they treated that poor child, Albert; even the teachers ignored him, or punished him for nothing. The shame would have been unbearable."

There it is again, that word for what I was made to feel. *La honte.* The shame that followed me here from Paris. The shame that made me lie to my daughter, that made me deny her her father. I hate myself for succumbing to it, for letting it run my life.

"And what would have been the point?" Soizic continues. "He never came back, did he? You were left to face it all on your own."

"That wasn't his fault!"

"He should have been more careful. He should have taken greater care with you."

"No! I should have taken greater care of him. It was my fault. All my fault." I've made a mess of everything, and now I'm afraid I'm about to lose my daughter.

Soizic looks at me for a long moment. "You have to forgive yourself, Élise."

"What?" How can she talk to me about forgiveness? "Let's go," I urge. "I need to see her." I long to hold Joséphine in my arms, with an ache that's physical.

Soizic starts the engine and pulls away. My hands are clasped tight on my lap, bony white knuckles looking up at me. My need to be with Joséphine is urgent, but Soizic is driving so slowly, as though she doesn't want to get home. A pregnant silence fills the small space between us, and the ball of fear in the pit of my stomach grows.

"Is there anything else you want to tell me, Soizic?" I ask.

"Joséphine met her grandfather."

"*Quoi!* What on earth for?" I picture him now, screaming obscenities at her. Isabelle should have known better than to take her there.

"She wanted to meet him." She glances sideways at me. "I should let Joséphine tell you."

"Tell me what? What's happened?"

Soizic turns her eyes back to the road and stares resolutely ahead. "Let's wait till we get home."

"Please, just tell me."

"*Bien*, it might be better if you're prepared."

Her words send a shudder down my spine. "Prepared for what?"

"Joséphine discovered some letters."

"What letters?"

Soizic lets out a long breath as she changes down gear, taking the next corner. "Letters from...from her father. To you."

"Sébastian? What are you talking about? There were no letters. He never wrote."

"He did." She states it simply, her eyes focused on the road.

My heart flutters wildly, words clumping together in my throat, suffocating me.

"He wrote to you, but your father got to the letters before anyone saw them. He hid them."

"But I thought he was dead!" My voice comes out high-pitched and frantic. I try to breathe. "Stop the car!" I scream. I want to jump out. I want to run.

"Calm down. I'll pull over."

I make myself go numb while she looks for somewhere to stop. She pulls into a small track leading to a farm. As soon as she stops, I throw the door open and rush out, gasping for air. "I thought he was dead!" I scream.

I'm aware of Soizic standing nearby. She touches my shoulder, but I bat her hand away. "Is he not dead?" I scream at her.

"We don't know. We haven't opened the letters yet. They're addressed to you. Joséphine has them." Soizic speaks in short sentences, as though these things cannot be linked.

"Is he alive?" I ask, more to myself than Soizic. "Is he alive?" A burning desire to know fills me, taking over from all my fear, all my anger. "I need to see the letters." I step back toward the car. "Now."

We drive the next few minutes in silence, while I try to take it in. If he wrote letters, he didn't die. "My father hid the letters?" Can that really be true?

Soizic puts her hand on my knee, her eyes focusing on the road. "I'm sorry, I shouldn't have told you. I should have waited till we got home."

Tears stream down my face. "I didn't look for him! I didn't look for him," I repeat, more to myself than Soizic. Guilt and sorrow wash over me like a wave pulling me down under the water. I can hardly breathe, thinking about it. I bend forward, laying my head on my lap.

Chapter Fifty-Four

Brittany, June 1963

Élise

"Élise." Soizic's voice is full of concern. "We're nearly there."

I lift my head up. How will I hold myself together?

We turn into the drive. Joséphine is standing there, the wind whipping round her, blowing her fair hair off her face. She looks so pale and fragile standing there in a faded summer dress. In her hand she's holding a large brown envelope. The letters are in there. I know they are.

My heart pounding, I open the door and step out of the car. "I'm sorry, Joséphine." My hand hovers in the space between us, wanting desperately to reach out, to touch her, to hold her, to see what's in the envelope. But she recoils from me, fury burning in her eyes.

"Why didn't you tell me?" Her words are sharp, but I feel the hurt behind them.

"I wanted to! I wanted to, Joséphine." My words come out in gasps. They don't tell her what I want to say; how desperate I'd been to speak the truth, how hiding it had eaten me up from inside.

"You should have." She states it simply, as though it would have been that simple. She can't understand how it was for me, for all of us.

My eyes leave her. I stare at the envelope in her hand. She lifts it up but doesn't give it to me. "Did Soizic tell you about the letters?"

I bite my bottom lip hard and nod, as though our roles have been reversed, and I'm the child now.

"I knew she would." She hands me the envelope. Then she steps back, scratching her forehead with her little finger, just as she used to do when she was small and confused about something. "It seems this family has even more secrets." Her eyes sweep over the envelope.

I turn it over in my hands. I feel the life vibrating inside it; the answers to the questions I've been asking myself ever since that early morning they took Sébastian away. I look back at Joséphine, but her eyes are blank. I'm desperate to open the envelope, but at the same time afraid.

"Élise." Soizic speaks from behind me. "Why don't you go inside and open them upstairs."

"Go on then," Joséphine says. "Go and open them. It's none of my business, after all."

I hear her pain. "Come with me, Joséphine. We can open them together." I hold the envelope tight against my chest with one hand, and in the other I take Joséphine's hand. It feels stiff and resistant, but she doesn't pull away. "These letters are addressed to me, but they belong to both of us. It's not just my story. It's yours too." I feel her hand soften. There should be no more secrets between us, and I want us to do this together, to find out the truth together. We walk into the cottage, Soizic following behind.

"I'll get lunch." Soizic stays in the kitchen, while Joséphine and I go on into the living room. I drop her hand and open the large brown envelope, tipping it upside down onto the coffee table. Thin blue envelopes fall out. There must be more than one hundred.

I stand back, clasping my face, a wail rising from my belly. I bring a finger to my lips, pushing them together, swallowing my howl. A sob escapes.

Thankfully Joséphine stays where she is. If she so much as touches me, I'll lose control. I fall onto my knees in front of the table, but I dare not touch the pieces of fragile paper, afraid that if I do, they'll disappear, that somehow they're not real, that this is all a dream. I stare down at the table, and I feel time shift. The world tilts, and I'm slipping backward. I focus on Joséphine, on her being here with me, and I try to hold on. I reach out a trembling hand, willing her to take it.

She does. And I'm brought back. Clutching her hand, I force words out from my tight throat. "How many?"

"One hundred and one. I'll put them in order." She deftly moves them around the table, laying some on the floor to pick up later and put them back in their correct place. The only sound is my breath pounding in my ears, but her slow measured movements calm me, and I find myself beginning to breathe steadily again.

"This is the first one." Joséphine lifts it up. "It's dated May fourteenth 1945."

"Just a month after you were born," I murmur.

She watches me closely. "It will tell us where he went, what happened to him after the war."

I nod, taking it from her and turning it over in my hand.

It's tightly sealed, and I have to tear the corner so I can slip my finger in and open it. My eyes fly over it, craving to know. Where did he go?

Lise, my love,

I don't get further than the first line. Closing my eyes, I hear his voice whispering in my ear, *Lise*. My body crumples in on itself as though it's lost its core.

"What does it say, Maman?" Joséphine's voice comes crashing through. I look up at her, then back at the letter, wanting and not wanting to read his words, knowing they'll break my heart all over again. I begin to read, first in my head, then aloud to Joséphine.

The war is over! We have peace, and I'm going to find my way back to you. I'm in England. A prisoner, but safe and well. Ma chérie, tell me you're all right. Please tell me they didn't hurt you.

Instinctively my hands fly to my head, grateful he didn't know what they did to me. I carry on reading.

I have been a POW since last September, but I should be released soon, and I'll be on the first boat back to France. Back to you.

Did he really come back for me? A tear escapes from the corner of my eye and slides down my cheek toward my mouth. I wipe it away with my finger. I should have waited for him in Paris. Bitter tears of regret and loss slide silently down my cheeks onto the thin paper, smudging the black ink. Through them, I read on.

You are behind every single thought I ever have. Every single thing I ever do. I dream of how I will find you again, how we will be able to love each other freely. This is what makes me want to live.

"But where is he now?" Joséphine wants the facts. She needs to know if she has a father. She hands me another envelope. "Read this one, Maman. It's the last one."

I take it from her and open it.

Part Four

1944

Chapter Fifty-Five

Paris, August 17, 1944

Sébastian

The men held Sébastian tightly as they dragged him out of Élise's apartment. For her sake, he didn't make a sound when they kicked him in the kidneys and thumped him in the face with balled fists. He took it all in silence as they dragged him away, out onto a quiet side street. They were going to shoot him where there would be no witnesses. He closed his eyes when they threw him to the ground, and he prayed, *Please God, keep Élise safe.* A blow to the head came swiftly. He felt himself disappearing.

He woke to find himself on a hard concrete floor. He didn't know how long he'd been lying there, but it felt like a long time. His ribs throbbed painfully, and his eyelids were swollen shut. He didn't bother trying to open them. His hands were tied behind his back and his legs bound together.

Lying on his side, he folded his legs, bringing his knees against his chest. A chill spread through his aching bones, and he began to shiver uncontrollably. The metallic taste of blood made him want to vomit. A door clicked open. Or was it closing? He heard footsteps next to his head, and readied himself for another kicking, but instead someone put something cool against his lips. Water trickled into his mouth, and he tried to swallow it, but his throat was swollen. He spluttered and choked. Arms pulled him up. He managed to swallow, and some of the cool water dripped down the back of his throat. He attempted to open an eye, to see who was next to him, but all he could make out was a blob of brown hair; everything else was fuzzy and blurred. Hands dropped his head back down onto the hard floor, and he felt himself slipping back into oblivion.

When he came to again, he was alone. His shoulders had stiffened up, and he wriggled his wrists, trying to free them from the rope, but the more he twisted, the tighter it became.

Abruptly the door opened, hitting him in the face. He heard a man laugh. Then light came streaming in, burning into his eyes. Strong arms hoisted him up. His ribs throbbed painfully, and his head felt like it had been split with an ax.

"He looks a mess. We should clean him up." Someone pushed him into a chair, but he couldn't sit up. "They shouldn't have beaten him up like this."

"It could have been worse. At least he's alive."

"Yes, we'll still be able to use him. Pascal wants to do a prisoner exchange."

Sébastian's head swam, the men's voices floating around him as though they were coming from another world. He felt himself topple to the side. Hands caught him, and he was held upright as someone wound rope around his body, fixing him to the chair. His ribs throbbed painfully, and he readied himself for the first slap around his face.

But the slap never came. Instead he felt a wet cloth on his face, and the same voice as before spoke.

"She snitched on you, thinking we'd spare her whore of a daughter." He laughed a gruesome, dirty laugh. "Why would we keep a deal with a fucking collabo?"

Élise's mother had handed him over! Waves of anger and deep sadness washed over him; that she would be driven to do that to protect her daughter. He could have told her these bargains were never respected. What would happen to Élise now? He closed his eyes, trying to block out the images of what they might do to her. He no longer cared for himself. Only Élise. *Please don't hurt her,* he begged in his head. *Anything but that.*

They untied him, and left him in the cellar with only one bowl of water, half a dry baguette, and a bucket to pee in. Two days later, they led him through the streets, a gun pointed at the back of his head. His ribs ached, and a pain shot through his side like a knife twisting in. Every step made him wince, and he tried to focus only on the ground beneath his feet, not on the people in the streets. Frenchmen were busy pulling up paving slabs, building barricades, but they stopped when they saw him being marched past. "*Sale Boche! Putain de Nazi!*" they shouted.

They led him in through a side door of the Hôtel de Ville, where they threw him into a room with a load of other German soldiers. They left them there with no food or water, while shots rang out and the fighting went on without them out in the streets of Paris. The smell of stale sweat, urine, and foul breath reached his nostrils, making him want to vomit again. He buried his nose in his inner elbow, trying to quell the feeling, holding a picture of Élise in his head. He saw her in men's pants, a thick brown belt, shirt loosely tucked in, scratching her forehead with her little finger, a smile playing on her lips, as if in holding this picture in his mind, he could make it come true. He blocked other thoughts, praying that they wouldn't hurt her, now they had him.

He must have slept. He didn't know how long, nor how many days had passed. The next thing he knew, five FFI men marched in, holding bottles and waving rifles.

One of them raised his bottle, drinking straight from it. *"Vive la France!"*

Another held up his, toasting, *"Vive la France!"* They jeered at the prisoners. *"Putains de Nazis!"* They put their arms around each other as they sang "La Marseillaise." *"Formez vos bataillons, marchons, marchons!"*

The German prisoners remained still and silent, not wanting to incur wrath from the drunken Frenchmen. Sébastian let their slurred words wash over him, his swollen eyelids beginning to close again. Just as he was about to let go, an explosion shook the building. The drunken FFI men stopped their singing and threw themselves down. Sébastian, already on the floor, pulled himself up squinting, as he looked out of the window. Red flames rose into the black night sky, streaking it as though the heavens themselves were bleeding.

"Fucking bastards!" a French voice shouted out. "They're bombing us! They're bombing Paris!"

A boot landed hard in Sébastian's stomach. He rolled over, expecting more blows. But instead, he heard the men leaving, the door slamming closed behind them, the key turning in the lock.

For a moment, no one in the room moved, then an SS

officer stood up. "It's not over yet!" He held his head high, his voice ringing out loud and clear. "We still have our soldiers all over Paris." Sébastian's heart sank. He'd dreaded the Nazis planting explosives, knowing only too well they were capable of it.

"It's too late," one of the men sitting on the floor mumbled. "There's no point. We should surrender."

The SS officer approached the man, standing over him. "Traitor! I'll have you court-martialed if you say another word like that."

The man laughed loudly and cynically. "Court-martialed? Don't you get it? You're a fucking prisoner! We're all prisoners. It's over! We've lost!"

The SS officer pulled his foot back, ready to let it fly into the man's stomach. But the man was quicker, grabbing his boot. The officer hit the ground with a horrible thud. The man jumped on top of the officer, holding his face between his hands, screaming at him. "We've lost! We've lost the fucking war!"

The other men stared—too tired, too hungry to join in. Sébastian turned away.

The door was suddenly thrown open. Two FFI men walked in. The man leapt off the officer.

"Ten more prisoners!" One of them waved his rifle around. "Just SS this time!" The other FFI man moved among them, checking out their collar badges for the SS insignia: two jagged black lines, like streaks of lightning.

"Where are you taking us?" one of the officers dared ask.

"Prisoner exchange." The FFI man laughed a dirty, mean laugh. "If you're lucky."

For the next few days the remaining prisoners were left with no news. Sébastian kept away from the other men, nursing his broken body, trying to overcome the pain and hunger that swept through him in vicious waves. They were given water and bread, but Sébastian didn't have the energy or the strength to fight for his share. One of the prisoners noticed and brought him some water. "Drink," he said. "Or you'll die."

Sébastian had to get back to Élise. He couldn't die, so he drank. "Thank you," he murmured. On the next night, even through the thick stone walls of the Hôtel de Ville, Sébastian could hear the crowds outside going wild. Then they went quiet while one loud voice spoke out. He couldn't hear the exact words, but he guessed it was de Gaulle. Sébastian looked around at his fellow prisoners, at their grimy, weary faces as they closed their eyes. He pictured Élise out there, celebrating, praying it was true.

The crowd cheered again. The speech must have come to an end. Sébastian's eyelids lay heavy over his eyes, and he let himself drift off to sleep.

Two days later, five men with rifles entered the room. "*C'est l'heure!* You're being resettled." The shortest one stared at them coldly. "That's the word you used, isn't it?" He put his face up to one of the prisoners, jeering at him. "Isn't that what you said, when you sent thousands to your camps?" The Frenchman poked his rifle under the prisoner's chin. "We'd better get our people back!"

"*Allez*, let's go!" Another Frenchman poked the butt of his rifle into Sébastian's back, shoving him over to the door. The other Frenchmen pushed the group forward, and they shuffled along, out of the room, down the stairs, into the daylight. With their hands on their heads, they were herded through the streets, unable to defend themselves as people spat at and cursed them. One of the jeering crowd approached, putting his face right up to Sébastian's, so close Sébastian could smell the venomous hatred on his breath. *"Sale Boche!"* The man hissed then spat in his face, his spit landing on Sébastian's nose. Sébastian made no attempt to wipe it away. Then a woman walked up to him, slapping him hard round the face. His throat was parched, he was weak with hunger, and the hot sun burned into his skin, but he looked out for Élise. If only he could see her. If only he knew she was unharmed.

They were marched through the streets until they came to the Vélodrome d'Hiver, the enormous indoor cycling stadium where thousands of Jewish prisoners had been held during the massive round-up of '42. It seemed fitting that the German POWs should be brought here now. A hush fell upon the large group as they were led into the stadium, where they sat or fell wherever they found themselves, their uniforms now disheveled and filthy. Gone were the smart, proud soldiers who'd marched down the Champs-Élysées four years ago. They'd been reduced to a quivering, frightened mass of weak and exhausted prisoners.

Sébastian's throat ached with thirst, and he tried in vain to swallow. He had to get water. Pushing himself onto his feet, he ignored the spinning in his head as he put one foot in front of the other, aware that he was staggering rather than walking. He held his head up, looking for a bucket of water, or better, a tap. But as his eyes scanned the huge velodrome, all he saw were thousands of desperate, defeated men.

Four days later, Sébastian and the rest of the German POWs were herded out of the velodrome and shoved onto busses that drove them out of Paris. Sébastian was one of the last to be pushed aboard, and there were no seats left. Jammed up against the other prisoners, the smell of stale sweat reached the back of his nose.

"What do you reckon?" an officer croaked at no one in particular. "Russia, Britain, France, or even America?"

"Better hope it's not Russia," a tired voice answered as the bus started up, jolting everyone forward.

"Or Britain," someone else said.

"We'll probably die on that putrid island," another man moaned. "They'll have no food. They'll leave us to starve."

"Or work us to death," the officer added.

"For fuck's sake!" someone shouted. "It's not over yet. This is just Paris! We still hold the rest of France!"

Sébastian closed his eyes, distancing himself from this crazy talk. Gradually, the bus went quiet as it rumbled along the roads taking them to God knows where. Some began to doze off where they were standing; exhausted, starving and thirsty. Sleep was their only escape now.

Eventually the bus came to a halt at the port of Le Havre, and they were herded out onto one of the Liberty ships. Sébastian felt small and insignificant as he stared at the enormous liner, and he mounted the gangplank with heavy legs, knowing that every step he took was taking him a step further from Élise. He paused, turning around for one last look at France. "I'll come back, Lise. I promise."

Chapter Fifty-Six

England, September 1944

Sébastian

Sébastian's knees had seized up after standing in line for three hours. He shook his legs out as he gazed at row upon row of German POWs on the racecourse at a place called Kempton Park. Ragged, dirty uniforms hung off the exhausted prisoners; some had kitbags, others cardboard boxes tied with string. Sébastian couldn't imagine how they'd managed to keep hold of their belongings through all the chaos of the last few weeks. They were all mixed up: officers, Wehrmacht, SS. Many looked down at their feet, others at each other, hoping to find a face they knew; officers seeking each other out, SS searching out SS. Sébastian stared blankly ahead, not wishing to make eye contact with anyone. The vinegary, acidic smell of filthy clothes and unwashed bodies grew unbearable as the morning dragged by. The track was eerily quiet, only a few hushed words reaching his ears, the atmosphere hanging thick and heavy, a light drizzle floating around them. Sébastian foresaw the endless waiting that lay ahead of him now. How long would it be before he'd have news of Élise? How would he be able to contact her?

He stared at the large makeshift tent he was shuffling toward, then there was more waiting as he lined up in front of a long wooden table where British army personnel were taking down details.

"Name?" The army man didn't look up when Sébastian approached the table.

"Kleinhaus, Sébastian."

"Date of birth?"

"Twenty-fourth June, 1920."

"Hitler Youth then." It was more of a statement than a question, and Sébastian nodded.

"Speak up."

"Yes, sir."

Sébastian left that tent, joining the line for the next, where they had to strip and shower. Sébastian couldn't help staring at the SS tattoo on the underarms of some of the men. One of them caught his eye. He took a step nearer Sébastian, holding out his wet arm. "Yes. SS!" he whispered threateningly in Sébastian's ear. "It's not over yet."

Sébastian looked him in the eye, refusing to be intimidated. "It won't be long now though," he answered, holding eye contact.

Anger flashed in the SS man's eyes. "We've only lost a battle. We haven't lost the war!" He poked his finger into Sébastian's chest. "And you'd do best to show your loyalty."

Sébastian took a step back, turning away. There was no point engaging with madmen.

Naked still, they were given a medical check-up, then

doused with DDT powder and gentian violet for lice. Brown POW uniforms with yellow diamond patches sewn on the back of the jackets and the trouser legs were thrust into their arms. Sébastian had just exchanged one uniform for another, and it made him feel like a cog in a machine again. Would he ever be free?

He spent the next five days thinking of Élise as he was shunted from one line to another, exhaustion and worry making his bones ache. He wished he had a photo, but all he had were memories; Élise staring defiantly at him, daring him to talk. Élise, her eyes wide with fear as she followed him out of the Gestapo headquarters. Élise lying in his bed, her head on his chest, running her fingers lightly down his ribs. Élise begging him to come home with her. He always stopped there, at that fatal moment.

On the fifth day he was put on a train to Northwich, wherever that was. He stared out of the window at the narrow terraced houses with tiny yards, backing onto the railway line, hardly a tree in sight. It all looked so tired and gray. As the train chugged into the countryside, the space opened out, and he saw large fields, separated by thick hedges, rays of sunlight breaking through the heavy cloud, illuminating streaks of green. Some of the men had already formed groups. Like it or not, they'd need each other, but Sébastian wasn't ready for that. He just wanted to be left alone.

When the train finally ground to a halt, the prisoners were marched out of the station toward a waiting lorry. A group of local lads hissed and shouted at them. "Bloody Krauts! Got what you deserve now!" Spit landed on Sébastian's cheek, and as he wiped it away, he saw a small boy in his mother's arms waving a British flag.

The lorry drove them to a mansion set in large grounds, where concrete huts with corrugated iron roofs had been erected. A smartly dressed British officer addressed the prisoners, an interpreter standing next to him, translating into German. "Welcome to Marbury Hall," the interpreter said, loudly and clearly. The prisoners stood by silently, and Sébastian waited for the officer to bark orders at them, but instead, he adopted a different tone, more like that of a headmaster than a commandant. "You men have only ever known dictatorship. And I feel sorry for you. But here, in Great Britain, you will learn about democracy."

Some of the prisoners looked at each other, lifting a cynical eyebrow. Sébastian stared blankly ahead, knowing that once this little speech was over, and the men were left to themselves, it was the Nazis he'd have to watch out for.

Indeed, once they were assigned to their camps, Sébastian's worst fears were confirmed; his was the west camp. For the pro-Nazis because he'd been part of the Hitler Youth.

As soon at the men were let out to wander around the camp, some sauntered over to the barbed-wire perimeter fence, greeting *Kameraden* with the Nazi salute. Sébastian closed his eyes, dreading what would happen if he was greeted by an SS officer. He wished he could have told the commandant they'd put him in the wrong camp. It was madness putting all the Nazis together. Fuck! How was he going to survive?

That evening they were put into huts of fifty, camp beds in two rows, and at the far end five tables with benches. When they sat down for dinner, two of them were sent into the kitchen to fetch the food and a large pot of tea. Acutely aware that he was surrounded by Nazis, Sébastian stared down at the table, trying to make himself invisible. That night he hardly slept a wink, hushed conversations reaching his ears, secret little groups already forming.

The next day everyone was put to work building more huts. It was a relief to be busy, and as he mixed cement with another prisoner, he took a deep breath, looking around.

"Raining again," his fellow prisoner commented, gazing at the gray sky.

Sébastian studied him. He didn't look mean; it might be okay to talk to him. "Looks like it. How long have you been here?"

"Two weeks. They picked me up in Ostend. I was on the run." He leaned against the cement mixer. "It was a relief in a way. I was starving. But I wasn't expecting this." He glanced around. "It's fucking scary."

Sébastian was surprised that he'd openly voiced his fears.

"You should be more careful," the man continued. "You haven't been joining in. You're distant. They don't like that. You'd better watch out or they'll have you in one of their kangaroo courts. They hang people like you."

"What about the guards?"

"They put it down to suicide. They don't care. One less Nazi." He shook his head. "We're fucked."

Another prisoner strode toward them. "*Heil Hitler!*" He raised his arm in salute. Sébastian's new friend lifted his arm in reply.

But Sébastian just stood there staring at the Nazi. He couldn't do it any more. He physically couldn't do it. Not even to stay alive for Élise. For a minute they outstared each other, Sébastian's heart beating hard and fast.

Quick as lightning, the Nazi made a grab for the other prisoner's arm, bending it and twisting it behind the man's back as he got him into an arm hold. "Look and learn!" he shouted over the man's screams. "We'll be coming for you next."

The man's screams grew louder, tearing through Sébastian. This was typical Nazi intimidation; going for someone else and making you watch. Anger and hatred pumped through Sébastian's veins, adrenaline bursting into his heart. He grabbed the shovel from the cement mixer. In one swift movement he brought it behind his head, then down with all his might, whacking the Nazi across the face, catching him off guard. The injured man clutched his head, falling to the ground, blood pouring out from a gash on his cheekbone.

"Fuck! Fuck! What the fuck did you do that for?" the other prisoner shouted.

Sébastian lifted the shovel back up, looking around, ready to defend himself. The rest of them would be after him now.

He was right. A group of about ten prisoners ran at him, their faces red with fury. He stepped back, holding the shovel in front of his face. But the first blow came to his stomach, the second to his kidneys. He closed his eyes, collapsing to the ground.

The guards appeared, shouting and lashing out with truncheons, pushing the prisoners to the ground, knees painfully digging into their backs, handcuffs trapping their wrists. Sébastian expected to be thrown into solitary confinement, but instead, he was dragged into an office.

"You hit a fellow prisoner." The officer sitting on the other side of the desk addressed him in German.

Sébastian was doubled over in agony from the blow to his kidneys and could barely get his words out. "He's a Nazi...sir."

"I know that! That's why he's here. And it's why you're here!"

"I'm not." Sébastian tried to stand up straight.

"Not what?"

"Not a Nazi, sir."

The officer tapped his pen against his forehead. "But you were, weren't you?"

"The Hitler Youth was obligatory, sir."

"And now you want me to believe you're no longer one of them, is that it?"

Sébastian took a painful breath in. "I never wanted to be."

The officer shrugged.

"They'll kill me, sir, if you keep me here."

The officer studied him. "And what makes you think I give a damn?"

"The commandant said he wanted to teach us about democracy." Sébastian found his breath again. "He said we had known nothing except cruel dictatorship. I want to learn, sir." It was the truth. He did want to learn. And he wanted to stay alive to get back to Élise.

The officer sighed. "We put you Nazis together so you could fight it out among yourselves." He paused, putting his hands, palms down, onto his desk as he leaned forward, staring coldly into Sébastian's eyes. "However, we might consider transferring you to another camp."

"Yes please, sir."

"We can't send a load of Nazis back to Germany. It will only start up again. We have a reeducation plan."

"Thank you, sir. Thank you."

"You want to be reeducated, do you?"

"Yes, sir."

"Right then. Ashton-in-Makerfield."

"Sir?"

"Yes?"

"Will you be transferring the other prisoner?"

The officer frowned. "Hans?"

"I don't know his name. The other man. They'll kill him too if you don't."

The officer let out a long breath. "Bloody Nazis. They don't know when to stop."

Chapter Fifty-Seven

Ashton-in-Makerfield, April 1945

Sébastian

Ashton-in-Makerfield gave Sébastian and Hans some much-needed time to heal, and to reflect, as it did for many of the men there. They were given language lessons and encouraged to read in English. Sébastian was glad to put his mind to something and enjoyed the learning, but Hans found it hard. Both of them were billeted out to the Joneses' farm, where they worked all day long, six days a week. The hard physical labor was a good tonic, and things settled down into a routine, with soccer on Sundays.

They'd been there for about eight months and were sitting down to breakfast one of these Sundays when an officer walked in. "Everyone into the film room. Now!"

The prisoners looked up, unused to being shouted at.

"I said now!" The officer marched to the tables. "Get your ass off those chairs!"

The prisoners jumped up and in single file, they followed

him out of their hut, into the long narrow room where they watched films and documentaries. It was already full of men from the other huts, and they sat in silence, guards standing at the end of each row, watching them with cold, stern faces. The atmosphere was tense, and Sébastian guessed one or several of them had done something wrong. He wondered if there had been an attempted escape.

The film reel started with its familiar whirring, but it wasn't a film this time. It was a black-and-white photo. Sébastian's first impression was of skulls with dark hollow eyes. Then he saw dirty gray striped jackets and pants hanging from skeletal bodies. "These are the Jewish prisoners you sent to the camps." A senior guard tapped the projection board with a stick.

There was a collective intake of breath. How was it possible for people to be that thin, and still be alive? Sébastian rubbed his eyes, as though he could erase the image from his mind. A sharp tap from the baton of the guard at the end of the row made him look back up.

"Eyes forward!" another guard shouted.

A feeling of dread spread through Sébastian. There was more to come. The whole room had gone deathly silent, the sound of their breathing too loud. All of them had known what Hitler thought of the Jews—vermin, rats, a scourge on the Aryan race. They'd all attended biology lessons on the superiority of their race and the way it was being contaminated by the Jews. "With Jewish blood dripping from the knife" went one of their songs in the Hitler Youth. So why should they be shocked to see how the Jewish prisoners had been treated? But still, they were.

Sébastian sensed Hans's eyes on him, but he kept his fixed on the screen, holding his breath. When the next photo clicked into place, he saw a large open ditch filled with skeletal bodies. Thousands of them. Sébastian heard more intakes of breath around him. He stole a glance at the other men's faces. Some were tight-lipped, others wiped their eyes, and he thought some were crying.

"What the hell?" Hans murmured, swallowing loudly.

The guard tapped the screen again. "When the Allies liberated the camps, this is what they found. Hundreds of thousands of bodies like this in mass graves."

The third picture showed what looked like large shower blocks.

"What the hell is that?" Hans whispered.

A terrible sense of foreboding seeped through Sébastian.

The next picture showed a shower block again, this time filled with naked dead bodies piled up, one on top of the other. "This is Auschwitz!" The guard shouted. "A death camp! On arrival at this camp many of the prisoners were sent straight to the gas chambers. This is one here. Poisonous gas was released through these outlets." He pointed to what looked like shower heads. "The room was tightly sealed, and they pumped the gas in till all the prisoners were dead." He paused, staring at the men sitting in their neat rows, then he tapped the wall with his baton. "It's what we call mass murder. What the Nazis called *The Final Solution.*"

Sébastian buried his face in his hands, rubbing his fists into his eyes till they hurt. He'd rather physical pain than the pain that pierced him now. What was the difference between a Nazi and himself? He remembered the "action days" when the Gestapo and SS would descend onto the streets. "*Rein!* Get inside! Close your shutters!" Everyone would run inside, terrified, closing their doors behind them while Jews were dragged from their homes and thrown into the waiting trucks. One day, Sébastian had been peeping out through the curtains when he saw them pull old Mr. Baumeister out by his beard; the man who used to give him money to run and get bread for him, the man who told him he'd be a fine athlete one day. He never saw Mr. Baumeister again, and when he'd asked about him, his father told him to shut up. When the Jewish children had disappeared from his class, where did he think they were going? It was something many of them had chosen not to think about. After all, they were powerless against the Nazi machine.

The photos changed life at the camp. The guards stopped being so friendly, looking away now from the prisoners instead of engaging with them, their lips tightly closed. And a week later when they were driven to the farm where they worked, the locals shouted insults at them. The farmer's wife, Mrs. Jones, stopped making them tea in the afternoon. A collective sense of guilt spread among many of the prisoners, even the young lads, who were only eighteen or nineteen and had only known dictatorship and war. Sébastian's yearning for Élise grew more intense than ever. The thought of her alone, learning of the horror that had gone on, then imagining he'd been killed or sent to Russia, filled him with worry. He had to get out soon, he had to find her.

Chapter Fifty-Eight

Ashton-in-Makerfield, September 1945

Sébastian

Germany finally surrendered on May 8. And it was now September. But Sébastian was still a prisoner. He'd thought POWs were supposed to be released once hostilities were over. He had to get back to France, to Élise. He'd written to her every week for the last four months, but had had no reply. He'd tried Yannick Le Bolzec too, but had no reply from him either. He needed to find out what had happened.

"Coming for a game of soccer?" Hans nudged him.

"Later. Library first. I'm going to look at the papers. You should come too."

"Sure." Hans surprised him. "Why not?" He gulped back his tea. "God, it's bitter."

"It needs sugar. At least put some milk in it."

"I'll never get used to it." Hans stood up. "Come on then, let's go. We've got half an hour before this lot get moving."

The other men were still hunched over their breakfast bowls, slowly munching their way through the bland porridge. Sébastian picked up his empty bowl and dirty cup, taking them into the kitchen. Hans followed.

"See you for the game later," Hans said to his friend on washing-up duty.

"Once I've cleaned up after you lot."

Sébastian and Hans walked out into the sunshine, along to the small library at the back of the British barracks. In reality it was just three shelves containing secondhand books that the locals had donated, and a couple of faded flat cushions on the floor. But they did get the papers. Sébastian picked up *Punch*—one of his favorites with its colorful, funny images that made a mockery of everything. Back in Germany one would have been shot for lesser crimes. He sat down on a flat cushion, bringing his knees to his chest as he opened the paper. "Look here." Sébastian waited for Hans to sit down. "It's incredible."

"What?" Hans crossed his legs, spreading the *Telegraph* out onto the concrete floor.

"They're criticizing their own prime minister."

"Yes, they're allowed to." Hans absentmindedly turned over the first page of his paper. "What do they say?"

"That he should let us POWs go. It's in the Geneva Convention." Sébastian read from the paper. "Prisoners of war should be repatriated once hostilities have ceased."

Hans took a deep breath. "Didn't they end months ago?"

Sébastian read on further. "But the prime minister, Attlee, says it's not a law, it's just, how do you say? Advice— just a guideline." He frowned. "Is that right? Is the Geneva Convention just guidelines?"

"I don't know." Hans shrugged. "I guess so. If that's what it says."

"Attlee says countries that have suffered because of the Nazis have a right to compensation—war reparations. And POW labor is compensation." Sébastian closed the paper.

"What? So we're compensation now." Hans laughed bitterly. "We work too hard. That's our problem. We're too good at following orders." He glanced at Sébastian. "But you know what, I bet the food is better here than we'd be getting in Germany."

"How long can they keep us here?" Sébastian heard the desperation in his own voice. For God's sake, he didn't even know whether Élise was dead or alive. Not a day went by when he didn't think about her, didn't worry about her.

"Hans." Sébastian stood. "You go on ahead without me. I want to ask the commandant something."

"I hope you're not going to start quoting the Geneva Convention at him."

"See you later, Hans." Sébastian left the library and walked over the freshly cut grass to the British barracks, knocking once on the commandant's door.

"Yes?"

Sébastian stepped into the office, giving a brisk nod. "Good morning, sir."

The commandant leaned back in his chair, looking at Sébastian over the top of his spectacles. "What can I do for you?"

"Sir, I have a question. Please."

"Yes?"

"When will we be released, sir?" He shot out the question before he lost his nerve.

Silence filled the room as the commandant stared coldly

at Sébastian. Finally, he spoke. "I have had no instructions regarding your release."

Sébastian gathered his courage. "But, sir, hostilities ended months ago—"

"I'm well aware of that." He cut him off. "But as I said, I haven't received any information regarding your release. Is that all?"

"Do you have any idea, sir?"

"No, I do not." The commandant got up and walked to the other side of the desk, opening the door, making it clear it was time for Sébastian to leave.

"Thank you, sir." Sébastian shot him one last glance before walking away. He no longer felt like playing soccer. Frustration and a feeling of powerlessness seeped through him. He was at the mercy of the British government now, and as fair and friendly as they might seem, he was still their prisoner. His frustration turned to anger, and he began to think like a prisoner. He began to think of escape.

When they worked at the Joneses' farm, they weren't watched all the time. Only Hans and Sébastian had been billeted there, as it was a small farm, and Mr. Jones worked alongside them, but sometimes he needed to go into town for something. But there was still Mrs. Jones, who started coming out again in the afternoon to bring them a cup of tea. And there were the three daughters. They seemed to be outside a lot, putting out washing or just walking through the fields, sometimes chasing each other, or pushing the younger one on a swing hanging from a large oak tree. They often glanced over at Sébastian and Hans, shyly at first, but one of the older two had started to raise her hand in greeting, causing her sisters to laugh. No, it would be no good trying to escape from there in broad daylight; too many eyes were watching them. It would be better to make a break for it at nighttime, under the cover of darkness.

Chapter Fifty-Nine

Ashton-in-Makerfield, December 1945

Sébastian

Sébastian had been hiding a cutlery fork in his shoe for the last few weeks. Whenever he had the chance, he walked around the perimeter of the camp, looking for a place out of sight, where it might be possible to dig under the wire. He'd located a spot behind one of the huts. Every time he walked past, he pretended to be doing up his shoelace, and he had a little dig with the fork. The earth wasn't too heavily packed, and he thought he could dig into it and release the wire. If he left at nighttime when no one was looking, it would give him the whole night to get away. He could cover a distance of about thirty kilometers in that time. Time to get to another village, change clothes, and get on a bus or a train heading south, to the ports. He'd been saving his shillings from the small amount of money they were paid for their work, and he guessed it would be enough to get him some food, maybe even a bus ticket.

He figured Christmas would be the perfect time; the nights were long, and the guards would be in better humor; less vigilant when they'd had a drink or two, getting ready to enjoy the festivities. He'd learned from last Christmas how important it was for the English. He had to give it a go.

So on Christmas Eve, after dinner, when the guards had had a little drink among themselves, Sébastian waited for the right opportunity. He looked over at the door. The guard who usually sat there was at a table instead of at his post, his head bent over a group of prisoners; it looked like he was teaching them the words to "Silent Night." Sébastian glanced around. No one was looking. Casually, he walked to the door.

"Where are you going?" The guard who'd appeared to be engrossed in singing, jumped up.

Sébastian put his hand in his pocket and pulled out a few shillings. "Need a smoke," he said. "Have you got any?"

"Sure." The guard offered him the open packet. "It's Christmas. Just take one."

"Thanks." Sébastian pulled one from the packet and stepped outside. He lit up, wondering if the guard would be waiting for him to come back in. He guessed he would, after all that was his job. So he wandered around for a few minutes, looking around to see who could be watching. The searchlights were left on all night long, but no one was behind them. They weren't expecting anyone to escape. He could use that to his advantage, but it meant he'd have to walk out with nothing but the clothes on his back and the little money in his pocket. He weighed up the risk and quickly decided he had to do it if he wanted to see Élise again.

He walked back into the hut, surprised to see the guard

wasn't there. Glancing around, he realized he wouldn't even stop to think that Sébastian hadn't come back in. He'd forgotten all about him. Quick as lightning, he stepped back outside. He didn't run. If someone stopped him, he would just pretend he needed some air. But nobody stopped him, and he soon came to the wire fence. Using the fork, he tried to dig into the ground; a pathetic idea really, given that the ground was frozen hard. But the wire wasn't buried deep, and he managed to pull it out from the earth. Then, flat on his belly, he slid under.

Once out, he stood up, looking around. He shivered and started running. He'd have to keep moving all night long, getting as far away as possible, and not freezing to death. He ran through the forest, keeping a good but steady pace, heading south. If he could keep this direction, he would get as far away as possible before daybreak. Soon he came to a clearing and a tractor path. He ran along the muddy tracks, thinking that maybe he could even cover forty kilometers before daybreak.

After about two hours he saw some speckled lights ahead. It must be a small hamlet of cottages. Maybe he could pick up a few eggs from a henhouse. He slowed down as he approached from the back of the houses. Then he heard a door open, laughter spilling out as people left by a side door. He crouched down, watching as the door shut and it went dark again. He had a feeling people around here didn't lock their doors. He decided to hang around for a bit, just to see.

It wasn't long before he saw two people come out of a cottage and cross the road. From his hiding place behind a tree, he saw them go into another house. More people appeared, going into the same house. Was it a party? He waited a few minutes. This was his opportunity. Stealthily, he slithered through the grass till he was alongside the house that had just been vacated. Quickly looking around, he dashed across the garden to the front door. He put his hand on the door handle and pushed. It opened. Creeping in, he closed it gently behind him. It was dark in the house, and he felt his way along the wall. He would find a room at the back of the house, where he'd be able to put a light on without it shining out onto the street. He soon came to a half-open door. He slipped through, closing it softly behind him before feeling for a light switch. Suddenly the room was filled with bright light, and he blinked, waiting for his eyes to adjust. When they had, he saw he was in the kitchen. He opened a cupboard, looking for something to eat.

A noise behind him made him freeze.

"What the hell?" A man stood facing him.

Sébastian's stomach jumped into his throat. "I mean you no harm." He put his hands up.

"Hey!" the man shouted loudly. "Get down here, Jeff!"

Sébastian turned and ran. A blow to his back sent him reeling to the ground. A large man jumped on him, pinning him down. "It's a Kraut!" He pulled Sébastian's head back by the tuft of his hair. Out of the corner of his eye Sébastian saw the other man approaching.

A foot landed in his mouth. "This is from my father!"

They rolled him over and kicked him in his ribs. "Hit by one of your Kraut bombs!"

Sébastian tried to curl into a tight ball, to protect himself. But the blows continued to fly. His head spun with pain. He couldn't open his eyes. He felt himself slipping into unconsciousness.

"Okay, that's enough," one of them said. "Let's call the police. They can take him back to that bloody camp."

Chapter Sixty

One Year Later

Ashton-in-Makerfield, December 1946

Sébastian

"It'll be Christmas again soon." Hans attempted some banter as the truck pulled off, taking them to the Joneses' farm. "I wish they'd let us go for Christmas," he continued when Sébastian didn't reply. "I'd love to see my mum's face if I turned up on Christmas Eve."

"Maybe next Christmas." Sébastian sighed. He'd still had no news from Élise. It was slowly killing him.

"You're kidding, right? It won't be long now."

Sébastian didn't answer, he was thinking about last Christmas and his botched escape, after which he'd lost all of his privileges. He was surprised the punishment hadn't been harsher, but the officer in charge had said that his injuries and stay in the hospital had probably taught him what he needed to know.

Hans nudged Sébastian. "Don't look so glum. I bet we'll be home in the new year."

Home. Sébastian found it touching that Hans still thought of home back in Munich. He himself had lost all sense of home. All he could think of was Lise. Wherever she was would be his home. Indeed, maybe home wasn't a place at all, but the people you wanted to be with.

The truck pulled to a stop outside the farm cottage, interrupting his thoughts. Hans and Sébastian jumped out the back and walked directly toward the cowshed where they always began their day's work.

"Sébastian! Hans!" Mr. Jones shouted over to them. "Can we have a word please?"

A word? Sébastian had been in England long enough now to understand that a word meant a whole lot more than just one word and was almost certainly related to something they'd done wrong. They turned around and walked toward the cottage.

"Good morning, Sébastian, Hans." Mr. Jones's voice was bright and cheerful. "Come in. We have something to ask you."

Hans raised an eyebrow. They'd never been invited in before. It wasn't allowed.

He must have noticed their hesitation because he quickly added. "It's okay. They've just lifted the ban on fraternization, in time for Christmas. Come in. My wife's got a brew on."

Hans smiled. "Thank you, Mr. Jones."

They followed him through the back door into the kitchen. It was light and warm inside, and the smell of baking bread welcomed them in. Mrs. Jones was putting a tea cozy over a large teapot. "Want a cuppa before you get started today?" She smiled.

"Thank you," they mumbled together.

"Lads." Mr. Jones put two mugs down. "We'd like to

invite you for Christmas dinner. Each family in the village is allowed two guests from the camp, and we'd like you to come to us." He looked at them expectantly.

"Thank you, sir," Hans said quickly.

"Yes, thank you, sir," Sébastian added. "That's very kind of you."

"No. You've been a great help to me. I couldn't have got through the harvest without your hard work. I appreciate it."

"It will be an honor." Hans spoke his best English. Sébastian felt a rush of pride in him, knowing how much harder it had been for Hans to pick up English than it had been for him. Being bilingual seemed to give Sébastian a certain facility for learning a third language.

Mr. Jones smiled. "That's settled then. Drink up and let's get on with the milking."

When Sébastian and Hans got back to the camp that evening, they heard that there'd been a steady stream of villagers all day, inviting POWs to spend Christmas Day with them and their families. It was very kind of them, but it wasn't what Sébastian wanted. He wanted to be freed, to be free to find Élise.

Hans suggested taking the family a present. Some of the men had been making beautiful carvings out of old pieces of wood. One had even made a child's rocking horse, but neither Sébastian nor Hans had such skills. Hans suggested buying something from one of the more artistic men, but Sébastian wanted to keep hold of his money. "Surely we can nail something together," he insisted.

Hans looked doubtful, but then his eyes lit up. "A picture frame. It will be easy; we just need to find straight pieces of wood, or we can cut them. Let's go and see what they have in the workshop."

When they got there, it was already a beehive of activity, men standing around waiting their turn to use the saw or the lathe. A pile of cast-off wood leaned against the corner wall. Quickly Hans went through it, coming up with a bent and broken wooden frame. "Perfect!" He held it out for Sébastian to look at.

"Yes, we'll be able to make two out of it." Sébastian nodded his approval.

So on the morning of the twenty-fifth, they found themselves lining up for the camp showers, everyone wanting to look clean and smart for their first social engagement in England. At midday, all the prisoners left together, walking two by two to the homes of their hosts. Sébastian wondered how they should greet them—probably a simple handshake; somehow he knew that to kiss the women on the cheek like they would have done in France would be inappropriate here, and they didn't want to get off on the wrong foot.

He opened the small gate, and they walked up the short garden path but before they even had time to knock on the door, it was opened by Mr. Jones, already holding out a hand in welcome. "Hello, lads. Come in. Come in."

Sébastian offered the bottle of homemade elderflower wine they'd bought from the camp shop and the wrapped picture frames. "Happy Christmas."

Mr. Jones took the bottle. "Thank you. It's much appreciated."

Mrs. Jones appeared, wiping her hands on her apron before she took the present. "You shouldn't have!" She showed them through to the parlor. A line of three daughters surveyed them curiously, and there seemed to be a kind of unbreachable space around them, but they were smiling. Sébastian had only ever seen them from a distance, and it felt slightly unnerving to be this close, as if they'd only existed in his imagination before. He looked around, thinking how different it was than a German home. A sideboard was covered with framed family photographs and little china ornaments, and ribbons of Christmas cards hung from the walls. There was no Christmas tree, just two candles on the mantelpiece next to a sprig of holly. A brightly colored paper chain was strung across the room from the chimney to the curtain rail. It looked childish and cozy all at the same time, stirring a longing in Sébastian for family, for home, and a yearning for Élise that hurt.

"Have a seat." Mr. Jones uncorked the bottle while Hans and Sébastian sat on the settee. "Happy Christmas." He handed everyone a glass of wine.

"Happy Christmas." They raised their glasses, and Sébastian noticed Hans's eyes fixed on the eldest daughter. He wanted to nudge his friend, tell him not to make it so obvious.

"Excuse me, I have to go and check on the dinner." Mrs. Jones left the room.

The atmosphere felt thick with the unsaid. But then they talked about the weather and the food at the camp. Cooking smells wafted into the room; not entirely pleasant, but something harsh and acidic, like heated vinegar.

Mr. Jones turned to look at his guests. "Should have got a few turkeys for the farm. But there were none to be had this year, not for love nor money!"

"That's okay." Sébastian felt bad for him. "We're honored to be here."

When Mrs. Jones called them into the dining room, Mr. Jones sat at the head of the table, assigning seats to the rest of them.

Mrs. Jones apologized. "I'm sorry I can't give you a proper Christmas dinner. It's the rationing. I could only get tripe."

"This is wonderful." Hans smiled a wide smile. "It looks delicious."

"We wanted to give you a home-cooked meal, before you leave." Mr. Jones cut into his tripe. "It shouldn't be long now."

Mr. Jones was wrong. Another Christmas came and went before Sébastian finally clutched his release papers in his hands, with only one thought in his head—to find Élise. With tears in his eyes, he threw his arms around Hans.

But Hans had gone pale and quiet. Sébastian leaned his forehead against Hans's. "Hans, it's over! It's over. We're going home!"

"Home?" He looked at Sébastian through watery eyes. "That's what I'm scared about."

"Come on. You couldn't wait to get back to Munich."

Hans pulled away, wiping his eyes. "I'm afraid of what I'll find." He let out a long breath. "What about you?"

"I'm not going back to Dresden." They all knew Dresden had been razed to the ground, but that wasn't why Sébastian wasn't going back. "I need to get to France. Come on, let's get out of here." Quickly they strode back to their hut. All Sébastian could think about was packing and getting on his way.

"At least come for a drink," Hans begged Sébastian as he watched him throw his few possessions into a duffel bag. "We have to celebrate. You can't leave like a thief in the night."

Sébastian paused for a minute. "Just the one then."

Hans put his arm around him, and they left together for the pub. It was already rowdy when they got there, and they found Mr. Jones sitting on a stool at the bar. He stood to greet them, shaking their hands warmly. "What'll you be having, lads?" Without waiting for an answer, Mr. Jones ordered pints. When they arrived, froth spilling over the edges, Mr. Jones raised his glass. "To unlikely friendships."

"To you and your beautiful country." Sébastian lifted his pint.

"Yes. Bloody good thing we didn't let you Krauts get your hands on it!"

They laughed together, without any awkwardness, in that humorous British way Sébastian had come to love. Then knocked their pints back in one.

"Good on you, lads." Mr. Jones turned around to order more drinks.

Five pints later, the farmer put his arm around Sébastian's neck. "You're a good lad. Why don't you stay on here?"

"What?"

"I'd give you a decent wage."

"That's very kind of you, sir."

"When I get a good worker, I like to hang on to 'em. Not everyone has the stamina for farm work. But you do. What d'you say, then?"

"You've been very good to us." Sébastian took a large swig of beer. "But there's something I have to do. Someone I need to find."

"Someone?"

"I promised I'd find her." It must have been the beer making him open up and talk like this.

"Lovers' promises." Mr. Jones knocked his glass against Sébastian's. "Ain't nothing sweeter. Good luck to you, lad. But if it don't work out, you know where to find us, eh?"

Chapter Sixty-One

France, January 1948

Sébastian

Sébastian was wearing civilian clothes. No one knew who he was; he was just a man traveling to France. For the first time in his life, he was free, but as he walked up the gangplank of the ship docked at Portsmouth, he wondered what his freedom would be worth if he wasn't free to love Élise. Doubts swarmed in his mind as he thought about what could have happened to her, the reasons why she never wrote back. After they boarded, he didn't follow the other foot passengers to the restaurants or the cabins on board, but instead found the stairs leading up to the deck, and even though it was dark and cold, he walked to the bow of the boat, leaning out, looking across the sea toward France. Exhaling slowly, he watched the men lifting the heavy ropes, as thick as necks, off the enormous cleats as the horn blew and they pulled away from England.

When the lights of England had faded, he went back

inside and tried to get comfortable in one of the seats in the bar area, but he was too excited and anxious to sleep properly. He dozed, and when they pulled into the port of Le Havre at six a.m., it felt as though he hadn't slept at all. The cafés and boulangeries were just opening as they left the ship, and he walked into the first one he saw and ordered a coffee and baguette at the bar, where it was cheaper. No one so much as glanced at him, and he took his time, savoring proper coffee and French bread. He'd never got used to the milky tea they drank by the gallon in England.

When he was finished, he walked to the railway station and bought a ticket for Paris. He found a seat on the train by the window and leaned his head against it, so he could rest. But sleep didn't come to him. Instead his mind replayed every conversation he'd ever had with Élise. "Do you believe in love at first sight?" she'd once asked him, and like an idiot he'd told her no, he didn't. But he did. He'd loved her from the moment he'd first seen her in the bookshop, and he knew he would never feel the same way about anyone else. But had she known? Had she really known how he felt? With the years that had passed he'd begun to wonder if he'd told her properly. Some words were too hard to speak, and he wasn't sure they'd ever left his mind and made it to her ears. But then he'd found the courage to write them down and send them to her. Had he frightened her off with their intensity? Words. Words. They were all that was left when all else was gone. "You just don't want to run away with me, do you?" she'd said, and he'd thought she was joking, but what if she'd been serious? What if she'd thought he didn't want to? When it was what he'd wanted more than anything else in the world.

As the train trundled through the countryside, taking

him to Paris, he grew excited and nervous in equal measure. He imagined that whatever Élise had had to endure in the last few years would evaporate once he took her in his arms. They would begin again. They would marry. As soon as possible.

A ring. He needed a ring.

He quickly left the train when it pulled into Saint-Lazare station, and he walked round the corner to the department store, Printemps. The jewelry was right there when he walked in, on the ground floor, as if inviting him. He stared down through the glass counters at the gold and silver rings, inlaid with sparkling stones.

"*Bonjour, monsieur.* Can I help you?" the woman behind the counter asked.

"*Bonjour, madame.* I need a ring. A wedding band, something simple."

"*Oui, monsieur.*" She brought out a tray lined with blue velvet on which lay a selection of gold bands.

He pointed to the thinnest one. "Can I see this one please?"

She picked it out and handed it to him. It was so light he could hardly feel it and turning it around in his fingers, he glimpsed the discreet price tag. Two hundred francs. He only had three hundred francs to his name. To spend two-thirds of his wealth on a ring seemed absurd. But he wanted it to be the first thing he bought as a free man.

"I'll take it." He pulled out his wallet. "Will you put it in a box?"

"Of course, monsieur."

She placed the beautifully wrapped package in his hand, and he held it for a moment, thinking that this was the first step toward the life he wanted to live.

★　　★　　★

He decided to save on the Métro fare and walk toward Saint-Sulpice. As he wandered through the streets of Paris, he recognized the city he'd fallen in love with when he'd first seen it at the age of sixteen—twelve whole years ago. Women in smart heels and scarves bustled by. Cars hooted, barges and boats steamed up and down the Seine. The City of Light had come alive again. Even the air smelled different, and he breathed in deeply, savoring the smell of fresh bread, and the faint lingering scent of cigar smoke mingling with that of the flowers standing in large pails outside the *fleuristes*. Smells of freedom; being able to eat what you liked, to choose your own life, and most importantly, to choose who you loved. He stopped to buy roasted chestnuts from a man hunched over an old metal cylinder, fiery hot coals smoldering as he threw the chestnuts onto metal gauze. He imagined his arm around Élise, eating them warm out of newspaper together.

When he reached Place Saint-Sulpice, he slowed down, anticipation and fear pulsating through his veins. He hurried over to Rue Henry de Jouvenel. The large burgundy front door stared at him imposingly and somewhat uninvitingly. He ignored his feelings of apprehension and pressed the silver button to the side, putting his other hand on the door and pushing it open. He noticed the concierge flicking her curtain aside as he walked past her window, through to the apartments. He remembered Élise's front door was to the left, and he knocked on it twice. Then he waited, his heart in his throat. But there was only silence. He knocked again. This time he thought he could hear someone coughing. Abruptly the door opened, and a thin man peered at Sébastian through narrowed eyes.

"*Bonjour, monsieur,*" Sébastian started. "I'm looking for Élise. Élise Chevalier."

The man coughed, the sound painful and dry, then he put his hand up his sleeve and pulled out a handkerchief. He rubbed his nose. "Who are you?"

Sébastian put out his hand. *"Bonjour, monsieur.* I'm Sébastian." He didn't want to say his surname; didn't want to introduce a German word into the conversation. This man was probably Élise's father, and he was ignoring Sébastian's hand. *"S'il vous plaît, monsieur,* I'd like to talk with Élise."

The man shook his head and coughed again.

"I've come from England," Sébastian continued, wary of telling him too much.

"Pas possible." The man stared at him.

"I'm sorry. What do you mean?"

"Pas possible!" He raised his voice.

Sébastian had to get past the gatekeeper. He had to see her, or at least find out where she was. "Please," he started. "Could you tell me how Élise is? Is she all right?"

The man's forehead crinkled into a deep frown. "All right?" he repeated as if the word was an insult in its superficiality. "All right? *Non!"* Sébastian felt the blood drain from his face, dreading what was coming next. "The Résistance got her."

"What do you mean?" Sébastian stumbled back.

"They came for her. Dragged her out through the window." His eyes were cold and expressionless as he looked at Sébastian. "Revenge attacks."

"Where is she?" He just wanted her to be alive.

"Les résistants de la dernière heure," he continued as though Sébastian hadn't spoken. "Everyone became a *résistant.* It was all over by the time I got back from Germany. De Gaulle took charge. Installed law and order." He paused for breath, as though his words had taken all his strength.

"Where is she?" Sébastian repeated desperately.

"It was too late for Élise though. They took her away."
He paused. "She was shot."

Sébastian stumbled, his knees giving way, his muscle
tone going slack. He crumpled down to the floor, pressing
his fists into his eyes till everything went the color of dark
blood. No! It wasn't possible. He would have known.

The man cackled, a nasty dry sound. He straightened his
crooked back and looked at Sébastian. "You should leave."

Sébastian buried his head in his hands. He couldn't get
up. *Lise! Lise!* He'd lost everything that mattered to him in
this world. Nothing made sense anymore. An image of her
dead body exploded into his head, blood spilling out from
under her head, congealing in her hair. His Lise.

Her father turned away and walked back through the
door, closing it behind him with a sharp click.

Sébastian didn't know how long he sat there in a crumpled heap, but he was vaguely aware of the inside door
opening. "You can't stay here." It was the concierge, looking down at him disdainfully.

He put his hands on the floor, pushing himself up, his
heart pounding with the effort. When he was on his feet
again, he couldn't speak. Numbly, he walked through the
outer door, no longer the same man who'd walked in only
fifteen minutes ago.

Sébastian stumbled through the streets of Paris. He had
no direction. No will. He was an empty man. He walked
and walked, the cold wind and his hunger nothing compared
to the pain and loss he felt inside. He found himself once
again in the 5th arrondissement, near the Panthéon. Near
the bookshop. But he couldn't bring himself to go in. The
familiarity of the bell going, seeing Monsieur Le Bolzec,
would kill him.

He carried on walking as the pale sun sank behind the Haussmann buildings, and then he found himself on the steps leading to Sacré-Coeur. He walked into the church. He was so exhausted he couldn't see straight and was only vaguely aware of a few people kneeling down, praying. He slumped onto one of the pews, waves of fatigue washing over him. Then he remembered the ring. He pulled the box out of his coat pocket, opening it to look at the simple gold band. He got up and walked over to the statue of Saint Pierre, where he lit a candle, but he didn't say a prayer. He kissed the ring and dropped it into the offertory box where people left money for the candles. Then he went back to the pews and, sitting down heavily, he leaned back and gazed at the vaulted ceiling. This time Jesus seemed to look down on him with pity.

Part Five

1963

Chapter Sixty-Two

Brittany, June 1963

Élise

Where are you, Lise my love? Why haven't you written back to me? I pray to God that nothing has happened to you. This thought fills me with terror. Where are you? Where are you? I should be released soon. They can't keep us here much longer.

I lean forward on the armchair, the last letter from Sébastian hanging damp and crumpled from my hands. "I don't understand. Did he come back to Paris?" My heart beats fast and hard as I imagine him coming back to Paris, finding me gone. But he could have followed me here. Maman would have given him my address. Wouldn't she? Why didn't he come? Why didn't he find us?

"Joséphine, what happened to him? Where did he go? Why didn't he look for us?" My voice comes out high-pitched, frantic.

"He came back to Paris," she states matter-of-factly.

I stare at her, gulping the hard lump in my throat. "How do you know?"

"Your father saw him." She bites her bottom lip, and I know she's holding something back.

"My father?" Confusion clouds my mind.

"Yes, he— Sébastian, came to your apartment." She hesitates again. "Your father told him you'd been shot. That you were dead."

"Dead!" I shake my head. "He told Sébastian I was dead?" I don't understand. And then it hits me. Of course he would. He would have done anything to keep a Boche out of the family. Anything.

A small crease appears between Joséphine's eyebrows. "It's not something you'd expect a father to lie about, is it?"

I sit there, frozen. My own father! He'd stolen everything from us. The life we could have had. Rage burns in my chest, quickly turning to hatred. I loathe that man with all my being.

"Sébastian might still be alive," Joséphine murmurs, and I'm brought back here, to the room we're sitting in, to my daughter, to the letters.

Sébastian could be alive? I don't dare believe it. Joséphine shouldn't get her hopes up like that, and I don't want to imagine the impossible. Anything could have happened since Sébastian's last letter, fifteen years ago. "No," I say. "I don't think so."

Joséphine leans forward, looking me in the eye. "I want to find him."

"Find him?" I repeat as though I can't understand the words.

"There's an address on the letter you're holding. I can write to it, ask if he's still there, or if they know where he's gone."

She makes it all sound so simple, as if it were only a matter of getting an address. I don't dare voice my fears. What if he has another family? A wife? "Joséphine," I say softly. "We don't know what's happened since this last letter."

"Whatever has happened, he's still my father."

"Yes, yes, of course he is."

"I want to find him." Her voice is determined.

"Let's wait a bit." I'm not ready. The thought of making contact terrifies me. "You need to get your exams out of the way."

"Don't worry about my exams." Her voice is cold, as though it's none of my business. "I can write to the last address. That won't take up much of my time."

"Okay, we'll write to the last address then. We could do that." I concentrate on the practicalities. Anything else is too hard.

The last address is a farm in Ashton-in-Makerfield, wherever that is. Joséphine writes the letter herself, using her English–French dictionary.

Nearly two weeks later, when her exams are over, and I come back for the weekend, Joséphine is waiting for me at the cottage. She's holding a letter in her hand, and her face is flushed with excitement. "Maman," she says as soon as I get out of the car. "This letter came from Mr. Jones."

I freeze, suddenly cold. I want to know. And I don't want to know. "Let's go in first."

"He's living in a place called Coventry," Joséphine tells me before we've even sat down. "The address is here."

An address. How is this possible? All this time I've been mourning him, and he wasn't even dead.

"Mr. Jones said he went there when he came back from France in 1948," she continues.

"How does he know he's still there?" We have to think this through.

"He says he is."

"I'll write to him." I imagine the letter I'll send, explaining everything, telling him he has a daughter.

"No!" she blurts out. She lowers her voice. "Don't write, please."

"But, Joséphine, *ma chérie*..." I have to write.

"No, Maman. He might not want to meet me."

"What do you mean? Of course, he'll want to meet you."

Joséphine shakes her head sadly. "He might have another life now. He might not want to see us."

"No. He'll be overjoyed to find out he has a daughter."

"No! You don't know that!" Joséphine stares at me. "You might scare him off."

"What?" I half laugh. The idea is ridiculous. "He's not like that," I repeat. "He'll want to meet us."

"You don't know anything about him now. The last time you saw him he was twenty-four. He's forty-three now."

"Joséphine, whatever's happened, he'll want to see us."

"You don't know anything! You hid him all my life, and now you're going to write to him and frighten him away. What if he's married? What if his wife won't let him meet us?"

Confused and conflicted, I stare at my daughter. "You don't want me to write?"

"No. I want to go there."

I don't understand. "You just want us to go, without writing first?"

"No. I want to go, on my own." She stares at me with cold eyes. "I don't want you to come with me. He's my father, and I want to do this alone. I'm not a child anymore. You can't protect me from everything."

My excitement in finding Sébastian evaporates, and I'm left with a sinking, empty feeling. *She doesn't want me there.* My own daughter. *She doesn't want me to be part of this.* She's all hurt and defiance.

Sébastian is alive. But I feel my world slipping away.

"I've already got my passport," she adds.

My heart twists as she provides further proof that she doesn't need me anymore.

Chapter Sixty-Three

England, June 23, 1963

Joséphine

Soizic drives Joséphine to Roscoff, where she'll take the night ferry to Plymouth. When it leaves port, she goes out on deck in the dark, staring out into the night, watching as the lights of France gradually fade away. She has a small cabin to herself, and as she lies in her little bunk, she lets the motion of the sea rock her to sleep.

She's woken abruptly at five thirty in the morning by a loud tapping on the door. *"On est arrivé!"* a voice shouts. *"C'est l'heure de se lever!"*

Joséphine drags herself out of bed and quickly pulls on her dress. Leaving her cabin, she sees other passengers already milling around, starting to gather in the lounge area. She wonders if anyone else might be going to London and if she could get a lift, but she's too embarrassed to try out her schoolgirl English on them. The foot passengers are herded down to the car deck, then across the tarmac and into a square building, where they shuffle through customs and passport control. When Joséphine hands over her brand-new passport, the lady smiles. "First time in England?"

"Yes, madame."

"Enjoy yourself then. And by the way, we don't say 'madame' here." She laughs lightly.

Joséphine walks outside to see the sun just beginning to peer over the gray buildings. A row of taxis wait in a line. Joséphine approaches one. "Hello. The railway station please." This is the first whole sentence she's spoken to an English person and she's relieved when the driver nods his head and pulls away without asking her to repeat herself.

The next obstacle is buying the train ticket. This proves more difficult as the woman selling the ticket babbles away; something about changing trains.

"Can you write it, please?" Joséphine smiles her sweetest smile.

The woman kindly obliges, and Joséphine is soon on a train, watching the English countryside fly by. After her early morning start, she's tired and hungry. Digging into her bag, she pulls out the croissants Soizic packed. As she eats them, she looks at the piece of paper the lady gave her. Paddington, 11:10. Euston, 12:15. She has a good hour to make the change.

When she gets off at Paddington, the station is packed and she stops for a moment, taking it all in as men in gray suits rush past her. She follows the taxi sign and soon finds a row of black cabs. It's all so different than her little seaside village, but she's enjoying the adventure. She shows the taxi driver her piece of paper, and he nods then takes her case, placing it on the floor in the back of the cab. She sits on the large leather seat, feeling like a queen as she stares out at the tall angular buildings. Soizic gave her some extra money in case she needs to find a hotel for the night. *A hotel! All on her own! In a foreign country!* She feels very grown up.

The cab pulls up outside a station, and she pays the driver then walks away, heading for one of the booths where she can ask about the train to Coventry.

"Platform twelve," the lady at the booth says. "Leaves in five minutes."

Five minutes! She has to run. Turning away from the booth, her eyes dart frantically around the station. She sees platform number ten and runs toward it, searching left and right to see where twelve might be. There it is! She runs through the gate just as the guard blows his whistle, jumping into the first carriage, heaving a sigh of relief. Four men sit in seats facing each other. The younger one smiles at her. "Looks like you just made it," he says as the train pulls away.

Joséphine doesn't understand the words, but she gets the gist and nods to him as she sits down, her case between her knees.

"Do you want a hand?" The man stands up, indicating her case.

"Thank you."

He lifts her case onto the rack above their heads. "Going far?" he asks as he sits back down.

It must be a question about where she's going. "Coventry."

A tiny line crosses his forehead. "Where are you from?"

She remembers this question from her school English. "France."

He grunts then opens his paper, burying his head in it. She seems to have disappointed him. Maybe it's her accent, or did she misunderstand something?

Feeling self-conscious, she takes out the book from her

handbag—*La Gloire de mon Père*, a book she happened to be reading when she found out about her father. Funny that. She pretends to read it, but really her mind is far too restless to concentrate. Her stomach rumbles, and she puts her hand over it, blushing as the young man looks up from his paper.

In fact, Joséphine has a cheese and ham baguette in her bag but is too embarrassed to take it out and eat it in front of everyone. By the time they pull into Coventry, she's hungry but too nervous to eat now she's so close. She gets in another taxi, showing the address. The taxi driver attempts to make conversation. "I'm sorry, I speak only a little English," she replies, repeating the phrase she learned at school.

She's soon deposited outside a gate leading to a tall house, which is joined to another. It's not a small cottage, like theirs in Brittany, but neither is it very big. It's the kind of house a family would live in, and Joséphine hesitates outside for a moment, trying to breathe calmly as she gathers her courage, her hunger forgotten. She pushes the gate open and walks down the short path to the front door. A bronze knocker in the shape of a sheep's head stares at her with expressionless eyes, and a shiver of apprehension runs down the back of her neck. She braces herself as she picks it up and raps twice.

An old lady opens the door. "Hello."

"Hello," Joséphine replies. "I am looking for Sébastian Kleinhaus."

"Sébastian?" she repeats. "He doesn't live here."

"*Zut.*" Joséphine suddenly feels deflated and worn out. "Where he lives?"

"Just three doors down."

Joséphine frowns. "Pardon?"

"I'll walk you there." The woman pulls on a jacket hanging on a hook by the door and slips on some shoes. Then she steps outside and walks down the path. Joséphine follows, her heart thumping hard as she realizes this lady is leading her toward her father.

"How do you know Mr. Kleinhaus?" the lady asks as they turn right outside the gate.

"He…he…" She can't just blurt it out, can she? "My mother knows him before the war."

Joséphine feels the lady's eyes on her and is relieved when they turn up a path toward another house. Without knocking, she opens the front door. "Maggie!" she shouts out. "It's Judy. I have a visitor for you."

A woman holding a baby comes down the stairs. "Hello." She stops and looks at Joséphine.

"This young lady is looking for Sébastian."

Joséphine puts out her hand, expecting it to be shaken. But it takes a few seconds for the woman to untangle a hand from the baby and limply shake Joséphine's. Could this be her father's wife? She's pale, her smile tight. "Hello," she says, putting her hand back around the baby. Could this be Joséphine's half brother?

"I want to talk to Sébastian Kleinhaus." Her English words feel clumsy and abrupt. She's sure there is a more polite way to ask, but she doesn't know the language well enough.

"He's at work. He'll be back this evening. You could come back at seven thirty." She glances at Joséphine's case and frowns.

"Thank you." Joséphine picks up her case and turns around. It's three o'clock now. Four and a half hours. She only has to wait four and a half hours, but right now it feels like an eternity.

Chapter Sixty-Four

Coventry, June 24, 1963

Sébastian

Sébastian pulls into the driveway at six thirty. Margaret is in the kitchen, holding the baby on her hip as she prepares the dinner. Her lips are pursed, and he knows she's worried about the baby's wheezing cough. He walks over to her, putting his arm around her waist. "How's the little lad today?"

Maggie turns to him, relaxing her lips and smiling. "He's breathing more easily. But I want to keep him upright." She kisses his cheek. "Happy birthday."

"Thank you." Sébastian takes Luke out of her arms, holding him against his chest, stroking his back, breathing in the clean fresh smell of him. The baby squirms but doesn't make a sound.

"Someone came to see you today." Maggie looks him in the eye.

Sébastian plays with Luke's tiny fingers, holding them,

then dropping them, watching them curl back up. "Who?" he asks when she doesn't volunteer anymore information.

"A woman." She looks at him intently. "A Frenchwoman."

Sébastian's pulse races and his throat feels thick. He swallows. "Who?"

"She didn't leave a name. I forgot to ask. I was busy with the baby."

"What did she say?" He hears the tremor in his voice.

"Her English wasn't great. I told her to come back at seven thirty."

Luke coughs quietly, and Sébastian feels his little body go limp as though the cough used up his last reserves of energy. His breathing sounds shallow.

Maggie holds out her arms, taking him back. "I'm going to give him some more cough mixture. Would you put Philip to bed?"

"Dada!" Philip, already in pajamas, toddles in, holding out a dinky car.

Sébastian bends down, taking the car from him. "Is this for me? Thank you." He collects his son in his arms and takes him upstairs.

On his way back down the stairs, he looks at his watch: seven o'clock. Maggie has set the table for dinner, and they eat together, but the atmosphere is charged, and Sébastian has lost his appetite. He can't help looking at the kitchen clock, waiting.

At exactly seven thirty, the doorbell rings. Taking a deep breath, he walks to the front door and opens it.

A young woman stands there. Sounds of cars, of neighbors calling out, all fade into the background, the years ticking backward, taking him back to Paris. His head feels light, as though he's in a dream. The woman on his doorstep is Élise. But not Élise. Her hair is nothing like Élise's. It's blonde and wavy, and her eyes aren't green like Élise's were. The color is all off, but it's in her face. And it's striking. She's hardly even a woman; more of a girl. She must be related to Élise in some way, but he can't imagine how. He puts his palm over his thumping heart and takes a step back. "Hello?" He adds inflection, turning it into a question

"*Bonjour*," she replies. Then she scratches her forehead with her little finger; a gesture that takes him back in time— back to Élise. "Can I talk to you?" she continues in French.

He opens the door wider. He wants her to come in so he can shut the door behind her. So he can sit down and put the pieces of the puzzle together. For a moment he wonders if she could be Élise's younger sister, Isabelle, all grown up, but Isabelle was ten in 1944 so now she'd be nearly thirty. The girl on his doorstep is nowhere near thirty.

She steps over the threshold, into his home, and he shows her through to the living room. For a moment they stand awkwardly, and he sees her casting her eyes around, taking in all the details, the family photos on the mantelpiece, the tiny china dogs in the glass cabinet, and he sees it all through her eyes. His family.

"*S'il te plaît, assieds-toi.*" He invites her to sit down, automatically using the familiar form of the verb.

She smooths down the back of her dress and perches on the edge of the settee, like a bird on a branch, ready to take flight at the slightest disturbance. He wants to put her at ease, but he doesn't know how. He wishes he'd asked to take her light summer jacket from her. "My wife told me you came earlier today." He tries to make his tone warm and casual, tries to hide the tremor stirring in his throat.

She just looks at him.

"Would you like a cup of tea?" he asks.

She shakes her head, her bright blue eyes turning a shade darker, and he can see she's waiting for something. "You look like someone I once knew," he says. Her eyes let in a little more light. "Élise," he continues. "She..." He doesn't know how to say it. How to say that she died. Some words simply can't be spoken.

He wishes she'd help him out, but her eyes give nothing away. "She and I were very close." God, it sounds feeble. He decides to change tack. "What can I do for you?" What's wrong with him? Now he sounds like a salesman.

"You were in Paris during the war, weren't you?"

Sébastian nods, his head swimming with confusion. He hasn't been back to France for fifteen years.

She frowns, a delicate line forming between her eyebrows. "You went back after the war?" It's a statement, but she adds inflection at the end, turning it into a question.

Sébastian studies her. There's something about the shape of her face, and her eyes. "Yes, I went back, after they released me." He glances out of the window, his mind whirring backward. He shifts in the chair, leaning forward, resting his head in his hands. "What's your name?"

"Joséphine," she answers.

"Joséphine," he repeats as if testing out the name. "Who are you, Joséphine?"

She answers with a question. "When you said you went back to Paris after the war, what happened?"

"There was nothing left for me there. I came back here." Sébastian looks into her eyes, and it's as though he's seeing into Élise's all those years ago.

"You don't know who I am, do you?"

It's not quite true. He does know. He does, and he doesn't, because it's not possible. "Are you related to Élise?"

"She's my mother." She sighs then looks away. "Her father lied to you," she speaks in a low voice. "Maman didn't die. She had me in April, eight months after you left Paris."

It hits him with full force. He jumps up, his breath blocked in his throat. Then air gushes back into his lungs, bruising them with its force. She's his child. Élise's child. Their child.

"Is Élise still alive?" he asks desperately.

She nods.

Sébastian brings his trembling hands to his face. A whole life flashes before him. The life he could have had. The life with Élise and their child. "But I wrote to her! I wrote!"

"She never got your letters. Her father hid them."

Sébastian puts his hand on his chest, over his thumping heart. He closes his eyes, unable to take it in. He opens his eyes. Joséphine stares at him. He turns to the pictures on the mantelpiece, his family. Then he looks back at Joséphine. He can't put the two together.

Joséphine follows his eyes to the mantelpiece. "Why didn't you look harder?" She gets up and stands in front of him. "Why didn't you find us?"

"I believed him. I believed that crazy man. I thought she'd been shot." His head feels thick with confusion. He doesn't understand now how he could have taken her father at his word. And he doesn't understand how it's taken this long for the truth to come out. "How did you find me?" he stutters.

"The letters. I found the letters last month when I went to Paris, when I met my grandfather for the first time. They made Maman cry."

"Where is she? Why didn't she come? Why didn't Élise come with you?"

Joséphine's eyes travel back to the photos on the mantelpiece. "I wanted to come on my own." She pauses. "I didn't want her to be here if…"

"If what?"

"To find you had started another family."

Sébastian closes his eyes again, imagining the pain Élise will feel when she learns that he got on with his life. "I never forgot her," he says quietly. He wants to hold his daughter. He wants to tell her that all these years, he's missed her with all his being, that his life wasn't complete without her. Without Élise.

The door opens with a creak. Maggie stands there. She looks exhausted. "I've made a bed in Luke's room." She looks from Sébastian to Joséphine. "For our guest."

"Thank you, Maggie." Sébastian switches to English. He can tell by the look in her eye that she already knows who this girl is. She must have known as soon as she saw her.

"Will you stay the night?" he turns to ask Joséphine in French.

"*Merci*, thank you." She blushes, and Sébastian wonders if she had made plans to stay elsewhere.

"I'm very tired," Maggie says. "I'm going to bed." Without waiting for a reply, she turns on her heel and disappears.

Sébastian and Joséphine are left there, facing each other. For a moment neither of them speaks. She's so still and quiet, and he's reminded of the way Élise was with him when they first met. He'll have to take it slowly.

"Would you like something to eat?" He feels more comfortable dealing with the practicalities.

"*Merci*," she says.

She follows him into the kitchen, and they stand there awkwardly for a moment. "I can make toast." He takes the loaf of sliced bread from the bread bin, switches the oven grill on, and places two slices under it.

"What did you do during the war?" Her question comes abruptly, just as he's looking for the butter dish. He freezes, then taking a deep breath he turns to face her, realizing this must have been going through her head ever since she found out about him.

"I was in the Hitler Youth when the war began." He has to start at the beginning. "Do you know what that was?"

"Not exactly," she admits.

"It was a program for children under the age of eighteen. Hitler's way of producing a young, loyal army. I was sixteen when it became compulsory to join." He feels he's making excuses for himself, and this isn't what he wants. "Some kids resisted. They formed other groups, like the Leipzig Meuten or the Edelweiss Pirates; they refused to conform and wore different clothes, listened to jazz, even wore their hair long." He stops, thinking how they were sent to prison, how they probably died there. He turns the bread over. "But I didn't join one of those groups. I was a conformist. We all were in my family." With a jolt, he realizes he's talking about her family too—her grandparents. "I was sent to Paris as a translator. And that's where I met your mother."

"Yes, she told me. What did you have to translate?"

"Letters mostly. Denunciation letters." She looks at him as if expecting more, but he can't justify himself. "Joséphine." He can't make her like him; she'll have to form her own judgment. "I'm not going to pretend I was a brave man. I was just another sheep, and I was terrified from the time I was sixteen till the time I met your mother. It's a long time to live in constant fear, and I'm not proud of it. I think many people did things they regret now. I'm not making excuses."

He looks at Joséphine. "I was no hero." He holds eye contact. "I'm sorry." The words catch in his throat. He's never apologized before, never asked for forgiveness. He wipes his eyes, swallowing the hard lump in his throat. "I'm sorry," he repeats.

"I don't know much about the war. People don't talk about it. Maman never told me you were my father."

Sébastian drops the piece of toast he's just picked up. "What?"

"She pretended my father was some Frenchman called Frédéric. I only found out it wasn't true last month when I found my birth certificate."

"Last month?" The words catch in his throat.

Joséphine nods. "Yes, I went from having a French hero as a father to having a...a German. She thought it was better for me if I didn't know. You know, if no one knew."

Élise had denied his existence. How could she have written him out like that? What did she do with all her memories of him? Had she managed to wipe them out? He can't begin to understand how that would be possible. He, himself, had treasured every single one, playing them back, even after he'd met Maggie. He could never have let Élise go like that. A deep sense of hurt and betrayal burns through Sébastian.

Chapter Sixty-Five

Coventry, June 24, 1963

Sébastian

Maggie has left the bedside lamp on, and she's moved Luke's crib to the end of the bed. Sébastian looks at his sleeping son and places a hand on his tiny chest, feeling the rhythm of his regular heartbeat.

He moves to his side of the bed and takes his clothes off, folding them over the back of the chair and putting his pajamas on before slipping into bed and switching off the lamp.

Maggie rolls over to face him. "You were a long time," she whispers.

"I made toast. Joséphine was hungry."

"Will you tell me about her?"

He's so tired, he wishes he didn't have to explain tonight. But this isn't something that can wait till the morning. "Maggie," he says. "Élise didn't die." Maggie knows about Élise, or rather, she knows what Sébastian chose to tell her.

Just the bare facts. Even if he'd wanted to, he wouldn't have been able to tell her how he felt about Élise. "Her father lied to me. She wasn't shot."

"She's still alive?"

"Yes." He lets out a long breath, composing himself before saying the next words. "She had a daughter, Joséphine. My daughter."

"I knew," Maggie whispers in the dark. "I knew as soon as I saw her."

"Élise never told her about me. She told Joséphine someone else was her father." The words tear at his heart. How could she have wiped him out of their lives like that? "She only found out a month ago."

Maggie turns over onto her back, reaching for his hand under the covers. But Sébastian doesn't move. He lies with his eyes open in the dark, thinking of how much he sees of Élise in Joséphine, in the way she cradles her chin in her hands when she's thinking, her eyes deep and penetrating. In the way she smiles with her mouth closed, tiny dimples appearing in her cheeks. Her expressions give her away, just like Élise's did. Sébastian came to learn how Élise could be saying one thing while thinking another, how she tried to hide her fear and insecurities, pretending to be confident when really, she was trembling inside. He sees how Joséphine has done the same in making this trip to England, how scared she must have been standing there on his doorstep, not knowing what to expect. As his thoughts turn to Élise, the hurt inside him grows. Did she come to hate him? It makes him wonder what Élise has told Joséphine. Has she told her about the time she kicked down the sign forbidding Jews? How he'd rescued her from the Gestapo headquarters? Or the picnic in the hotel room when they had dreamed of a whole life together? He wonders if Joséphine is pleased with what she's found, or if she was hoping or expecting something else.

"Are you thinking about her?" Maggie's question draws him back to the present.

"Yes," he admits. "I was thinking about both of them."

"Does she look like her mother?"

"Yes, she does."

"She has your eyes. Like Philip." She hesitates. "Did Élise ever marry?"

"I don't know. I didn't ask." But somehow, he does know. He knows she didn't. And he knows the question Maggie wants to ask but dares not.

"This won't change anything for us." Sébastian tries to put her mind at rest. "It's in the past. I've already grieved for her." He squeezes Maggie's hand under the covers, but he doesn't turn over. He carries on staring at the ceiling in the dark.

Chapter Sixty-Six

Coventry, June 25, 1963

Joséphine

When Joséphine first wakes, she thinks she's home in Trégastel, and then it comes back to her. She's in England, and her father is here in this house. This thought sends a thrill through her, but at the same time she feels a pang of homesickness for the familiarity of the little cottage, for Maman and Soizic. She hears sounds coming from downstairs: a child chattering, crockery being moved around, her father's voice.

When he answered the door yesterday evening in a dark suit and a navy-blue tie, she'd thought how clean-cut and refined he looked. He didn't look like the kind of man who'd get angry or shout and swear. And then he made her toast in the kitchen, still in his suit. But she sensed a froideur from his wife, Maggie. She hopes she won't be left alone with her and the children for the day. With only her school-girl English, communication is limited; and the words she hears are hardly recognizable from the lessons at school. She gets up and goes to the bathroom where she washes then she pulls on the same dress she wore yesterday and walks down the narrow staircase, treading gently, not wanting to disturb.

"*Bonjour*, Joséphine," her father greets her as soon as she steps into the kitchen. "Toast?"

She knows this word now and smiles. "*Oui, s'il te plaît.*" Automatically, she's used the familiar *tu* instead of the formal *vous*. His smile tells her that he's noticed.

"Sit down," he continues in French. "You can sit next to Philip."

At home, in the morning she would greet Soizic and her mother with a kiss on each cheek. But instinctively she knows this is not expected here, and so she just says hello to Philip and sits on the stool next to him at the kitchen counter. He's in a high chair and waves a piece of floppy toast at her as though in greeting. His cheeks are covered in sticky jam and bread crumbs.

"Tea?" her father asks.

She usually has a bowl of Ricoré in the mornings—a mixture of chicory and coffee—but she imagines they don't have that here. "Yes, thank you."

He boils some water and pours it into a teapot, covering it with some sort of wooly jacket. It all feels so different than home.

"I've taken the day off work." Her father turns round to face her. "So we can spend some time together." He says it so simply, so warmly, as though wanting to spend time with her is the most natural thing in the world. Joséphine looks at his hands as he pours her tea. His fingers are long, and there's a small brown mark in the shape of crescent moon between his first and middle finger. She lifts her own hand up, looking at the brown mark at the base of her first finger. It's the same. Her fingers are the same. Her eyes sting with unshed tears. Quickly she blinks them away and turns instead to Philip, who's poking her arm with a spoon.

"I guess this is your first time in England," her father says.

"Yes."

"I'll take you into Coventry today. Show you what a modern English city looks like."

"Thank you." A jolt of excitement runs through her as she thinks about exploring this new place.

He turns to pinch Philip's sticky cheek. "Shall we take the little lad with us?"

Philip grins as though he understands.

"How old is he?" Joséphine asks.

"He was two last week. You can speak to him in French if you like. I do sometimes. He seems to get it as well as the English."

"What about German?" Joséphine asks impulsively. "Do you speak German with him?"

"No," he answers. "I think two languages are enough for one little boy. Don't you?" He looks at her quizzically.

"Yes, I suppose so."

"We have a lot to talk about, Joséphine." He puts his hand on her shoulder. "I'm looking forward to today."

There he is again, telling her how much he wants to get to know her. She can't help feeling a warm glow inside.

Chapter Sixty-Seven

Brittany, July 1, 1963

Élise

It takes a whole week for a letter to arrive from Joséphine. I haven't been worried; she's a sensible girl; it's just that when she left, she was still quietly angry with me, and I've been dying to hear from her, to know that she's okay.

The envelope is addressed to both Soizic and me, but when I open it, I find two more envelopes inside, one with only my name on it. I stuff it in the front pocket of my dress and open the other one. I read it aloud to Soizic.

Chère Maman, Soizic,

It feels like my world has been turned upside down, and I'm not the person I thought I was. There's a whole other side to me that I didn't even know existed. It's like I grew up with only one half of me there. I'd like to stay here longer. My father has a wife, two children. I'd like to get to know them better.

My heart plummets into the pit of my stomach. I feel sick. A wife! Two children! How can she casually tell me Sébastian has a family as if it were the most natural thing in the world? The words blur then swim. I reach for the edge of the table and hold on, forcing myself to take hold of this piece of information and put it in perspective. Sébastian started his life again. He let me go.

Of course, I'd considered this possibility. But I'd never believed it. And there it is now, staring at me in black and white. How can he have married someone else? Had children with someone ese? It was supposed to be us.

I look at Soizic, and I see it in her eyes. Pity. I have to get away from her.

But before I can open the door, she puts her hand on my shoulder. "Joséphine will come home soon. She just needs some time."

"Time!" I snap. "That's what you took from us!"

She drops her hand, and her eyes turn cold. "I gave you a home when no one else would."

"Yes! But at what price?" I stare back at her. "You made me pay for it!"

The blood drains from Soizic's face. Her lips tighten and close.

"You made me lie to her!"

She turns away as though I'd slapped her. Then, swiftly, she swivels back round to face me. "It was a small price to pay! She grew up without the burden of the past. And she's alive. She's alive!" The last word comes out as a sob, and I know she's thinking of her own daughter. The daughter who has haunted our lives here, whose grave we are not worthy to visit, neither Joséphine nor me.

Soizic composes herself, the blood returning to her face.

"The war wasn't even over when you turned up on my doorstep. We had to protect ourselves and Joséphine. It was the only way."

I can't talk about it, not now. I push past Soizic and walk quickly out of the house and down to the sea. The tide is far out, and the wind is against me, raking through my hair, blowing it off my face. I stride forward along the beach toward Île aux Lapins, once more accessible. After I've removed my shoes, I walk across the wide path of shingle and sharp broken shells, and I climb the largest boulder at the far end of the island, pushing my feet against the rounded holes and edges, pulling myself up with my hands. Finally, I come to the highest point, and I sit there, looking out to sea, letting my thoughts in. Thinking how I denied my daughter her father, pretending he never existed. How I traded him in for a home. Roughly, I wipe away tears of self-pity, and I curse myself for listening to Soizic. I'd longed to tell Joséphine the truth about her father, but I'd rationalized my feelings, telling myself it was best for everyone if Joséphine didn't know, not yet, that it was better to wait until she was old enough to understand. But now it feels as though the wind is gusting through the walls I built around us, blowing up years of debris into my face, choking me. Why hadn't I listened to my heart instead?

I think of Sébastian. What's in his letter? I don't blame him for starting his life again, I just wish I could have done the same. But I was living as though I were a shadow of myself. I became terrified of men, and then I grew to despise them. The only man I might have let near me was Sébastian, but since I believed him to be dead, I shut down that part of myself. Joséphine was all that mattered to me, and to see her grow up in safety was all I wanted.

The sound of children playing makes me turn around. I see a woman chasing two young girls behind a rock. They scream with delight as their mother catches them. I used to bring Joséphine here; we'd build sandcastles in the damp sand, catch crabs in the rock pools, only to release them later and watch them scamper sideways back into the sea. I wonder if she'll remember those moments, if she'll remember the cakes I baked for her birthdays, the stories I told her in bed. Or will she only remember that I lied to her? Soizic says she needs time, but I know the damage time can do. How it can take your loved ones so far away there's no coming back. Have I lost my daughter now she's found her other family? The family that never kept secrets from her.

"*Les filles*, time to go back!" I hear the mother shout. "The tide's coming in."

The girls run to her, one on each side, taking her hand. I watch them walk away, along the shingly ridge between the island and the beach. The waves are splashing up, closing in on it. I watch it getting narrower and narrower. And I take out Sébastian's letter.

Chère Élise,

He always used to call me Lise. Writing Élise puts the distance between us, and I can hardly bear to read the next words.

You are alive! And we have a beautiful daughter! This fills my heart with gladness. But also with sadness, that we never found each other again. I never stopped thinking about you, and I never stopped loving you.

Why does he have to say that? He must have stopped loving me. He married someone else.

I was an idiot. I was an idiot to believe your father when he told me you'd been shot. I was overwhelmed with grief and couldn't see the truth. Please forgive me.

The writing becomes hazy as my eyes fill with tears. I look away, blinking them back, and I read further down.

I could never love anyone the way I loved you, Élise. But someone came into my life.

I can't read on. I look up through blurry eyes; the tide has come in and the sandy path has disappeared. The mother and her daughters are walking down the beach, holding hands, swinging them, as though they have not a care in the world.

I should go back while the path is only covered in shallow water, but I can't seem to move. I'm frozen. I sit on the rock, the letter crumpled in my hands, and I gaze out to sea, focusing on nothing. I feel myself disappearing. Fading into nothing. Suspended in time. I have nowhere to be, nowhere I want to go. I listen to the waves rolling in, gathering in strength, and still I can't move. The wind whistles through the rocks, around their sharp edges. The stray blades of grass are bent backward by the wind. The same wind gently caresses my hair, whispering to me, and I realize I am no longer afraid. There is nothing left to fear. The truth is released. I listen to the timeless rhythm of the waves, lapping against the rocks, pulling back, then coming in again. I feel weightless, as though I could float away. I close my eyes and sync my breath with the sound of the sea.

Chapter Sixty-Eight

Coventry, July 4, 1963

Sébastian

Joséphine has been there for ten days when a knock on the door breaks into what has become their morning routine. The postman stands there, holding out a brown slip of paper. "Telegram," he announces, passing it to Sébastian.

Sébastian takes it. It's so short, his eyes have read it before his mind catches up with the fact that it's not actually addressed to him. It's addressed to Joséphine.

> Your mother has had an accident. In the hospital.
> Come home.

Élise! Élise is in the hospital! He shuts the front door, his pulse racing. What could have happened? What if she's been in some horrific car accident? How is he going to tell Joséphine?

He walks back into the kitchen, clutching the piece

of paper. He holds out the telegram in trembling hands. "Joséphine. It's your mother."

Without a word, Joséphine takes the paper from him. She reads it in a second, then drops it. "What does it mean?" Her eyes are wide with shock.

Maggie bends to pick up the piece of paper. She looks from Sébastian to Joséphine and back again. The hush in the kitchen lies thick and heavy.

Philip shouts, "Dada!" as if to bring everyone back.

Sébastian springs into action, putting his arm around his daughter, attempting to reassure her. "She's in the hospital. They'll be looking after her. She'll be okay." His words are pathetic-sounding, and he hates himself for uttering them, for selfishly keeping Joséphine here when she should have gone home.

"Élise is in the hospital?" Maggie asks for confirmation.

"Yes," Sébastian answers. "Joséphine has to go."

"You could use the neighbors' phone," Maggie suggests. "Call the hospital." She's right; he could.

"Do you know the name of the nearest hospital?" He turns to Joséphine, relieved to be able to do something practical.

"Yes, it's in Lannion."

"I'll go next door and call them."

"Can I come with you?" Joséphine's voice is faint.

He nods, and they walk out of the front door together.

The neighbors are having breakfast, and when they see the look of panic on Sébastian's face, they tell him of course he can use the phone, even if it's to call France. Sébastian calls the operator first, retrieving the number of the hospital. Then he dials the number, his first finger trembling as he puts it into the zero, rotating the dialing disk till it clicks, then putting his finger into the next digit. It seems to take forever, his heart pounding with each rotation.

"*L'hôpital*," a woman's voice answers.

"*Bonjour, madame*," Sébastian starts. "I've just received a telegram informing me that Élise Chevalier has been hospitalized. Could you please tell me if she is with you?"

"Who's calling please?"

What is he to her now? He hesitates. "I'm calling on behalf of her daughter who's with me. Joséphine Chevalier."

"Yes, Élise Chevalier is here."

"Can you tell me how she is?"

"She's still in a coma."

"A coma?" He grips the phone tightly, sweat breaking out under his hairline and on his palms.

"Yes, I'm sorry. Didn't you know?"

"No. What happened?"

"She was found out in the sea, off Île aux Lapins. The lifeguards brought her in."

In the sea! He wants to ask what she was doing out there. Instead, he says, "We'll be there tomorrow." His heart pounding against his ribs, he wipes the handset on his pants before putting it back in its cradle and turning to Joséphine.

"A coma?" she murmurs, her face deathly pale.

"We'll leave today, Joséphine." He takes her in his arms, holding her tight against his chest. She doesn't make a sound and she's rigid as stone.

Chapter Sixty-Nine

Coventry, July 4, 1963

Sébastian

He has to take Joséphine home, back to her mother. In a secret part of his heart, he wanted to make this journey with his daughter, but not like this, not in this state of panic and terror.

He packs his bag quickly, hesitating when he looks in his sock drawer. He doesn't know how long he'll be gone. He feels Maggie's eyes boring into his back and turns to look at her. "I . . ." But he doesn't know what to say. "I'll come back as soon as I can." He doesn't even know what that means. Does it mean when Élise has come out of her coma? What if she doesn't? Does it mean once he feels ready? What if he never does? What if he can't leave again?

This is ridiculous, he tells himself. It was another life, another time. He loves Maggie now. He's doing this for Joséphine, and once she's safely home, he'll come back. He wasn't there when she was growing up, but he can be there for her now. He has to do this. He has no choice.

"Sébastian." Maggie walks further into the room so she's standing right next to him. She leans her head on his shoulder. "I hope she'll be all right." He's not sure if she's talking about Élise or Joséphine.

That afternoon Maggie drives them to the railway station. Joséphine sits in the back of the car, Philip on her lap, while Luke is wrapped in his blanket, asleep on the back seat. Sébastian keeps his hand on Maggie's knee the whole way, wanting her to know that his heart still belongs to her, but it seems like such a small pathetic gesture. Why can't he just tell her? He's tried, it's just that the words wouldn't come.

Maggie parks the car, and they get out of the back, except Luke, who's fast asleep. Sébastian leans toward Maggie and kisses her briefly on the lips. "I love you," he whispers as he pulls back.

He feels Joséphine tense up. Then he turns to Philip, who's holding Joséphine's hand, though looking a little sulky. He picks him up and hugs him. This will be the first time Sébastian has spent a night away from his family, and it feels wrong to be saying goodbye to them like this.

"Goodbye, Joséphine." Maggie takes her by the shoulders. "I hope your mother will be better soon." Joséphine kisses her on the cheek, and she and Sébastian walk into the station. Sébastian looks back over his shoulder, but Maggie is already settling Philip back into the car.

Joséphine and Sébastian sit opposite each other on the train. Joséphine stares out of the window as the countryside flashes by. It reminds Sébastian of his first train journey in this country when he was scared and alone; unsure what treatment he would receive at the hands of the English.

"Do you think she'll be all right?" Joséphine asks abruptly without looking at him.

"Yes, I do." But of course, he has no idea, and Joséphine knows that. She's just asking for comfort and reassurance, and Sébastian does what fathers do; he comforts his child.

"She's a good swimmer." Joséphine repeats for the hundredth time. "The current must have been very strong."

"Yes, there are some currents that whirl around under the sea, that can pull you right down. There's a name for them, but I can't remember it."

She turns to look at him quizzically as though wondering how he would know that. Then she stares out of the window again. "It's so neat, isn't it?" she says in a faraway voice.

He follows her eyes, taking in the green fields, divided into parcels by bushes and stone walls.

"Do you like it here?" she murmurs without taking her eyes off the passing scenery.

"Yes. It's my home now."

"What about Germany?"

He's already told her about his parents—her grandparents—and his beloved grandmother, who were killed during the bombing of Dresden. "There's nothing left for me there."

"Will you tell me about it? The war. Everything." Joséphine swallows. "And Maman. Will you tell me what she was like?"

Sébastian smiles a small smile. "I see a lot of her in you. You have her eyes. And that same way about you of getting to the truth, she always questioned everything, like you do. She had a way of looking at me...as though..." He feels slightly ridiculous saying it, but says it anyway. "As though she could see right into me."

"I know what you mean." Joséphine surprises him with her words. "She always seemed to know what I was thinking." She pauses, scratching her forehead with her little finger. "That's why it was such a shock to find out what she'd been hiding from me."

Chapter Seventy

Plymouth, July 5, 1963

Sébastian

Sébastian has booked separate cabins on the ferry crossing even though it costs double. He can't suddenly be the father she's never had, and he's wary of frightening her away with too much intrusiveness, too much familiarity. Sometimes he catches her looking at him curiously as though she can't quite work out who he is. He loves to look at her, but often averts his eyes when really all he wants to do is soak up her presence.

He wonders what she was like when she was learning to walk, to talk. What kind of questions did she ask? What were her nightmares? Her passions? Her insecurities? What was her first word? He's missed these formative years. He sees the young woman she is, but he'll never know the layers of the child concealed within. He imagines her to have been full of enthusiasm and curiosity, overflowing with incessant questions, long blonde hair flying behind her, skinny legs dancing, running along the beach. It fills him with melancholy and a yearning for more. He wants to know his daughter in a way that is beyond his reach.

They're both tired, but they still go out on deck, watching the crew pulling in the thick heavy ropes as they are cast off from the deck. The horn blows, and the pilot gives the engine a blast as the ferry pulls away. They stand close to each other, and he feels Joséphine shiver. He wants to put his arm around her and tell her everything's going to be okay, but that would be presumptuous and superficial, as though he could know. He doesn't know, and it terrifies him.

When all the lights from the land have faded, they go back inside to their separate cabins. Sébastian lies on his bunk letting the rhythm of the waves lull him to sleep. But he wakes a short time after, fully alert, worried about Élise and what they'll find when they get to the hospital. What does it mean, to be in a coma? Is it like deep sleep, giving your body time to recover? She *must* recover. His mind turns to Maggie; he felt bad leaving her with the children, especially since Luke's been ill. It's a relief to know her mother will be staying to help. All night long he drifts in and out of sleep, thinking of Élise, then Maggie, then Joséphine, and Élise again.

Early the next morning a loud horn signals their approach into the port of Roscoff. Sébastian dresses quickly then goes out to the corridor. Joséphine is already sitting on one of the chairs in the lounge area. She looks nervous and tired but is wearing a clean blue dress, a light brown silk scarf loosely tied around her neck. He takes a minute to observe her before she notices him standing there, then she turns and acknowledges him with a sad smile.

He sits next to her. "How did you sleep?" he asks.

"Okay." Her dull eyes tell a different story, but he doesn't say anything. He takes her hand and holds it while they wait to disembark.

They don't talk as they shuffle off the ferry and through passport control.

When they get outside, Joséphine points to an old green Renault 4CV, where a woman with gray hair is leaning against the bonnet. A younger woman stands next to her, dark hair falling around her shoulders. The resemblance to Élise is striking. A pang of longing shoots through Sébastian as he's reminded of all the years he missed with Élise—when she was in her late twenties, her early thirties, her late thirties.

"There's Soizic, and Isabelle." Joséphine walks quickly toward them, and when she reaches them the old woman wraps her arms around her, enveloping her. Sébastian follows behind and sees that his daughter is sobbing.

Isabelle smiles at him, taking a step nearer, and instinctively he knows it's all right to kiss her on the cheek rather than the formal handshake. He's grateful for this small gesture which says so much.

However, when Soizic steps back from Joséphine, she holds her hand out, barely making eye contact. "*Bonjour, monsieur.*" Her tone is cold. She turns to open the passenger door, standing back so Joséphine can get in. Then she walks back round to the driver's side and lifts the seat so he can get in the back with Isabelle.

"We'll go straight to the hospital," Soizic announces as they drive along the winding roads.

"Thank you." Sébastian tries not to let this woman make him feel intimidated and alienated. "We've been so worried."

"She got cut off by the tide," Soizic continues. "I don't

understand why she left it so late to come back. She must have fallen asleep in the sun."

"Maman never sleeps in the day." Joséphine winds her window down, and the air rushes in.

Sébastian is confused. Soizic is saying Élise must have fallen asleep, and Joséphine is saying that cannot be the case. So what did happen? Did she fall asleep? Or did she deliberately not leave the island in time? Why would she put herself in danger like that?

"I came as soon as I heard," Isabelle speaks into the silence. "Maman would have come too, but Papa is very ill."

A chill runs down the back of Sébastian's neck at the mention of Élise's father. Joséphine doesn't ask after him, and neither does he.

When they get to the hospital, they're met by a nurse who takes them down a long windowless corridor. It smells of antiseptic, bleach, and boiled cabbage, which Sébastian tries to ignore as they walk toward number thirty-two, Élise's room.

Chapter Seventy-One

Brittany, July 6, 1963

Sébastian

Élise. His Lise. She looks so peaceful, as though she were only asleep. The years slip away, and he's reminded of how he watched her sleeping on his bed in that hotel room for the last time. He holds his breath, looking at her dark hair fanning the pillow. It's longer than he remembers, and her smooth ivory skin is unlined. Long silky eyelashes curl onto her cheeks, adding the only color to her pale face.

His fingers tingle with a longing to reach out and touch her, but he dares not. He realizes he's been holding his breath. It comes back in a rush, thumping in his ears. Joséphine leans over her mother, putting her hands on her face, tenderly stroking her forehead then whispering something in her ear.

Soizic taps Sébastian on the shoulder. "Let's leave them for a minute."

Sébastian ignores her. He's only just got here, and he doesn't want to leave.

"Come on," Soizic insists. "Isabelle can stay with her."

He turns to look at Soizic and understands that she's telling him his place. Reluctantly he pulls his eyes away from Élise and follows Soizic out of the room and down the corridor, where they sit on plastic chairs. He takes out a packet of cigarettes, offering one to Soizic.

"I don't think you should smoke in here," she says curtly.

He stands up. "I'll go outside then." Without waiting for an answer, he walks back toward the door they came in through. He's glad to get away from the old woman; she's not hiding her distaste for him. He can feel it as though it were physical. He walks over to the area of shrubbery and lights up, inhaling as he looks at the clear blue sky. *Lise. Lise.* He's come back. Eighteen years too late. Damn it! Damn it all! He kicks at a loose stone, mixed emotions flooding him. Regret. Guilt. Anger. Fear. He's terrified Élise won't wake up, that he won't be able to talk to her again, that he won't be able to explain.

He thinks of the wedding ring he bought for her, the one he left in the offertory box. He thinks of the candle he lit for her. And he asks himself why he didn't look harder. Why, oh why, had he believed her father? Why hadn't he at least asked to see her grave? He turns his eyes to the ground, his shoulders slumping. Why had he given up so easily?

He longs to talk to her. He has to tell her that he tried to make the best of his life, but that he always held her in his heart, that he never forgot her. He lights another cigarette, trying to still the anxiety pumping through his body, and he paces around the patch of shrubbery again and again.

"Monsieur Kleinhaus." A voice behind him makes him turn around. "You can go and see Élise now." Soizic can hardly look him in the eye, but at least she's come to get him.

"Thank you." He throws his cigarette butt on the ground, grinds it in with the tip of his shoe, then follows her back into the hospital. The vein next to his temple pulses hard, almost painfully, and he can feel a migraine starting.

Isabelle is no longer there, and Joséphine is sitting on a chair next to the bed. She turns to look at him when he walks in, and he sees her face is red and blotchy, her eyes swollen. He places a hand on her shoulder. And he looks at Élise.

Joséphine stands up. "I'm going outside," she whispers.

Without taking his eyes off Élise, Sébastian sits in the chair Joséphine's just left. He strokes the hair back from Élise's face and leans over her, kissing her on her forehead, just like he used to. His lips linger there, all the things he wanted to tell her spiraling round in his aching head, and he doesn't sit back up. He closes his eyes, and he feels his breathing change. As he inhales, his breath seems to go deeper, reaching into his body, into the back of his head, filling every cell with oxygen. It feels like minutes pass before he finally exhales, and as he breathes in again, a sense of peace and calm comes over him, as though he's come home at last. His head is lighter, his migraine gone. He doesn't move but stays there, soaking up this feeling of being in the right place.

Then he remembers the little box in his pocket. He sits back up and takes it out. He lifts out the silver chain with the single ruby rose, and he places it around Élise's neck, moving her hair out of the way so he can do up the clasp. "I told you I'd bring it back to you," he whispers in her ear, half expecting her to answer him, to thank him.

He hears the door click open, and without a word, Joséphine slips back in. She stands next to him. He reaches out for her hand, squeezing it softly, just to let her know he's there for her.

"Do you think she knows we're here?" Joséphine whispers.

"Yes, she does." Sébastian raises his voice to a normal level. "And I'm sure she's smiling inside." He lets go of Joséphine's hand and takes Élise's. "She'll wake when she's ready."

"She has to." Joséphine's voice is desperate.

"She will." And in that moment, he truly believes it. He has the strongest feeling that Élise is just giving them more time to get to know each other, giving Sébastian the space to be a father to their daughter.

"I was so horrible to her." Joséphine's voice trembles, and he knows she's trying not to cry. "I didn't understand why she was hardly here for me, why she had to work for another family. And why she didn't even tell me about you. I was angry with her." Tears slide down her cheeks. "Is it my fault?"

"What do you mean?" He tenses, afraid of what she's going to say.

Joséphine sniffles, gulping back tears. "Do you think she wanted to die?"

"No! No!" It's crossed his mind, but he hasn't let himself entertain this thought, not seriously, and he can't let Joséphine think this. "Of course not," he insists. "She wouldn't do that." Lise would never do that, would never abandon them like that. "She has you." He stands up and grips Joséphine's shoulders, turning her round to face him. "I know she loves you."

"But I told her I wanted to stay in England." She gulps back more tears. "I wanted to hurt her."

Sébastian pulls her into him. "It's not your fault."

Chapter Seventy-Two

Brittany, July 5, 1963

Joséphine

The next evening, Joséphine sits at the kitchen table watching Soizic shelling peas onto an old newspaper. There's so much she'd like to ask her, but she doesn't know how. She wishes she'd talked to her mother before dashing off to England, even let her mother talk, but she hadn't. She became uncommunicative and sullen, like a sulking child. And now all the questions she'd like to ask Soizic die on her tongue before she can get them out.

"Where's your father?" Soizic looks up.

"Gone for a walk." He'd asked Joséphine if she wanted to go with him, but she preferred to stay and talk to Soizic. She needs to know what made her mother go into the water like that, with all her clothes on, on her own. She has to find out.

"Never thought I'd be cooking dinner for a Boche!" Soizic shakes her head.

"A Boche?" How can Soizic talk about him like that? "He's my father."

"Yes, and that's the only reason he's here." She shakes her head again. "For the love of God, I don't know why I'm doing it."

"Maybe you've forgiven him," Joséphine ventures.

"No. No. Only God can forgive." She sounds resigned. "All we can do is accept. I've accepted that he wasn't much more than a boy when the war began, that he didn't have the courage to do the right thing."

"Maybe sometimes you don't know what the right thing is." Joséphine is thinking of how she wanted to distance herself from her mother, how she wanted to get to know her father instead, of how she knowingly hurt her mother.

Soizic shakes her head. "No, I think we know what the right thing is, we just lack the courage to do it."

Is that what happened to Joséphine? Had she lacked the courage to confront her mother? Had she run away instead? She's not sure. She wipes her eyes, swallowing her tears. They won't help anyone. "What was the last thing Maman said to you?" There, she's said it now.

Soizic goes very still, and Joséphine feels the air between them swell and grow heavy. "We'd just got your letter from England, and the one from your father," Soizic finally says. "She was upset."

"Because of me." Joséphine swallows again, forcing the next words out. "Because I wanted to stay with...because I didn't want to come home." The tears she's been holding back burst from a place deep inside. There's no stopping them now. It was her fault. She knew it was.

"No. No." Soizic gets up and comes round to Joséphine's side of the table. She envelopes her in her warm solid arms, rocking her gently. "It was me. She was upset with me. Because I wouldn't let her talk about him. Your father. I wouldn't let her tell you the truth about who your father was."

"Why?" Anger mixes with guilt, and Joséphine pulls away from Soizic. "Just because he was German?"

"Yes." Her answer is plain and honest, and Joséphine senses no shame in it.

Soizic puts her hand up her sleeve and pulls out a handkerchief. She wipes Joséphine's eyes. "You haven't lived through a war." Her tone is soft. "You don't know what it was like. I hope you never have to witness the violence, the cruelty. Ask your mother. We had to protect you from it. If people had known your father was a Boche, you would have been made to suffer, even as a child. But for it to work, everyone had to pretend, especially you. And the lie worked, didn't it? You had a safe, peaceful childhood." Soizic is breathing quickly as though exhausted after her little speech.

Joséphine feels her mouth setting in a hard line. "Safe, peaceful childhood? Is that what you think I had?" She wipes her eyes. "I was lonely. I thought people were whispering behind my back, and I didn't know why. I thought there was something wrong with me."

"What? But you never said anything."

"No one ever said anything! But there *was* something wrong with me, wasn't there? I just didn't know what." She pauses. "People knew, didn't they?"

"No! We never told a soul." Soizic lets out a long breath. "I suppose people draw their own conclusions when they see a blue-eyed, fair-haired child, born in 1945. No father."

"It never crossed my mind that I had a German father. I

just swallowed your lies." Joséphine buries her nose in the handkerchief, sniffing back more tears. "I still don't understand why you took us in."

"My brother, Yannick, asked me."

"So, you didn't even want to?"

Soizic shakes her head. "Not at first, no. But when you were born, I felt differently. Yannick knew I would. He always seemed to know what people needed before they did." She hesitates. "He knew I'd come to love you, like a daughter." Her voice cracks on the word "daughter."

"But it wasn't my father." Joséphine speaks slowly, digging deep for the courage to say what she wants to say. "It wasn't him who killed your daughter." There, she's done it now. She's stepped onto forbidden territory. Holding her breath, she waits for Soizic to reply.

Soizic lets out a breath, filling the air around them. But no words come.

Joséphine coughs. "It wasn't his fault."

Soizic stands and walks back round to the other side of the table. Without looking at Joséphine, she folds the newspaper around the peapods, picks them up, and takes them over to the sink. She throws them into it. Then she turns around to face Joséphine. "Your father wasn't the one who arrested Mireille, nor was he the one who interrogated her, or killed her, but he was part of it. He belonged to them— the Nazis. Every single last one of them is guilty."

Joséphine can't stand to see the hurt and pain burning in Soizic's eyes. She looks down, ashamed at how she's forced Soizic to remember.

"They kept Mireille for three days." Soizic's voice is hoarse, ragged with emotion. "Three whole days."

Joséphine swallows hard, then wipes her eyes and walks

toward Soizic. She puts her arms around her and holds her tight as though she'll fall into fragments if she lets go.

"She didn't talk," Soizic whispers through her tears. "She never talked."

Joséphine doesn't let go of Soizic when convulsions shoot through her. She holds her tighter. She knows the story. She knows how they sewed her daughter's lips together then hung her from a butcher's hook. And she understands how some things can never be forgiven.

Chapter Seventy-Three

Brittany, July 7, 1963

Sébastian

Sébastian should have brought a sweater; the early evenings are cool, and the wind is strong, blowing sharp grains of sand into his face. It must be time to head back now anyway. Soizic is cooking dinner. He wouldn't be surprised if she slipped something into his portion; her animosity is visceral. Thank God, he's booked into a hotel for the night; dinner will be hard enough. He's only doing it for Joséphine, and he knows Soizic is too.

Turning around, he heads back to the cottage. When he opens the kitchen door, he sees Joséphine and Soizic huddled together by the sink, crying.

"Has something happened? Élise?" he asks desperately. "Is Élise...?"

"There's no news." Joséphine pulls back and looks at him through wet eyes.

This isn't his place, here in their home. He should leave.

"I'm sorry, I've intruded," he says. "Don't worry about dinner, I'm not hungry. It's probably better if I go now."

No one answers.

"I'll come back in the morning." Without another word, Sébastian turns around and walks out.

The next morning, he gets up early and walks along the beach before going to the cottage. He thinks about going back home to Coventry, where he's needed. He's seen Élise, but there's nothing he can do now. They've lived without him all these years, they'll manage now. He'll stay just one more night, and then he'll go. He can always come back when Élise wakes up from the coma. This is how he has to think; she *will* wake up.

He arrives at the cottage and is just about to knock on the kitchen door when it opens, banging him on the nose. Soizic stands in front of him. "I'm sorry," she mumbles. "I'm running late this morning. I'm just on my way out to see to the cows." She pauses. "There's coffee on the stove if you want some."

"*Merci.*" It's the most she's ever said to him. "Do you want a hand?" he asks impulsively.

She looks him in the eye. "What do you know about cows?"

"I worked on a farm in England."

She looks surprised. "If you like," she eventually says in an exasperated voice, as though she'll just have to put up with him.

Sébastian follows her toward the cowshed. It will be good to have something practical to do. They go into the shed, and she passes him a little wooden milking stool. He sets it down next to a cow then sits on it; it's so small he has to fold his knees against his chest. He warms his hands together then puts his fingers on the teats and pulls gently. The cow moos loudly, but the milk starts to flow into the pail below. It all comes back to him, all that time he spent in England, all that time when Élise was raising Joséphine on her own, believing him to be dead.

Lost in his thoughts, he almost forgets where he is. Then he hears Soizic's voice behind him. "I think that's all she's going to give you today." Sébastian stops milking and looks up. Soizic is studying him with an expression he can't quite read. Then she speaks. "My mother always said you can't go far wrong with a man who can milk a cow."

Sébastian's face breaks into a smile, and he laughs. It feels good to laugh. He laughs some more. Then he realizes Soizic is joining in. He catches her eye, and she abruptly stops. But they had a moment, and it lifts his tired heart.

"Would you give me a ride to the hospital this morning, please?" he asks.

"Yes, I'll take you now, before Joséphine gets up. She needs to rest."

After a quick coffee, she drives him in. They don't talk, and he knows better than to push it. He thanks her and gets out of the car, heading toward the main door. The receptionist greets him, then a doctor with a clipboard walks toward to him. "Monsieur," he says. "I believe you're here to see Élise Chevalier?"

"Yes, that's right." Sébastian's pulse races. Why has the doctor come to greet him like this?

"I've been in to observe her this morning." The doctor walks forward and Sébastian has to walk quickly to keep up. "She's showing some minuscule movement," he continues.

Sébastian's heart leaps.

"Very, very tiny, but her eyelids have been moving, indicating REM sleep—dream sleep."

"Thank you!" Sébastian walks more quickly, desperate to get to Lise.

Chapter Seventy-Four

Brittany, July 8, 1963

Élise

Bright sunlight streams through large windows, shining onto Sébastian. His hair is combed with a neat side part, and he's smiling at me. He's happy. There's a woman with dark blonde hair standing by his side, holding out her hand. I take it, and I can tell she's a good person, that she loves him. It's okay for me to leave him now.

I'm weightless, and I float out of the room. Now I'm swimming in the sea, following sunbeams glinting off the water. I roll onto my back, the water moving like silk over my body. I gaze up at the cloudless sky. There is no sound, only peace. This is where I want to be.

A voice sends shock waves through me, shattering the silence. The sea rolls under me. It's parting. I'm falling, falling. I look at the sky again, but it's turned dark and threatening. The water tugs at me, pulling me down. I try to kick, but I can't find my legs. I'm a dead weight, sinking, sinking.

The voice echoes through me again. But I don't want to listen to it. Using the last of my strength, I reach out, searching for the warmth of the sun. But my arms won't move. My eyes are covered in thick, clinging mud. I'm being sucked down, sucked into darkness. I try to cry out. *Help! Help!* But no sound comes. I use all my strength to force a scream from my throat, but it only comes out as the tiniest squeak. I'm going to die here. I feel it coming for me. Death. A huge, frightening void. I try again. I scream. But the scream stays inside me.

The voice comes again. "Lise."

Lise. There's only one person in the world who calls me Lise. But he's not here. Sébastian's not here. He's in that sunny room with his wife.

"Sébastian!" I try to scream, but mud fills my throat. He can't hear me.

"Lise." His voice is clear now. But I still can't see him, and the cloying darkness is pulling me down. I'm so weak, so tired. I feel myself letting go, falling, falling.

"Lise. I'm here. I'm here." His words are close. But why won't he save me? Using all my force, I try to hold on. I try to lift a hand, to reach out and touch him.

I feel his finger. I have to hold on to it. I have to. But the thick wet mud fills my mouth, my nostrils, wanting to suffocate me. I have to move my hand. I put all my will-power into it, all my strength. Still, it won't move.

Mud fills my throat. I can't breathe. I cough. It burns my throat. I cough again. I cough up the thick mud that wants to kill me. I cough and splutter. Water flows up through me, drowning me. Air. I need air. I gasp. A deep breath floods my lungs. They're going to explode. And then I breathe. I breathe. I'm breathing.

He's holding me. Sébastian is holding me. I cling to him. I grip his arms, my fingers digging in. He holds me tight, his arms wrapped around me, his hands clutching me. His body shudders unevenly, and I realize he's crying. My wet cheek lies against his, and I taste the salt of our tears on my tongue.

Commotion, people shouting, clanking noises try to break through, but I won't let them. I block them out, and I hold on.

"Thank God. You've come back, Lise." I swallow his words whole, desperate for more. "You're safe. Lise," he whispers in my ear. "I'm here."

I want to answer him, but my throat is still thick with mud. No words can get through. Hands on my shoulders pull on me. They're pulling me away from him. My voice is released. I scream.

"Lise." He's still holding on to me, but his voice is stronger now. "It's okay. The doctor just wants to check you."

Where am I? Am I stuck in a dream? Or have I died? I try to ask, but I can't find my voice.

"Shh, shh, Lise. I'm not going anywhere. I'm staying here with you."

I open my eyes. The mud has gone. And I see him. Sébastian. But there's something different about him. His face is fuller, more settled. I look into his eyes; they're the same. The same blue as Joséphine's. Where is she?

"Joséphine," I murmur, her name bubbling up in my throat.

"Joséphine is fine," he says. "Our daughter. She's just like you."

"Where? Where is she?"

"She'll be here soon." He grips my hand.

Then I see it. The sea. The waves washing over me. The current pulling at my legs. Pulling me down. Gasping for air.

Someone shines a bright light into my eyes. It hurts, but I don't have the strength to pull away. "How are you feeling, madame?" The question is too complicated for me. I cough again. "The lifeguards brought you in. Do you remember what happened?" Suddenly I do. The letter. The tide coming in. Covering the path. The cold. The dark. "Did you bang your head? Do you remember falling into the sea?"

"Yes," I murmur. It comes back to me in patches. I tried to keep warm, but there was nowhere to go. Just rocks. And the dark. There was no moon. I couldn't see. Then it comes flooding back to me. Jumping in, trying to swim, the waves crashing over me, the jagged rocks. "I dreamed I drowned."

"You were lucky a fisherman spotted you. You had a narrow escape. We need to do further tests tomorrow." The doctor looks at Sébastian.

Sébastian. Is that really him?

"Don't leave her alone for the moment. Once she feels stronger you could help her get up, but she's not to leave the room."

It is him! It is Sébastian. It's not a dream. He's real.

"Lise." He takes my hand, holding it against his cheek.

"Where have you been?" I close my eyes, my head throbbing against my temples.

"I'm here. I'm here now."

"I waited for you." I concentrate on his eyes, trying not to give in to the pain in my head, trying not to slip away.

"I tried. I tried to get back to you."

I try to breathe into my head, to stop the spinning. He squeezes my hand, and it keeps me here.

"Lise, all those letters I wrote. You never got them."

I close my eyes again, swallowing the hard lump in my throat, words blurring and swimming in front of me. "The letters." I try to concentrate. "I read them." I feel sleep waves coming, a release from the pain, but I want to stay here now, with him. I take a deep breath, forcing myself to hold on. "Where did you go?"

"I'm here. I'm here now." His voice is hoarse, and I know he's summoning these words from a place deep inside. He puts his hand gently around the back of my neck, holding me tight against him, and I feel his love like a physical force, beating in my heart. "I never left you," he murmurs.

I want Sébastian to stay with me. I want to know everything about him, but I'm so tired. I lean into him, closing my eyes again, and now my head feels light, as though a huge weight has been lifted. Waves of sleep draw in. I resist them. "Tell me," I murmur. "What happened that night? The night they took you away."

He takes my head and lays it softly on the pillow. "You're tired, *ma chérie*. Rest now."

Chapter Seventy-Five

Brittany, July 9, 1963

Élise

The next morning Sébastian walks into my room with Joséphine. They look like they've been together all their lives, smiling at me in the same shy way.

I hold my hands out to them. Sébastian takes one, Joséphine the other. I drink in this magical wonderful feeling of being held between them.

Joséphine lets go of my hand and puts her arms around me, burying her face in my neck. I feel her begin to tremble, her tears soaking into me. "I'm sorry, Maman. I'm so sorry."

I hold her tight. "But, Joséphine, you have nothing to be sorry for. I should have known the sea better than that. It was my own stupid fault."

"But you got my letter." She sobs. "It was horrible—the way I told you about…" Her words tumble out. "I didn't mean it. I wanted to come home."

"I know you did. I know you were just angry with me."

"But I shouldn't have told you about... about his other family."

"No," I say. "You were right to tell me." I look over her shoulder at Sébastian, and the look of discomfort in his eyes tells me everything. This is something we'll have to get out of the way, something we'll have to talk about. His new life. Without me.

"How did you like England?"

She moves back, wiping her tears away. "I missed you. I missed Soizic."

"You must tell me all about it." I want to hear her stories, but my head is throbbing again.

As if on cue, the nurse walks in. "*Bonjour, tout le monde*," she says. "I hope you're not overwhelming madame here. She needs plenty of rest. I'm just going to run some checks on her. Would you mind stepping outside?"

Joséphine and Sébastian stand up. Sébastian flicks his gaze back to me. "I'll come back."

"*Au revoir, Maman.*" Joséphine kisses me on the cheek, and then they're gone.

After my checks, I drift off to sleep again. Then the nurse comes back in to wake me for lunch. I'm not hungry, but when the hot dish of carrot puree and lamb arrives, I find my appetite. It's good to eat, and I feel better already. I'm just finishing my *fromage blanc* when Sébastian walks in.

My heart leaps at the sight of him, and a smile stretches across my face. It's matched by his, and he walks further into the room, moving my lunch tray out of the way, so he can sit on the bed. He takes my hand, bringing it to his lips. "You've got your color back." He strokes my cheek with the back of his hand.

I reach out and take it in mine, holding it tight. "What happened, Sébastian? What happened?"

"You got caught by the tide. You thought you could swim for it."

"No." I grip his hand tightly, looking into his eyes, and it's as though I'm looking back in time. "What happened to us?"

The only sound is his breathing. My breathing. His silence is his answer.

"Will you stay a while? Just a short while, here with me?" I can't bear to lose him all over again. Not yet. I'm not strong enough.

"Yes, yes, of course." I hear the warmth in his voice. "I'll stay as long as you need me."

I want to tell him I'll never stop needing him, that I'll need him forever, that I've always needed him, but I bite my tongue and swallow my words.

"Isn't our daughter incredible? And brave, coming all that way to England on her own." He kisses me on the forehead. "I wish I'd been here when she was growing up. I would give anything to have been with you both. I'm so sorry you had to do it all on your own."

"I had Soizic."

He smiles a crooked smile. "That couldn't have been easy."

"Sébastian," I say, enjoying the sound of his name on my tongue. "It was never the right time for us, was it?"

He squeezes my hand, and his eyes turn a shade darker. The silence between us swirls. So much to say. And so little.

"What's your wife like?" I force myself to ask as naturally as possible, but still, I hear the false note of brightness in my voice, and I know he hears it too. But this is the kind of question a long-lost friend would ask, and that's what we are now. Friends who were once in love. A lifetime ago.

The question seems to have startled him. "Maggie?" Her name slips off his tongue with such familiarity, such warmth, it makes my heart ache. "She's kind. She has hazel eyes, straight brown hair." It's a vague description and doesn't really tell me anything. It's not what I'm after, but I know he doesn't want to hurt me, he doesn't want to tell me how happy they are together, but I feel it. And I need to hear it.

"Where did you meet her?" I help him out.

"At work." He seems relieved to have something concrete to talk about. "I went to Coventry. It was blitzed during the war." He pauses, and I understand that's exactly *why* he chose Coventry. "I was working on design patents for motorbikes. I still am."

I wait for him to get back to the subject of his wife.

"Maggie was making tea in the little kitchen next to the secretarial pool." He hesitates, and I can tell he's unsure whether to go on, so I say nothing. "I'd been there about a month," he continues. "I hadn't made any friends, not really. People were polite and respectful with me, which was already something, I wasn't expecting more than that. It was a kind of penance for me—to go to Coventry."

I nod, understanding his need to make this pilgrimage.

"But Maggie was different. She wanted to know where I was from, though she must have already known. Everyone knew I was German." He pauses. "She told me I was the only man to set foot in the kitchen, and hadn't I noticed? She made me laugh."

I want to tell him to stop. I've heard enough. But I just look at him, trying my best to keep my eyes expressionless, while my heart is breaking all over again. He goes quiet as though he's read my mind. Then I turn away and stare resolutely at the hospital parking lot, my eyes unfocused, trying to push my heartache back down where no one will see it. I feel his eyes on me, but I can't look at him. Not yet.

Chapter Seventy-Six

Brittany, July 9, 1963

Sébastian

Sébastian has to use the payphone in the village to call the neighbor at home, who fetches Maggie. He has ten one-franc coins ready; that should be more than enough.

"How is Élise?" Maggie asks immediately.

"She's okay. She came out of the coma yesterday."

"Yesterday? Is she all right?"

"Yes, she's getting stronger every day." He should tell her he's coming home now, but he's not ready. "How are the children?"

"Luke's cough has gone completely. He's much better." The relief in her voice travels down the line. "Philip doesn't stop talking. You know what he's like. He likes to babble on." She laughs, and Sébastian's heart fills with love for his family. "When are you coming home?" she asks.

"Next week, I think." It's a guess, but he doesn't know what else to say.

"Next week?" Her surprise resonates down the line. "What about work?" She's reducing it to practicalities.

"I'll call them. Don't worry."

Silence echoes back down the line. He shoves another franc into the slot, wondering what he can say to reassure her. "I'll come back as soon as I can." He cringes at the inadequacy of his words. "I'll wait till Élise comes out of the hospital."

"When will that be?" Maggie's voice has an edge to it. She's not going to put up with any ambiguity. And neither should she.

"Soon. I just want to make sure Joséphine is settled. She's had a lot to come to terms with. And she gets her exam results next week. I'd like to be here for that."

"She can always come and visit." Maggie won't let him find excuses. "Philip would love to see her again. He's become quite attached to her. He talks about her, he calls her 'Yo-feen.' It's very cute."

"I know." But he knows he can't take Joséphine away from Lise. She needs her daughter near her.

The next day Sébastian visits Élise. She's allowed to leave the room as long as she stays in the hospital, so he takes her arm and they walk to the lounge area, where they find a table by the window. They sit opposite each other, their hands on their laps. But this doesn't feel right to him, so he reaches across the table, his palm open. She places her slender hand in his and he wraps his fingers around it, caressing the back of her hand with his thumb. Neither of them speaks, then he smiles. "I'm so glad Joséphine found me."

"She didn't want me to come with her."

"She's got a strong character. Just like her mother." He

squeezes her hand. "I was an idiot for believing your father when he told me you'd been shot. I can't believe I didn't see it now."

"I don't think I can ever forgive him for what he did."

He nods, acknowledging her pain. "I wish we'd run away, like you wanted to," he whispers in a dreamlike voice. "Taken horses, lived in the forest until it was all over. At least we would have been together, just like you said."

"We couldn't have known someone would give you away."

He puts a little pressure on the back of her hand. Does she know? Does she know it was her mother? He doesn't want to tell her now. He doesn't know what it might do to her in her fragile state, but the question lies there.

"Do you know who it was?" she finally asks.

He shakes his head, unable to speak a lie.

But she sees through him. "You do know, don't you?"

He shakes his head again, looking down at their entwined hands.

"Who was it? Was it Isabelle's friend, Marie?"

For the third time he shakes his head.

"It was my mother, wasn't it?"

This time he finds he can't shake his head.

Élise lets out a long breath. "Deep down I think I always knew."

"She was trying to protect you."

"What! By having you killed? No, she was thinking of herself and being accused of collaboration afterward. She wanted to gain credit with the Résistance."

"No. They offered her a deal. Your safety for handing me in."

"My safety?" She laughs ironically. "That's a good one." She pauses. "I wonder if Isabelle knows."

"I'm not sure. You can ask her; she's coming in later then she's going back to Paris tonight. Your father is ill." He pauses. "Lise." He wants to know. He has to know, but he doesn't dare ask. The air between them expands with the unsaid. Then he finds the courage. "What happened after they took me away?" He feels Élise go very still. He can't even hear her breathing. "Lise, what happened? Tell me."

And so she tells him. She tells him how they dragged her from her home, how they stripped her down to her underwear, how they shaved her and branded her on the forehead. He screws his eyes shut tightly, as though he can rid himself of the terrifying images crashing through his mind. He takes in a breath and stands, sweeping the hair back from her face, kissing her softly on the forehead, where they must have painted the swastika. "Forgive me," he murmurs.

"It's not you I need to forgive."

"I should never have exposed you to that. I should have known." He swallows the hard pebble in his throat, cursing himself, cursing her mother for giving him away. In doing so, she'd betrayed her own daughter. How could she have been so stupid?

He wants to hold Lise, stroke her beautiful hair, soothe her pain, but he's too late, and he's worried it would seem like pity. "Lise," he says. "You've been so brave."

"No, I've been hiding here ever since."

"You came here and lived with a woman who had every reason to despise and hate you, but you did it to keep our daughter safe." He lifts a strand of her hair and kisses it. He still can't stop the images flooding his mind. Men stripping her, taking razors to her head. "I should have been there. I should have stopped them. Who was it? Who did it?"

"I don't even know. Men. But there were women in the crowd. Everyone was there."

Sébastian buries his head in her hair. "I want to kill them."

Élise pulls back and looks at him. "And so the never-ending wheel of revenge turns."

"I'm sorry. It's just…" He wants to punch the wall. But instead he tries to calm the rage beating in his heart. "How did you get through? How did you…?"

"I'm not sure I ever did, not really. It threw me into survival mode. I didn't want anything anymore, only for Joséphine to be safe." She pauses, her forehead creased. "It took away all my dreams." She lets out a long breath. "Horizontal collaboration. De Gaulle made it a crime: '*indignité nationale*,' he called it. They didn't try prostitutes though." Élise smiles faintly. "They were just doing their job."

"Like the police," Sébastian says, fury still burning in his chest. He squeezes Élise's hand, a terrible sense of injustice making his heart swell. Were the police punished for collaborating? Of course not, but then they'd been ordered to. What choice did they have? "It was all so wrong." He drops his head as though in defeat.

Then he looks up. "Lise, has there been anyone else?" He immediately regrets asking. He doesn't even know where the question came from. It's not the point. He's so clumsy. It's none of his business.

"No," she answers. "No one."

He wishes there had been. He can't stand the thought of her extinguishing that part of herself. It doesn't seem right, that he got on with his life, even found love, while she was living out her life alone.

"I don't think I can forgive my mother. Or my father."

Lise interrupts his train of thought, bringing the conversation back to her parents.

There's a bleakness in her voice, and he wants to make it better. "Your mother was trying to protect you," he says again. "You know how it was, all those different factions, she could have made a deal with one group, only for another to go back on it. I don't believe she gave me away because she wanted me dead." He hesitates, seeing a parallel between the way Joséphine felt toward her mother when she found she'd been lying to her all her life, and the way Élise feels now toward her own mother. "Sometimes people do the wrong things for the right reasons. I imagine your mother has punished herself enough."

"You think I should forgive her?"

Looking her in the eye, he nods slowly.

"Then Joséphine will forgive me?"

"Joséphine has already forgiven you."

Lise smiles. "Has she?"

"Yes. We've all done things we regret." He pauses, giving himself time to think. "Maybe it's time for you to talk with your mother, give her a chance to explain herself. She must have been terrified for you."

Chapter Seventy-Seven

Brittany, July 10, 1963

Élise

Joséphine walks into my room, wearing the light blue summer dress I bought for her birthday, the one I picked out specially because it matches her eyes. She has a healthy glow about her, and her face is lightly tanned. I guess she's enjoying having some time outside, while she waits for her exam results.

"I picked you some flowers." She brings her hands out from behind her back, flourishing a bouquet of pink and purple flowers. "They're from the field," she says, as if I didn't know.

I hold out my hand and take them, bringing them up to my nose, breathing in their fresh sweet odor. "Thank you." I kiss her on the cheek. "They're beautiful." I put them in the carafe of water on the bedside table. "I'll get a vase later."

She laughs, a light happy laugh. Then she puts her arms

around me. We hold each other tight, and I soak up the sensation of her soft skin next to mine, the warmth of her body, her lemony fresh smell. My daughter.

"Joséphine," I murmur. "How are you?"

She pulls back. "I was so scared." Her eyes fill up. "I thought...I thought you were going to die."

I take the summer scarf she has loosely tied around her neck and wipe away her tears. "No, I'm not leaving you. Joséphine, I'm sorry, I'm sorry I lied to you."

"I'm sorry I didn't ask you more questions, Maman, about what you did during the war. I'm sorry I was so angry with you. Isabelle said I should ask you."

"Did she?" I think of telling her about what Sébastian and I did together, how we saved the children, but it seems so long ago now.

"What did Isabelle mean?" she insists.

And so I tell her.

"All those hidden stories." A small crease appears between Joséphine's eyebrows. "It's as though...as though I only half knew you." She pauses. "I wish I'd known about everything. I wish I'd known you properly."

She rubs her eyes in an endearingly childish gesture. "Imagine how different it would have been if no one had ever lied. Lies are like stealing. You steal the truth." She's so wise for her years. "But you've given it back now." She smiles. "And I've got my father back." She pauses, the smile dropping from her face. "I just wish..."

I know what she's going to say, and I don't want to hear it. I take her hand, rubbing it between mine, like I used to when she'd come out of the sea with freezing fingers, and I try to think of something to say that will stop her from saying it. But I'm too slow.

"I wish," she forges ahead, "I just wish he didn't have another family."

There, she's said it now. Of course, part of me wishes the same, but I have to be the adult here and see the way forward. "No," I say, "it means you have brothers, and…"

"And what?"

"It means he was happy. I'd rather think of your father as happy during those years than alone and sad. At least I had you."

"But it wasn't enough, was it?" I notice she's turned it into a question rather than a statement.

"It was. It was enough for me. I was happy." I bring her hand up to my cheek and hold it there, while I look into her eyes, imploring her to believe me.

"But there was something missing. There was. I felt it," she insists.

"Yes," I admit. "The story of your father was missing. Children pick up on these things, and you knew something wasn't right." I pause, remembering my times of sadness, and I tell myself how important it is to be honest with her now. "I didn't enjoy leaving you on Sundays. But I always looked forward to my weekends, to coming back to you. I missed you so much."

"But why did you work so far away, for all those years?"

"It was all I could find at the time, and the Beauforts were good to me. I suppose we got into a routine, and I could see that you were happy and well cared for. I saw how much Soizic loved you…loves you, and I was content that everything was going smoothly."

"But were you happy, Maman?"

"Yes, I was. I was lonely at times, but you gave me so much happiness, so much pleasure, it was all worth it. And we had our Augusts together. That was the best part."

Joséphine smiles, her tears nearly all dried up now. "Yes, we had some great summers, didn't we? I loved those long evenings when we'd stay on the beach as long as we wanted."

"And we're going to have more. We have a lifetime of summers in front of us." I take my daughter in my arms, my heart overflowing with love. And I think, *What would have happened if I'd drowned?* How could I have been so caught up in my own grief that I couldn't see hers?

Chapter Seventy-Eight

Brittany, July 12, 1963

Élise

Soizic comes to pick me up from the hospital with Joséphine. I sit in the front of the car, gazing out at the fields and little stone cottages, catching glimpses of water as we cross the small bridge, taking us across the estuary into Trégastel.

"We've prepared your favorite dinner." Joséphine's excitement rings out.

"What's that then?" I'm curious.

"*Confit de canard* and green beans. Then *tarte au citron*." She sounds triumphant.

"It *was* supposed to be a secret." Soizic laughs.

Confit de canard; the dish I chose the only time Sébastian and I ate together in a restaurant. Funny how she came to decide that was my favorite. Actually, I prefer lamb, but I don't tell her. "I can't wait," I say. And I can't. I can't wait for the four of us to sit down at the table together, like a family. I'm assuming Sébastian will be invited. If he isn't, I'll insist. I won't let Soizic leave him out. Not ever again.

In the late afternoon, while Joséphine and Soizic prepare the feast, Sébastian and I walk barefoot along the beach, through the shallow waves, letting them break over our feet. He splashes me playfully, and I splash him back, then he takes my hand, as if we're old friends, easy in each other's company. The warmth of his touch spreads through me, electrifying me, making me feel alive in a way I haven't been alive in years. I know he feels it too.

I pull my hand away, pushing my hair behind my ears as I stare out to the horizon, reminding myself not to get too close. He puts his hands in his pockets, looking out to sea. "It's beautiful here," he says wistfully. I watch him squinting at the sunlight shimmering on the sea, and I know what he's thinking. This is where he wants to be. With me. With his daughter. But there's another part to the story. His sons. His wife.

"Yes. It's beautiful." My heart is full, just with him standing there next to me. I long to reach out and touch him, caress the stubble on his cheek, stroke his lips, but I don't. "Sébastian," I say. "Shall we go back now?"

"Back now?" he repeats as though he can't quite understand two simple words.

"Yes, back home."

"Home?" He shakes his head as if shaking out a thought. "Yes, of course." I hear the twinge of regret in his voice. Quickly turning around from the horizon, I walk away.

But he grabs my hand. My stomach lurches, and I turn around, facing him. He puts an arm around my waist and pulls me toward him. I feel his warm breath on my cheek. He puts the other arm around the back of my neck and his lips touch mine. We stand there, the sea swirling around our legs, lost in our kiss, and I feel him breathing life back into me. I hear the seagulls screech and the waves hitting the shore, but it's as though these sounds belong to another world.

Chapter Seventy-Nine

Brittany, July 13, 1963

Sébastian

After breakfast at the hotel, Sébastian walks to the cottage, but instead of going inside, he goes into the cowshed, inhaling the earthy honest smell of the animals. Lise has taken Joséphine out shopping: "A girl's trip," she said, smiling. He was glad to let them go, glad to have some time to himself. He needs to think. Really think.

He wants to take Lise in his arms, kiss her again and again, whisper in her ear how much he loves her, has always loved her. He aches to do it, a physical ache that makes his body heavy. But he's torn. Behind every smile, every laugh, every conversation, lies a turmoil. He doesn't speak of it to Lise, but she knows.

How can he leave her? It will break her heart. It will break his. They could pretend they'll be good friends, even great friends. But they were always so much more than that.

And she'll know that every night she goes to bed alone,

he'll be going to bed with his wife. It will only hurt her unless she can break away from him. Unless she finds another love. He has to want that for her. But does he? Could he bear the idea? He has to *really truly* want that for her. But he can see she doesn't even want that for herself.

Someone coughing behind him makes him turn around. Soizic stands there, her head cocked to one side as though weighing him up. Neither of them speaks.

Then a cow makes a long deep moo, as though to fill the silence.

"Do you want a coffee?" she asks.

He nods, and they walk into the kitchen, where she passes him the coffee grinder. "My wrists aren't what they used to be," she says.

"While I'm here," he says, "I could do some of the heavy work for you. I could probably mend the wall where it's started to crumble."

She laughs. "Oh, you could, could you? There's an art to building a stone wall like that. You're an office worker now, aren't you?"

"Not exactly. I'm an engineer."

Soizic purses her lips together. He turns back to the grinder.

"Why did you go back there?" she asks.

"To England? It seemed like the right thing to do. My atonement."

Soizic shrugs a shoulder, as if dismissing what he's just said. "And that's where you met your wife?"

"Maggie. Yes." Her name hangs heavy in the room. Sébastian finishes grinding the beans and hands the grinder back to Soizic.

"What's she like?" she asks.

Sébastian is surprised by her question. "She's kind. And strong, and patient."

Soizic passes him a cup of coffee. "When are you going back? You shouldn't leave it any longer. It will only get harder."

"I know." He looks at her. "But I don't know how to leave."

Soizic sighs. "Well, it's a step up from being dead. At least you're alive."

He can't help smiling at her pragmatism.

"Sometimes loving someone doesn't mean being with them," she continues.

He understands why she's insisting on this point. Both her daughter and husband were taken away from her in the cruelest way, and she would have been happy just to know they were alive somewhere. "Élise will still be here, but your life is somewhere else now. The longer you leave it, the harder it will be for everyone. *Courage*, Sébastian," she murmurs. "You have to tell her soon."

It's the first time she's used his name, and he knows it's her way of saying she's accepted him.

Chapter Eighty

Brittany, July 15, 1963

Joséphine

Monday morning, Joséphine wakes early, excitement and anticipation running through her. Today her parents will be taking her to school to find out if she's passed her *baccalauréat*, just like all the other kids. She imagines her school friends seeing Sébastian and working it out, and she doesn't care what they think. She'll be leaving this small town soon, this place where everyone always wondered if she had a Boche for a father, but where no one dared say it out loud.

Soizic drives them to the school, her father in the front seat next to her, while Joséphine and her mother sit in the back, their hands on the seat, interlaced, neither of them saying a word. Joséphine knows her mum understands how nervous she is, how important this step is for her, the way she looks at her and winks, squeezing her hand. *It's going to be all right*, she's saying with her eyes.

Soizic parks the car. "I'll wait here." She turns back to face Joséphine. "*Bonne chance.*"

"Aren't you coming in?" She wants Soizic there.

"No, you go with your mum and dad."

"But..." Joséphine wants to tell her how she's been like a parent to her too, that she needs her to be there for everything to be complete. "I want you to come." She sits back in her seat.

"You are so *têtue, ma chère.* As stubborn as a true Breton." Soizic smiles at her, but there's a touch of sadness in her smile.

"I'll stay here," her father interrupts. "You go, Madame Le Calvez."

"No!" Joséphine feels like crying. She doesn't want this. She wants them all to go in together.

Her mother squeezes her hand again. "Soizic," she says softly, leaning forward, talking in her ear, though they can all hear. "You've been like a mother to Joséphine, and she wants you there."

Soizic doesn't move, and for a moment the silence hangs heavy like thick fog.

A knock on the window makes them all jump. Hervé's face appears. "Are you coming in?" he shouts through the window.

Soizic winds the window down. "*Bonjour,* Hervé."

Joséphine's father gets out the other side. He hasn't met Hervé yet and holds out his hand across the bonnet. Hervé takes it and shakes it, then her father lifts the front seat so Joséphine and her mum can get out. They stand there a minute, waiting for Soizic.

"Come on then!" Hervé pulls Joséphine's hand.

"Wait." Joséphine turns around and sees Soizic slowly getting out, as though her body has become too heavy for her. Joséphine takes a step back toward her and kisses her on the cheek. "*Merci*," she whispers.

Holding her head high, she walks into her school with her mother, father, Soizic, and Hervé. Her family.

The *baccalauréat* results are on a list stuck to the wall for the world to see. A group of students are already gathered around. Squeals of delight, long heavy sighs, even swearing from some of the boys, "*Putain!*" and "*C'est pas vrai!*" It all reaches Joséphine's ears, but she stands back, just watching for a moment, waiting till she's ready.

One of the boys turns round and sees her. "*Salut*, Joséphine. Have you seen? You've got—" Then he notices the man next to her. The boy turns back round, looking at his friends. "Joséphine's here," he says. They all turn around to look at her.

"*Salut, tout le monde*," Joséphine says. "This is my dad." She turns to look at him and smiles. "We finally found him." She turns back to her peer group, waiting to see their reactions. Some are stony-faced, others blank-faced, and others are smiling. "He's been in England all this time. He was sent there as a POW."

One boy stares coldly at her then walks away, a girl follows him, then another boy. One of the girls Joséphine hardly knows walks toward them, holding out her hand. "Pleased to meet you," she says, shaking Sébastian's hand. Other students say *bonjour*, and then they all go back to checking the list on the wall.

"Look, Joséphine," the first boy says. "You got eighteen! The second-highest score."

First a shiver runs through Joséphine, as if none of this is real. She freezes, her heart stops, then in a burst it beats hard and furious, her future unfurling before her. She can go to Rennes now to study literature. "Yes!" she shouts in English, jumping into the air.

The next morning Joséphine's father takes her to the jewelers. He says he wants to buy her something special to celebrate her results. They settle on a simple silver bangle, then walk back home through the narrow winding lanes.

"Joséphine," he says. "You know how proud I am of you, don't you?"

She smiles shyly. "I guess so."

"And you know how glad I am that you found me."

"Yes," she says slowly, wondering where this conversation is going.

"Joséphine, I have to go back to England."

She stops in her stride, and the air around them goes still. She knew he'd have to go back, but she's not ready yet. He's only stayed ten days. Ten days out of her whole life.

Taking a deep breath, Sébastian turns around and carries on walking.

"What?" she shouts after him. "Are you just going to walk away again?"

He stops, then turns around to face her. "I never walked away. You know that." He speaks softly. "Joséphine, you've seen your brothers. You know them now. And you know better than anyone what it's like to grow up without a father. I can't do that to them."

"But what about Maman? You love her, I know you do."

"Yes, I do, and I love you. But I also love my wife, and my children." He frowns. "I can't stay."

"Can't you just go back and see them sometimes?"

"No." He shakes his head. "You know that wouldn't be enough."

"So you're going back to Margaret?"

"Yes."

"But you don't love her, not really. I've seen you with Maman. It's completely different."

"Joséphine." He takes her hand. "I got here too late to be there for you when you were growing up. I have to be there for my boys, and for Maggie."

Joséphine lets out a long heavy breath. "It's not fair."

He sighs softly. "Oh Joséphine, what is fair? There are only choices, often difficult ones. I haven't always made the best choices. I have to get this one right."

"But this might not be the right choice! Maybe they'll be all right without you."

"You know that's not true. They need their father, just like you did. I'll still be here, for you. I'll come and visit you at university, and you can come and stay with me, for as long as you like."

"Have you told Maman?" she asks abruptly.

He shakes his head. "I'll tell her today."

"When are you going?"

"I'm on the night boat tonight. Madame Le Calvez has agreed to take me."

"Tonight?" Joséphine's eyes water over as she stares at him. "Tonight!"

He puts his arm around her, but she's unyielding. "I thought you were going to come to Rennes with me."

"I will come, once you're settled in. I can't make this any harder for your mother than it already is."

She pushes his arm away. "Just go then! Just go!" She walks away, her arms swinging defiantly by her sides. She knows she's behaving childishly and unfairly, but she just can't seem to help herself.

Chapter Eighty-One

Brittany, July 16, 1963

Élise

Sébastian comes back alone; he's not sure where Joséphine is, but he says he thinks she wants some time alone. I can see he's worried about her, and I tell him she still has a lot to come to terms with, that time to think it over will be good for her.

"It's such a beautiful day. Let's make a picnic." It's an impulsive idea of mine, but it's exactly what I want to do today. "We could have it on the beach," I add.

Sébastian's worry lines break out into a smile. And once again I see the young man I knew nineteen years ago. "That's a wonderful idea." He puts his arm around me, as though we were a couple, like any other. We walk to the local shops together to get the supplies, starting with the boulangerie for the baguette and tarts, then we go to the fromagerie to get a perfectly ripe Camembert. Just the épicerie left now. They have a small selection of wine.

"What was that wine we drank when we had our picnic in the hotel?" I ask him.

He looks taken aback and hesitates before replying. "Château Margaux." He smiles.

"We should get a 1944," I say.

"Well, actually we should get a 1939. That was the one we had."

"Not too old?"

"No, but we'll have to ask."

As it turns out, they do have a bottle, but at a ridiculous price. Still Sébastian wants to buy it. I try to stop him, but he says, "No, it's priceless."

We return home with our supplies. "Isn't it amazing," he says as we walk back, "how much everything can change in eighteen years? We can buy whatever we like, go wherever we like, eat whatever we want."

Love whoever we want, I want to add, but of course I don't. It's the only freedom we don't have. I want to hold him close, caress the back of his head, feel him melt into me, climb into the same bed every night, but I can do none of these things. "Yes," I say instead. "Isn't it wonderful."

Back at the cottage we pack our supplies into a knapsack. I carefully wrap two wine glasses in napkins. We can't drink Château Margaux, 1939, from plastic goblets. Then we set off along the *sentier des douaniers* toward Perros-Guirec, following the well-trodden path between the granite boulders on the beach, between the pine trees and along the cliffs. We talk about Paris; reliving the secret meetings, the fear, the excitement, the bookshop, and then what happened to our dear Monsieur Le Bolzec. We go quiet for a while, remembering him. "We should find his grave," I say. "I'd like to lay some fresh flowers down for him."

Sébastian looks at me, but he doesn't say yes, we should. He says nothing.

We finally get to Perros-Guirec, where we find a shady spot in front of overhanging trees at the far end of the beach. Sébastian spreads out the picnic rug, and I open the knapsack, setting out our little feast. Earlier I slipped in the book of poetry by Victor Hugo, but I hesitate to take it out. I just wanted to have it with us. The wine is full-bodied and well rounded, and the cheese melts on my tongue. I lie on my side, my head balanced on one hand, taking in Sébastian, while he gazes out to sea, sipping his wine. He's taken his T-shirt off, and his skin is smooth and slightly tanned, a few golden hairs on his chest glinting in the sun.

"Sébastian," I say. "What are you thinking?"

He turns toward me, the intensity in his eyes burning into me.

I move closer, touching his shoulder with the tip of my finger. I feel him tremble, and I can't help but move nearer, bridging the gap between us. He's just a breath away. Lightly I touch the hairs on his chest, longing to hold his body against mine.

"Lise," he says in a sigh.

I kiss his lips, as though I can kiss away the words I know he's going to say.

"You're always in my mind, behind everything I ever do, everything I think."

I kiss him again.

He pulls back. "Lise, I have to leave."

I sit up, staring ahead but seeing nothing. The wind caresses my hair, whispering to me as silent tears fall. I can't look at him. If I look at him, I won't be able to let him go.

"Tonight," he says. "I'm leaving tonight."

I carry on gazing out to sea, my heart aching with a loss so deep, I can hardly breathe.

He kisses my cheek. "I've always loved you. I always will."

If I turn around and wrap myself around him. If I cling to him like I clung to him in the hospital. If I kiss him again and again, he won't be able to leave me. I know he won't. I think about how much I need him, how empty my life will be without him in it. I could do it. I could. But I love him too much. And so I say nothing. I don't even move. I turn myself to stone.

I feel his lips touch my cheek, and I catch his oaky, musky smell. "*Au revoir, Lise. Je t'aime*," he murmurs. I hear him packing up the picnic, and I know he'll leave me with only the rug I'm sitting on. It takes all my strength to sit there and not throw my arms around him, not beg him to stay.

"Lise, I can't stay. I can't leave my boys without a father." He strokes my hair.

I flinch. He feels it and quickly drops his hand. "I'm sorry. I'm so sorry."

Shut up, I want to scream at him. But I hold my silence. I imagine I'm one of the granite boulders, and I don't move a muscle. He has to go now. He must. Or I might crack.

I feel him walk away. But I don't look, and the emptiness inside me expands till it swallows me and there's nothing left. But I keep breathing.

I get up and walk into the sea, feeling the waves splashing against my legs. I sit down in the shallows, watching the waves swirl around my dress. I splash water onto my face, letting it mingle with my tears, tasting the salt on my lips. I don't know how long I stay there, trying to make sense of it all, trying to be braver than I ever wanted to be.

Then I hear my name being called.

I turn around and see my daughter. My beautiful daughter. "Maman, Maman!" she cries.

This is my name.

I stand to meet her, and she throws her arms around me. "Maman," she says. "I love you." It's the first time I've heard her say these words since she was small. "I love you, Maman," she says again, as though she knows her words are breathing life back into me.

I clasp her, spinning her around and around, as though she were a little girl. To me she is weightless. She is all light, and air, and love.

Sébastian brought her back to me. And he left her here with me, where she belongs. "Joséphine," I say, "You're here."

"Yes, Maman, I'm here. I'm here!"

I stop spinning and kiss her damp cheek. I stroke her unruly hair. She is my family, and she's come home. I pull her to my chest, holding her close as I blink back tears. Through blurry eyes, I look over her shoulder and see a pair of doves standing in the shallows. Cocking their heads, they look at me then spread their wings and soar away—brilliant white against a blue sky. As they grow smaller and smaller, a sense of freedom sears through me. I'm finally free from the web of lies. I pull Joséphine closer, my heart thumping in my throat, and I inhale deeply, letting the air fill my lungs with its life-force. This life. This life full of possibilities. This life I want to live.

Epilogue

Early November 1963

It's a crisp winter's morning, the sun bright but not strong. I shiver, then put my arm around Joséphine as we wait for the train. "I haven't been back to Paris since I left with you inside me." I laugh, though it's not funny.

She gives me a serious look. "Will you be all right?"

I look down at the telegram from my mother again.

Papa died Friday. Funeral Tuesday. Please come.

My father—Papa; I haven't called him that since I was a child. Old memories of him surface; Papa picking me up from school on a Saturday morning, taking me straight to the patisserie, letting me choose a cake for my mother's birthday. Papa singing loudly in the bath. Who was this man who was my father?

The train pulls in and we board an empty carriage. Joséphine sits by the window, and I sit next to her, resting my hand on her knee. I need to feel the physicality of her. I need to know she's here.

As the countryside gives way to concrete and buildings, as we get nearer to Paris, something flutters in my stomach. The shame and fear I felt when I left is with me still.

As if she knows, Joséphine puts her hand over mine. "We're nearly there," she murmurs.

I don't move as the train slowly shunts forward, the platform coming into view. When it draws to a stop, she picks up our little suitcase with one hand, taking my hand in the other. "Come on, Maman."

But I'm frozen in my seat, unable to move. Paris. Too many memories. It terrifies me.

Joséphine puts the case down and sits next to me. She puts her arm around me and gives me a squeeze. "It will be all right," she tells me.

I look at my beautiful, sensitive daughter through blurry eyes, and I know that with Joséphine by my side I will be ready to face the memories. I kiss her on the cheek. "Let's go," I say. "Let's see Paris."

We get off the train, and it's like stepping into a different world. It's not the Paris I remember. People rush by—chatting, shouting, laughing. Gone are the sinister uniforms, the black boots, the half-starved, petrified citizens. I stand still for a moment, absorbing the energy, the joy, the freedom, and I wonder how it could have happened here. How was it possible?

"Élise!" someone shouts. Isabelle runs up to us, throwing her arms around me then Joséphine. "I'm so glad you came."

We walk to the apartment through the Jardins du Luxembourg, along the tree-lined avenues, where the leaves are turning shades of ruby red and burnt orange. I ask to sit on the bench opposite the perfectly cut grass where I once kicked down that sign. I stare at the empty space, remembering Ellen.

I look up, half expecting to see Nazi soldiers, but there are only children running ahead of their mothers and couples arm-in-arm strolling through the gardens, as though they have not a care in the world. Closing my eyes, I lean back on the bench and breathe in the warm smell of autumn blowing on the breeze.

We don't talk, but Isabelle takes my hand, and I take Joséphine's and together we walk through the gardens, toward our old apartment. Crossing Place Saint-Sulpice, my pulse begins to race and I'm short of breath. We cross the square and round the corner onto our little street. I freeze. The iron balustrade is still there. Closing my eyes tight, I try to block out the memory of the men pulling me down, the loud thud as I hit the ground, the pain shooting through my elbow, the shouting, the chanting... *Stop!* I shake my head as though I can shake the memory out.

Joséphine looks at me with concern. "You're so pale, Maman."

I nod, looking at the large burgundy-colored front door. Nothing has changed. And everything has changed. Isabelle pushes on the door, and we go through to the entrance. There's our name, *Chevalier*, on one of the postboxes. I imagine my father with his little key, opening it, taking out all the letters that came for me, hiding them away.

The glass door on the other side of the entrance opens. My mother stands there, looking thin and fragile as she glances from one of us to the next, such sadness in her eyes. Suddenly, I'm reminded of Joséphine coming to me in the sea when I felt broken, and I remember what she said.

I step toward her and take her hand. I bring it up to my lips and kiss it softly. Isabelle takes my other hand, and the three of us hold on to each other. Then Joséphine joins us, wrapping her arms around our backs. And the circle is complete.

Author's Note

This book was first inspired by my great-uncle, Wolfgang, who came from Eastern Germany, and who at the age of fifteen was required to join the Hitler Youth. In 1943, he was taken prisoner by the British army in North Africa, from where he was shipped off to the American South to work in the fields. Later, he was transferred to Coventry, England, still as a POW, and it was while working on a farm in Kenilworth that he met my great-aunt, Dorothy. Wolfgang didn't like to talk about the war, and he never spoke German to his children. Sadly, he passed away in 2017, but happily Dorothy is still healthy and well today and will tell you how everyone loved Wolfgang "like a son."

Their story intrigued me, and I always wondered how the local population felt toward such marriages. I went on to read *Trautmann's Journey: From Hitler Youth to FA Cup Legend* by Catrine Clay, a true account of a young German soldier who first came to England as a POW, but then made his home there, playing for England in the FA cup—a brilliant and inspiring book.

Acknowledgments

My heartfelt thanks go once again to all my wonderful writing friends, who are so much more than that: Ian, Shelley, Maz, Ellen, Melissa, Rachel, Haze, Nancy, and Connie. Thank you for being there for me and my many drafts. You make the writing come alive.

I am very fortunate to have such a great publisher, and I thank Sherise Hobbs at Headline Review for being with me every step of the way. Thank you, Sherise, for your passion and dedication to "the story." When it came to putting the finishing touches to the book, Flora Rees, my copyeditor, did a brilliant job of making sure it all fitted together perfectly. Thank you, Flora, for your attention to detail and your suggestions. I would also like to thank my wonderful agent, Sheila Crowley, at Curtis Brown for all her support and hard work. I wouldn't be there without you!

At home, I'd like to thank Christian for being there through the thick and the thin, good and bad, happy and sad.

Reading Group Guide

Discussion Questions

1. In Monsieur Le Bolzec's bookshop, Sebastian ponders his loneliness and the alienation he feels when he is ostracized by the French customers. How did this scene make you feel, reading from the perspective of the occupier versus the occupied? Did Sebastian's sadness surprise you?

2. Later, when speaking to Monsieur Le Bolzec, Sebastian says he's never allowed to take off his uniform. Monsieur Le Bolzec remarks that Sebastian—despite his position in the German army—is "no freer" than the French. What did you make of this observation, that Monsieur Le Bolzec and Sebastian were both prisoners in different ways?

3. Why do you think Monsieur Le Bolzec gave Sebastian a copy of *The Picture of Dorian Gray* to read? And what did you make of Sebastian's comment that sooner or later, like Oscar Wilde's famous character, the "surface is bound to crack"? What was the author foreshadowing here?

4. The author writes about the principles of Nazism, saying that based on Hitler's teachings, there was "no room for misunderstanding, or even understanding" individual needs when it came to the well-being of the state. What do you think the author meant by this?

5. In the Sacré-Cœur Basilica in Montmartre, Sebastian thinks back to when he attended church as a child, when he was comforted by the thought of God watching over him. As a soldier, however, he felt like the likelier scenario was a reality lorded over by the Greek gods, since they enjoyed playing with people "as though they were pawns on a chessboard." What was the author intimating here, and why do you think Sebastian felt this way at that point in his life?

6. Inside the cathedral, Sebastian looks through a stained-glass window, and meditates on the idea that God isn't there for people like him, but for the "innocent, those looking for comfort, not reason." Did you feel, however, that Sebastian was innocent in some ways, despite the uniform he wore? Why or why not?

7. The author discusses Hitler's use of propaganda during World War II, noting that truth was "far less important than success" to the Third Reich when it came to communicating with the German people. How is propaganda used today, and how do you think about it in relation to something like "fake news"?

8. Sebastian and Elise's relationship was a forbidden one, viewed as abhorrent, traitorous, and dangerous by people on both sides. Did you agree with their naysayers, or did

you feel that their relationship related more strongly to the Victor Hugo epigraph at the beginning of the novel, that love is worth fighting for no matter what, as "there is no other pearl to be found in the dark folds of life"?

9. Elise, in an attempt to alleviate the shame she felt at having to live among the Nazis, helped smuggle Jewish children out of the city, putting her own life in significant risk. Even so, she feels that her help is "tiny...nothing compared to others." Sebastian feels similarly—like he isn't doing enough—when he burns the denunciation letter that would jeopardize the children Elise is trying to save, "watching the paper glow orange then turn to black as it disintegrated into ash." Do you agree with Elise and Sebastian's assessments of their work here? Or did you feel they were committing very impactful acts of rebellion?

10. In the bookshop, Monsieur Le Bolzec speaks to Elise of Sebastian: "It's a funny thing, nationality. What does it really mean to be French? Or to be German?" Do you agree or disagree with this statement? As a translator in the German army, born to a French mother and a German father, how did this statement make you feel about Sebastian's character? How might conflicts disappear—or, conversely, arise—with this kind of thinking?

11. Monsieur Le Bolzec tells Elise that reasons behind actions matter: "When you get to my age...you realize [that] there's a story and then there's the story behind it." How did these words affect Elise going forward, and the way she interpreted Sebastian's actions? Has Monsieur Le Bolzec's statement rung true in your own life?

12. In times of war, do you believe that all those involved are victims—but that some victims are more innocent than others? Why or why not?

13. When Sebastian sees Josephine for the first time, he's struck by a number of emotions: surprise, hope, confusion, happiness, wariness. Josephine had a similar experience when Elise confirmed that Frederick was not her biological father. Have you ever been in a situation where you were completely blindsided and emotionally scrambled? How did you process what happened?

14. When Josephine first travels to Paris, she is delighted by the prospect of exploring the city and all it has to offer. What is a great adventure you've had in your own life, and how did it impact you going forward?

15. Sebastian makes a very difficult decision at the end of the novel. Do you feel he made the right choice? Ultimately, how did the ending of the book make you feel?

VISIT **GCPClubCar.com** to sign up for the **GCP Club Car** newsletter, featuring exclusive promotions, info on other **Club Car** titles, and more.

 @grandcentralpub   @grandcentralpub   @grandcentralpub

About the Author

Ruth Druart grew up on the Isle of Wight, leaving at eighteen to study psychology. In 1993 she moved to Paris, the city that inspired her to write her Paris-set novels.

RuthDruart.com
Facebook @ruth.druart
Instagram @ruth.druart
Twitter @RuthDruart